EXPLORER

EXPLORER

Douchan Gersi

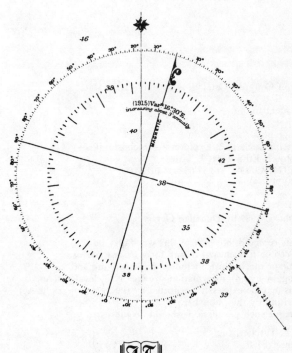

JEREMY P. TARCHER, INC.
Los Angeles
Distributed by St. Martin's Press
New York

Library of Congress Cataloging in Publication Data

Gersi, Douchan.
  Explorer.
  Bibliography.
  1. Gersi, Douchan. 2. Explorers—Czechoslovakia—
Biography. 3. Ethnology. I. Title.
G239.52.G47A3 1987 914.37′044 87-10120
ISBN 0-87477-430-6

Jeremy P. Tarcher, Inc.
9110 Sunset Blvd.
Los Angeles, CA 90069

Design by Robert Tinnon
Photographs by Douchan Gersi
Illustrations by Slim Mzali

Manufactured in the United States of America
10 9 8 7 6 5 4 3 2 1

First Edition

To the people of tradition—the so-called "primitives"—whose destiny changed mine.

To Maroussia and Maeva, my daughters, so that they will better understand my long absences.

To my father, who went traveling into the hereafter.

To my mother, who's waiting for my return.

Contents

Acknowledgments

Struggling with my memories and the English language has not always been a joy for me or my many helpers. My gratitude goes to Patricia, who has borne my sleepless nights, and my family and friends in the United States and abroad whom I have neglected during my sojourn as a writer. I am grateful to Jeremy Tarcher, my publisher and friend, who encouraged me to continue fighting with the white sheets of paper; to Gregory Armstrong, who helped carve my first rough paths through the written jungle; and to Kip Hargrove, who shouted warnings and pointed out obstructions on the paths. Also to Lynette Padwa, who supervised the often chaotic pages, and to Bud Sperry for his helping hands.

Others who have my gratitude are Darrell Burstein, my doctor, who kept me in good shape physically and mentally, and Stacy Williams, Ed Solomon, Mary Ann del Pizzo, and Christian Berglas, who waited while I used their computers. My thanks also to Slim Mzali for his drawings and to Mick Viet for his help.

Gratitude is also owed to the anthropologists and explorers whose ideas and experiences have helped inform mine.

Finally, I would like to thank destiny, which has allowed me to survive for so long in spite of my risk-taking and occasional foolishness.

Author's Note

In this book I describe only a few of my many expeditions throughout the world. These adventures in the Philippines and Borneo took place between 1967 and 1977, during which time I also traveled to New Zealand, the Polynesian islands, the Melanesian islands, the Sahara desert, Molokai Island, a few African countries, New Guinea, and Peru. I have chosen to pass up those adventures in this volume in order to create a story with a continuity that rarely happens in actual time. Here I tell of my time among headhunters whose lives and values I have come to appreciate and admire no less than I do those of the European-based culture in which I grew up. I love the tribal peoples whom I call "the people of tradition." It is my hope that by reading of my adventures in seeking them and living among them, you will come to value them as well.

By Way of Introduction

Better to be crazy for one's own sake than wise for others.
FRIEDRICH NIETZSCHE

When people ask me, "What do you do for a living?" and I answer, "I am an explorer," they usually roll their eyes and form the kind of smile they would give to a little boy who has said, "When I grow up, I'm going to be a cowboy and fight Indians!"

And yet, indeed, I am an explorer. An explorer-filmmaker. I have friends in the jungle of New Guinea who eat their enemies; I have friends in the tropical forest of the Amazon who shrink human heads. I am the blood brother of a headhunter in the Philippines, and I belong to another tribe in the deep of Borneo. I was accepted among the Tuareg—the so-called "Blue Men of the Sahara"—warriors of the silence, stones, and sands. And with them, I have crossed their North African desert from West to East, passing by Timbuktu.

I own a white camel in the Sahara desert and a horse in Afghanistan. I have traveled on the backs of elephants, ostriches, and water buffaloes. I have entered the underwater world in pursuit of the lost cities of Atlantis and have searched for "El Dorado," the Inca treasure, in the Peruvian Amazon. I have studied with great magicians hidden in South America, Africa, and Haiti, and have approached the secrets of Voodoo and other forbidden religions of the world.

Sometimes people say, "You're a hero!" But is the man a hero who pees in his pants when African elephants charge him? Is he a hero who falls to his knees and cries like a baby when a band of headhunters advance on him with spears? Is he a hero who thinks only of reciting his childhood prayers when he is lost, starving, naked, alone in the middle of an uncharted jungle?

Others have said to me: "You're insane—a crazy man!" But is he insane who lives out his fantasies and makes even his wildest dreams come true? Is he insane who is always happy where he is, yet is ready to move on physically and psychologically? Is he crazy who knows that beyond the closed door there is a secret, beyond the horizon there is the forbidden, irresistible song he must hear?

And once drawn into adventure, I adapt myself to many things I wouldn't have believed possible when living in my own culture. For instance, I think I have tasted almost everything that can be eaten by humans: ants and large fat worms in New Guinea; snakes and long water lizards in Borneo; rats, flying termites, and giant grasshoppers in Africa; sand lizards in the Sahara desert; dogs and cats in southeast Asia; and elsewhere tortoises and turtles. Still, in a Parisian gourmet restaurant, I once nearly became sick when I found a hair in my soup.

When living in modern civilization, I hate danger, love luxury, and for my personal comfort need baths, clean clothes, and even nice scents on my body. But as soon as I'm on an expedition, I find that adventure without danger is not appealing. Then I don't mind wearing filthy clothes, not being able to brush my teeth, resting on the dirt floor of a crowded hut, sleeping under a tree, having my face covered with malaria-carrying mosquitoes. This attitude is necessary, for one of the most difficult requirements of the explorer's life is to adapt to extreme and often intolerable conditions. The price of entering the unknown is misery in many forms: shaking with malaria; guts aching from constant vomiting and bloody dysentery; skin crawling with ants, leeches, and fungus; muscles shouting, "Not one more step!"

On an agonizingly long journey, sometimes one must keep alive on a handful of food once a day or even once a week, surviving like an animal, becoming an animal to survive. And yet, I love the smell of the hot sand, of sweat; I love the heat, and I love the caress of tropical rain. Surrounded by the empty horizon of a desert or inside the vegetal cathedral of a rotting jungle, I feel at home. Not because I have found the ultimate happiness, but because I am truly searching for it.

One way I make myself able to grow in wisdom is by putting my own balance in jeopardy. My inner conflicts, stirred by emotional violence, push me closer to the truth. Each experience is good because it helps me to grow. By challenging myself I push back the barriers of my limitations; I push back weakness, ignorance, and fear. I come to the reality of being just another insect leaving tracks on a muddy soil. And yet, in my attempt to fulfill the possibilities of life, I try to become a man-god, my fingers reaching out to the cosmos, my heart plunging into universal love.

Of course, it's never easy to abandon a safe place, a home—where heart and mind, often at great cost, have achieved a fragile balance—just to follow a dream. But follow a dream I must, in order to fully test myself and my values. And in the testing I change the perceptions I have about others, about myself, and about everything.

I erase the given values of my own culture in order to live according to the values of another. I merge into the new and become new myself. I suppress my modern consciousness to be able to assume completely the mind and logic of the tribe. Then, like a baby, I learn how to breathe all over again, how to talk, feel, think, and see. I learn to carry my emotions and my feelings wide open on my skin. Because the heart always speaks the truth, it speaks the only language understood by those human societies that the twentieth century has forgotten. With the heart you can talk to people with whom you share not a single word. Then, by learning one word and then another, the spoken language changes from a "no trespassing" sign to a "welcome" mat.

This physical and intellectual adaptation to another human environment helps me retain my sanity by allowing me to acknowledge the primitive in myself. As I move from modern civilization's last outpost to a tribe's environment, I can detoxicate myself from my cultural identity. However, when I return to my own civilization I experience a real culture shock and must learn to accept my civilized self again. And only then am I able to appreciate all that I have learned elsewhere.

I think of Melville writing in *Moby-Dick*: "Whenever I find myself growing grim around the mouth; whenever it is a damp, drizzly November in my soul . . . then I account it high time to get to the sea as soon as I can." For me it is not the sea, but the contact with my brothers, those known as *aborigines* or *primitive people,* whom I call *people of tradition* because they have been able to maintain their primal identities in an age when even the stars have been marked with the bootprints of modern man. The people of tradition are one of the principal reasons that I value life. They restore me. They are my church and my religion. It is in order to write a love song to the people of tradition that I am an explorer.

I don't go to bring them our civilization or progress, or other beliefs governed by other gods, or other dreams. And I don't go to change their values. I just want all of us and our descendants to know the treasures of knowledge that these people have preserved from age-old times, so we can learn more about ourselves and our own past and perhaps regain some of the values we have lost. Sooner or later, the twentieth century will take their territories and their lives. It would be a crime against human intelligence if their heritage were totally lost. Aware of their fragile future, I want to put down and film as much of the appearance, activity, heart, and soul of these people as possible, so that one day the children of their children will be able to know how their forefathers lived.

My dream is to present these people of tradition as they are, with the sound of their heartbeats and the moaning of their dreams, so that, instead of wanting to change them, we will change our perception about them and about all human beings who are different. The Creator, whatever that term means to us, has given us a world made of differences: water and fire, valleys and mountains, day and night, man and woman, and a multitude of human and cultural differences. We owe it to the Creator to retain and protect these differences.

It is my duty to bring to you a sense of the glories of these differences. Just letting you know of the existence of these miraculously different people will assure their survival in your memories. And at the least, they will not have survived this long in vain. If there is somewhere a paradise for people of tradition, I wish to be a part of it.

But it's not out of disdain for my own culture that I love entering the secret, forbidden dreams of the people of tradition. It is also because I am addicted to curiosity. I want to know everything, and everything amazes me. A cat running, the smile of a child, the birth of a flower, the endless pictures my TV set sends me. I love to travel back in time into a natural wilderness, into the purity of human societies which deal with life according to ancient traditions; because there, perhaps, I may find answers to the never-ending questions of the spirit—"What is God?"; "What is the meaning of life?"; "Who am I on earth, in the galaxy, in the cosmos?" But each time I think I have reached the Truth, a new teaching reveals another truth behind it. And I am once again riding a merry-go-round of questions, of uncertainties, quests, despairs, angers, frustrations.

To civilized men, my quest may seem naive. They prefer the cement jungle and *its* wild animals. Good. More blank spots on the map for me. They have watering holes, I have oases. They have flow charts, I have flowing rivers. They have credit cards, I have trinkets and beads (including those of sweat) that buy my survival in my jungles. I prefer to follow the rules dictated by my heart instead of by logic and reason. I want to create my own paradise. I pray to live fully. I cry for freedom.

CHAPTER ONE

Childhood and Initiation

We are told that talent creates its own opportunities. But it sometimes seems that intense desire creates not only its own opportunities, but its own talents.

ERIC HOFFER

Perhaps destiny made me a nomad, condemned to wander in exile, endlessly searching for a better place to live, to dream, and to love. I was born in Bratislava, Czechoslovakia, in 1947; when I was still a baby my parents decided to leave everything—wealth, fame, social success, and an easy life—in their wild escape to freedom, for the communists had taken over and were about to close the border. Our long exile led us to a boat that took us to what was then the Belgian Congo (now Zaire), on the African coast.

To help Maman down the gangplank, an African took me in his arms and carried me to the wharf. As it was the first time I saw a black face so close to mine, I wet my finger and went over his face with it. I had a double surprise: my finger was still white and his skin still black. This was my first discovery in Africa. I was one year old.

In his book *When God Was a Woman*, Merlin Stone wrote: "So many of the stories told to us from the time we are just old enough to understand deeply affect our attitudes and comprehension of the world about us and ourselves. Our ethics, morals, conduct, values, sense of duty and even sense of humor are often developed from simple childhood parables and fables." The eleven years of my childhood spent in that African country were something like a fable. Papa was my god, and Maman my angel. I grew up in the bush closer to the natives than to the "civilized" people. Papa preferred to raise his family away from civilization's folly. Instead of buildings and freeways, I was surrounded by a magical forest and wild animals.

I was charmed by danger for the first time when I was about two or three years old. One afternoon I was playing inside our house. Maman, taking care of my little sister, was outside on the veranda. Alarmed by a sudden silence, she entered the house and found me sitting on the floor face-to-face with a cobra that stood erect, its hood unfolded, less than three feet in front of me. We were both slowly moving from side to side as if hypnotized by each other. Without making a sound, my mother went out of the house and came back with a machete. She crept upon the snake from behind and cut off its head, saving my life for other cobras and other dangers.

The region where we lived swarmed with so many snakes that we had to be on constant alert. When it's cold, snakes will enter beds for a little heat, so one of Maman's evening rituals was to examine our beds for reptiles. And the morning ritual consisted of searching our shoes for deadly scorpions.

I remember long evenings on the veranda where we had our dinner. There, amid the symphony of the tropical night, my parents told stories about their childhood and about our homeland. Their tales were often interrupted by the sound of drums echoing from village to village, tomtoms telling their own stories. Sometimes the drums sent prayers to the moon and stars, or messages to the divinities, thanking them or asking for favors. Sometimes the drums cried, mourning a deceased one, or shouted in joy, announcing a birth.

Occasionally we heard piercing squeals and ferocious barking, and knew our guard dogs were fighting with wild dogs or a hungry leopard, for our farm sheltered thousands of chickens, hundreds of ducks and pigeons, and a few dozen pigs. Following Papa, who grabbed his gun and ran to them as fast as possible, we would carry buckets of water to throw on the fighters to separate them. That was the only way to give Papa a chance to shoot the intruder without wounding our own dogs.

For years, our only light at night was provided by kerosene lamps. After sundown, hundreds of nocturnal insects buzzed around the lamps and smashed their heads against the hot glass chimneys. That was when we got our best lessons in the natural sciences. We collected giant colorful night butterflies and other strange insects and learned to name all of them. For the next day's dessert, we caught large flying termites; cooked as the natives do, they taste like salty nuts.

Soon, collecting nocturnal insects was not enough to quench my curiosity. I wanted to collect birds, but for this I needed a rifle. The proliferation of snakes pushed my father, when I was only five years old, to give me an air rifle powerful enough to kill big snakes and birds the size of eagles.

Although I had often accompanied Papa on his hunting trips, my first kill made a big impression on me. I remember it was a small red bird that hid behind a leaf. Too nervous to startle the bird into flying so I could see my target, I aimed at the leaf and shot. The red bird fell dead.

I rapidly began to develop my skill as a hunter. One year later, my expertise saved my mother's life. She and some natives were building shelters for our pigs when a snake, disturbed from its nap, bit her twice on the foot. She was already trembling with pain and fever when Papa, alerted by the workers, came and found her. He drove his knife into her wounds to deepen them and began to suck the venom out. Then they left for the closest hospital, about an hour's drive away. Papa asked me to find and kill the snake as fast as possible, and then radio the hospital physician the name of the species to which the snake belonged. Since antivenom serums are made of snake venom, knowing the species of the snake would enable the doctor to inject my mother with the right antidote.

I took my rifle and ran to the place where the workers, armed with their machetes, were still searching for the snake. It took us a while to find the long fat highly poisonous *black mamba*. As soon as I shot it, the workers jumped on its still-moving body and, with their machetes, sliced it to pieces to punish it for biting Maman. I radioed the hospital and the antivenom serum was ready when my parents arrived.

I was a hunter, yes. But I never had the feeling that I was really killing anything—except snakes. Instead, I was preserving forever the beauty of my prey, sending them into eternity. For me, hunting was deeply linked with observing the beauty of the animal world. Each species of snake was kept in a big glass container filled with alcohol. As for the bird specimens, Maman showed me how to preserve them by injecting them with a formaldehyde mixture.

Every day or so, I went back to the bush. Alone, rifle in hand, a bag hanging on my shoulder, I penetrated the unknown, pushed back the borders of my wild territory. I loved to be deafened by the crazed beating of my heart whenever I was surprised by a new discovery or frozen by apprehension. Often I was intimate with fear and panic during these expeditions. Each new sound that entered my ears was rapidly analyzed.

When I could identify it, I always felt better, but I felt the deeper elation of fear when it was unknown.

If I followed a bird or an antelope for hours and couldn't find my way back, I lived with the joyful panic of feeling lost. I became a prisoner of the curiosity that moved me toward any new noise, be it squeal or roar. Then, afterward, I was intoxicated again by the satisfaction of having overcome my dread of the unknown. I loved to watch small animals and birds; above all, I loved to approach them silently without alarming them. I learned to master the tremblings of my limbs, to control my heartbeat and my breathing, to wipe away the sweat that burned my eyes.

Hunter though I was, I dreamed of becoming a musician. Every Christmas Eve, Papa listened to the voluptuous melodies of Gypsy music, and I would see the tears escaping from his eyes as he shuddered to the melancholy of violins crying their emotions. I asked him once, "Papa, are you sad?" After a few seconds to pull himself out of his memories, he looked at me and said, "I am not sad. If you cry only when you are sad or because you are in pain, then you will never know how great and amazing life can be. I cry because the sound of these violins is so beautiful, it carries emotions better than any words, any language." That same night, I decided to become a musician . . . to be able to make people cry of happiness. I was seven.

A year or two later, bored with playing with my two little sisters, I asked my father when he would make me some brothers to play with. I knew his dream was to have enough sons to man his own soccer team. Realizing I just lacked friends to play games with, he said, "Do you remember how to go to the river a mile north from the house? The river where we went a few times to fish? Well, go down this river. After a small walk—an hour or so—you will find a village. There you can easily find many friends to play with."

Armed with my rifle, I set out the next day intent on a long and adventurous expedition. But hardly had I passed the border of our estate when my heart started to beat like all the tomtoms of Africa—those drums that almost every night reverberated from trees to stars. Filled with apprehension, I finally reached the river, but did not go farther. I sat on the bank of the river and waited for the courage to go on. I waited for it until the shadows grew long. Then, disappointed at myself, I slowly went home, carrying in my heart the heavy weight of my cowardice.

After dinner, Papa asked me if I had found any new friends. Ashamed by my behavior, I lied. "Well . . . not really . . . yet. I reached the river . . . but then . . . I found some birds so magnificent and strange that I followed them, and . . ." My story was a success.

The next day, I was determined to reach the village. Concentrating my thoughts on something other than what I was doing, I reached the river and began to push back that invisible but strong barrier of the unknown by moving in the direction of the village. In the excitement of overcoming my fear I found courage, but unfortunately my cowardliness possessed me once again. I stopped, sat, and waited, dreaming of courage and of my new friends to be.

That night after dinner, to save my honor I had to lie again, pretending that I had reached the village and had played with my new friends. Papa said, "I don't like to have you so far from home. Tomorrow, tell your friends' parents that I want to talk to them. I need some additional workers for the farm. If they could move here, your friends would be right here."

I was caught in a trap. Even if I lied again to my father and he believed me, I would still have to face myself and my own reality in the twilight that precedes my sleep. My father used to tell me, "Whatever you do belongs to you, even the truth about yourself. You must be your own judge and the only judge of your behavior. If you can fool others, don't ever fool yourself. You must always be aware of who you are and in your life act in such a way that you will never be ashamed of who you are. One of the many ways to meet yourself is at the twilight of your day, when you are slowly about to lose control of your body. There, meet with yourself and with your self-awareness, enter your own consciousness, face your own reality. Don't ever forget that you will be able to accept and love others only if you have accepted yourself." Another day he told me: "When you must make some decisions, don't wait for help from your guardian angel, for you *are* and *must be* your own guardian angel." Thus, because of my father's teaching, I never could escape this encounter with myself that came just before I entered the world of dreams. So I was left with only one choice: to go to the village.

Thinking that it would help me make friends faster, I took along my soccer ball instead of my rifle. I reached the river and then followed its current. Yet even though my heart drummed in my head, something fed my courage. Was it fear of having to face my father as a coward? Was it the thought of his belt against my buttocks when he found out about my lies? Or was it the humiliation of having to face myself again, just before sleep? The image of my aching buttocks was nothing compared to the pain of feeling lonely with my failure, my eyes burning under dried tears.

I came to the front of the village. And everything suddenly looked so easy! So many worries for nothing, I thought to myself.

Following some instinct, but mostly copying my parents' respectful attitude when we visited native villages, I stood in front of the village and waited. Soon the villagers came and looked at me with curiosity and kindness, especially the women and children of my age. Language was not a barrier. At a very young age, I had had to learn the many languages in all the different provinces of the Belgian Congo (Zaire) where we had lived. Slovak was my first language, the one used by the family. Swahili, the Bantu language used in a large part of Africa, became my second while we were living in Katanga. Later, I learned to speak French. And in the Kasai region, where this adventure took place, I had to talk Tchiluba. Perhaps being Slavic gives me an ease with languages. They say in Slovakia: "The more languages you can speak, the more times a man you are." And, "If you speak the language of your enemy, you are already his conqueror."

A family invited me to share their food. And I found new friends. The only problem was that they were not willing to play my games. I had to play theirs, especially the very wildest one played with a bow and real arrows. Two boys, each standing in a circle five feet in diameter drawn on the ground about 100 feet apart, faced each other. Each was armed with a bow and some three-foot-long arrows sharp enough to kill a bull. The rules of this game were simple. Each boy in his turn had to send up an arrow in such a way that it would fall into the opposite circle. If he did so, he won a point. Meanwhile, his opponent had to avoid the falling arrow without leaving the boundary of his circle. If he succeeded, then it was his turn to send an arrow into the opposite circle. But if he jumped out of his circle, he was automatically the loser, no matter how many points he already had collected, and he had to give his place to another player. It was a game of skill, dexterity, and, moreover, a game of self-confidence and self-control.

The boys offered me the honor of being the first bowman. Instead of asking them to wait a few minutes so I could practice with the bow, I accepted their invitation right away. That was my mistake. Not used to the bow or to the weight of the arrows, I missed the circle of my opponent. That instantly brought laughs of derision from my new friends. My opponent became the bowman. He sent his arrow so high into the sky that I could not see it fall. Panicked by the fear of being wounded, I jumped out of my circle. And the laughter became frenzy when the arrow drove into the ground outside my circle. I was put out of the game, I was a loser, nothing else, no matter that I was their guest. Then I asked them to play my game with the soccer ball. They did so, but rapidly changed the rules, and I did not have a chance to touch the ball once.

It was a long walk home.

"So, how are your new friends?" my father asked. At least I had the courage to tell him of my disappointment. "If you want them to play your games according to your rules," he said, "you must, first and always, succeed in theirs. You must become the best in what they do. Only then will you be accepted and will you gain their confidence and respect."

The next day, I went back to the village. I played their games and succeeded even in their wildest one. And I gained all that my father said.

I loved my childhood, but unfortunately, a few years later, the devil slipped into my paradise. Papa, who had never been sick, suddenly became seriously ill, a victim of cancer. Accompanied by Maman, he went to be treated in Paris, leaving behind my two sisters and me, for he thought he would soon recover and come back to us. But after several radium treatments, the Parisian physicians told him his condition was incurable. Not willing to give up, Maman moved Papa to a hospital in Belgium. Two months later, however, she called us to join them, for, in spite of hope, faith, and prayers, Papa was to die. He was not yet forty-four years old. Maman was thirty-four, and I, twelve and a half.

That same year, 1959, the rebellion for independence was bathing the Belgian Congo in blood. Soon that country became Zaire and the new government confiscated all of our possessions. The Belgian citizens were compensated by Belgium but we were without citizenship papers. We lost everything. Wishing to keep our freedom, Maman refused to take refuge with her family in Czechoslovakia. So, without money, as refugees of the United Nations, we had no other choice than to live in Belgium where, in spite of having been raised as a countess, my mother had to take a job.

My father's brutal death broke to pieces the charm of my adolescence. I had to leave the world of naïveté to enter adulthood and confront the reality of survival in modern civilization. I was unhappy. I badly missed the world of my childhood and didn't know what to do with my life or what to do for a living. I thought about many different possibilities: one day an archaeologist, the next an actor, then a mystic, a professional hunter, a composer, a physician, a writer, a musician, etc. So, besides conscientiously studying math and electronics during the day (to ensure my future, as my mother put it), I took evening classes in speech and in drama. I spent my nights writing poems and nurturing my dreams of adventure with my memories of Africa. At seventeen, in a state of utter exhaustion from lack of sleep, I came down with a meningitis that almost took my life away. I recovered and was very encouraged a few months later when a Belgian publisher published my first book: a collection of poems that I had written in French.

At eighteen, tired of living with hand-me-down furniture and clothing given to us by various aid groups, I decided to look for an after-school job. I approached a Belgian organization called "Exploration du Monde" (Exploration of the World) that was hiring six explorer-filmmakers a year to present their documentary films in a three-month lecture tour in the important cities of Belgium and Luxembourg. For the smaller cities, they used the services of an in-house staff of lecturers. I passed their test for this job and was booked for a three-month tour, five lectures a week.

In France there is a similar organization called "Connaissance du Monde" (Knowledge of the World), which puts on programs in France and Switzerland, and through various affiliates, in all the French-speaking parts of Africa, Canada, and the Caribbean. It may seem strange to Americans, who aren't big fans of documentaries, that in those countries people go to the movies and pay the price of a feature film to see a ninety-minute documentary. The explorer is on the stage, narrating his own movie, and the audience has the opportunity to meet him and buy his book during the intermission. An explorer-filmmaker usually gives three lectures a day: an early matinee for schoolchildren, another at 5:00 P.M. for old people, who prefer not going out at night, and a show at 9:00 P.M., to which people come dressed as if for a concert or live theater. And depending on the size of the city, the lecturer sometimes stays more than one day. If not, the next day he moves to another city, sometimes hundreds of miles away or more. After paying for his travel, accommodation, food expenses, and agent's fees, he is often left with the proceeds of his lecture tours and book sales as his only resources to finance future expeditions. No profit here, but by being willing to struggle financially, the explorer protects his freedom to choose his own subjects and make movies in his own way.

The movie I was given to lecture with was called *Summits and Marvels*, showing the natural beauties of the Alps. It was made by Samivel, a French moviemaker who is considered in Europe to be a master of the documentary.

My first lecture was in a prison. I was welcomed by two convicts who were sent to help me with my technical equipment. With them were two guards who escorted us to the prison theater, through a giant corridor fifteen feet wide and more than twenty feet high. Every fifty feet or so, the corridor was interrupted by a huge mesh wall in which there was a guard door that had to be opened by a large key. The noise of key, door, our steps, and the sound of people talking echoed endlessly through the corridor. After the last door, we passed through an enormous quadrangle, like the inside of a honeycomb, lined with three tiers of cells. Then we arrived at the theater, where the prisoners were waiting for me. As I entered I could see all their eyes fixed on me. A guard stood next to my table beside the screen. "In case you need help," he explained. Four more guards were in place at the doors.

The film went on, and I began reading my commentary. The prisoners listened in rapt silence until I came to these words: "It is in nature, and especially in the mountains, that a man can meet himself. Those who are prisoners of the cities and of their ways will never be able to experience this magical feeling of being close to the Creator. There between the sky and the earth is the ultimate door to freedom."

At these words the audience exploded with sound. The prisoners yelled, laughed, applauded. They whistled and smashed their shoes on the floor. Immediately the lights came on, and the guards ordered silence. I stood there wishing I were invisible.

"Thanks for your overwhelming applause, but the movie isn't finished yet . . . shall we?" I said with difficulty, my voice dry in my throat. The lights went out and I finished the lecture, adapting the text to my audience with greater care. It was a skill that also served me in the jungle.

Later, I frequently had to face hundreds of wild teenagers, boys and girls almost my own age. But they hadn't come to experience the magic poetry of the mountains; instead, in the darkness, they savored the pleasurable explorations of youth.

Thanks to the lectures, I was able to meet Samivel. A real friendship developed between us, as well as a kind of father-son relationship. Although Samivel was aware that I knew nothing about filmmaking, he asked me to become his assistant for a movie about Provence, the southwestern region of France, that he was scheduled to start when summer began. I was excited about the idea but couldn't say yes right away, for the answer depended upon my mother allowing me to stop my studies for a whole year. To my surprise, she said yes. "But after that, back to school," she added.

Samivel's crew was composed of only two men: him and me. In the beginning I was happy just to carry the equipment, load film into the cameras, and use the tape recorder. But seeing him filming, being his pupil for the making of his movie, aroused in me a vocation. And the day I shot my first picture, I felt as if the camera were a substitute for the rifle I carried as a child.

Photography, according to filmmaker Chris Marker, "is hunting. It is the hunter's instinct without the desire to kill. It is the hunting of angels. . . . One tracks, aims, fires, and click! Instead of a dead man, one makes something eternal." Instead of freezing life to send it into oblivion, my shots were to preserve life. My trophies were to be thousands of slides and hundreds of hours of film.

I decided that the first step in my vocation would be to make documentaries. Making these films is creating eternity by fighting time and space. It is collecting what exists at the time of the shooting, what may have existed since time immemorial, but what will no longer exist in five, ten, or fifteen years. Being a filmmaker has become the substitute for being the musician that I dreamed of as a child. Pictures were to be my music, my way of composing symphonies and rousing emotions.

For a whole year, Samivel patiently passed his knowledge on to me. Thanks to his talent and teaching, I became a reputable cameraman. When his movie was finished, two French explorer-filmmakers asked me to be their cameraman. Jacques Cornet was going to Afghanistan, Gabriel Linge to the Philippines. I chose the Philippines because Gabriel was the first one to leave.

"I thought we had a deal concerning your studies," said Maman. After a short pause, she added, "How long will that trip be?"

"Four months," I said. "Only four months, I expect."

"When would you leave?"

"In three months."

"That's another school year lost."

"No, Maman, as soon as I return, I'll go back to school and study hard to catch up."

Maman accepted. But I knew she was suffering, for she felt I had responsibilities toward my two young sisters and herself. In memory of my father, she had kept her widowhood and had no other entertainment than to take care of us. Therefore I felt, in order to gain a complete freedom, it was time to find the perfect someone to whom I could give the familial leadership. So my elder sister and I decided to marry Maman off. We enrolled her in all the clubs at the parish where we were living: the Choral Society, the Sunday Walkers Society, etc. At the bridge club, she fell in love with a widower, and they married just before I left for the Philippines. I was free!

CHAPTER TWO

My Brother the Headhunter

Too many people are thinking of security instead of opportunity. They seem more afraid of life than death.

JAMES F. BYRNES

The Philippines. An archipelago of 7,106 islands, 7,107 at low tide. Several very large islands covered with jungles and cities. Many without names. Some of rock and sand. Others with beaches and coconut trees. Hundreds belong to sultans whose kingdoms cover the entire southern part of the archipelago going toward Celebes and Borneo. Some shelter Moro guerrilleros. Others harbor vast colonies of pirates. Others are the temporary homes of the Badjaos, the nomads of the seas.

I love the Philippines. It has a smell of adventure. Everywhere. Even when only daily life is happening.

I had been in the Philippines for four months when one day my car broke down in the country. I had gone there to film rice harvesting. Forced to abandon the car, I found a bus to take me back to Manila.

Under the palm-thatched roof of the bus stop, people were jam-packed to avoid the strong noon sun. All around me were mothers with their sleeping or crying babies. On one side, a Filipino was caressing his fighting rooster. On the other side, a too-fat pig that a lady tried to push into a too-small bag pissed on my foot. In front of me, surrounded by a large, noisy audience, two crouching men were playing a game, moving their pieces—bottle caps and small stones—on a checkerboard drawn on the ground. Bettors had placed money on each side of the board.

As I watched, a sexually excited rooster chased a hen through the middle of the game, scattering the bottle caps and pebbles.

It took five minutes of loud arguments between players and assistants before the pieces were put back in their places. Then, another hen raced through to seize a dead worm. Later, a mother chicken, followed by five or six chicks, jumped on the game and shit on it, barely escaping a blow sent by one of the players. The play went on like this until the bus arrived in a cloud of dust and chicken feathers. To stop the bus the driver stalled the motor. "No brakes!" explained a Filipino standing next to me, laughing.

The bus was already full, but we all got on anyway. Inside, my nostrils were assaulted by a dozen different smells: sweat, heat, humidity, pigs, and the feces of all the different animals that also traveled on the bus. My ears thought I was in the middle of a market. My eyes discovered only one small, narrow place to sit, close to the window on the back bench of the bus. This place was free only because the other passengers had the kindness to squeeze themselves even more tightly together. To get to it I had to clamber through a central alley crowded by boxes, bags, and animals. As I gingerly made my way to the back, the driver attempted to start the engine by coasting down the steep road. I heard the same Filipino say, "And of course, no battery!"

My humorous Filipino informant was trying to keep his balance on top of the bags in the central aisle, as I squeezed between the window and a woman who had disappeared behind a mountain of bags on her knees. On the very top of her belongings was a wicker cage with a couple of ducks, their heads emerging through a hole. Each time the bus horn sounded, they tried to relieve their nervousness by nibbling on my hair. As I examined the open windows, wondering what could be done for protection in case of rain, I heard the voice of my Filipino fellow traveler: "Somewhere beneath the bags and the chicken under your seat you will find a piece of wood to put on the window in case of rain. But nobody uses it because of the heat."

Watching my hopeless attempts to dodge the hungry ducks, he added, "Five more hours to Manila. I guess you will never forget this trip."

Before we reached Manila, I knew everything about the life of the talkative Filipino, who was twenty-six years old and called Luis. He was a civil employee and had great pride in his country. When he learned I was a filmmaker, he said I should go north of Luzon—the main island, where we were—into the

Ilocos Norte, where rumors told of tribes who lived in the jungle and still practiced headhunting. It was said that Japanese soldiers who had been left there from World War II were being hunted for their heads. And, more recently, people have disappeared there, victims of a tribe called *Apayaos*, about whom very little is known.

"Have you been there?" I asked.

"Never," he said. "It's covered with a wild and dangerous jungle. Tribesmen are said to be ferocious."

"Would you go there?"

"Why not? One day, perhaps."

That day would be sooner than he expected.

I had come to the Philippines as Gabriel's cameraman more to make a travelogue than to explore. Although we had penetrated a quiet forest to film a group of *Negritos*, an ethnic group of black pygmies, I was already bored with the prospect of continuing to photograph picturesque sights and scenes. I proposed to Gabriel that we explore the jungle of Ilocos Norte and search for headhunters. He refused: "I am not interested in risking my life!"

My duty toward Gabriel ended four months later. I was free to return to Europe with him or stay longer. Although reason and promises indicated that I should return to Belgium and complete my education, I felt compelled to strike out into the unknown. I felt that in taking some kind of extreme risk I would fulfill my destiny. In short, I was twenty years old and looking for adventure. So, despite my lack of money, I decided to stay.

"You've really decided to meet headhunters?" said Gabriel, who, like all my other friends, thought I was crazy. But since nothing could change my mind, he left my return ticket to Europe in one of my pockets, and in the other, a few free local tickets offered by Philippines Airlines. He also arranged for me to continue to have the use of a Renault for as long as I wanted.

"Here's two hundred dollars," he said. "Sorry I can't lend you more. Shooting my movie cost much more than I expected."

An explorer-filmmaker is never sure he will come back alive or, if he does survive, that he will bring back what he was searching for. If he finds something amazing, and comes back alive, there is no security that the movie he shot will be exploitable or even usable. Film can be damaged by the humidity and

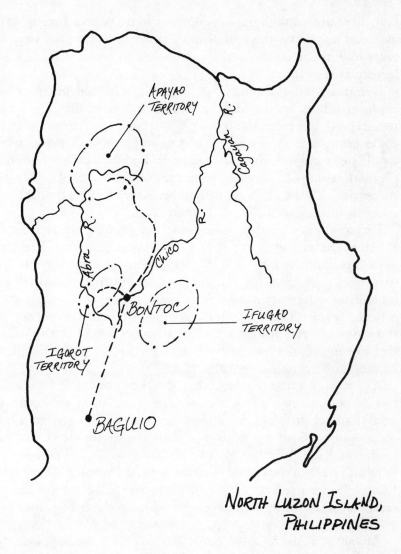

Map of the Philippines. Dash line indicates the trail of the expedition.

heat. Cameras can break down. There are no guarantees in the jungle and, consequently, financing an expedition is a risky investment. Unless it is considered an advertising campaign, no company is philanthropic enough to finance the crazy dreams of an explorer-filmmaker. Each new expedition is a financial headache. Each departure for a new dream is a financial risk. Each return from a trip is a nightmare until the explorer-filmmaker makes sure that the pictures are of a good quality and that there are enough quality pictures to make a feature-length movie. Then starts the hell of daily survival during the time it takes to edit the movie, write the book, and wait until the first lecture is scheduled.

Generally, an assistant or cameraman who accompanies an explorer-filmmaker in his expedition will have all of his expenses paid, but receives no salary. So it's certain that those who come along are driven by a common passion. Besides, who would be ready to endure such dangers and difficulties if not for the realization of a dream? If the movie is not exploitable or successful, it's the explorer-filmmaker who loses his money; his companions, after all, lived their dreams.

I have always tried to take along companions as assistants. When there is danger, one person can save the other. When one person is depressed, the other always seems to have the energy to restore him. Sharing danger and adventure in itself is an incredible source of energy. Who could resist such an opportunity? Everyone! I couldn't find a companion ready to journey to the jungles of the headhunters. Finally, I called Luis, the talkative Filipino I met on the bus. He said that he had a vacation coming and accepted my offer.

As I hung up the phone, I thought about how the whims of fate—a coincidence, a stroke of luck or misfortune, an accident, a mechanical problem, an unforeseen encounter—so often become key tools of an explorer. How much they change the course of a life. Without my car's breakdown in the country, I wouldn't have taken the bus to Manila, and I wouldn't have met Luis, who aroused in me the desire to explore the jungle in search of headhunters. Between Manila and the headhunter region lay 300 miles, and perhaps thousands of years.

At 4:00 A.M., my small Renault was ready for the trip, heavily loaded with reserves of gasoline, backpacks, strong walking shoes, and, of course, a couple of heavy, sharp machetes. I carried a still camera and a small tape recorder that Gabriel had left with me.

I had to hurry. Luis was waiting for me with a 4:30 breakfast on the other side of Manila. Moreover, to reach the poor district where he was living I had to detour twenty miles to avoid Tondo, another poor district reported to be very dangerous.

When I arrived Luis was in front of his house, a wooden shed surrounded by chickens and mud. This two-room "house" sheltered his wife, their two kids, the two sons of one of his brothers, another brother and his mother-in-law, and a cousin who had moved in "for a week" three years before. The walls of the room where Luis and I ate breakfast, while his whole family watched silently, were covered with old newspapers and several pious pictures representing the Holy Virgin. Three oil lamps hung from a ceiling covered with thousands of small black spots of fly shit. The place would have been sinister if not for all these smiling faces.

"So, you're going to visit the country?" said Luis's wife, whose eyes sparkled with goodness. "The country?" I asked, looking at Luis who suddenly interrupted me, saying, "Yes, we're going to visit the country!" On our way out after the farewells, Luis whispered to me, "I don't want them to worry about us."

Our first destination was Baguio, where Luis had some relatives. Baguio is 200 miles north of Manila on the way to the mountains. The town is built in a crater at an altitude of 4500 feet in the mountain fief of a headhunter tribe called the *Ifugaos*. But the Ifugaos no longer hunt human heads, or chase away the rich people from Manila who come to Baguio in summer for the cooler climate. Peaceful coexistence between the exotic mountain dwellers and the worshippers of the urban god of money has made Baguio a city of remarkable contrasts.

My first stop was at the Catholic mission, where I hoped to get information about the region I wanted to explore. If the headhunters still existed, the missionaries were likely to know where they were located. Missionaries have always been a priceless source of information for anthropologists and explorers. They were often the first ones to enter uncharted regions and contact unknown tribes. To bring a new religious faith to these so-called "primitive" people, missionaries learned to speak their language, and lived among them. Although their vocation was not ethnology, some missionaries recorded their observations of the traditions and customs of the tribal cultures even as these traditions were being destroyed by the religion the missionaries imposed.

At the church I met an old priest who, before retiring in Baguio, used to climb the wild mountains and walk through marshes and rivers of the jungle in search of "lost souls" to baptize. He said he had tried to reach the headhunters of the Ilocos Norte but had been turned back by their spears. "I bet that there are still some tribes actively hunting heads in the heart of the Ilocos Norte—like the Apayaos. Of course, the government will never acknowledge the fact. They believe it makes their country look backward. I hope you find them and are accepted."

The sky became darker as we left Baguio. Then the heavy clouds exploded with brutality. While all the children played, jumping and screaming under the pouring rain, the winds started their own wild games, chasing one another. They whirled, blew, ruffled the corollas of coconut trees, uprooted trees, pulled away the palm-leaf roofs of houses, tore off people's cone-shaped hats. Then, as suddenly as they started, the games of nature stopped, leaving the good smell of the wet soil that started to steam under the sun. Rice swamps reflected the sky and the swollen clouds again. Roads and small villages were transformed into sloughs. But the wet children were still there, screaming and splashing in roadside ditches filled with brown water.

As we went into the mountains, everything changed. No more straight roads across rice paddies spreading out their sparkling geometry as far as the eye can see. We left behind the coconut trees with green heads lending color to the heavy clouded skies. No more silhouettes of peasants in conical hats or buffalo with big white birds strutting on their heads and backs. No more children running behind the car. No more *sari-sari*—small huts transformed into a shop/bar/restaurant, where one can eat or drink at any time, day or night. No more crazy brakings to keep alive suicidal hens which waited until the last moment to cross the road. No more swerving to avoid 300 feet of road covered with fish or half a mile covered with paddy rice, drying in the sun. We left the caravans of kamikaze buses that charged down the middle of the road, their roofs covered with people sitting atop luggage, bicycles, goats, pigs, and chickens tied down by one leg. No, nothing of that here.

Civilization has yet to disturb the fragile quiet of the mountains. Even the weather is different; it turns cold and humid at night. The scenery bathed in mist gives a surrealist impression. The almost continuous rain of the last few days had transformed our road into an obstacle course of muddy holes. Each puddle we crossed threw a splatter of ocher mud on the windshield. The holes sucked greedily at our wheels as if to take them into the bowels of the earth. I drove down the steep roads, zigzagging between holes and trucks that came sideslipping down the incline. Three times I grazed the edge of the cliff. Once, I lost control completely and came to a stop just as the car was about to drop into a ravine. All that held us to the road was the thick mud clinging to the undercarriage of the car.

Finally the rain stopped and the sun started to lift the fog. At last we saw what Filipinos call the eighth wonder of the world. In front of us, for miles, covering both sides of the valley, were six-thousand-foot mountains whose flanks were carved with hundreds of large flooded terraces sparkling like mirrors, reflecting the sky and its cloud sculptures. Giant staircases of terraces led up to the summits and disappeared into the swirling fog: celestial paths to infinity, linking earth with heaven. The silence around us was broken only by the whisper of the wind playing in the grass.

These sculptured mountains are essential to the survival of the people of this region. Each terrace is a large rice paddy. The terraces were created over two thousand years ago in an effort that rivaled the building of the pyramids. First they were cut out of the mountains. Then, to retain the tons of mud and water, each one was surrounded by a fifteen-foot wall of large stones. Each wall has a double function: buttress of the terrace above, and foundation and support of the one below. An ingenious system of dikes and canals allows water from the higher terraces to irrigate the lower ones. It is estimated that if the lengths of these walls were added together, they would equal half the circumference of the earth.

This empire of carved mountains is the territory of the Ifugaos, who, it is said, practiced ritualistic headhunting until the 1940s. One can see their traditional villages, made up of five or six houses on pilework, set deep in the valleys or hanging precariously from the mountainsides near the rice terraces.

These men of the mountains still work these terraces with their water buffalo, sloughing through knee-high water in the sticky swamps, hoping not to be bitten by the venomous snakes that take refuge there. During the planting season the men's families join them. Some of these people are said to have webbed toes.

At noon of the second day out of Baguio, we reached Bontoc, a small town in the territory of the Igorots, where we stumbled upon a market. I immediately stopped the car and, with Luis, sauntered along in the crowded atmosphere.

I love markets. They reflect a people's state of mind, their primal interest in life, their needs, their emotions, and their problems. Markets reveal their religion, magic, witchcraft, and other parallel medicines. They show the variety of ethnic groups living in that region, the characters of their different identities, the languages and dialects.

Markets are a feast for eyes, nostrils, and ears. Colors of clothes and goods. Bad odors and smells of perfumes, spices, fruits, and other merchandise. Sounds of children's cries, screams of vendors vaunting their commodities, squeals of all the different kinds of animals contained in pasteboard boxes and willow cages. Some are familiar to our Western culinary traditions: pigs, ducks, chickens, rabbits. Some are more exotic to us: snakes of all sizes, giant lizards, monkeys, even puppies and kittens. By comparing the prices, it was easy to see which ones were considered delicacies. I have tasted all of them at one time or another. Whereas for some exotic foods it is hard to compare the taste with something familiar, one can say that a cat tastes like a rabbit, dog meat is closer to pig, snake resembles chicken, some water lizard is like fish, and the crocodile's tail is as delicious as lobster.

From the native pharmacopoeia's great variety of products, each of which is supposed to remedy a specific problem, I recognized *baluds,* the most popular aphrodisiac in the Philippines. The balud is a duck's egg cooked before it hatches, when the baby duck inside is already completely formed but without feathers, and the beak, the claws, the skull, and the rest of the bones still have the consistency of cartilage. It has the fine taste of a country egg. But it is disgusting when it has been cooked later than it should be and the baby duck is already covered with feathers, its beak, palmate feet, claws, skull, and bones harder than cartilage.

In Manila one can buy these aphrodisiacs anywhere at any time. In the districts containing dance halls, bars, and bordellos, one can hear the piercing voices of vendors yelling "Balud! Balud!" At that signal, especially around two or three in the morning, one can see older men chasing the vendors to buy a few baluds to improve their ability to make love.

Besides the small number of Filipinos who have settled here and the local Igorots (ex-headhunters) wearing modern clothes, other tribesmen who came down from their faraway villages were harbored at the Bontoc market. Even some Ifugaos were there to exchange their goods. None of the tribesmen wore shoes, and only a few wore shirts and trousers. The majority still dressed according to their old traditions. For a man, this was a long, thin piece of red cloth attached around the waist and passed between the legs and buttocks, hiding just the sex. A small straw cap, ornate with wild boar's tusks, was worn tilted back on the head. The scanty loincloth revealed the tattoos decorating their bodies.[1] In their villages the women are half-naked, but in the marketplace their only visible tattoos were those on arms and hands, the rest covered by a kind of shirt and a colorful traditional long straight cotton skirt which they weave themselves. Some women wore tiaras on their long black hair, made of snake's vertebrae threaded together. The only jewelry others wore were golden bracelets around their wrists.

The majority of the women smoked pipes turned upside down, in case of rain. Perhaps for the same reason, when they smoked a cigarette, they always put the burning part inside their mouth. The men preferred to chew tobacco instead of smoking it. However, the men's and women's favorite habit was to chew the betel, a veritable institution all over Asia. The betel is, in fact, made of four different ingredients: the arec nut, which is wrapped in a betel leaf, and a tobacco leaf on which is applied a little bit of quicklime. Betel is a variety of pepper plant native to Malaysia. The arec nut is astringent; the quicklime liberates the alkaloids from the betel and the nicotine from the tobacco. These alkaloids are a powerful stimulant, accelerating the heartbeat, producing euphoria, and diminishing hunger. But this tonic has negative aspects: the betel reddens the lips, the saliva, and the gums, while the quicklime blackens the teeth and slowly burns them away completely. Chewing betel is for Asia what masticating *cola* nuts is for Africa, what chewing *khat* leaves is for Arabia, and what chewing *coca* leaves is for some South American countries.

Markets are a perfect place to make new contacts and friends. Not only are they places where people come to buy, to sell, or to exchange but also gatherings where people come to meet one another and talk. I have never left a market without having talked to people who offered invitations to their homes. That day in the market—by accident or by fate—Luis and I met Bong.

1. For more explanation about meanings of tattooing, see note 1 at the end of this book.

Bong is an Igorot. He was about seventeen years old—he didn't know with precision—and was a student in the Catholic mission. On the condition that we would take him to a distant village to visit his grandfather, whom he hadn't seen for a year, he agreed to be our interpreter and guide. For that family reason, the school gave him one week off.

We continued north from Bontoc at 3:00 A.M. The road, nothing more than a track carved in the muddy soil, crossed valleys and mountains covered with jungle. Twelve hours later, it became completely impassable. We abandoned the car and, each carrying his personal belongings, followed a small path down a steep hill leading to Bong's grandfather's village deep in a valley. On the way down the cliff several caves attracted my interest. Bong was too far ahead to answer my questions, so I decided to explore for myself. Inside, laid out in the hollows of large tree trunks that had been scooped out like canoes, were human skeletons, some quite recently dead, with hair and flesh still on their bodies. Unwittingly, I had found my way into a burial ground. Seeing the remains of people who had once lived, ate, laughed, made love, I experienced both fascination and fear. I don't understand death; I don't understand how life can suddenly end, just like that.

Luis's call interrupted my thoughts and I became aware that what I was doing could arouse anger among the natives. Terrified, I jumped out of the cave, hoping that nobody had seen me.

Bong's grandfather's village was visible from the place where Luis and Bong were waiting farther down the cliff. Following a steep zigzagging ancient path, it took almost a half hour to cover a few hundred yards.

Trailing Bong, Luis and I entered the village which was comprised of huts, all of different shapes—high, low, square, and rectangular—that unlike those of Ifugaos are built directly on the ground. We were welcomed by a dozen barking dogs that created a panic among the great number of chickens and pigs that had been resting peacefully in the shadows. Most of the men and women were still at work in the fields, so there remained only the old women cooking food in front of their huts, and others taking care of small babies. Old men talked together under a palm tree. Children scurried out of sight as soon as they noticed us.

Soon Bong found his grandfather, an old man with tattoos covering his body. When he saw his grandson, tears of joy came to his eyes. Bong kissed the old man's hands almost rapturously. After they talked, the old man approached Luis and me, stretched out his scrawny hand to us, and spoke. Bong translated: "This village is your village because you have brought a great joy into my heart. After he moved to the city, I thought I would never again see the son of my son." He pointed to a hut. "That was my house." Then, putting his hand on my shoulder, he added, "Now it is our house! Come in."

"Our house." This house literally became ours. This sharing expression is one of the touching ways people of tradition indicate they have accepted you. Everything considered theirs is now ours. There are no exceptions.

This act of sharing is part of their social organization because only the principle of sharing can ensure their survival. Igorots, like the majority of people of tradition, live in a clan system that is an extension of the family structure and is based on family unity. The family unit is the smallest form of social organization, consisting of the father, the mother, and the children. Clan members have common blood ties, up to the fifth and sometimes sixth degree, and include those who are related by marriage. The elders are called the *parents* (old men are called *father;* old women are called *mother*). All the younger members are their children and call one another *brother* and *sister.*

To strengthen clan unity, tradition spiritually links all the members to one another, so that clan unity is formed not only by familial ties but also, and most of all, by magical bonds. For the stronger the clan unity, the more securely the clan system will ensure survival of all its members by providing them with protection, shelter, and food.

The clan unity principle doesn't eliminate individuality, individual possession, or personal wealth. Clan unity manifests itself in the collective responsibility of members for one another's safety. Furthermore, each member is equally responsible for the actions of every other member of the clan, sharing equally in the consequences of victory or defeat of their clan by another clan, or in the disgrace or honor coming to their clan. When any one of them commits a crime or a misdeed against another clan, all the members of the clan will be troubled equally, and all of them are liable to vengeance from the relatives of the victim. If the victim is someone of their own clan, all the members must avenge him. In cases of murder, it is a collective disgrace not to avenge the victim.

The clan must always provide its members with shelter. Someone building his hut will always be helped by all the members of his clan. In exchange, at his turn, he will help everybody else. In addition, all clan members collectively face the consequences of any hardship or misfortune, such as a fire, a death, or the destruction of a crop, which may occur to any one of them at any time.

Generally, the totality of the land belongs to all clan members. Sometimes, however, because of a complicated system of inheritance, certain lands are privately owned. Except for the very old, the very young, and pregnant women, everyone, including a private owner, shares in the work of the fields, whoever the fields belong to. Even the owner of a private field will work in others' as well as in his own and in those belonging collectively to the clan.

All crops produced by the clan's land are shared equally among clan members. Private plot owners, in their turn, will share among all clan members a part of their privately produced crops. After sharing, they retain what remains, but in time of short supply, their private reserve will feed all clan members. Crops or products of hunting and gathering are divided in equal parts, although in some clans, the chief or the shaman gets a slightly bigger share. Sharing always includes every single clan member, regardless of what crimes he may have committed against his clan or whether he has worked or not. Participation in personal and collective work is not an obligation, but instead is taken for granted as something everyone does. Even shirkers will be fed by the clan, although they lose valuable prestige. Only expulsion from a clan terminates the obligation to share.

Expulsion or death is the ultimate punishment for the worst crime a clan member can commit against his community. A murderer of a member of his own clan, or an adulterer, will receive the death penalty; the adulteress, if not killed by her husband, will be expelled from the clan, as will a thief. However, depending on its own laws, each clan—or each culture— may have a different notion about what is the worst crime a member can commit against his community.

This principle of unity, such as collective sharing, can be extended by peace treaty to involve more than one clan of the same tribe and, sometimes, even a clan of another tribe.

Before showing us into our new home, Bong's grandfather yelled something to his neighbor, an old woman who was cooking some food in front of her house. "Great," Bong said. "We'll eat!"

The Igorot hut's main structure is made of tree trunks and completed with bamboo sticks. Inside the square-shaped house is one solid tree trunk, erected at the center, that supports the roof structure. Two such supports are needed for the rectangular-shaped huts. The frames of the roof and walls are covered by thick layers of palm fronds. Lacking inside separations, the whole hut is essentially used as a bedroom, although in times of rain it serves additionally as kitchen, dining room, and living room. The furniture is rudimentary. In Bong's grandfather's hut, a few mats on one side were used as beds. On the other side was a bench, a few small baskets, and two old native chairs. A cooking hearth for use in rainy weather was set in the middle of the room close to the center pole. The skulls of a pig and a buffalo were hung from the roof just over the hearth, along with a large bag of talismans to ward off evil spirits.

Because Bong's grandfather was a widower, his food was prepared by the old woman next door. She served traditional food in two cast-iron cooking pots called *payoc*. One pot contained the *tenafo,* the rice, and the other, the *otag,* dried meat of a water buffalo or a pig, served with a sauce. Otag can also be made from wild boar or deer, which may be obtained from a hunting tribe in exchange for rice. Smaller animals, such as chickens, snakes, ducks, and monkeys, are boiled or roasted fresh. Vegetables are served on large banana leaves covered with *kamote,* sweet potato. To wash down the meal, the old woman brought us two large, tall, hollow bamboo tubes, one filled with water, the other with *basi,* a very thirst-quenching native beer made of fermented rice, with about the same alcoholic content as wine.

Crouching over the food served in common pots, we all ate with our fingers. But with style! The societies of tradition have their own rule book of *savoir-vivre.* Only the right hand is used to touch food. With your fingers, you take a small portion of rice and squeeze it until it becomes a ball that you can soak in the sauce. Grabbing a piece of meat doesn't require quite so much skill. As you eat, it is polite to make little noises to show your satisfaction and to please the host.

This first meal with Bong's grandfather was very important

because it made me his protégé, and that changed my relationship with the members of his clan. As I knew from my childhood in Africa, a foreigner becomes a welcome guest by accepting the first meal and sharing it with his host. A guest is put under his host's protection. If someone from the village physically or morally hurt me, it would be as if he had hurt Bong's grandfather. If someone from another clan insulted or killed me, I would be avenged by the host's clan in the same way that a blood member would be. All over the world, all societies of tradition have such laws of hospitality.

Now that I was accepted into the tribe as a guest, I was not only fully protected, but everything for my comfort in the way of food and accommodation would be taken care of by the tribesmen. This situation, however, would continue only for a limited time, depending on tribal custom, from a minimum of twenty-four hours up to a whole year.

A tribe does not automatically include a foreigner under its hospitality laws, but there are ways to encourage it. For instance, I increased my chances greatly by bringing Bong to his grandfather.

On the other hand, being a guest is not enough in itself to secure a longer stay than the period allowed by the laws of hospitality. And when the time comes, the tribe will usually make a guest know whether or not he's welcome to leave. That demand will be strictly enforced if, during his stay, his behavior has disturbed the traditions and thus jeopardized the harmony of the village. The way a guest behaves will determine his chances of extending his stay, so when I arrive among tribesmen my first priority is to be sensitive and receptive to their way of life. For me the success of an expedition is measured by the freedom to stay as long as I want among a tribe, studying and filming them without hurry.

I said earlier that one of the explorer's main tools is coincidence. Intuition, the ability to function by following one's primal instincts, is another. Before setting out on my expeditions, I try to learn as much as possible from studies, books, and other explorers about the customs of the area I intend to visit. Once there, I try to get more information by questioning missionaries and neighboring tribes. And yet, all that is not enough. Books and studies, if any exist, are not always accurate.

Even if there have been other explorers expert in that area, they are not always known. You can't find them in the yellow pages—and even when they are available they will not always share all they know because it's still part of their own study. If any missionaries are available, their knowledge may be scant. Neighboring tribes may not know much about other tribes, or they will say anything just to please you. Hard facts are scarce in the jungle. That's why I have to use my intuition when I arrive among tribesmen; I must feel what they want from me and how to deal with them. Among these people who live in concert with nature, I gain respect, friendship, and perhaps the right to stay alive—not with the knowledge given to me by modern civilization but with my guts, the primitive within myself.

I observe their behavior, and I act as they do, in strict conformity with their traditional social practices. I accept whatever is offered me, be it food, drink—or women, in case they also practice sexual hospitality. Even if I am not required to share in their daily labor, I ask permission to participate in the work of the fields or in their hunting and fishing parties. I try to help treat illnesses with the medicines I have brought along.

I make myself aware of their taboos so I can avoid violating them. For example, their religious traditions may have decreed that some part of the village or some house cannot be entered or certain trees cannot be touched. Because taboos can differ radically from tribe to tribe, learning about them requires considerable vigilance. Whenever in doubt, I abstain from entering cemeteries and places of worship and from touching whatever seems to be surrounded by a special aura, venerated by people, or decorated with offerings.

Allowing for exceptions, if a guest breaks a ban by ignorance, the tribe will usually forgive him, for even though tribal social organization gives him the same rights as if he were a member, he is allowed some leeway in the strict religious prohibitions that apply to actual members of the tribe. Once I broke a taboo that I thought would cost my life. In Haiti where I was filming a Voodoo ceremony, the *hougan* (the priest) had warned me many times that, as soon as the ceremony started and until it ended, it was forbidden for any uninitiated person to move outside the large sacred and magical white circle that was drawn around us. "Why?" I asked. "It's dangerous!" was all he said. While filming the Voodoo ritual, I inadvertently stepped outside the circle just in front of the priest. His reaction was instantaneous. He called a few of his assistants who brutally grabbed me and carried me into a dark room, part of the *houmfort,* the temple. I was more surprised than scared, but rapidly became more scared than surprised for, over the noise of the drumbeats keeping time to the ceremony outside, I heard snake whistlings coming from the corners of the room. Partially blinded in the sudden darkness, I moved to the middle of the room and stumbled upon a bed onto which I quickly jumped. Getting used to the darkness, I saw a dozen human forms that, whistling, were crawling on the floor and onto the bed. I was surrounded by men and women in deep trances, possessed by Djamballa Vedo: the male energy of fecundity, symbolized by a snake. Fearing their reaction, I was too scared to push them away from me. Still whistling, they pulled me down on the bed and crawled all over my body. I lay with them for more than twenty minutes before they silently slid back to the floor. I stood frozen on the bed and waited for the ceremony outside to end, wondering what would be my next psychological ordeal. After an hour, the drumbeats stopped. Two men brought me back to the center of the temple where I had to completely undress. The priest gave me a ritual bath "to purify me," as he said, from the evil *loas,* or spirits, that touched me when I moved out of the magic circle of protection.

Another thing I do during that period of hospitality is to learn, as fast as I can, as much of a tribe's language as possible so I can express myself without a translator, even if one is available. Translators' services can be a double-edged sword if my words and those of the people I meet are misinterpreted. A first contact with tribesmen may be jeopardized if my interpreter belongs to another tribe or to the same tribe but another clan. Even if he is a member of their clan, they may not have positive feelings for him, for whatever reasons, and this may diminish my chances of gaining acceptance. So, using sign language and drawings I make on the ground, I do my best to communicate with tribesmen on my own. Then I begin to learn their language, starting with the most useful words, such as *water, food, tree,* that I can pick up quite fast. The mind remembers very quickly when one is alone among people who speak a foreign language. Necessity stimulates the talent.

Because of the trading contacts people have with their neighbors, there is a good chance that when I reach the next tribe I will find there a tribesman who understands at least a little of the language of the tribe from which I have come. After they accept me, I quickly learn their language and then move on, linguistically hopscotching from tribe to tribe. In this manner I am able to cross a region made up of various tribes speaking different languages.

Understanding a language is generally easier than speaking it. Often I discover only afterward, when reading books or talking to scholars, much that I heard but didn't really understand at the time I was living among a tribe. So, to bring back an accurate report of their customs and life-style, I always record on tape the tribesmen's answers to my many questions. Later, missionaries or other people who know the language make clear what were mysteries to me.

Learning a people's language always pleases them. They feel proud that a foreigner shows interest in their culture. Every night around the campfire or inside a hut, they teach me new words. Then, all together, as if we were in a classroom, they ask for and learn words from my language. And if they laugh at me because of the clumsy way I pronounce their words, it's not mockery but genuine amusement, just as their attempts to pronounce my language amuse them. Their great sense of humor invites jokes which, unfortunately, I am rarely able to tell because I lack the vocabulary. But by behaving in funny ways, I make them burst out laughing. In fact, almost everything amuses them, as if they were children. And in many ways they are. Comparing their state of mind to ours, they have remained at the level of childhood where the power of belief and magic is part of their everyday life. Their reasoning, even if it follows another logic, is not a matter of intelligence, but of imagination and faith.

Laughter is a tool of communication. It erases suspicion, builds confidence, and establishes ties between people. To make people laugh is the best way I have found to make myself rapidly accepted among a tribe and to acquire special friends and allies. And these are important to have whenever a tribal council is deciding whether to extend my stay at the end of the grace period covered by the laws of hospitality. Then my behavior will be ruled by strict observance of their social laws. While continuing to have the same rights as other tribal members, I also acquire new obligations and duties. I gain the right to have a hut of my own. If none is available, the community will help me build one. If I continue to harmonize and contribute, it is possible for me to become, one day, a full member of the tribe by a process of initiation.

After four days in the village, with visits to a few others, the time came to give Bong a ride back to his school in the town of Bontoc. On the way, he introduced Luis and me to another Igorot village. He prepared the way for us, so that on our return from Bontoc we could make use of a network of clan loyalties that could lead us to the Kalingas, an isolated tribe living farther away from civilization.

Since visiting the mountain tribes, Luis strangely had lost the humor that had so pleased me when I first met him on the bus trip to Manila. Now he was always silent and rarely posed questions to Bong about the customs of his tribe. Luis was an educated adult, a man of the cities who had never experienced a stay among traditional peoples. He was shocked by their life-style and felt kinship more with me than with the natives. He became more and more like an outsider just at the time I was feeling closer to the natives. Like most urban Filipinos, he didn't recognize any common bond with these tribesmen. Although he seemed to recognize their deep happiness, he was embarrassed by the archaic conditions in which they lived. At times he complained to me about their unwillingness to cooperate with the efforts of his government to move them closer to modern civilization.

After delivering Bong, we drove a half day along narrow, bumpy dirt roads no wider than our wheel base, often scraping the bottom of the car's chassis. We had left Bontoc far behind before we realized that we had lost the right tracks somewhere along the way. As I was about to make a U-turn, a half-naked tribesman burst out of the bushes, told us he was a man from the Kalinga tribe, and asked for a ride to the road's end. Seeing an opportunity to be invited among his tribe, we took him with us. When the tracks ended, the man said to follow him down the valley. So, Luis and I, carrying our bags, abandoned the car and began to walk along an ancient trail. After three days in rain and fog, going up one mountain and down the other side, passing through villages, some perched on mountain flanks and others nestled in valleys, we reached the home of our new friend.

The Kalingas are taller and stronger than the Igorots, and have smaller waists and broader shoulders. Their dark skin and straight noses make them look rather like North American Indians. Still considering themselves to be warriors, Kalingas continue to be feared by Igorots and Ifugaos. Not long ago—before they were forced to become farmers to survive—they had been hunters. Hunting was the first and the oldest form of survival and the only one ever practiced by warriors. To be a hunter is to have another state of mind—even in our society, *hunter* has remained synonymous with *adventurer*. Among traditional people, hunters generally enjoy more prestige than do farmers and cultivators. A hunter sees breeding livestock—because it involves traveling with the animals—as preferable to cultivating a field, which, in his eyes, represents the lowest responsibility a sedentary people can have.

Composed of several huts, some on pilework, others on ground, the small Kalinga village was vibrating as if tomtoms were beating everywhere. But the beatings were not drums, just women crushing wild rice in front of their huts. As they faced one another in pairs, hammering their high wooden pestles into the long mortars in rapid rhythm, the sparkling sweat on their half-naked bodies accentuated the tattoos that covered their abdomens and arms. Kalinga women are widely regarded as great beauties and were often the objects of tribal wars with neighboring Igorots and Ifugaos, who risked their lives to kidnap them.

When the Kalinga who brought me to the village noticed me admiring the beautiful breasts of one of the women, he warned me: "Don't look at our women! Kalingas don't like that." I wanted to answer that I was looking at them with an anthropological eye, but instead, from that moment, I never stared directly at the women but observed them with my peripheral vision.

I noticed a group of men gathered around a large circular platform called the *ato,* which was surrounded by three separate poles. As I was to learn, a human head is buried underneath each pole. Generally, the ato is a circular platform about fifteen feet in diameter made of one large stone. Sometimes it is surrounded by a circle of large flat stones where the men sit. A human head is also buried under each stone. The ato is a place of worship where the council of elders and wisemen meet with the *pangollo,* the chief of the village, to have discussions and make political decisions. Without an ato a village would not even exist.

There was action in the ato. Some of the people there were angry, some excited, some laughing. There were no placid faces. Our Kalinga friend, wondering as much as Luis and I about the reason for the meeting, left us and entered the crowded ato. After a while he came back and, using gestures and the Kalinga language mixed with Igorot words, gave us an explanation.

"One year ago, during a dispute, in spite of a peace treaty tying the two villages, a man from our village was killed in an Apayao village. The murder broke the peace treaty. Our clan must have revenge. An eye for an eye, blood always calls for blood. The men are meeting to make plans to catch the murderer and behead him. His head will be brought here and offered to the *fedohing,* the keeper of the peace treaty (who can also be the *aman-a,* the shaman). Only when the head is delivered can the peace treaty be resumed."

"What will happen if they don't find the killer?"

"We will kill three other members of their clan."

"What is going on now?"

"Our shaman is performing an *eyag,* a magical ceremony to question the divinities about the best way to find and attack the murderer."

"Can we see?" I asked.

"No!" he answered.

Although revenge is part of their social system, tribal people are not eager to die themselves. They will seek to delay the danger of their obligatory revenge for as long as possible, and then go to the shaman to find out if the time is right—hoping that the omen is wrong or that the culprit has died a natural death in the meantime.

Among the Ifugaos, to select the man who will be responsible for exacting vengeance, the shaman, carrying a rooster, enters the circle formed by all the volunteers who sit on the ground. He makes invocations and asks the spirits to guide the choice of the rooster. After its cry, a sign that vengeance must be taken, the shaman beheads the rooster with an axe and lets its body run around until it collapses. The man closest to the rooster's fallen body is the chosen one. This man then picks up the rooster and throws it to another man who will be his successor if he cannot fulfill his duty. The two of them have six years to avenge their clan's honor. The number of men who must be killed in revenge depends on the social importance of the original victim.

Often these acts of vengeance lead to tribal war. However, to avoid it the tribes have various ways of attempting to save even the worst relationship they have with another clan. For instance, I learned later that the vengeance of the Kalinga clan could have been avoided if, as soon as the murder had been committed, the Apayao clan's keeper of the peace treaty had come to offer the keeper of this village a large cast-iron cooking pot, at the same time saying, "I am bringing you this *payoc,* which is not broken. I wish it to be the same for our peace treaty." Because the Apayaos had neglected to do this, the Kalingas sent a messenger to their village to get back their *polting,* the long, large machete that is exchanged to symbolize the peace treaty.

Violence, in traditional societies, exists to enforce morality. Other than a sudden act of violence engendered by passion—besides killing her lover, a man may kill his wife if she is guilty of adultery—violence is dictated more often by their code of honor than by their own tempers. But violence can be caused by fear—fear of gods' reprisals or fear of outsiders. A tribe's belligerence toward a foreigner is more likely provoked by fear of him than by the tribe's inherent ferocity.

Knowing they were neighbors, I spent the next three days asking our Kalinga friend about the Apayaos. He finally confirmed that they still hunt human heads. He said that their headhunting is most intense during the season when flowers bloom, because that is also the wedding season, and before a young man can be married, he must behead a man. I asked if at this time of the year the jungle was safe. "The territory of Apayaos is very large," said the Kalinga. "It covers deep valleys and high mountains." Then he made me understand that the blooming of flowers had ended here and in some other parts of the forest, but elsewhere—depending on various factors influencing the climate, altitude, terrain, and humidity—flowers might be about to bloom.

Perhaps it was this uncertainty that made Luis change his mind about accompanying me. Was he suddenly afraid to risk his life just for the thrill of meeting a tribe of headhunters? I don't know, but he came to me and said, "Let me introduce you to Amok. He'll bring you to the Apayaos. You can see the headhunters on your own."

"But what about you, Luis?" I replied, very surprised, since just the day before he had expressed his excitement about meeting headhunters.

"I have taken too much time off from work. I—I really must go back to Manila. Don't worry, just leave me on the road and I'll catch a truck. You will have no problem. Amok will be more helpful than I would, because he speaks the language. But maybe you shouldn't go."

"Don't worry. Nothing will happen to me," I answered.

I shared Luis's increasing sense of danger. But whereas it drove him back to the city, it only reminded me of the heart-pounding pleasure that I had in the bush as a child. I could no more have turned back than he could have gone on. In fact, his decision to go back made my desire to go on even stronger.

Three days later we were back at the car. Leaving Luis by the side of the road, Amok and I drove off. About a mile from a small Kalinga village, the path became completely impassable. Amok went and made arrangements to leave the useless car under the chief's protection. I loaded my backpack with a change of clothes—one extra shirt, a pair of underwear, jeans, and socks. I added a pack of tobacco leaves and betel nuts to be used as gifts; my sleeping bag; the cassette tape recorder; a still camera; and only three rolls of film, for that was all I could afford. Amok carried a small bag with some rice and a few pieces of dried meat. Armed with our machetes, we started to cross miles of rice fields. Later we entered the deep jungle, walking north. The North was mountains covered with jungles. The North was where I had a meeting with my destiny.

It is always dark in the interior of the jungle. The dense tops of the trees form a roof, which prevents the sunlight from coming through. But I was surprised to find walking through the jungle easy. The giant tropical trees were spaced quite far from one another. Apart from lianas hanging down from branches, there were few thick bushes choking the space. Only rarely did we have to use our machetes to carve through the vegetation, because this jungle was made of primary forest. The other kind of forest, more difficult to cross, is called the *secondary* forest. It is crowded with thorny vines and lianas that weave from tree to tree, feeding on their sap and ultimately strangling them to death. The secondary forest is cloaked with thick, dense plants, struggling with one another for survival and fighting for life with giant trees whose foliage blocks the sunlight.

Another thing that surprised me was encountering so little of the jungle fauna. Besides the noisy swarms of malaria-carrying mosquitoes, and monkeys we rarely saw but often heard moving from branch to branch, there were multicolored birds, insects, and colonies of ants of all sizes up to one inch long. And yet we know this jungle contains snakes, wild boars, deer, black panthers. At the slightest noise, they all freeze, merge with the dense vegetation, and become invisible. If I had been there to explore the animal world, as I did later in other expeditions, I would have had to build a place to hide and wait, silent and motionless.

Though the fauna is often invisible to the eyes of a neophyte, its sounds are everywhere, the principal performers being monkeys and birds. The jungle is a vast symphony whose music and volume vary from place to place and with the time of day.

We pitched camp around 4:00 P.M., for night falls fast, and when the sun goes down, the jungle is pitch black. Using thin branches, Amok built the framework of a small hut on foot-high pilework to keep us away from the damp and the bugs, and covered the roof and sides with palm fronds and large tree leaves. Then he cooked the rice and we ate it with the dried meat. We didn't need to carry more than a gourd of water because streams and small rivers run everywhere throughout the jungle.

I drank, and always do, directly from rivers and streams without boiling the water or treating it with chemicals. Initially, of course, I often suffer acute diarrhea, but the right medicines ease the pain and get me over the first crisis. In this way I build up antibodies that I will need in the wild when I am accepted among natives with whom food and drinks will be shared. Treating my water with chemicals would kill my natural resistance; boiling water would not build up a new resistance. And when I ran out of chemicals or could not boil water, my system would be defenseless against germs. Acute amebiasis cannot be afforded in the middle of nowhere, when one needs all one's resources to survive.

I didn't sleep well that first night in the jungle because the sounds were much louder than in the daytime, and my mind kept imagining my meeting headhunters. I fantasized about what my first contact with them would be like, and I especially wondered what their reaction would be when they saw a white man, if they hadn't seen one before.

Soon after I fell asleep, I awoke with a strong need to urinate. It was so dark around me that I was scared to get out of the hut, and I was reluctant to go near Amok, for whenever he had to pee he always went far from me. Uncomfortable, I went back to sleep.

The next morning was very cold as it always is in jungle, due to the humidity of 90 percent or more. Thus, my clothes were wet and were to remain so for the whole trip. Soon they were covered with mold, which ate them away.

Yet I always love the mornings. Heated by the invisible sun, the soil and the wet vegetation start to smoke, slowly plunging the jungle into a translucent fog that disappears as the plumes of steam rise to the tops of the trees and, caught there, rest like strands of plaited hair. These columns of steam carry up the aromas of the jungle floor, a profusion of smells, each one different from the other—some vile stenches, some rare perfumes. After a while I learned to recognize the acid smell of the fungi, the sour odor of the jungle creepers, the heavy aroma of the soil, the subtle perfumes of fruits and flowers. This feast of smells is strong and powerful in the jungle because each odor remains prisoner of the place where it springs up. Smells and noises don't travel very much through the density of the vegetation, but remain amplified by the closeness of the space. Sound is also amplified. Sometimes, a single leaf falling from a tree can startle you, because its fall resounds like a clapping of hands.

It was raining again, the kind of rain one finds in Europe or in New York in winter, cold and thin. So we stopped for a short break. Whether attracted by our body heat, our smell, or some unknown vibrations, a multitude of leeches instantly came toward us. Those that had been on the branches over our heads seemed to hurl themselves down on our bodies. Those on more distant perches flung themselves on top of those who were already wiggling toward us on the wet, leaf-covered soil. As soon as they reached our skin, they searched for the tenderest part. Then they attached themselves with the tiny suckers on their heads and proceeded to make small holes with the three teeth-like blades in their mouths. Though we saw them all around us and brushed many off our clothes and boots, we felt no bites because of an anesthetic in their saliva that also prevents coagulation: the wounds bleed for hours and often become infected. Amok taught me never to tear away a leech, but to burn them off with cigarettes or to put salt on them. When neither remedy is available, natives detach leeches by passing a machete or knife between their skin and the leech.

At the end of the day, Amok asked me to undress. I did so and several leeches inflated with blood fell down from my shirt. They had reached my skin under the clothes, quenched their thirst and, unable to escape, took a nap in their trap. We found a few others still at work. Some were crushed between my toes. They had entered my boots through the small lace holes and reached my skin by passing through the weave of my socks. Because of their incredible ability to make themselves as thin as needles, leeches can be deadly to people. They can enter the anus and penetrate the viscera. Then, when they are so inflated with blood that they are unable to exit, they die while still in the viscera, causing their victims rapid and deadly septicemia. When crossing swamps, the natives protect their buttocks with a mixture of tobacco and water; but tobacco burned my skin, so I rubbed my buttocks and testicles with wet soap. When the soap was gone, I blocked my anus with adhesive plaster.

I must admit I wasn't prepared to undergo such an expedition in a hostile jungle. But I was driven by instincts forged at the time of my childhood. Almost every smell, scent, sound, and feeling took me back to my African boyhood, back into the atmosphere of those exploratory expeditions when curiosity was my means of vanquishing cowardice. It was as if I walked in two different dimensions of space and time. I was at the same time in both Africa and Asia; I was in both my present time and my past. I was child and adult, walking side by side. I was neither a neophyte nor a "professional," just a follower of a mysterious call, with no sense of uncertainty or error or danger. It was as if the danger were not intended personally for me.

Before Luis left, he had given me some information about Amok. Amok, a Kalinga, had spent much of his boyhood hunting with an Apayao friend. That friendship between a Kalinga and an Apayao was possible because their clans were tied together by a peace treaty. One day, his friend married a woman from another Apayao clan. To satisfy both clans, long in dispute, the newly married friend moved to his wife's distant village. When Amok learned of my desire to meet Apayaos living far from civilization, he saw an opportunity to meet his friend again by taking me to that village. The only problem was that he had never been there before and didn't dare ask directions from other Apayao villages for, he said, "They are not good people." So we had to follow a path marked in his memory years ago.

After almost eight days of walking up and down mountains covered with deep jungles, and crossing rivers (a journey we could have made in only three days if I had been able to walk as fast as he), Amok announced, "I know where we are. My friend's village should be behind this mountain."

I asked him: "Have we been lost for the past week?"

"Yes," he replied, "but now I know where I am!" We were, he said, still two days from the village of his friend. Astonished by his precision, I asked him how he could be so sure. He explained that a rock of a certain form, a river having a specific color and making a distinctive noise because of the stones in its stream, a tree having a particular aspect, the number and shapes of mountains—all were landmarks of a path.

When we left Amok's village, he didn't speak a word of English and I spoke only a few words of Kalinga, yet after a few days we communicated well. Need and desire create a language all their own.

As we approached a narrow, calm river, Amok warned me to be careful of crocodiles, yet he walked right into the water. I yelled after him that we should build bamboo rafts. He called back to me there was no need because the river was not that deep. How could I tell him that for me, a foreigner, crossing this river infested with crocodiles seemed suicidal? Seeing me hesitate, he came back laughing and asked, "Don't you have crocodiles in your country?" I suppose that he assumed everything was the same everywhere.

"We don't have crocodiles, but big fish that can eat men!" I said, because I didn't want to appear a wimp.

I took out my handgun that I had hidden in my bag since the beginning of that trip. I'd had the feeling that if natives saw it they would interpret my carrying a weapon as a sign of hostility or possibly fear of facing the same dangers they confronted with only their spears.

Amok reacted instantly when he saw my gun. "No good to show that to Apayaos. We must not enter the village of my friend with that."

I had hoped to keep my gun hidden until I was accepted by the tribe; then I would use it to help them hunt. But perhaps that was a bad idea. Anything as powerful as a gun might only have disrupted the delicate fabric of their society by creating a need they would not be able to fulfill after I was gone.

"No need for the gun," Amok said. "Watch me." He reentered the water and waited until I joined him. Then, as we made our way across, he pounded the surface with the palms of his hands. The reverberation from the water was intended to scare off the crocs. Apparently Amok's technique worked, for we were able to cross the river without being eaten. Nevertheless I was happy to be on dry land, at least for the moment.

Amok was still visibly upset that I was carrying the gun, so I wrapped it in a T-shirt and buried it next to a tree that I marked with my knife, hoping to recover it on my return.

Nights were now easy to handle. As soon I lay down I fell asleep, overcome by exhaustion. No more fantasizing about anything whatsoever. And when the need to have a pee woke me, I moved out of the hut; as the nights went by, I moved progressively farther and farther away. One gets used to danger.

When we reached the mountain summit in the late afternoon, through a break in the vegetation we could see a village perched on the opposite slope. But it was not the village of Amok's friend, which he said was set in a valley between stony cliffs.

"Probably behind this mountain, in the next valley," Amok claimed.

But I had had enough of walking through the jungle. I had come for headhunters and I didn't care which village they were from. I refused to go farther and begged him to introduce me to these villagers. "You can go visit your friend, and I will stay here. Pick me up on your way back."

"They don't know you, and they don't know me!" said Amok, a little upset. "You and I are not Apayaos! Who knows what they'll do?"

"Okay, okay, Amok. We'll see tomorrow," I answered, to calm him.

"Yes, yes, tomorrow. It isn't good to approach a village at night. Night is the time of evil spirits. If we disturb the spirits, they may make someone sick and we will be blamed for it." To illustrate his meaning, he drew a finger across his neck.

I slept poorly through the rainy night.

In the morning, the sun arose strong and bright, and early it became so hot that even the birds, monkeys, and insects became silent, as if they were unwilling to compete with the sun's voice.

I took a mirror out of my pack and checked my face to see if

I was looking too wild for my first meeting with headhunters. While I was doing this I suddenly became aware that the jungle was totally silent. Startled, I looked around and my gaze was caught by some magnificent orchids hanging from nestlike parasites attached to trees. Flowers! I thought while my heart began to race. Amok and I were surrounded by flowers. Flowers everywhere. Flowers of all colors. Flowers meant the wedding season had started. In our walk through the jungle I had completely forgotten to verify if it was a safe season for us to visit headhunters. Panic drove my heart into a frenzy. Injected into the blood by fear, adrenaline always fills the brain with a cloud that muffles thought. I could not move or say to Amok, "We're in great danger. We'd better get out of here before. . . ."

A sharp noise interrupted the merry-go-round in my brain. Two half-naked warriors emerged from the bushes, armed with long spears and wearing only pieces of cloth covering their genitals. Their hair reached to their shoulders and they had tattoos on their bodies. They were smaller than the Kalingas and had more Asiatic features. Walking slowly toward us they stopped about ten feet in front of Amok, who immediately began talking. I didn't like the nervous sound of his voice. I had a presentiment that I was being watched from behind, but when I turned, nobody was there.

Still speaking with Amok, the two warriors didn't take their eyes off me. With the mirror I still had in my hand, I looked over my shoulder. What I saw released a double dose of adrenaline. Partially hidden in the vegetation were more warriors, spears in their hands. I wanted to run but it was all I could do not to collapse. I was rejecting the very encounter I had been looking for.

Finished talking with Amok, the two warriors approached me wide-eyed, joined by the others who had hidden behind us. Staring at me, they jabbered away clearly amused by my terrified expression. One of them laughed as he reached out to touch my beard with his fingertips. The ideas that flash through the mind in moments of terror are inexplicable. As he pulled my beard, I thought of those times in school when I stood in front of the teacher without my homework done, waiting for the worst. As I felt the present terror I would have given anything to be back in school.

Another warrior smiled as he also touched my beard. I saw his teeth darkened by the use of betel. Then he gently patted my cheek and, nodding at me, picked up my pack and started to move away with it. Amok said, "They want us to go into their village."

Instead of killing me, the fierce headhunters became my porters.

My entering the village escorted by the warriors provoked an amazing reaction among the people. Naked children and half-naked women instantly flew away from my sight, but I could see them watching cautiously from various hiding places. Men prudently followed us up to the ato, where I was presented to their chief. I spoke greetings in Apayao that I had learned from Amok, and then offered the chief my tobacco leaves and betel nuts. When he took my gifts I knew he would be friendly, for if he wished to be my enemy he would have left them on the stones. Besides, from the way he shook my hands I knew he was pleased. He gestured for Amok and me to sit next to him on the polished stones.

The ato filled with village notables, mostly old men, who sat around us. The chief asked me many questions; Amok handled our side of the conversation. My pronunciation of the few Apayao words I knew made them roar. Two men brought rice alcohol in calabashes, more tobacco leaves, and betel nuts. Everybody talked at once. We drank, smoked, and chewed betel. When a stranger is invited to share these stimulants, it confers honor and assures peace, as did smoking a pipe to the North American Indians. To my great relief, I realized that our acceptance was assured and that I could relax.

The small village, which was surrounded by coconut trees, was composed of about ten huts built on platforms supported by four or five eight-foot-tall tree trunks. The roofs and the external walls were covered with large woven palm leaves. Each house had one to three small windows and a door that opened onto a small balcony, which was easily reached by stairs carved into a tree trunk ramp. The huts were built around a bare, hard-packed dirt plaza approximately 150 feet in diameter.

At the edge of the village were the ato and a windowless long, low hut, about five feet high, which was built right on the ground. Between the entrance of that hut and the ato was a wooden pole with chicken feathers attached to its top. I learned later that the head of an enemy was buried beneath this pole that symbolically links the human world of the village to the divine one of the gods. Like the totem in the northwest coast American Indian cultures; "old trees" for African tribes; and the *poteau mitan,* the pole in the center of the Haitian Voodoo temple, this pole was the center of their universe. It was the magic axis between man and gods through which man's prayers reach the gods, and the gods' graces reach down to man.

Before nightfall we moved away from the ato and took seats facing the entrance of the low hut. A woman tended big pots full of food that were cooking over the campfire in front of us while others were cooking for their own families in front of their huts. Slowly, the night enveloped the whole village. In the surrounding jungle, the nocturnal symphony began with the calls of toads irregularly breaking the rhythm. Although the stars remained hidden behind the darkness of heavy clouds, I was able to see giant bats flying zigzag above the houses, capturing insects. I was deeply and fully enjoying the smell of the night that the increasing humidity was releasing. The strong and fresh perfume of the jungle forest mixed with the sour scent of burning wood and the strange odors of cooking food.

My reveries, enhanced by the rice alcohol, the strong tobacco, and the betel, were interrupted by the terrified barking of a dog one of the headhunters carried. Approaching the large iron pot, he caressed the dog, spoke to it, and then dropped it alive into the boiling water. The dog's scream rapidly drowned. At first surprised, I soon became hurt by what I saw, deeply hurt, but I couldn't jump up to help the poor animal as I normally would. I looked away thinking, Do I feel upset when a live lobster is thrown into boiling water? Here, although dogs are more useful as guards, they are no more loved or respected than pigs or chickens. They are a survival food in case of starvation, and a gourmet food for great occasions.

Later the boiled dog was taken from the pot and cut into pieces which were laid, hairy skin and all, on a banana leaf. Fighting to overcome my disgust and nausea, I didn't realize that everybody was politely waiting for me to begin eating before they themselves did.

"Eat!" Amok whispered. "Eat, we are waiting for you!" Aware of my hesitation, he added: "You must eat, this repast is a *tanid,* a purifying ritual that will protect the party from the malevolent spirits."

The faces around me, lit by the campfire, had lost their smiles.

They looked upset. Amok look worried. I ate! Although I normally would have asked what it was I was drinking, I decided not to find out what was in the refreshing brown liquid they offered me. Later I learned that the drink was the blood of a water buffalo mixed with the juice of some herbs to prevent coagulation.

Late at night, Amok and I were taken into the hut that had no windows. The entrance was small and narrow, as in an igloo. A campfire inside filled the first room with smoke to chase away mosquitoes and other night insects. Above the fire, skulls of a water buffalo and a pig hung as offerings to the divinities of rain and storm. These skulls were also a display of the wealth of the clan, since they showed how many animals had been sacrificed. Next to the skulls was a large wicker bag that contained human skulls yellowed by smoke. Opposite the main entrance was a small entry to the dormitory. Here the quite young and quite old village males—the bachelors and the widowers—sleep side by side on small carpets of palm leaves.

This was the men's house. No woman could enter, except into the first room and then only during certain specific religious ceremonies. The women also had their special house, where the unmarried females and widows lived together. This house was forbidden to men, except for bachelors who could come at night to seduce women.

At puberty, boys and girls leave the family house and move into the men's or women's house and begin a long process of initiation. While the teachings given by the older women to the girls mostly concern their sexual education, boys are initiated into the sacred. The elders also teach them how to assume the responsibilities and the offices they will hold after entering adulthood.

In spite of the huge quantity of rice alcohol I had drunk, I had a hard time finding sleep—not only because there were too many of us in the men's hut and it was extraordinarily hot but because I was simply too excited. It couldn't believe that I was really among the Apayaos, headhunters, whom legend had portrayed as bloodthirsty and dangerous savages. It seemed strange and for some reason worrisome that I had so easy a time being accepted among them.

After the too-early awakening next morning—people moved

out of the dormitory at sunrise—Amok and I shared a breakfast
of rice and leftovers from last night's dinner with a young man
not older than eighteen who had slept next to me. His name was
Kuru. I wanted to make friends with him because Amok was
now going to his friend's village, promising to come back soon.
Nervously I asked, "How soon is soon?"

Amok said, "When I finish visiting my friend."

When Amok left it was as if I had lost my link with my own
civilization, even though he wasn't even part of it. He represented the guarantor of my security, my culture, my knowledge.
Now, I was among the headhunters on my own, and yet I felt
safer than in the jungle.

I was in a society where there were no civilized controls, no
authorities, and no laws other than those created by relative
strength and power. Still I felt more secure than in our societies,
where an individual is in theory protected by the policy and
laws that reinforce ethics and morality, but can lose his or her
life because of the senseless violence that is everywhere. In the
jungle I belonged only to myself, and my life was dependent
upon my actions. It was up to me to enforce my right to exist.
If I imposed myself on the Apayaos with my personality,
strength, and behavior, they would respect me for what I am,
and acknowledge my right to stay alive.

I was aware that Kuru's feelings of liking me were not enough
to make him a friend and ally. So, I resorted to intuitive feelings
as to what would please him. My first move was to show him
that I wanted to know more about his people. Pointing two
fingers at my eyes and the other hand at the village, I made him
understand my desire to visit his home.

The village was very clean. Apart from a few dogs,
there were no other animals running among the houses. Chickens, used only as sacrifices to the gods, were kept in wicker cages
that hung from beneath the huts on pilework. Behind the
houses, pigs oinked from large, deep holes dug in the ground to
keep them from running throughout the village or into the
jungle.

During the day most of the villagers were away performing
various duties—hunting, fishing, and cultivating their fields.
The village was deserted, except for the old, the children, and
some women. A few of the women were weaving palm-leaf

baskets, as they sat and chatted together beneath a house. While the children still kept a safe distance from me, every time I looked at the women, there was a better reaction than the day before. Now they laughed before rapidly disappearing into a hiding place where they could peer at me. Not trying to hide their nudity, they reacted shyly because I was a foreigner; moreover, according to Kuru I was the first white man to have visited them. Very few of the villagers had ever seen a white man.

Among people of tradition, nakedness is not something that provokes any embarrassment. Instead, they might be embarrassed by what is missing from their body, such as specific tattoos or other designs applied to the skin.

It is difficult to say whether or not Apayao women are pretty. Talking about female beauty is always a challenge. Beauty is evaluated according to various criteria and values that vary from one culture to another, from one kind of education to another. In one place a woman is cute when her breasts are flat and hanging; in another place she becomes pretty only if her body is covered with tattoos or if her skin is lighter or darker. As far as the Apayao women are concerned, after a while I became attracted to their muscular bodies, developed by the hard work they shared with men, enhanced with tattoos covering their hands and bare breasts. Even though their teeth were darkened by the use of betel, I started to find them seductive.

While walking with Kuru, I tried to learn the places or things in their village that could be considered taboo, so that I could avoid violating them. Because of offerings of rice placed at its foot, I assumed that the wooden pole erected between the ato and the men's hut was such a spot—Kuru confirmed this later.

I wanted to know everything and Kuru wanted to show me everything, so we spent the rest of the day walking around the village and up to the fields. All the while I made him laugh a lot by trying to pronounce the new Apayao words I had asked him to teach me.

Sitting next to Kuru, I ate dinner with the bachelors and widowers who lived in the men's house. Taking turns, each of them tried to increase my vocabulary. Rapidly the crowd around us grew bigger. Attracted by our laughter, almost all the married men, after they finished sharing dinner with their families, came and sat around us and were soon joined by their wives and kids. And I had to learn more new words to please everyone. Unable to write the words down fast enough, I took from my backpack my small cassette player, put it on "Record," and set it in the middle of the crowd. The arrival of this mysterious thing shut all mouths and aroused curiosity and suspicion. I spoke a few words I had just learned, rewound the tape, and pushed "Play." Performing levitation would not have provoked greater surprise. My voice coming from that object was incomprehensible. Mouths hanging open, all silent and admiring, they stared at my cassette player. Suddenly there was an explosion of laughter, screams of admiration and of surprise, raucous throat clearings, noisy spittings of red saliva, repeated tongue clickings . . . and everybody talking at once while cautiously touching the cassette player with their fingertips. Many got up and went to call in their relatives or friends. Even the chief was called over. Later, when they finally calmed down, I recorded the chief's voice and played it. Then, at their request, I did the same for each and every one. That was the playful atmosphere I was to live in every evening. Except that, soon accustomed to its magic, they became uninterested in the cassette player.

Much later, as we were again drinking rice alcohol in front of the men's house, I heard voluptuous music that seemed to come from the jungle. With gestures, I showed Kuru how much I liked it and asked if it were played on a flute. Communicating in the same manner but punctuating with words, he informed me that the music came from a nose flute, blown with one nostril only, played by a lover to seduce his girl. After a few days I learned that among Apayaos, sexual freedom is practiced before marriage. These melancholic sounds are sometimes intended to lure the girl from her house for a sexual meeting in the forest. The trysts are perilous because there is always some danger of an attack from an enemy tribe, so the women's house is the real center of romance. According to this clan's customs, a man may enter into the women's house, court, and make love, but only at night and if his lover is expecting him. Otherwise he'll be chased away by the women. Kuru proposed to visit the women's house with me.

As I started to climb the stairs to the balcony of the women's house, Kuru, who was already at the entrance, asked the women if we could visit their place. Several answered in the affirmative. He beckoned me to follow and then disappeared into the large one-room hut. Scarcely had I reached the balcony when a young man, visibly angered by my arrival, jumped from the house and vanished into the night. It was clear that my presence was not universally pleasing.

The room was dark except for the left corner near the entrance where, set on the floor, a coconut half-shell holding a burning wick floated on a pool of oil. Around it were seated two old and three young women, chatting, chewing betel, and spitting red saliva between the bamboo boards that formed the floor. The youngest was weaving a conical hat. In front of them, next to the oil lamp, was a small open box containing betel nuts, lime, and pepper leaves.

The women greeted me, laughing. The oldest, in charge of the women's house, offered us betel to chew as we sat down next to them. I looked around and saw many women sleeping side by side on the floor, while others courted face-to-face with their boyfriends.

For Apayaos, as generally among all people of tradition, mating is very important. Men woo their lovers in the fashion of animals and birds. While the fauna's mating games are limited by the instinct of their species, seduction techniques among human beings are more varied as instinct is augmented by imagination. One young man was making his partner laugh. Some were singing improvised poems or reciting ancient ballads. Others made music with the nose flute or a jew's-harp made of bamboo. I saw bodies moving closer, caressing each other in the dim light.

In public, Apayaos are very reserved about anything related to sexuality. Not only did they conceal acts of tenderness and loving gestures, such as kissing and hugging (except toward children) but they were also reserved in their conversation. Some specific words are never pronounced or are replaced by euphemisms or other phrases. For example, the words *sex act* are replaced by *dispute*.

Though outwardly reserved sexually, people of this tradition consider sex to be very important. According to their primal myths, the world itself was created by a sexual union between two cosmic realities. The sex act, in itself an act of fecundity, enabled the creation of the world. Fecundity, having engendered the cosmos, is therefore the primordial force that brings together the rhythms of nature and those of human life. It plays an essential role in their social and religious institutions, as well as in their daily lives, and is worshiped by almost all people of tradition. That worship is called *cult of fecundity* and involves various fertility rites. The sex act is the main one, not only because it enables the human beings to procreate but also because there is a direct connection between the sex act and the desired fruitfulness of nature, as both are regulated by the same force. Thus sexuality and a life of plenty are synonymous.

Their period of sexual freedom allows people to try more than one lover. There is generally very little risk of a woman becoming pregnant within these periods of intense sexual activity and frequent change of partners, unless they want to. For the great majority of tribes practicing sexual freedom, birth control is a matter of survival. Women can prevent pregnancy by eating a mixture prepared with abortive plants that provoke menstruation, interrupting any possible pregnancy without risk or pain.

When a couple feels well-mated, the boy will ask the girl to marry him (never vice versa). If he is too shy, he will have an intermediary, usually the old woman in charge of the women's house, ask for him. Often before proposing, the boy will wait for the girl to become pregnant so that he is sure she can procreate. If the girl accepts the proposal, the boy must go for a *kilib,* a human head hunt, before informing his parents about his nuptial intentions. This bloody trophy will be the proof of his courage, showing that he is a fearless fighter, that he can protect his family and all members of the clan, and, in short, that he has become a man.

Once informed there is to be a wedding, the shaman performs divination rituals to determine the best date within the flower season and a time when the moon and the constellation of Orion are visible—the moon marking the beginning of a cycle. Indeed, since there is a direct connection between the fecundity of humans and the fecundity of nature, there is also a direct connection between cosmic cycles and human sexuality. Therefore all fertility rites, including weddings, are regulated by astronomy.

On the day set for the wedding, the boy's parents visit the girl's parents, bringing bags filled with rice cakes. Depending on the number of guests participating in the feast, the girl's parents cut the throat of a dog, a pig, or a water buffalo. During the feast everybody discusses the value of the *toduk,* gifts given by the boy's parents to the parents of the girl. This kind of reverse dowry can consist of ancient Chinese jars that are used to hold water and rice, Ming porcelain dishes, clothes, weapons, animals, and sometimes pieces of land, if they are privately owned by the family. Besides the dishes, there are jars beautifully decorated with colorful enamels, which would cost a fortune in our countries. They were brought into the Philippines between the fourteenth and seventeenth centuries by Chinese traders who exchanged them for spices and other goods. Their makers, highly cultivated Chinese artists from the Ming dynasty, would be surprised by their current use.

The families' joint agreement about what constitutes the toduk "legalizes" the marriage. Until this toduk is fully paid, the young couple must stay with the girl's family. On the day of the last installment, a new occasion for a feast, the couple may go to live with the boy's family until the birth of their first child. After that they can move into their own house.

The day after my first visit to the women's house, I indicated to Kuru my desire to accompany him when he worked in the community rice field.

Although the Apayaos are essentially hunters, this clan had a common rice field large enough to produce all the rice needed by the community. It was cultivated on mountainous slopes, and because rains were slowly taking away the soil and leaving behind only rocks and stones, the people had to prepare a new portion of jungle for planting every year. The previous day they had cut about one hundred trees and burned them. We set to work to clear away the unburned branches and trunks. I spent my whole day walking bent over, my feet in ashes, my hands black from handling the charred wood. But the day gave me the opportunity to meet a co-worker, Mutu, a young Apayao girl. She was there with a group of other young girls and women, walking bent over, feet and hands powdered with ashes, but laughing, chatting, sometimes singing. I thought about my family and wondered what they were doing while I was working hard and sweating, just for the pleasure of sharing the life of headhunters. Were they watching TV or taking in a movie? Perhaps in search of a restaurant they were wandering through the city that was illuminated like a Christmas tree. Maybe they were already asleep. I daydreamed of home and watched Mutu.

I don't know why I looked at Mutu more than at the other girls. She was neither prettier nor more friendly to me, but I immediately liked her and saw that the feeling was mutual. Back in the village she disappeared from my sight but remained in my mind.

Seeing that I was eager to join the village life, early the next morning Kuru asked me to accompany him on a hunt. I was not too happy about the prospect. Besides the fact that I was losing an opportunity to see Mutu, my back and legs were as sore as if I had been beaten with a thousand sticks. But I followed him.

Armed only with his long spear and a large *bolo,* a kind of machete, Kuru spent the whole day running up and down mountains, chasing wild boars. I ran behind, trying to stay up with him and wondering how I would escape from repeating this excruciating ordeal the next day if Kuru caught nothing today. Then I heard the shrill squeal of a wounded animal. When I reached Kuru I saw that he had succeeded in wedging a wild boar against a small cliff and had thrown his spear into its back. When the animal fell, Kuru approached it, machete ready to behead it if the boar made a move to run away. The animal was in agonized death throes. My friend caressed its back, whispered some incantations, and only then cut its throat.

When I asked him later what the incantations were about, he explained he had to beg for the animal's forgiveness so that its spirit would not take revenge on him. Some tribes even start their incantations as they hunt the animal and continue these prayers until the wounded animal dies. Some Papuans of New Guinea practice a similar ritual, cutting a small hole in a tree to help the soul of the tree depart safely before they fell it.

Unfortunately, the death of the wild boar wasn't the end of my suffering. Now we had to bring it back to the village. To ease our trip back, Kuru, who said this was the biggest beast he had ever killed, cut it into two halves. I inherited the part with the head. As I struggled back to the village along slippery hillsides, across a river, and through the damned bushes, I thought about my friends in Brussels who would someday tell me, "How great your experience with headhunters must have been. I envy you, I really do!"

When we came back with our bloody prey, almost all the villagers came and surrounded us admiringly. Mutu was there too. They asked Kuru questions and laughed while he told his story. I bet he told them how great I was, running behind him.

As I was leaving the small stream where I cleaned the sweat, blood, and dirt from my skin, I again met Mutu who was carrying some items to wash there. She had become very attractive to me. I could not help staring at her well-formed breasts. I smiled. She smiled also, but covered her mouth, embarrassed. When she passed, I turned my head back and saw that she too had turned back to look at me before disappearing into the bushes. Without any purpose other than to see her once more, I went back to the stream and washed my hair again, of course not too far from where she was beating her clothes with a stone. I finally made so bold as to tell her with gestures and words that I wanted us to meet there that night, and I disappeared.

When I came back at night, not only was she there but she called out to me, for I had passed near without seeing her. Scared to be doing something that might be disapproved of by her people, I stayed close to her but without any motion that would indicate I wanted to seduce her. Finally she was the one to move up against my body, and I just followed the rules of lovemaking.

I don't know how old she was, aside from being young and no longer a virgin. Mutu was very sensual, but she refused the mouth kiss with the touching of tongues and exchange of saliva. That is not practiced at all in her culture, although in others it can be the primary source of eroticism. She already had a good knowledge of lovemaking, and she was very attentive to my reactions without jeopardizing her own pleasure. In most traditional cultures, eroticism has not been murdered as it has in ours.

I made love with Mutu a few more times during my stay in the village and made love to other girls who invited me. We met in the privacy of the jungle, for I never again dared go at night to the women's house for fear that someone might see me trying to seduce a girl who was already courted by a young warrior. One thing that I was not afraid of was venereal disease, which does not exist among tribal people unless brought by modern civilization.

Four days after my coming into the village, even the women and children had become my friends, and I felt I really had become part of their community. Headhunters they might be, yet perhaps because they sensed that I was trying to live in accord with the rhythm of the village they were all smiles and friendliness to me.

Our humanity is made of many different logics, each culture possessing its own. A culture's logic regulates the system of thoughts, filters the feelings and emotions, and transforms perception of the world. Since I hadn't come here to judge, I tried to cut all ties linking me to my culture and memories in order to strip myself of thoughts that might act as a screen between myself and this new world. My desire was to die to what I had been in order to be reborn into this new culture with its own knowledge and logic. I wanted not only to understand these people but also to experience their life as best I could.

One morning, no one left the village to work. Instead, they gathered in front of a hut.

"The man died during the night," said Kuru, taking me into the midst of the gathering. There, members of the old man's family were sacrificing dogs and pigs to the divinities, by cutting the animals' throats. These animals would later feed those who came to mourn.

Although it was very spacious, about twenty by twenty-five feet, the single room of the dead man's hut was crowded. He had been dressed in the ceremonial clothes, a woven shirt covering the body down to the traditional long narrow red piece of cloth that hides the sexual organs. His body was laid on his mat in the middle of the noisy gathering. While some people talked in loud voices and others cried or lamented, the dead man's son chanted next to the corpse, enumerating the virtues and the great deeds of his father's life. This chanting was to continue for the entire five days of the funeral ceremony. Ceremonies last a minimum of three days, but may go on as long as the family of the deceased can continue to feed the gathering.

The first person to feast was the dead man himself. His sister approached his corpse and opened his mouth with her fingers, pushing aside his tongue so that the man's wife could give him his last meal. Force-feeding him rice and meat, she pushed the food deep inside his throat with her fingers, filling the mouth again and again. To end this final meal she poured in some rice wine. After this, the old wife closed the mouth of her husband with a long thin piece of cloth and gagged him so that he would retain the food.

Before rigor mortis could take hold, the deceased was set on a funerary chair. The room fell silent. No more talk, no more crying, just eyes emptied by sorrow staring at the dead man who seemed quite lifelike as his closest relatives tied him upright to the chair of death. Two days earlier he had been laughing and teaching me new words. Now he sat there like a sleeping prisoner, his hair perfectly combed.

Abruptly, two men entered and cleared a small space in front of the dead man. Then they started a dance, which is supposed to be the outward expression of mourning. However, unlike a funeral march, it is vigorous and full of life, more than a Greek dance where the men slap their thighs, knees, and calves. Here, face-to-face, they dealt each other alternating slaps on the thighs. This performance aroused loud lamentations and crying, but also comments and laughter. (I have noticed, among people of tradition, that laughter is an integral part of all their emotional manifestations, whether expressing sorrow or facing the sacred.) Meanwhile, tobacco, betel, and rice wine were distributed to all participants.

For five days and nights of chanting, crying, laughing, drinking, smoking, and eating, friends and relatives came to visit the dead man, whose last sleep was honored with the endless chants that spoke highly of him. This constant attention was required so that parts of his body would not be stolen and eaten by the *anitos,* the evil spirits.

According to the cultures of tradition, death is the separation of the soul from the body. The body is dead forever, but the soul goes back to the primordial world, also called the *world of the invisibles,* where the divinities, ancestors, and souls of the dead continue to live. In that invisible world, life is lived in the same way as it is on earth except that, as it is an eternal paradise, there is no struggle for survival.

For the Apayaos and for many other cultures, there is no hell. The mistakes a man commits in his lifetime are punished by his clan and fully atoned for by the man while he is alive; they do not mark his soul with sins or interfere with his life after death.

The funeral rituals performed by the family of the deceased are intended to chase away malevolent spirits and to help the soul of the deceased depart the world of the living, reach that place of the invisibles where its ancestors live, and be accepted among them. If the prescribed rituals have not been perfectly executed, the soul will not make the journey to its ancestors safely, or, if it does, it will not be accepted. In either case the soul of the dead person will return to the world of the living, bringing disaster or illness to the members of its family. In this manner the soul will express its vengeance and will let its family know through the shaman what other rituals are required in order for it to forgive them and go to join its ancestors.

Besides chants, prayers, and magical incantations, the funeral rituals are composed of offerings of clothes, food, beverages, and animal, or sometimes human, sacrifices. The acts of sacrificing and offering have the same meaning. They are intended to transform what is sacrificed or offered from "being visible" to "being invisible," and to send it into the world of the invisibles, so that the spirits, ancestors, and other deceased souls can enjoy it. Sacrificing, or "offering," liberates the quintessence or astral body, the level of existence that animates the material or physical body. Without this quintessence, a material or physical body ceases to exist. It is assumed that if the quintessence of something has been sent as food, the divinities and the ancestors will actually be fed by it. A dress will actually be used as a dress. An animal will serve as an animal.

On the fifth day, as they had no more food left, the relatives planned to carry the deceased away. Still attached to his funeral chair and swollen by heat and the decay of his organs, the body was covered with a shroud. But even here, in the depths of the Ilocos Norte, the dead do not wish to leave family and home. So a chant was spoken to soften his resistance and chase him away. I recorded parts of the chants and later I met a student who spoke Apayao and translated them.

> We are leaving you forever. By performing all the rituals and sacrificing the animals, we have given you the prescribed funeral. . . . Now you must go. And do not curse us, but beseech your ancestors to give us happiness and prosperity.

Now the whole village, about sixty people, gathered in front of the dead man's house. Then, following behind the relatives who carried their dead parent sitting on the funeral chair, they made a long procession through the village and entered the jungle. The chanting continued:

> You have all that you need: rice, chicken, and pigs to feed you, and the clothes to wear during your stay in the dwelling place of your ancestors. You leave your earthly goods with your children and relatives, so that they can enjoy life in the same way you enjoyed it while you were living.

After twenty minutes of an easy walk through the jungle, we reached a small and narrow canyon leading to a high stony cliff. As the path started to climb and became harder to follow, we left behind more and more of the old people and young kids who had already formed the rearguard.

> Beseech your ancestors to give us happiness and prosperity and protection against our enemies; make abundant game for our hunt. . . . Take away rats, insects, and other predators that destroy the rice plants. . . . Prevent diseases from killing our poultry and our animals. Send them fertility so that we will be able to make more sacrifices for you. Give us good health so that we will live as long as possible, continuing our traditions and offering sacrifices.

We were down to about thirty in number when, slightly covered by hanging vegetation appeared the entrance of the sacred cave, a fissure like a vulva high in the stony cliff. From there on, the path climbed hard, zigzagging between heaps of huge rocks. The procession stopped.

> We are saying farewell forever. . . . This is the last place we can go for guiding you to the dwelling place of your ancestors. . . . Go and live with your ancestors forever.

The shaman and those carrying the funeral chair started the hard climb. They were the only ones allowed to go farther and enter the sacred cave. And none of them would ever reveal anything about the rituals performed there.

"Kuru, have you been up there before?"

He shook his head. "It will be my turn only on the day I have to carry a close relative."

I longed to see inside.

Once back in the village, we all cleaned our hands, faces, and feet to wash away the death and the sins committed by the deceased in his lifetime. Then a big feast began to mark the beginning of the mourning, which ends on the day when the deceased's soul is said to have reached the dwelling place of his ancestors and to have been accepted by them. That time is announced by the shaman after he contacts the ancestors and divinities.

The rituals performed during the extended mourning are as

important as those performed when the body was still in the village. Not only will they help the soul undergo his very difficult trip but they will also prevent the soul from coming back to the village in a last attempt to stay among the living. Besides the rituals, during this mourning period, which can last a whole year, the people observe a variety of taboos concerning food and the behavior of the deceased one's family. For instance, they cannot cut their hair, and the closest female relatives cannot wear jewelry but must wear a girdle made of tree bark. Everybody respects these taboos, for if the deceased's soul fails in its attempt to reach its ancestors, it will come back to the village and torture those who have broken the rules of mourning, until they perform rituals again.

When the shaman signals that the soul of the deceased has begun a new life among his ancestors, a time of feasts and dances marks the end of the period of mourning, but not the end of relationships with the deceased. He has now become an ancestor, and according to the cult of ancestors, rituals will always be performed for them, for the ancestors help and protect the living, and are intermediaries between the living and the divinities. If rituals are not properly performed, the deceased's soul can do harm to the living and to all of their goods.

People who believe in the survival of the spirits of the deceased consider the violation of a tomb both a sacrilege and a most dangerous act, because a disturbed spirit can take revenge on the surviving family members by sending them maladies or calamities. If caught violating a tomb, a person would be in danger of being killed as a sacrifice to appease the anger of these disturbed spirits. Kuru told me all this, yet a few days after the funeral, my curiosity pushed me to explore the sacred cave. I am not proud of this, but I tell it because it is part of the story. I was aware that what I was doing was wrong and dangerous, but I felt that nothing could happen to me because I wasn't going there to disturb or steal but only to observe and learn.

After dinner one night when the moon was bright enough for me to find my way, I waited for the village to sleep. I slipped out of the men's house with my cassette player, thinking that if I were caught I could say I was out walking to record the night sounds. Deafened by my heartbeats and shaking with fear, I left the village and the barking dogs and entered the jungle as silently as I could, hoping that I wouldn't stumble upon any couples making love. Soon I reached the first heaps of rock scattered at the foot of the cliff and climbed the path leading to the sacred cave.

As I was about to enter, strong fears and sensations suddenly possessed me. I almost fled, but after a last glance over the canyon I drew back the natural hanging lianas that curtained off the cave's entrance and entered the darkness. Once inside and hidden from view by the vegetal curtain, I took from my pocket a matchbox, opened it with trembling fingers, and lit the first match. The whole cave burst into light. At first I thought the surfaces of the cave must be covered with tiny mirrors, but when I recovered from my surprise, I discovered that the walls were studded with phosphorus, pyrites, reflective crystals, and pieces of gold of great value.

In the glittering light I was surrounded by hundreds of eyes that silently observed my sacrilege. Without their funeral chairs, the corpses sat on the ground in the fetal position. Some had fallen on their sides, but those leaning against the walls of the cave or against other corpses sat up perfectly straight, chins on knees, hands holding tightly onto their legs. On closer inspection, I saw that they stayed in the fetal position because their hands had been tied to their lower legs. The majority of the corpses were perfectly preserved. There was no stench or putrefaction. They had hair on their heads as if they had been mummified. Was this natural mummification due to the cave's special atmosphere?

Dishes that had contained the last offerings of food were still there in front of each corpse. The dead men had their weapons, the dead women their jewelry. I recognized the dead man in whose funeral I had participated. If his hands had not been tied, it seemed he could have eaten the remains of his meal—the rice, meat, and rice wine that still awaited his pleasure.

All cultures of tradition celebrate their ancestors through the cult of the dead, and in that sacred cave I felt the truth of the belief that man really dies only when there is nobody who thinks about him any more. Somehow, I knew that continuous love and remembrance generate the energies that keep a soul alive. They are right—the Ifugaos, the Maoris, and the Dayaks—who can recite the names of their ancestors back for twenty generations.

Many cultures of tradition also believe that the gods themselves die when humans no longer honor them. When the people don't need him any more and he disappears from their memory, a god will lose his immortality. Kuru told me, "The gods need us as much as we need them. They are our hope for a better life, we are their immortality."

Once, while fishing in Borneo with a Dayak headhunter friend, he told me, "The Gods have created us so they will be fed by our offerings and will exist on the energies of our faith." Then he looked at me and added, "In exchange, they have created nature, to feed us, and paradise, where we will live like Gods." Five minutes later he said, smiling, "And I am so grateful to the Gods to be only a human, because . . ." he looked around us at the jungle and the river, and sighed, "because what a daily burden and worry to make all this work so perfectly."

In the midst of my thoughts I suddenly heard a strange noise, as if someone were coming from deep inside the sacred cave. I extinguished my match and waited, heart pounding, breathless. The noise came closer. My imagination went wild. I saw myself in the hands of the warriors, paying a bloody price for having broken the taboo. Overcome by panic, I tried to reach the cave exit in the darkness but stumbled on a body and, losing my balance, fell among those whose dwelling place I had profaned. Frantically crawling among the corpses, I finally reached the exit, flew out of the cave, hurtled down the slope, and hid in some bushes where I tried to calm down, promising all gods that I would never commit a sacrilege again. Then I wet my trousers.

Before heading for the men's house, I went to the small river next to the village and lay down in it to wash away death and my shame.

The following day I went back to work with Kuru and some other villagers on the new rice field. Kuru was what Americans might call "a great guy," young and strong, between sixteen and twenty years old. He himself couldn't tell me his age because among these people a person's life is not measured in years but by the number of his initiations. Kuru always took his time explaining everything to me. He showed me new plants and insects and new things to eat. He told me about manioc roots and how one can only eat them raw and in small quantities because they contain arsenic. For large quantities to be edible, they must remain in water for several days and then be pressed to get rid of the poison before cooking.

That morning, during a "betel nuts" pause, I took him aside

and explained that in some cultures there is a blood-mixing ritual that makes two people become brothers. He said he knew about that, but for his tribe the most important ceremony is adoption.

"Kuru, I would like to become your blood brother!" I said, putting my hand on his shoulder.

I asked him because of our wonderful relationship, and perhaps also because I was feeling guilty about having violated their secret cave. I felt I had betrayed the trust Kuru and his people had given me. Deep in my heart I hoped the blood brother ceremony would exorcise my "sin" and that perhaps I would be forgiven in case they happened to learn about the foolish thing I had done.

"I would like that also. Tonight we'll talk to the shaman."

The shaman is the keeper of the culture and traditions. By performing rituals, he protects or restores the multifaceted harmony existing within each of his people and in each one's relationship to his clan, the village, the tribe, their ancestors, their divinities, and nature. This effort to keep all invisibles happy or to beseech their favors means the shaman must also perform rituals whenever something very important is about to occur that could disturb the quietness, established order, and harmony between humans and invisibles—as, for instance, my adoption. The shaman can establish contact and question ancestors and gods. While in a trance, he can be the intermediary between them and humans.

All these shaman powers and abilities are essential because the people of tradition believe that all natural disorders, sickness, lack of rain, and so forth, are a reaction by the invisibles to a disturbance created by humans. When someone is sick, the shaman restores him by exorcising the disturbance and reestablishing the balance among him, the clan, and the cosmos. After performing appropriate rituals to appease the divine fury that causes the malady, he will cure the patient with herbs and other natural medicines.

One of the shaman's rituals—to keep the invisible presence happy and to ask for favors—is performed at the end of the rice planting. He intones the following incantation:

> I am calling the souls of the ancestors, I am calling the spirits of the Eastern mountains and of the Western mountains, I am calling . . . [He enumerates all the names of spirits, divinities, and

gods.] so that they all will come and be present at our celebration marking the end of the rice planting.

And when the shaman assumes all souls and deities are present, he chants:

Today we are celebrating this feast, inviting you to accept these sacrifices of chicken and offerings of rice that we have prepared for you. Be the protector of our children and of our brothers.

Informed of my proposition to become Kuru's blood brother, the shaman called Kuru and me to join him in the ato before nightfall. He was holding a live chicken. He asked us to be seated, and, crouching on the ground, he caressed the chicken and began to recite some invocations. Then he beheaded the chicken with his knife and threw a few of its feathers into the air, noting how they fell and positioned themselves on the ground. Then, cutting open the body, he made a long and meticulous examination of the gall bladder and the liver. When finished, he announced: "The propitious time will be in three days! So have said the auguries."

It is believed that turning to the auguries is the easiest way to involve the invisibles in the everyday life of humans. This forces the invisibles to get interested, and it guarantees that their anger will not be aroused.

Besides occurring in the livers and gall bladders of sacrificed animals, the auguries can be found at the right times in specific birds, snakes, and lizards, in the special screams of certain animals, and even in the movement of stones.

When two people blame each other for a crime, the shaman prepares a pot filled with boiling water. After having thrown a stone into the water, he asks the accused and then the accuser to plunge their hands into the boiling water to take out the stone. According to this painful method of divination, the culprit is the one who sustains the worst burns.

The most amazing session of divination I witnessed happened while the shaman was trying to decide what ritual to perform in order to heal a sick old woman. He filled a hollow coconut half-shell with rice wine and, while reciting prayers for about ten minutes, examined the surface of the wine. When he was satisfied he had found the solution, he used two different methods to obtain confirmation. First he attached a stone to a thin rope hanging from the roof. When the stone was motionless, he started to enumerate all the possible rituals that could be performed for healing. As he pronounced the name of the ritual that had been dictated to him by the surface of the wine, the stone began moving in a circle. I checked that no one was on the roof, and there were no visible ways the shaman could have mechanically started the movement of the stone. As the second test of confirmation, he took an egg and balanced the small end of it on the ground. Again he enumerated all the rituals, and to my astonishment, the egg tipped over as he pronounced the name of the very same ritual.

My initiation started the night before the day set by the auguries. I had already been taught the importance of the primordial myth and its consequences on the structure of the clan and on my behavior. Unfortunately, I didn't understand very much of what was said, and for some unknown reason my cassette player refused to record that night.

On the cloudy morning of my new birth into the community, I was awakened early by the beating of gongs. I could eat nothing and had to wait alone in the men's house until called by the shaman.

With drums of various sizes, many villagers followed wherever Kuru, a few notables, and the shaman led me. On our way to the little stream I noticed that a few pigs had already been sacrificed to the divinities; their meat was cooking to feed the whole village later. After a washing in the stream, my naked body was covered with mud the color of blood. Blood symbolizes death and purification—that which precedes and enables a new birth.

Then in the first room of the men's hut I had to lie down on the ground near the campfire, which all watched with close attention. If the fire had died, it would have been a bad omen for the whole clan. An old woman, my new "mother"-to-be, crouched above me in the position of giving birth. Meanwhile the shaman hung a coconut half-shell containing water and ashes above the entrance to guard against the anitos.

After the ritual enactment of my birth, a bunch of ginger roots wrapped in leaves was put next to me by the shaman. Ginger protects from negative energies, which can be generated not only by the anitos but also by the unhappy souls of the deceased, especially those who have committed suicide. Then he put a piece of an animal's internal organ on my chest, symbolizing the placenta, and another piece on my navel, representing the umbilical cord. My "mother" grabbed my testicles with both hands and, half-yelling, half-laughing, expressed her joy at having given birth to a male. Before she and I were washed, the shaman took away the placenta and burned it. He buried the umbilical cord in ashes kept in a coconut half-shell. Next, my "mother" offered me one of her long, flat, tired breasts which, as a baby, I had to suck.

Before leaving the men's hut, I was dressed with the traditional long piece of red cloth rolled around my waist. My "mother" had to cover her body to protect it from the gods' eyes and wore a large conical hat on her head to protect her from the sun god and rain god.

On the village's central plaza, some people were dancing to the wild beats of gongs. The shaman brought a giant Ming dynasty jar filled with rice wine. But before opening it, he attached a few betel leaves for protection. Then everybody started to drink, eat, and enjoy.

During the feast, Kuru took care of my needs. He was very happy, for this celebration was for him, too. Later in the day I was called back into the first room of the men's house with Kuru. The shaman notched Kuru's hand just above the wrist. Then he notched mine. The hot blood started to flow. For the symbolic blood exchange, Kuru's hand was joined to mine with a small cloth under which a piece of ginger was put against our skins as a magical protection. Then our wounds were covered with medicinal herbs, and we were allowed to go out and join the feasting crowd.

As the night was falling, the atmosphere of the feast became even more animated. All around the big fire, villagers celebrated, ate, drank, laughed, and danced; it looked like a Brueghel painting. Even children were overjoyed, imitating the women who were turning in a circle, clapping their hands. Beside them, the men jumped from one foot to the other, holding their machetes, symbols of the warrior. That's how we spent a great part of the night. Dancing, eating, chewing betel nuts, getting drunk with alcohol, and getting high on the smoke of a kind of cannabis which takes you right into paradise.

The next morning everyone was back at work.

A few days later, I witnessed a very strange bargain. We received a visit from three Apayaos belonging to another clan in a nearby village. They asked if any weddings were to be performed in the near future.

Our chief responded: "Only in many months, for two of our young warriors."

The answer seemed to please the visitors. "It's a good omen. We have in our class two men whom you can have for your next *kilib* [headhunting]."

Our chief accepted. The deal was made.

Ordinarily, when a bridegroom has to go headhunting, nothing will stop him from bringing back human heads. It is a question of prestige and courage. If he fails, he will lose his honor and his fiancée. So, he will choose five or six friends of the same age, who go only as helpers, for he who gets married must behead the enemy. To repay them for their assistance, he will later accompany those of his group when they get married. Probably he already assisted some who got married in the past and are coming now to help him in return.

After a last meeting with the shaman in the ato, the groom-to-be and his helpers go to a nearby village with which their clan has no peace treaty and wait, hoping to surprise a man wandering alone. If they don't, they will attack the village, but only if they feel they can win the battle easily. Otherwise they will go farther on to the next village, sometimes even far outside their tribal territory.

In order to avoid losing able-bodied young people, sometimes arrangements are made between two groups—one being in need of a human head, the other being eager to kill one of its members. This was exactly the sort of thing proposed by our neighbors. The two men had been judged guilty—one for adultery, the other for robbery—and sentenced to death for actions against the code of their clan.

Thanks to this friendly arrangement, one village will get rid of its two culprits, and two young warriors from our village will find human heads without jeopardizing their lives and those of many others. They will have their honor, get married, have many children, and be happy forever after. And the peace between villages will be preserved. Until the next wedding.

One afternoon a few weeks later, Amok came back from his friend's village. The time had come for me to depart. Perhaps Kuru secretly hoped I would take him with me. Perhaps he hoped I would stay with them, but when I told him

I was leaving he just whispered, "So, you go?" And I answered, "But I will come back one day." Was he aware that we belong to two different galaxies? He belongs to mountains and to divinities whose mystical language I cannot speak. I belong to the wind and to my own uncertainty. He belongs to these cultures of tradition where understanding is based on faith: believe first, and you will understand! I belong to a culture whose reasoning is based on scientific logic: understand first, and you will believe! The power of belief creating miracles versus miracles created by science. Our intelligence is kaleidoscopic, focused on many different things simultaneously, blinded by stress, and polluted by rationalism; yet it enables us to build spaceships to reach the heavens. Theirs is more like an ongoing meditation that enables meetings with the divine and a deep awareness of man's connection with the universe's eternal natural forces. Tradition provides tribal people with explanations for what to us are mysteries—the darkness beyond death, the afterlife, and the existence of God.

It is very difficult for us to accept that these illiterate people could have what we lost, as our religious principles became dogmatic, more moral than metaphysical. Their religious system provides them with answers; our religions keep us ignorant.

I was glad that Kuru didn't ask me to stay. How could I have explained to him, without hurting his feelings, that this first experience of living with his people had given me a deep desire to meet other people of tradition and penetrate their souls? How could I tell him that my thirst for living couldn't be quenched just by his friendship? I was glad he did not ask me to take him along with me, for what could I have said to dissuade him from that? Maybe he didn't want to leave his galaxy.

Farewell, my brother the headhunter. Perhaps one day our bloods will mix again. Maybe in heaven's paradise.

CHAPTER THREE

Kingdoms of Sultans, Pirates, and Guerrilleros

Most of the evils of life arise from Man's being unable to sit still in a room.

BLAISE PASCAL

The return to the car took only four days. It seemed much shorter, for I had lost all ties with reality and had the strange sensation of having only dreamed about my experience with Kuru and his people. I don't even remember anything Amok told me about his trip to the village of his childhood friends and their reunion. It was in that disoriented state of mind that I left Amok in his village and headed for Bontoc.

In the car, driving past a few trucks, and seeing many times some half-naked tribesman walking along the tracks with his spear on his shoulder, I slowly awoke to both the present and past reality. In retrospect all that I had experienced during the past several weeks seemed unbelievable. I couldn't wait to get home and tell my family. I couldn't imagine what their reaction would be. I had told them in my last letter only that since the documentary was finished I was going to visit a little bit of the Philippines before heading home. Not a word about headhunters, of course.

It was quite late when I arrived in Bontoc. As I wanted to say hello to Bong, I decided to spend the night in a small hotel near his school. Exhausted and dirty, I dropped my stuff in the room, searched for the one bathroom that served the whole hotel, and jumped into the shower . . . but too late: the reservoir which supplied it with water was already empty at that late time. But the jungle rivers had never run dry.

The wooden walls of my room were plastered with pieces of cardboard, religious pictures serving as wallpaper. Facing the door, a small window covered with a mosquito net opened onto the sticky night. I lay naked on the coarse sheets of the short, narrow bed, which creaked every time I moved. Still it was so good to be lying on a bed. Old newspapers were glued to the ceiling from which hung a long electrical wire with a bulb at its end, darkened by the droppings of thousands of flies.

In that atmosphere, with its exotic smells, I started to realize that I wasn't ready yet to confront the reality of the "civilized" world. I wasn't willing yet to give up the romance I had begun. I was eager to be with my family again, but I was not ready to return to Brussels, which was still deeply tinged with the suffering and sorrow of losing my father when I needed him so badly. It was still too marked with dark memories. But if I was not yet to return home, then where to go? As I was conjuring up my next adventure, the bulb above me died without a noise. Moments later I was asleep.

It was past 10:00 A.M. when the hotel manager awakened me. The reservoir that supplied the shower with water was not yet refilled. And it was too late to visit Bong, who was already in school. So I hurried on to Manila. By the time I had arrived I had decided to embark for the Sulu islands.

South of the Philippines, the 394 islands of the Sulu Archipelago dot the emerald sea between Mindanao Island in the Philippines and the islands of Borneo and Sulawezi (Celebes) in Indonesia.

This area had long fascinated me. In childhood I had read about the Sulu navigator-traders who used to sail to Malaysia, India, and the Arabic Middle-East to sell their wares—tea, coffee, spices, tobacco, sugar cane, and precious wood. I had been enthralled by the idea of that unconquerable pirate empire. The word *sultan* aroused my curiosity and passion.

In 1000 A.D. these Sulu islands, organized into a vast number of small and independent sultanates, had been subdued by the giant Malayan/Moslem empire which, for the next five hundred years, maintained control of the whole area from Borneo to the Philippines. The Sulu natives, who became Moslem, survived by being pirates, pillaging Malayan boats and fighting among themselves for power. Later all the sultans, while retaining their property, pledged allegiance to the powerful sultan of Jolo Island who fought and won against the Malayan empire, returning the entire Sulu Archipelago to the control of pirates. (The distance between Manila and Jolo Island is 750 miles but no gap of centuries. Today, pirates are everywhere.)

After Magellan's discovery of it in 1521, the Philippines became Spanish, but Spain was never able to subdue the Sulu islands.

With the protection of Allah, the pirates visited terror and death upon the conquistadores. In memory of their endless wars against the Moors who invaded Spain, the conquistadores called their new Moslem enemies the *Moros*.

Right up to our time, the Moros have refused to submit to any authority. Even the Philippine government is unable to subdue them. They call their islands "The land of the braves," and on their flag are two crossed sabers.

These people sail safely among the maze of coral reefs even in the face of violent typhoons that sweep the islands with winds up to one hundred miles per hour and bring as much as one and one-half inches of rain in a few hours. The record for rainfall is more than three feet of water in one day!

In going to the Sulu islands I didn't know that I was to exchange the quietness of the green jungle for a certain brutality that was blowing over these white-beached islands. I went there because of my ignorance. And ignorance, like accident and intuition, is another key tool of the explorer. There are so many places I wouldn't have gone, so many people I wouldn't have seen and met, so many expeditions I wouldn't have led if I had only known in advance what I was to experience.

My adventure began in Zamboanga, a small seaside city in the southern part of Mindanao Island. From there a single DC-3 flew two or three times a week to Jolo, which was still known as "the island of the unsubdued men." Five minutes after take-off, one of the airplane's motors burst into flames. Only the pilot's skill and the legendary maneuverability of the DC-3 enabled us to return to the airport safely. It might have been weeks before the plane was repaired, so the only way to continue my voyage was aboard a freighter which left Zamboanga at 10:00 P.M. and was supposed to reach Jolo the next morning. As I get seasick easily, I recoiled at the prospect, but had no option.

At night, like Hong Kong and Macao, the port was crowded with boats that seemed to be refugees from both world wars, and hundreds of native boats of all sizes and shapes, from junklike and sampanlike large wooden boats with masts to small one- or two-outrigger canoes. Scattered everywhere on pier, gangways, and decks were candles, oil lamps, and small fires over which food was cooking.

As the only apparent foreigner on board, I was the object of intense curiosity from the crowds of passengers who stared suspiciously at me while trying to find places among the mountains of freight on deck. The already overcrowded open deck was the only place on the freighter that passengers could find space—the ship's interior was crammed with cargo.

In spite of the utter confusion, a fairyland atmosphere prevailed on the boat. It was as if I were in the middle of a night market from *The Thousand and One Nights*. The men wore turbans, Chinese or western style shirts, and long sarongs attached to their waists. Each man was armed with a long saber, called a *kris*, which was protected in a sheath made of bamboo, hanging at his side. The blades of these sabers measure up to three feet long. Although deadly enough in themselves, in the old days the pirates used to cover their blades with *upas*, a poison whose making is still kept secret. The women wore long sarongs with beautifully adorned shirts. Instead of turbans, scarves covered their heads.

Every boarding passenger carried something: luggage, pieces of furniture, radios, babies, small children, pigs, chickens, ducks. It was amazing to see how much material each person could manage to carry on his back and head, in his arms, and hanging from his shoulders. Some were so bent and overloaded you could not see more than their legs. An animated pile of junk simply waddled toward you.

By the time I arrived the only place left was at the edge of the deck along a railing three feet high, which I knew couldn't possibly protect me from big waves. With the weight of the enormous amount of cargo, the deck was only three feet above the level of the sea.

As we left Zamboanga, the deck was transformed into a giant campground lit by electric flashlights, oil lamps, candles, and small fires set in little portable stoves. The light of the flickering flames revealed the exotic faces on the people who sat around the fires. The noise on the deck was that of a feast.

Soon, as candles and oil lamps were blown out by the winds of the open sea, the light of a million bright stars took over. Even the sea projected an opal glimmer. This phosphorescent azure of the tropic sea is not the reflection of the sky, but a real glow created by millions of luminescent plankton, called *noctilucae*, which float under the sea's surface. It is this phenomenon that causes the islands and boats of the South Seas to float at night between two colored depths: the sea and the sky.

Hoping that the sea would stay calm and the sky without rain, I put my backpack under my head and tried to sleep. With the sounds of the motor, the sea, the breeze, the people eating and talking, screaming children, crying babies, the distorted music of radios, barking dogs, squeals of other animals on board, mixed with the smells of the night, the sea, the food, and the fumes of candles, oil lamps, and stoves, I sank into a world of enchantment and dreams.

I was awakened by someone trying to steal my pack, which happily I was using as a pillow. I scowled ferociously at the thief and sought sleep once more. Then it happened again. Then again. No matter how venomously I glared at them, the thieves were unimpressed by my twenty-year-old capacity for ferocity.

I was again abruptly shaken from my sleep but now it was dawn, when the sun was beginning to blow out the stars and the glow of the sea. Cold, wet hands slapped my face. Yelling, I seized my pack by reflex and jumped to my feet. I heard laughter all around me. On the deck a flying fish was struggling frantically. It had landed on my face and hit me with its wings.

The beauty of the scenery soon made me forget my rough awakening. Far off, the sea and the sky were merging with the morning mist and changing color. It was difficult to see where the ocean ended and the sunrise began. As flat as a lake, the sea was stirred only by the jumping of flying fish, which drew long ripples on the surface. Not infrequently they would jump so high that they landed on the deck, like my recent companion. Later the water was churned by dolphins who escorted our boat until we approached Jolo, where the dolphins left us behind. I wondered what they knew.

When I saw how the disembarking passengers struggled against one another, as if to be first on the Jolo wharf was a matter of life and death, I decided to wait until last. But I soon regretted that decision because instead of struggling in the same direction, I now had to struggle against the crowd of boarding passengers who, in a pirate tradition, were taking the boat by storm.

Later as I wandered along the wharf, looking at people loading and unloading their canoes, I heard a voice shouting for help. A small group of men jostled toward me, fighting amongst themselves for the possession of a cane which they then managed to drop at my feet. I grabbed it away from a dozen grasping hands, and they fled as the old man approached. He was dressed like everyone else in a long sarong and turban, but the hilt of his long kris was magnificently wrought with pearls.

"Is this yours?" I said in English, offering him the cane.

The old man was surprised because, in this den of thieves, I had just helped him recover a cane with a gold pommel.

"Who are you? A priest? A military man? A teacher? What are you doing here?" he asked me, mixing a few English words with Spanish and Tagalog, the Filipino language. Behind the magnification of his thick glasses I could see his eyes were faded by the sun and the passing of time. He waited for an answer.

"Neither priest, nor soldier, nor teacher, I am just a traveler who wants to visit these islands!" Then, winking at him as if telling a joke, I said, "I want to meet a sultan, a real one. Salaam!" This Moslem word is used for both greeting and farewell. As I moved away, the old man grabbed my arm and said, pointing at his chest, "Me, sultan! Me, Sultan Kiram III." From the rest of what he said I picked out only that he had just arrived and would be going back to his own island soon, and that if I wanted to go along I was to meet him here on the wharf very early three days from now.

As I moved away from the wharf, I couldn't believe how great was the good star that leads my destiny. After giving me Luis, who brought me to the mountain tribes and Bong, it put a sultan in my path. Two years earlier, destiny had gotten me hired by the Belgian lecture tour organization where I met Samivel, thanks to whom I was here in Jolo and about to follow a sultan to his island. I finally really believe that the function of coincidence, or whatever other names it has—luck or fate—is to help us in our blind walk through the maze of life. The problem always is to be fast enough to grab its messages, decipher them, and follow them before opportunities vanish.

The three days I spent in Jolo were a nightmare. This "island of unsubdued men," this "land of revolt," still bathed itself in an atmosphere of brutal violence.

The sultan of Jolo had his residence here. Besides having authority over all the Sulu Archipelago's sultans, he was the official representative of the Moro people. Because the Filipino central government blamed him for not preventing his subjects from organizing guerrilla movements, the island swarmed with Filipino soldiers. They were everywhere. And since the military barracks were fully occupied, the officers took up most of the available hotel space throughout the small town. They were even in the small hotel where I was lucky enough to find, for three days, the last available room. Instead of *hotel* I should say *guest house*, because that's what hotels are called here. And aptly so, because they are large private houses made of bamboo and wood, to which their owners have added some amenities.

The first evening, I walked through the market as the sun was about to plunge into the sea for its daily bath. The song of a *muezzin*, calling for the evening prayers, attracted my attention and lured me to a mosque. Standing in the shadow between two houses, I watched the Moslem worshippers entering the prayer house for their holy meeting with Allah.

The spiritual and religious reverie that overtakes me each time I am in the vicinity of a place of worship was broken off by a man who suddenly appeared in front of me.

"Are you a Moslem?" he asked in broken English.

I shook my head.

"If you are not a Moslem," he said, taking a revolver from his robes, cocking it, and placing it under my chin, "then you are a Jew! I am going to kill you!"

"I am not Jewish! Let me—"

He stuck his gun at my throat and whispered, "Yes, you are!"

While he was raving about bad things done by the Israelis during the Six-Day War, I began to splutter out incoherent explanations, trying to figure out how to get out of this ridiculous situation without being killed.

Soon, with fear activating all the resources of my imagination, I somehow managed to concoct a story. "I am an active member of the secret movement of the Liberation of the Holy Crescent," I said. This aroused his interest and curiosity so much that he wanted to see the documents proving it, which I said I had left in the guest house.

"Let's go to your place together," he said, hiding his handgun beneath his robes but pointing it still at my side.

By the time we arrived in front of the guest house, he was calm and trustful. I told him to wait outside, because it would take me time to find the proof of my story.

Thanking heaven for having provided so many military men in Jolo that some were even staying in my small and cheap hotel, I knocked frantically on every door, hoping to find a military officer. At last I found one, asleep. With his help the man, who was evidently known to be unhinged, was put in jail for three days—the length of my stay. Later, to help me forget my bad adventure, the same officer proposed taking me on a one-day tour of Jolo. I accepted, thinking that at least with him I would be safe.

Starting early next morning, a military jeep drove us with an escort to different points around the island. The officer showed me the best places for taking photographs. Wherever we went, the soldiers, their guns loaded, assumed firing positions. Nervous and excited—I had never had an armed escort before—I remarked offhandedly to the officer, "Still troubles with the Moros, hm?"

"No, no, no! Crushed! They are all crushed! It's just a military exercise!"

A military exercise? I thought to myself. Whenever we stop off the road, the soldiers seem too tense and nervous to be just exercising.

After a tasty lunch of chicken and rice at one of Jolo's small military bases, the officer sent me aboard a military truck for more sightseeing.

"Sorry, I can't come along. Some administrative problems to resolve," he said before we left. "But afterward I'll join you wherever you are."

I rode standing on the rear platform of the truck. There in the open air I was able to see the scenery, and it was easier to shoot pictures. Anyway, with the driver and two soldiers in it, the cab was too crowded, too hot, and too noisy. We were driving off-road very fast. Not to be bounced from the truck, I had to hold firmly to the cabin roof. Behind me, another bodyguard stood clutching a heavy machine gun mounted on the rear end of the platform. We stopped not far from a small lake. I started to shoot some pictures. Since the bad idle of the motor made the truck tremble, the driver asked me through the rear window if he should switch off the ignition.

"No need! *Maramipong salamat!* [Thank you very much]," I said in Tagalog. I was occupied with my camera when I heard the sound of gunfire and men screaming. The truck lurched forward and threw me into the bushes. All around I heard more shots and machine-gun fire. I lay on the ground where I fell, not moving a muscle. Bullets hissed above my head. The gunfire seemed endless. My ears took a long time to accept the silence when it finally came. Paralyzed by fear, I didn't move, imagining that the rebels were still there, watching. I thought I could hear them moving. They must believe I am dead, I said to myself. Then I'd better act as if I really am dead, it's the only way to survive! My heart beat like crazy at even the slightest noise. I was ready to stay like that until nightfall.

Perhaps one hour later, I heard a truck coming. I remained absolutely motionless until I recognized the voice of my officer friend. "You're alive, thank God, you're alive! I'm sorry, so sorry!" he said, helping me climb into his military jeep.

My whole escort had been killed.

Still in a state of shock, I couldn't pay much attention to the officer's explanation. All I could make out was that my guards had been the victims of Moro guerrilleros.

Incredibly the officer offered to continue the tour.

"No, thank you! No more strolls in Jolo! No more scenic rides. I can't take these military exercises. I think I am going away. Back to Brussels and the calm!" I didn't care to meet sultans any more. I just wanted to get out of Jolo as soon as possible—that night, that moment!

On our way back to town the sky grew dark with pouring rain and the wind began to blow hard, bending the heads of coconut trees before sometimes breaking their trunks apart or uprooting them. For two days a heavy storm prevented all boats from sailing.

I was sentenced to Jolo. I stayed in my room, recovering from my terror. I tried to sleep but nightmares kept me awake. I was killed by Moros. I was killed by the man who attacked me in front of the mosque. Even my friendly army officer took a turn at taking my life away.

The tropical storm left Jolo early in the morning of the third day, and the sea calmed down. When I went to find out how soon the first boat could take me back to Zamboanga, I stumbled upon the sultan who was there at the wharf, waiting by his sailing canoe, which was already loaded. Destiny intervened once more, wrapping my recent terrifying experience with the sails of a new adventure, pointing me forward instead of back.

Our small boat was a *vinta,* a thirty-foot-long Southeast Asian canoe with a many-colored square sail. Long, heavy pieces of bamboo, attached by ten- to fifteen-foot arms on each side of the hull and parallel to it, prevent the canoe from capsizing in strong winds and rough seas.

A vinta has a kind of cover made of woven palm leaves to protect people in bad weather or at night, but since it is fragile and would blow away in a breeze, it is of use only when the boat is motionless. Otherwise, it is rolled up and attached to the arms of the two-balance system.

These very fast vintas are used for short hops from island to island. For trips across wider seas, the local navigators adapt this system of one- or two-balances to bigger and heavier boats. In fact, our modern catamarans are based on the design of the one-balance canoe, while the two-balance system has inspired the trimarans.

In all we were twelve men aboard the sultan's vinta. Some were crew members; others were obviously the sultan's body-guards. Like all the people of the Sulu islands they wore light, very ample pajamalike trousers, small braided jackets tight around the waist, and a large belt that held a kris, a dagger, and a few little boxes made of copper containing betel nuts and the other ingredients needed for their chewing mixture. Some had faded multicolored scarves wrapped around their heads as turbans. The sultan's clothes were similar but were made of more precious fabrics. They dressed like pirates in a play.

The bottom of the canoe was always filled with a bit of water. Raised above it was a floor made of bamboo laths on which we sat cross-legged along the hull and around the center of the vinta, crowded with a cargo of standard island goods: fabrics, krises, blades, radios, chickens, ducks, pigs, and even some bottles of alcohol (in these islands, some Moslems don't bother with the taboos of the Koran). In Jolo I had learned that the main industry of these islanders was pearl diving, so instead of buying with money, the Sulu people swap pearls and mother-of-pearl for their merchandise.

O̶ur exit from the harbor was slowed by the hundreds of vintas and other much larger wooden boats that, under full sail, were leaving for their destinations near or faraway. Some were to sail up to Irian-Jaya (Indonesian New Guinea), Sulawezi (Celebes), Borneo, or other Indonesian islands. Others were headed for as far away as China. These commercial sail-boats made their way cautiously, trying to avoid the crowd of small *lepas,* two-balance canoes that look like floating houses, which shelter whole families of the *Badjao* people, also called *Badjau,* which means *born from the sea*; the Badjaos are one of many sea nomad groups. Much smaller in stature than other Asians, they average five feet in height and are of Chinese, Malayan, or Negrito ethnic descent. One finds them along islands and coasts from the South Philippines and North Indonesia up to South India, where they are called *Moken.* Like all sea gypsies, the Badjaos belong to the ocean and lead their lives near it, beside it, and from it. Although some settle in villages on small islands, the majority stop on deserted beaches to give birth, bury their dead, or dream of the next voyage. Every family has its own boat that is literally its home. Since the head of the family is the rightful owner of the boat, when he dies it is demolished and then rebuilt as his coffin. The Badjaos sail in groups of three or four boats, joyfully calling to one another over the water as they sail toward their destiny.

While everyone in our vinta was busy talking with people from other boats, I looked at these sea gypsies sailing around us. Their dockside glances had given place to curious but friendly stares.

For me sailing has always symbolized the ultimate freedom, the call of the salt spray, the wind as the only master while floating between Neptune and the heavens. And when our sails were puffed out with the winds of dreams and freedom, when the noises of the harbor were fading behind us, replaced by the whispers of the sea, the breeze, the sail, and of the boats cleaving the waters, then I even forgot to be seasick.

Once again I tasted pure joy. I still couldn't believe that I was going to a sultan's kingdom with the sultan himself. I thought, How wonderful life is. And by living it to its extremes, it becomes even more wonderful. The prospect of entering the world I had dreamed of made me forget my brush with death. Now at last I was fully relaxed.

My serenity was abruptly disturbed by the unmistakable clicking of guns being loaded. Suddenly, except for the sultan and myself, every man had an M-16 rifle in his hand or flung on his shoulder. Yet, all around us I could see nothing but the open sea, with Jolo disappearing far behind, the outlines of several islands wedged between sky and water, and only a few canoes whose sails gave color to the horizon. So, who was I with? I knew they were Moros. I wondered if they were also guerrilleros. I looked at the sultan and expressed my surprise at the guns.

"What is your name again?" he asked, still using his broken English/Tagalog pidgin.

"Douchan! Dou . . . chaaaan!"

He conscientiously repeated my name several times: "Dou . . . ssan, Dou . . . ssan. You from France?"

"Yes!" I could never have explained that I had been born in Czechoslovakia and raised in Africa, and that I lived in Belgium.

"Very, very good!" he replied nodding, and turning to the others he added something else I couldn't understand but that made everybody laugh but me. Stretching out my hand, I touched and caressed the rifle that the man next to me was holding on his knees. "That also very, very good," I said, nodding and frowning to emphasize satisfaction. "But why that?"

"Bad peoples!" he said, pointing to the horizon. "Many bad peoples!"

"Bad people? You mean . . . pirates?"

"Pirates! Yes, yes!" he said, happy to be understood. Another man repeated, rolling his eyes, "Pirates! Many, many!" Then he burst out laughing, soon imitated by the others. And they began commenting upon this subject.

"Many, many pirates!" said the sultan, inhaling deeply the smoke of his cigarette. He cleared his throat noisily, spat a long stream of saliva into the sea, and started to tell me about them. At that time, I did not understand much of what he said, and happily so; otherwise I might have asked him to take me back to Jolo which, compared to what I was to learn later about these seas we were sailing, seemed so much safer.

The ocean from the Philippines to North Borneo contained three kinds of pirates. Organized gangs which worked for rich, well-protected Asian businessmen operated from boats disguised as fishing boats but propelled by powerful engines. Armed with machine guns and sometimes even small cannon, they pillaged mainly freighters and private yachts. Their bosses communicated with them by radio and took care of reselling the loot.

Less organized independents practiced piracy from junks also camouflaged as fishing boats. Other pirates worked from small, actual fishing boats. And some fishing boats were really just fishing boats, which always surprised everybody.

Looking at the sultan and his men, whose clothes belonged to the world of "Ali Baba and the Forty Thieves," I had a hard time believing that I wasn't dreaming. They were like an illustration in an old book.

The sultan began to question me about my country. I understood less than a quarter of what he asked, and he probably understood only a tenth of what I told him. After a while, to my relief, he nodded off to sleep, perhaps tired of not understanding me or bored by my conversation. Soon, except for the pair on watch, all the men were dozing, their rifles propped up on their knees. Each time we were approached by a "fishing boat," they quickly woke up, holding their rifles at the ready. Then, when we were alone on the sea, they gave in again to their drowsiness. I started to wonder what I would do if we were really attacked.

What the hell am I doing here? I thought as I tried to relax. If pirates attack us I'll jump into the water! I said to myself, Yes, that is what I'll do . . . unless it's infested by sharks. Sharks? That's a good question to ask the sultan as soon as he wakes up. Numbed by the heat of the day, my brain soon stopped thinking, abandoning me to somnolence.

A burst of rifle fire startled me out of my sleep, discharging adrenaline into my blood. I threw myself to the bottom of the canoe, where I froze, head down and breathless. This is it, we're being attacked! Expecting a hail of bullets but hearing peals of laughter and screams of joy, I slowly turned my head up and saw mirthful faces looking at me. I stood up, embarrassed but maintaining a very dignified air and as if nothing had happened and went back to my seat. Having nothing to say, I smiled and then noticed another vinta which was moving away, the people on board waving at us. When it happened again later, I realized that exchanging rifle fire between two boats while laughing and yelling screams of joy was only their way of greeting each other.

We stopped once on the beach of a deserted island to spend the night and cook rice and meat. Otherwise, the two days of the trip consisted only of noisy greetings from friendly boats, defensive posturing whenever a fishing boat came too close to us, attempts at conversation between my boatmates and me, and a lot of sleep, rocked by heat, silence, and the strong wind that kept us at a rapid speed.

A string of small islands appeared around 3:00 P.M. of the second day. With gestures, the sultan indicated to me that the islands were his.

The sultan's village.

"How many do you have?" I asked, holding up three, four, then ten fingers.

"Many, many!" He turned and said something to his people. Counting with their fingers, all began to recite names together. I guessed they were the names of the sultan's islands. When the recitation ended, forty-one fingers had been counted.

About half a mile from the island where the sultan had his residence, my companions fired their rifles to announce our arrival. A few minutes later we heard a fusillade of greeting in return.

From far away the village looked as if it were built on a giant pier, fifteen to twenty feet high, thrusting out over the sea. As we got closer, I could see that the village was composed of two separate platforms linked together by a narrow footbridge. Most of the villagers' houses were built on the platform which extended inland from the beach; a mosque was at the far end. The sultan's palace covered the other platform built half over sand and half over water. It was a very large bamboo house, about fifty feet square, completely surrounded by a large veranda. A tree-trunk staircase connected one side of the veranda to the sea below where canoes docked at the pilework.

About fifty people, including women and children, crowded together on the balustrade to watch us arrive. All the men, even the young boys, carried automatic rifles. Just as we reached the palace, all of them fired into the air, cheering and laughing.

Carrying large sabers wedged in their belts, the men in the village were dressed like those with whom I had traveled. The women wore silk trousers tight at the legs, and jackets with narrow sleeves and gold buttons. Some women wore magnificent saris of silk woven with gold.

The palace was made of thick bamboo logs tied tightly side by side; the outer walls were covered with a canvas of woven *nippa* leaves. The nippa is a kind of palm tree which grows in water. When woven, the leaves make a waterproof surface good for roofs, walls, baskets, and hats. The few windows of the palace were just one-foot-square holes, with shutters that could be closed for protection against pouring rain and strong winds. At the rear of the palace, very small compartments provided quarters for the servants and guards, and storerooms for food and other goods. There also was a very large kitchen with a door that led outside to the back of the house. The rest of the palace was one large room about fifty by twenty-five feet, which became by turns the dining room, living room, and council chamber. And at night, with mats hung from the bamboo roof to create for everyone a sense of intimacy, it became the bedroom for the sultan's entire family which consisted of eighteen wives and all their children—he could not say how many.

The crowd that had followed me stayed outside the palace and watched through the main door as I entered the large main room. Seeing that everyone was barefoot, I left my shoes outside.

It was not easy to walk barefoot on the floor, which was made of thin strips of bamboo attached side by side, with enough space between them for the betel users to spit their red saliva directly onto the beach or into the sea. During the day I could see the betel saliva swirling in the waves, among the crabs, and on the shiny sand. And at night, when lying on the floor, I had the feeling of sleeping right on the beach.

As I sat next to the sultan at the center of the room on a large vegetal many-colored mat, he proudly presented me to his court, old men who were the dignitaries of the village. Then the servants brought us a delicious meal of fish and rice, served on metal plates from Hong Kong that were painted with multi-

colored flowers, and accompanied by generous amounts of
Filipino brandy. The women ate apart, sitting together on the
other side of the room.

After dinner the sultan smoked opium with me; everyone else
chewed betel, except for a few old notables who smoked hashish.
Then the sultan summoned his senior wife, a small, shy, smiling
old woman with blackened teeth. He seated her very close to me.
I wondered what was going on, as I had been told in Jolo that
Moros were very jealous husbands who severely punished un-
faithful wives and their lovers, too. I thought he was testing me,
so I acted as if she weren't even there. But after the servants
hung the mats to create separate sleeping cells, the sultan insisted on leaving her with me for the night.

From my childhood in Africa and from the many books I had
read about the customs of cultures throughout the vast world,
I knew that many practice what is called *sexual hospitality*. In
some tribes, this custom doesn't necessarily apply to a man who
is obviously accompanied by his woman; in others, it also involves the female guest. Generally, sexual hospitality has no
other purpose than to relieve the guest's loneliness, honor him,
and provide evidence of the munificence of the host, who is
honored by his guest's acceptance of the gift. For some peoples,
the custom's main purpose is to bring new blood into the community.

The night was not easy. My "hostess" was not at all to my
taste but I knew I couldn't refuse her. It would have been an
insult, like rejecting a gift or a meal. I assumed that had I refused
her, I would have been summarily ejected from the island, probably without a safe escort, and abandoned on another island.

The much-too-short mats that hung from the roof, transforming the large room into a dormitory, did little to diminish the
communal feeling. The sounds flowed freely. Lying on the floor
I could see in the oil lamps' gleam everything that was going on
elsewhere. From the shadows, the members of the sultan's family watched, ready to evaluate their foreign guest's expertise in
the matter of sex. But I was with a woman for whom I had no
sexual desire. Moreover, just knowing that people all around me
were watching gave me a total impotence. I could hear their
whisperings of impatience and the stirrings of mats whenever
they moved a little in their hiding places. Since I didn't want to
be deported to an island in the middle of nowhere, I tried everything, including fantasizing, but without success. If only my

The author at age two previewing his
future.

What the Filipinos call the eighth wonder of the world: the rice terraces
built some 2000 years ago.

Bong and I asking directions from an Igorot.

In a cave near Bong's grandfather's village, a hollow tree trunk serves as a casket.

An Apayao men's house with low, igloo-style entrance.

A house in an Apayao village. The round cans on the
legs keep the rats from climbing in.

An Apayao woman with arm tattoos.

A well-tattooed Igorot makes up for his lack
of pockets by strapping his pipe behind his ear.

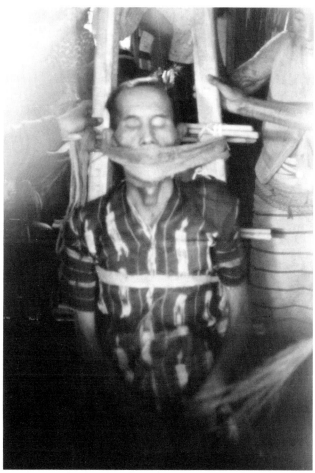

At the Apayao funeral the guest of honor, his mouth and
throat stuffed with rice, is prepared for burial.

Moro houses built on piling over a rocky beach near Jollo.

The kriss on this Moro guerrilla's waist is all he needs
to command respect.

In small double-balance boats, the Moros of the Sulu Archipelago travel hundreds of miles from island to island.

The Sultan's family greets us with shouts and shots.

The Sultan.

Dancing on the beach on my wedding day.

sultana would help by moving her body, or doing something, anything ... then perhaps. But she didn't. She lay there waiting shyly, as troubled by the situation as I was. Yet I had to honor her with majesty! Suddenly, I remembered a piece of advice given to me by a friend: "In this situation there is only one thing to do: drink lots of water!" For when a man has drunk a lot before going to sleep, when he awakens the pressure of his full bladder results in an erection! With gestures I expressed to my sultana that I was thirsty. She understood my message, stood up and disappeared, then shortly came back with a bottle of local brandy and another bottle filled with water. I chose the latter and emptied it. As expected, it eventually worked, helped on by a little imagination and the fact that my roommates had succumbed to sleep.

As the nights passed, I was able to abandon that technique born of desperation, for my later playmates were more and more to my taste. And after the first night, nobody wanted to watch me any more.

By giving me his wife, the sultan was not trying to satisfy any perverse needs for himself or his people—it was simple curiosity, not vice. He was only following the custom dictated by his traditional laws of hospitality. But knowing the Moros' jealous nature, I abstained from having any favorites and treated the women who came to me with an equanimity that matched their own. In the morning, I awoke alone and the ladies never gave me any special attention the next day.

I didn't stay very long on that island cut off from the modern century and my past, with no other foreigners, no telephones, no post offices or other references to remind me of my own cultural identity. Not missing my family, but thinking of them.

I didn't stay very long in that place where I had no great eagerness to go on with my career as a filmmaker, only regretting sometimes the lack of more film for my still camera or a movie camera to capture the life of these people. I had no ambition other than to be myself with them and enjoy them—no need but to absorb deep in my heart, my eyes, my ears, and my memory all that I saw, heard, and experienced day after day. I had no thoughts of tomorrow other than the hope to still be alive to enjoy.

No, I didn't stay very long. Just about eight weeks. Only eight weeks of living like a prince, not in wealth but in consideration and warmth. In those two months I shared the villagers' way of life, sometimes giving bits of advice to ameliorate this or that problem. And as our mutual vocabulary improved, I befriended the sultan more and more.

He had worries. One concerned the economy of his sultanate. For a long time, his wealth and that of all the other Sulu sultanates was ensured by the gathering of pearls, mother-of-pearl, coral, and the trading of shark fins, bird nests, and turtle eggs with the Chinese. But that commerce had been slowly undermined by plastics and other synthetic materials, as well as by the closing of the Chinese trade. So their most lucrative activities shifted to the less dependable: fishing and smuggling.

His second worry concerned the neighboring sultanate. Although the sultans of the Sulu Archipelago officially pledged allegiance to the sultan of Jolo through the payment of a yearly tribute, the islands were in reality self-governing; each sultan managed his territory as he wished. Not infrequently, two sultans would start a battle to extend their power over other islands. One way of extending power or avoiding a deadly confrontation was to effect a peace treaty with another sultan by marrying one of his daughters; this explained the number of wives in a typical sultan's harem. Still, one needed to be watchful, for in order to increase their wealth some sultans resorted to piracy, commanding groups of pirates who attacked not only local trading boats but also merchants sailing between the Philippines and Indonesia and any yachts or pleasure boats that dared to venture into these waters. The *Taosugs*, the Moro ethnic group among whom I was living, had always been known as great navigators and pirates.

I listened to the problems of paradise and nodded my head without offering advice. Because of their immense hospitality, I quickly settled into daily life among the Taosugs, observing, learning, and enjoying. For Westerners whose activities are patterned by the day/night cycle and the clock, the islanders' life must appear very chaotic, for instead of by sunrise and sunset, it is regulated by seasons, weather, tides, sea currents, and the movements of fish.

For some fishermen, the day begins very early. Long before sunrise they sail out to the far horizon where they harpoon rays, porpoises, octopus, and whatever else is attracted by the light of the oil lamps attached to the front of their canoes.

Others leave the village in early morning aboard vintas crowded with nets. Depending on the type of net carried, they sail in different directions to fish separately, not knowing if they will return at sunset or two days later. Or perhaps they stay together in groups of three or four boats, as is the case when fishing with a "spider net." A spider net is made of cotton intertwined with other natural fibers and stretches to about seven hundred feet in breadth. Held on the surface by floats and weighed down with stones and shells, a spider net forms an underwater wall, stopping and catching all fish, even sharks.

Later in the morning, the night fishermen return with their catch, which they share with relatives, exchange for rice, and sell at the local market. Bunches of men, women, and adolescents, wearing conical hats and carrying sabers, slowly descend from the high platform supporting the village, and head for the rice fields. Although the islanders are essentially people of the sea, due to economic changes they now more commonly own and cultivate their own rice fields.

As the sun starts its celestial ascent, groups of young and older men embark aboard their canoes, with knives, small baskets, and round diving goggles that they make themselves. These people often are Badjaos working for the sultan in exchange for protection, as some sultanates still enslave them.

Pearl or shell gathering is not easy. Ballasted with a big stone in order to reach the bottom faster, they dive thirty, forty feet down, sometimes more, holding their breath as long as possible to increase the quantity of their gathering. This kind of daily diving drastically lowers their life expectancy. Some whom I met on these gathering parties had already started to go blind, even young ones. The sea salt, the bright daylight, and the pressure of the depths had begun the destruction of their eyes.

Later in the day when the heat diminishes, vintas appear on the horizon, their square multicolored sails contrasting with a sky often loaded with swollen clouds. As the canoes come closer and hit the beaches, one can see their catches hanging on ropes, split in two, cleaned, and already drying in the sun. The less lucky fishermen will return sometimes very late at night.

Soon, with the return of peasants, fishermen, pearl and shell gatherers, the village comes to life again, echoing with radios whining the *imam*'s call to prayer, the greetings of barking dogs, children's screams, and the sounds of conversation mixing with the beat of pestles crushing rice in mortars. Then, little by little everywhere the lights of oil lamps, candles, and fires begin to mark the night, which slowly falls on the rising smoke and smells of meals cooking.

Later, men with men, women with women, they collect in small groups sitting in front of the houses or against the balustrade at the end of the platform, looking out at the fluorescent sea. There, with a background of *gamelan*, or gong music, coming from their radios, they gossip, laugh at fishing stories, and play cards, dominoes, or mah-jongg, always chewing betel or smoking.

After a day spent providing for food necessities, breaking off only to turn toward Mecca and say their ritual prayers, at night some played with their newborn babies; others, protected by the intimacy of darkness, made love—ensuring their own immortality and that of the family.

After I had been with him about four weeks, the sultan told me he wanted to make me *datu*, which is the local word for *sultan* but is also used to designate someone who is like a *vice sultan*. The latter station was what he intended to bestow on me.

I was surprised by his decision. Surprised, but proud. I didn't know exactly what led him to make it and didn't ask questions, but, as I soon learned, such an honor goes hand-in-hand with a price. Without asking for my concurrence, he told me that I was to marry one of his daughters. Uh-oh, I said to myself. Is he planning to keep me here for the rest of my life?

Whatever his reasons were, the sultan clearly wasn't leaving me a choice. I felt it was take it or take it. I didn't argue. I smiled, said thanks, and asked him which daughter. I got no answer— maybe he hadn't made up his mind yet.

I didn't question the implications of such a wedding—after all, according to the traditions of the Moros, it is not love between two persons that makes a wedding, but the need to combine two families or two powers. Although I didn't feel like being married at twenty, I could only accept it as a new experience. Considering the situation I am in, I said to myself, there is nothing left to me but to hope that she will be nice looking. And the day I decide to go, it is up to me to be as artful as a cartload of monkeys to find a way to say "bye-bye!"

Until that day when I was to meet her, the only thing on my mind was to guess which of his daughters would become my wife. I rarely saw any of them and hadn't tried to since the day the sultan seemed very much annoyed by my approaching them.

Every day I had to undergo special lessons to increase my knowledge of the Koran. Finally, the sultan introduced me to Leila, my fiancée. She was very young, not very tall but cute with her dark skin, her long black hair, and Oriental eyes without brows—the local standard of beauty called for shaving them. She was very shy, hid her mouth with her hand whenever she smiled, and her eyes were downcast almost the whole time she was facing me. A few times she stared at me intently without even blinking. I found it very provocative.

Apart from formally greeting her and asking how she was—and getting no answer—I had no opportunity to talk to her before the wedding, and we never did enjoy the usual courting procedures.

When a Moro boy has made his choice, he lets the girl know it by offering her some fruit. Eating a piece of fruit in front of him is her way of accepting his proposition. Then he will perform the same ritual with the rest of her family. If they too express their agreement, the boy and the girl will be considered engaged. Then the girl's family chooses from its male relatives the *wali*, or negotiator, who arranges with the groom-to-be and his family the value of the dowry they must pay to the bride's family. Depending on the wealth and social status of the recipients, this can represent a true fortune.

Once the dowry has been set, and paid, the wedding can take place. The betrothed are separated, the girl in a room with the women, the boy with the men. The priest performs the religious ceremony in the presence of the boy only. Afterward, the boy enters the room where the bride waits and, by placing his hand on her forehead, symbolically takes possession of her. Then, all day (or, in the case of politically important weddings, for several days) there is feasting and dancing. The first night, sometimes with an old woman as a witness, the groom must honor his wife on a small carpet that is later shown to everybody as proof of the girl's virginity. If she is not a virgin, the marriage can be ended and the boy's family can recover the dowry. However, if through the marriage the boy gains access to a higher social status, he sometimes keeps his wife and is entitled to ask for material compensation—a nonvirgin bonus—from his wife's family.

Except for the dowry that I didn't have to pay, my wedding

followed the traditional pattern. Leila, a gold tiara on her head, wore a sumptuous robe of blue silk woven with gold and studded with many jewels. I wore red trousers, a blue shirt of silk embroidered with gold, a long multicolored silk scarf tied around my waist, and a turban wrapped around my head. Wedged in my belt was a wonderful kris that the sultan had given me as the symbol of my new title and function.

I had put my hand on Leila's forehead, then on her hand—symbolizing marital power—and cups of water and rice, symbols of purity and fertility, were placed in front of us. We were invited to sit in the middle of the palace's large room where a woman began to sing love ballads, accompanied by a musician playing the *gambong*, a type of Indonesian xylophone. The sound of her voice blended with the melodious gongs coming from the village. Since Moros still live according to a feudal system, the people stayed outside the palace. Joined by natives from the other islands that belonged to our sultan, they had their own feast. Only important notables and guests, among whom were four other friendly sultans, came to visit inside the palace and brought us presents. Mostly for Leila, they brought sumptuous pieces of fabric, gold jewels, and other priceless goods, since with these gifts they hoped to gain the sultan's favor. Most of these rich and important guests wore magnificent, colorful clothes with gold buttons and richly decorated daggers, krises, or swords.

Later, inside the palace and outside around fires on the beach, people ate, drank, and danced to the sounds of gongs. The celebrating went on for three days. It was incredibly romantic. If only we had been in love.

When time came to honor my bride on the small, multicolored carpet, I began to come back to reality. It seemed so unbelievable, a dream. Until now I had lived these events as a spectator, not an actor. I couldn't remember if I had even talked to Leila at all. But once I found myself lying next to her and felt her trembling with tension, apparently afraid of what was about to happen, I truly started to feel sorry for her. I knew that I could not stay in this place very long, that sooner or later the need to leave, to go home and then on to other adventures, would overcome me. I wouldn't take her with me because I didn't love her, and it would be impossible for her to move from one civilization to another without great suffering. I asked her, "Do you have any regrets?" She said no. Despite her nervousness, she seemed full of desire. That helped, because without feeling that the desire was mutual I wouldn't have been able to take her.

The rug was shown. I wanted to stay with her a little longer and dream away the night with tenderness, but the sultan showed up and called me away. I followed him into a small room heavy with the smell of incense burning on the floor and of oily perfume that covered the sultan's body. He invited me to sit on the rug next to him. He was drunk.

"Women is okay! But now it's time for the real pleasure!" he whispered in my ear. Before I had time to understand his meaning, he began to caress my chest! My brain started working at full speed. I had to find a way to escape from his passion without hurting his feelings.

"You remember that I have told you I will always worship the religion of my ancestors," I said.

"Yes . . . but no problems!" he said, while his caresses began to creep downward.

"Listen! I want you, too! My desire for you is as strong as yours for me, since the first day I met you . . . but . . ."

Instead of listening to me, he sighed in passion. I stopped his hand.

"I'm sorry. My religion forbids sex between men. If I do it, my ancestors will never forgive. All my family and descendants will be cursed forever. That is what my religion says."

After a long pause he looked at me and whispered, "Nothing should trouble the peace of ancestors." Slowly, he got up and left.

The next three weeks were great. Although I avoided all situations where I might find myself alone with him, the sultan's behavior with me was as it always had been. There was no evidence of animosity. As my language got better I was able to communicate a little bit with everyone in the village, which made it easier to share in their activities. However, since they considered me one of them, I also had to submit to their daily religious ritual, to pray five times a day toward Mecca. Although they had a small mosque, these rituals never took place there. I must admit that I skipped a lot of them whenever I knew I couldn't be seen.

My princess was sweet but silent. Even though I asked her

many questions, she never said a thing, or else answered vaguely without unveiling her thoughts, remaining secret about her sentiments. In a culture where men and women never share entertainment together, she had been educated to obey and please her husband, that's all. And because women have their life apart from males, they always gather together, sharing their feelings and worries only with one another. Our relationship existed only at night and that was not enough.

One day I learned that a vinta of the sultan's was sailing early the next morning for North Borneo. I knew it was time to go and suddenly felt an irresistible desire to go home and see my family, to wander from café to restaurant, to go to the movies, and to chat with friends. But above all, just to go home. Without knowing the possible repercussions, I announced my decision.

"So, you must leave?" the sultan asked matter-of-factly.

"Yes. My father died not long ago so I must see my mother, my family."

He looked annoyed.

"But I will be back soon. I shall leave all my things here."

Leila was perhaps enamored of me, because of a girlish heart and the romance of our circumstances, but clearly she did not have time to truly love me. And as she had said nothing, I couldn't know. I knew she would marry again when her father wanted to secure a peace treaty with another sultan. But I felt bad. So bad that I didn't want to make love to her. She was the one to insist.

By four o'clock the next morning, the crew of seven men had already filled the vinta with various goods to be exchanged in Sandakan, the capital of Sabah, a small sultanate in North Borneo (at that time, 1967, still independent). In spite of the early hour, many people crowded the palace veranda. I saw Leila staring at me. The sultan came out holding my kris. "You must always keep this with you!" he said and, opening my hand, put a few big pearls in my palm. "Those are for your sisters." Then he gave me a giant one, "And this is for your mother!"

"I will be back. One day soon." My desire to return came from the depths of my heart.

The last words of farewell were carried away by the wind that puffed our sails. Soon we passed a small island that had been given to me by the sultan. The winds blew us rapidly toward the south; the kingdom of my sultan lay far behind.

Around 3:00 A.M. the next day, we were moving a few miles offshore along the southern coasts of Tawitawi, the last large island of the Sulu Archipelago before North Borneo, located between the Sulu Sea and the Celebes Sea where we were heading. The stars that guided the local navigators had disappeared behind heavy clouds. The only lights were an oil storm lantern attached to the front of our vinta and the opal glow of the coral sea.

The wind was growing stronger and the seven men on board started to argue about the possibility that we would soon be hit by a storm. The four who were positive about it wanted to stop on the island of Tawitawi, but the other three preferred to go on to Borneo, saying that the wind would take the storm away from our route. Unable to decide among themselves, they looked to me. I looked at the black sky. Just as I was about to choose for safety and security, the wind began to blow with fury. But instead of thunder, it brought the sound of gunshots. A bullet broke our oil storm lantern, throwing us into sudden darkness. We had been so busy with the sail and the arguing that nobody had seen the unlighted pirate boat approaching us from behind.

This surprise attack created such a panic that, instead of everyone grabbing rifles to fight back, only two men began to shoot, covering the others who were trying desperately to raise the sail for the boat to flee. With the wind and the rough sea, I suspected that we hadn't the slightest chance of escape. The pirate's boat, a large and high junk, was now less than fifteen feet away. Fumbling in the darkness, trembling with tension, and obliged to stay bent over, I couldn't find even one single rifle. I yelled to the captain who gave me a gun; I yelled to the others to fight back. Suddenly the shadowy conflict was lit by the beam of a searchlight mounted on the front of the pirate boat. I fired at it and missed. One of my companions fell, wounded in the shoulder. Another man hit the pirate searchlight with his bullet. I could see darker against the sky only the silhouette of the pirate boat but not the people on it, so I aimed just above their deck. The gunshots blended with the shouts of our men and theirs. Crawling on the bottom of the boat despite his pain and loss of blood, our wounded man supplied us additional bullet clips. We heard several shouts coming from the pirate boat, and they stopped firing, tacked, and moved away. It seemed they had not expected such a resistance. In all, the combat had lasted less than ten minutes.

The one-hour trip to Balimbang, one of Tawitawi's main port towns, was wild with joy, as everyone retold the story of the battle and his personal exploits at least a dozen times. If one could believe what each crewman claimed, at least one hundred people had been aboard that pirate boat and we had shot them all dead!

Privately I thought that all of us were still alive because those pirates were poor shots. I asked why the crewmen didn't respond to the attack by spraying the pirates with bullets, instead of leaving only two people shooting while the others risked their lives to prepare the boat for escape.

"It has always worked like that!" They explained that it is better to run than to fight because pirates never take prisoners. "But next time we'll do like you wish, and you'll be the one to give us the order to start shooting!" they said, and burst out laughing. Still shaken, I found it hard to join in.

The wounded man was taken to the town's community clinic. Although he was not badly hurt, it was decided to leave him with friends—where we had rested briefly—and to pick him up on the next voyage. As I relaxed, I began to realize for the first time what we had experienced. Once again my desire to return home overcame me.

We left Tawitawi the next day, our rifles and bullets always at hand. Thanks to a better wind than expected we sailed nonstop for two days and were to reach Sandakan the next morning. Although we had now arrived on the coast of North Borneo, the crewmen said we should not spend the night without our weapons by our sides. I hoped never to see another pirate.

The first explosion which broke through the peaceful early morning fog was so strong that the waters echoed for a long time. Three hundred feet away, a large junklike fishing boat with two masts and many sails slowly and silently emerged from the fog and approached our left side. At the second explosion a spray of water rose near our vinta. We all threw ourselves to the bottom of the boat and, fingers on triggers, watched cautiously as the junk came closer. Now we could see a small cannon on the front deck, with many people bustling about it as if it had jammed. The pirates numbered about thirty. Over my thundering heartbeats I could hear the clicks of their rifles. I gave no starting signal, as we had planned nothing between us. But all of us began shooting together with such precision and luck that almost every bullet hit its mark, throwing panic into the surviving pirates. No longer shooting at us, the pirates sailed their boat slowly past us and disappeared into the fog.

We looked at one another, secretly sharing the same idea: to become pirates ourselves, jump on their boat, and take what they had stolen for ourselves. But nobody gave the signal, and then it was too late. The junk and our brief dream of revenge were buried in the deep fog.

Everyone began hugging, screaming, and jumping with joy. Me, too. Not for one single second had I felt that I was killing human beings. I was killing danger. And danger has no human face.

Twenty years later, as I am writing this book, piracy still exists from the Philippines to Burma, and anyone who wishes to fight pirates can go there and do so.

CHAPTER FOUR

The King and I

The unknown is an ocean. What is conscience? The compass of the unknown.

JOSEPH COOK

Christmas was coming. After stopping briefly in Hong Kong and India, I flew home to Brussels. To welcome me, Maman had prepared chicken and rice. She was surprised when I didn't jump at it. "Maman," I said, "that's what I have been eating for months!"

My family couldn't believe my stories. For them it was like listening to someone reading from an adventure book. The next day I was elated, quietly walking down the street to buy fresh croissants. I was happy to taste peace again. Happy to be covered with my family's love and attention. Happy to rediscover my culture. Everything amazed me as if I had never seen it before. Yet I felt lost in the city. After my stay in the Orient, everyone appeared to be the victim of some terrible palsy which caused their limbs to shudder and their eyes to glaze. I asked myself again and again, Don't they know how great it is just to be alive?

I was thrilled just to be on my way to the baker, but walking back home with my bag filled with croissants, I began to suffer from a deep solitude.

To the degree that I had become used to the dangers of an expedition, I now feared civilization's dangers. For instance, I was now afraid to drive my car. A tire might explode! The brakes or the steering system might fail! Some other driver might hit me! I could drive no more than thirty miles per hour even on the highway.

A few weeks later when I had become adjusted, I started to feel as if my skin had become too small for my body. I was not bored, just anxious to regain the sensation of being alive. The compulsion to go farther rose up in me, like a fever. I was still too young to succumb to civilization.

"So, now you're ready to hit your studies again, right?" my mother asked. That I had met headhunters and survived pirates wasn't enough to make her forget the deal we had made.

"Well . . ." (clearing my throat noisily) ". . . as a matter of fact . . ." and I told her that Gabriel wanted me to co-produce and co-direct his next movie, about the Maori people living in New Zealand, where we would stay about seven months.

"Yes, but—" she started. Knowing it wouldn't be easy to change her mind, I interrupted. "Maman, let me finish, please!" I explained that by touring with this movie and giving lectures, I would be able to make a living soon. I added, "Besides, if I don't make it as I should and as you want it, I promise I'll go back to school!" And I knew I had to make it because my mother is not easily fooled. Even today I know I had better handle my life with straightforwardness and honesty, because whenever I am facing her she sees only her little boy, whom she always has to reprimand and to whom she still can't help repeating, "Don't eat so fast, it's bad for your stomach! Don't smoke and drink, it's bad for your health! Sleep more, you need it!" and so on.

As planned, Gabriel and I stayed seven months in New Zealand to make the documentary about the Maoris, among whom I celebrated my twenty-first birthday.

I came back home at the beginning of December that year. Gabriel's agent booked me for a three-month lecture tour in the smaller French cities with our movie on the Philippines. The tour was to start the next January. I needed a car, a 16-mm projector, and an entire sound system—tape player, microphone, amplifier, and speakers.

"Maman, would you help me to get a loan from a bank, please?" I won't tell you what she started to reply, but she did help me. Thank God.

Lecturing in smaller cities only, I wasn't making a lot of money. Since I was still living at home, I earned enough to cover all the tour expenses and make my monthly bank payments. But not enough to save enough to finance an expedition of my own.

At the end of that lecture tour, Gabriel Linge, still busy editing our two movies, sent me back alone to New Zealand for some additional shots of the Maori people and more close-ups of that country's amazing volcanoes.

Near Rotorua on the north island are powerful vapor streams, geysers, and boiling lakes of mud which explode every ten minutes or so in giant bubbles of vapor. There are also hot sulfur springs and many-colored mud ponds that bubble noisily and are blanketed by noxious sulfurous clouds.

My determination to get great pictures made me blind to danger, for the camera was a buffer between danger and me. Many times when filming I have noticed that I often take high risks without being aware of it. I am unable to see or evaluate the danger because the lens puts a distance between the event and me. To observe through the camera's eye is, in fact, like wearing a carnival mask. It changes one's perception of things, and they lose their intrinsic values and become unreal. The protective shield of the camera enables me to film scenes impossible to tolerate if seen with the naked eye; and later, if the scenes are bloody, I have a hard time looking at these pictures that I myself shot. I think it is this difference between camera view and personal experience that permits a sensitive and emotional person to be an excellent war reporter.

So, lured by their appealing yellow color, I slowly moved to the small pools at the far end of the fragile crust layer. And as I squatted next to one of them, taking close-ups, I felt a small vibration beneath my feet. Immediately I stepped back, but I was too late. I went through the layer of shale, and my left leg plunged up to the knee in boiling sulfur. Blinded by the hot vapors, I still had time to throw my camera toward the path at the other end of the crust layer. Then began a torturous crawl toward safety.

Almost immediately my foot doubled in size. The pain was intense. My foot felt alternately burning and freezing. Following the path, I had to crawl on my two hands and one good foot for about half a mile up to the camper where my girlfriend, a local university student, was waiting. She drove me to the nearest hospital, about an hour away.

"You're a lucky man!" said the doctor. "This saved your foot!" He showed me the sandal which he had taken from my burned foot. "With an ordinary shoe you would not have a foot any more, just bones. Just bones! You're really lucky, young man."

"How come?" I asked, panting with pain.

He explained: "A shoe would have kept in the boiling sulfur and cooked your foot longer and deeper. And when you took it off you would have found just the bones. The rest would come off with the shoe. It has happened to a few careless tourists. I've seen it."

My foot had received third degree burns. The doctor wanted to keep me until they could peel off the cooked skin. That would take two weeks. But the Maoris were having a wedding that I wanted to film, so after two days of arguments, the hospital staff made me sign a release form and let me go.

Obviously, shooting a movie on crutches was not easy, but I did it. Because I had to. Gabriel needed these pictures.

Three weeks later, consumed by high fever and horrible pain, I went back to the hospital and learned that my foot had become gangrenous. The surgeon wanted to amputate, but I was not ready to accept the idea of losing my foot. I desperately wanted to go back to Europe. Because of my condition, UTA (the French airline with which Gabriel and I had a deal for free tickets) refused to carry me on such a long trip, but they agreed to drop me in New Caledonia, a French island 1000 miles north. There I found an old surgeon, one of those taciturn renegades to modern society one finds living only at the edge of civilization, used to making do with whatever is available. Used to making miracles. I pleaded with him to keep my body whole somehow. I remember him saying, as I sank into the pentothal sleep, "I'll do my best."

To get rid of infection he had to cut away a great deal of my flesh. But my foot was still there when I awoke.

"Thanks for the miracle, Doc."

"I only got rid of the devil. You are the one who must make a miracle—that's why God gave us a will . . . to make miracles. It's up to you alone to keep your foot and heal it. But you must be ready to suffer."

The veins of the foot were destroyed, but with time the capillaries would replace them. The major problem was to avoid infection—burned or cooked flesh loses its ability to fight infection. Antibiotics help, but they slow down considerably the formation of new cells. So twice a day, for four weeks, the nurse peeled off the newly formed scab and presented my bloody wound to the healing sun.

I came to understand what the surgeon meant when he asked me if I were ready to suffer. Between the two peelings a day, which each time left the bed soaked with my sweat, I had hours to think about my future. I decided I was not going to spend my life working for other explorers, making their dreams come true. I felt ready to realize my own dreams by making my own movies. I decided to study and film as a first subject the Gypsies of Europe. They are nomads, and nomads have always fascinated me, maybe because their way of living represents for me a kind of ultimate freedom. Moreover, since it wouldn't involve so much travel and living expenses, filming little by little the Gypsies roaming throughout Europe would be more affordable with my limited income.

The day I made that decision I became impatient to heal enough so I could leave the hospital and move back home. To pay the medical expenses, I entertained from my hospital bed the local radio audience with tales of my adventures. And before leaving Nouméa, New Caledonia, I presented in the local theater a lecture with Gabriel's movies on the Philippines that I had carried along from Europe. When I finally got back to Europe, I didn't have enough time or money to lie with my leg elevated for six months waiting for complete reconstitution of my new veins and skin, as my doctor had advised. I had only one month to stay quiet and force my foot to return to its initial position, for I was booked on a six-month lecture tour of France. I spent my convalescence reading books about Gypsies and dating Daniele, a high school student I met at one of my lectures in Brussels. And four weeks later, only three months after my accident, I was off lecturing in France with a bare foot. I even went on a hunt, walking in the snow.

I believe that by forcing myself to use my foot I was able to accelerate the healing process. A few months later I had recovered the complete use of it. And when my lecture tour ended, I went off chasing Gypsy tracks through the south of France.

Two months passed. Summer began. Some student friends invited me to accompany them on a four-week trip to Tamanrasset, a small legendary town in the Hoggar mountain region in the heart of the Sahara desert. Although my work on Gypsies was keeping me busy, only one week after my friends made their proposition (and nine months after the boiling sulfur experience), I found myself with my girlfriend Daniele following their Land Rover and two VW buses on the way to southern Algeria. This is a region of dry rocky mountains and peaks much like those of America's Monument Valley but more massive and higher. Maybe I followed because I knew there lay the land of the Tuareg people, often called the "blue men of the Sahara."

It is amazing how much the whims of fate can give life a completely unexpected direction and a new, momentary vocation; change drastically old projects and beget new ones, and create other needs, fantasies, and dreams. That's what happened to me because my too-fragile car broke down in the middle of the Sahara Desert, where I met the Tuareg people. And I decided they would be the subject of my next movie.

The Tuareg people dwell far away from towns and roads. To find and meet them we would need to drive through the whole Sahara Desert. Since a vehicle with four-wheel drive would be the safest choice for that kind of Saharan expedition, I bought a secondhand Land Rover with a diesel engine. Transformed into a comfortless kind of motorhome, this car had already experienced the Sahara many times with its owner. That's why, excited by my project, he sold it to me, payable in two years. I used that car right away for my lecture tours, for I was able to save some money by sleeping and eating in it.

At the end of January of the following year, 1971, I married Daniele. I almost missed my wedding. I reached Brussels with just two hours to spare, exhausted after a whole night of driving the slow Land Rover six hundred miles up from Nice, on the French Riviera, where just the previous evening I had been lecturing.

"Still on for the Tuareg?" asked Daniele, after our wedding.

"More than ever."

"With what money?"

"I'll find a way, don't worry."

Sure enough, she didn't worry for me. She hadn't the time for that because she already had to worry about how to make herself comfortable with me. And that started a day and a half after the wedding on our honeymoon trip.

The uncomfortable and unheated Land Rover was our honeymoon hotel. The honeymoon trip was a three-month lecture tour through the foggy, cold, and rainy north of France.

In spite of spending cold and sleepless nights in the car and eating mainly sandwiches, I had not enough funds for my first expedition. I approached various corporations, but aside from Nestlé, which gave me two hundred pounds of food, no one wanted to finance my expedition. It was based on nothing more than the I hope that I would be able to meet the Tuareg. Moreover, I was still unknown. So I was forced to deceive the companies where I bought film and equipment by paying with bad checks. Knowing that my bank and all my creditors would soon write me letters of complaint and all of that, I asked my dear sister Patricia to answer as follows: "Very sorry about the trouble caused by my brother, but he left for the Sahara and there is no way to reach him before his return in one year or two. However, I can promise that as soon as he comes back, he will contact you."

And so at the wheel of my Land Rover—with Daniele and Philippe, a young French schoolteacher who was going to assist me, and with a small mountain of gear—I left Brussels for my first great expedition, a nine-month trip through the Sahara, in search of the Tuareg nomads. Although deeply in debt with only 50,000 Belgian francs (a thousand dollars) to cover the whole trip's expenses, I had a dream to follow and the will to reach it.

Everything went great. So great that when the movie on the Tuareg was finished, I went to visit my creditors and told them I was very sorry, I really was! I said I came back from my expedition with some amazing footage. But I said if they took legal proceedings against me, I would end up in jail. Consequently, I would not be able to edit my films, write my books, and go on my lecture tours. Thus, I would not be able to pay them back. However, if they gave me more time, I would pay back everything with whatever penalties and interest. They agreed. And I did.

The year after I filmed the Tuareg, I had not yet made enough money to continue my movie on Gypsies. So, without Daniele, I joined Samivel, the man who first taught me cinematography, and shot a movie with him about animal life in the French Alps. Camping in the mountains, we climbed cliffs to film eagles, ran behind chamois and ibex, and hid for hours on end to watch marmots and foxes.

Two months later I rejoined Gabriel, who was now making a movie in Hawaii. More than in the other islands it was among the recluses living in Kaulapapa that I found the true Polynesian atmosphere and warmth. Kaulapapa, a leper colony on a small peninsula on the island of Molokai, is completely separated from the rest of the island by a long, almost vertical cliff. The lepers are shunned by society, and their isolation has protected them from moral contamination and allowed them to safeguard the purity of their souls.

In 1973, although Daniele was pregnant, I could not resist going to Afghanistan and crossing the central mountain range on horseback. I returned in time to plan the birth of my daughter, Maroussia.

My wife and I had decided, with the gynecologist's approval, that the birth should take place in the least possible light. That idea had come to my mind because, as a child in Africa, I had learned that one of the men on our farm was a sorcerer; he could see at night as well as he could during the day. When I became his good friend, he explained that he had been born in complete darkness and had remained in that condition for about three weeks after his birth.

His answer had been good enough to satisfy me then, but as I grew older I started to wonder if it could be for humans the same way it is for cats. Nature keeps cats' eyes closed for a few weeks so that the most sensitive parts of their ocular system are not damaged by light. This enables them to function even in nearly complete darkness.

Many tribes all over the world give birth in darkness and wait before putting the baby into daylight. These people retain keen night vision. Later, on Easter Island, I was told by the old people that not only could their ancestors see at night but were also able to make paintings deep inside the darkest of caves. This is perhaps the explanation for the paintings found deep inside the dark Egyptian tombs, where there is no trace of soot, either in the painted rooms or inside the corridors surrounding them. I do not hold with the current theory that the artists used a complicated system of mirrors that reflected the daylight down the long passageways.

It seemed to me that our societies might be losing this ability because our newborn babies are bombarded by intense light, so I wanted to give my own child a chance to see at night. Our obstetrician was game for the experiment, but at the last moment he was called away and replaced by someone who told me I was crazy to make such a request. He claimed that, in case of problems, he could not save the baby in darkness. And so Maroussia was born in the light.

I was a very happy husband and father, a family man with all the responsibilities it implies. Still, I couldn't help dreaming of living another great adventure. After the deadly smiles of those devil-hearted sharks with human faces known as pirates, after the quiet smiles of the emerald seas, and islands where coconut trees bend and beckon with the breeze, after the romantic smiles of the Saharan warriors of love and silence, after Afghanistan and other countries burned by hot winds and bright stars, once again I felt a compulsion rising in me to reenter the living green cathedrals and live with men who still hunt heads.

I have been fascinated by them since my youth, when I was attracted by adventure books set in wild countries and amongst strange peoples. Or perhaps my fascination goes back farther. Astonishingly, my family coat of arms from the eleventh century shows a man standing with a human head impaled on a spear.

Going back to the northern Philippines would have seemed stale, but I didn't know in what other jungles I might find the headhunters. I thought of Borneo but the decision wasn't finally made until the day I visited King Leopold III of Belgium.

Since abdicating in 1951 in favor of his son Baudouin, King Leopold III had become known as a great explorer. He had cut new paths in the Amazon, in the jungles of New Guinea, and across some of the Andaman islands.

Although I had been keeping up a regular correspondence with him for several years (I had written him for the first time when I went to study the Maoris with Gabriel), I met the king for the first time only a year before my expedition in Borneo. That day I was received by his secretary who, seeing me in a necklace instead of a necktie, cautioned me in a friendly way, "Call the King, 'Majesty.' Talk to him in the third person. Stay polite, and everything will go well."

Then the secretary invited me to follow him to the king's office. He knocked at a large door; then after a second knock he opened it and said in a loud voice, "Majesty, Mister Douchan Gersi!"

The royal office was one thousand square feet, at least. Huge Persian carpets covered the floor. Orderly bookshelves, official pictures, and artifacts covered the walls. Additional books and photographs were arranged on small tables throughout the room. As I entered, the king, sitting behind a huge desk at the far end of the room, arose.

"Please sit down. We'll be more comfortable." His hand indicated some cozy divans and armchairs to my left, which were set around a small table on which all my books were spread out wide open . . . his way of making me feel at ease. He joined me and immediately asked me not to stand on protocol while we talked.

He was dressed informally in light gray trousers, a light blue polo shirt, and a dark hunter's jacket with leather patches at the elbows. His short gray hair contrasted with his deep blue eyes, which reflected a warm heart and the sadness of a man who had lived through too many agonizing dramas. However, as he began to question me about my adventures, asking for information about the smallest details and listening with a gentle smile, his eyes became younger and sparkled with his own passion for adventure.

After two or three hours of conversation, interrupted only by a servant who brought us drinks, he started calling me "Douchan." Then he invited me to enter his "world," another office, twice as large as the first one, in the basement. Whenever he was not playing golf or walking in his exotic gardens, this was the place where he spent his time writing, reading, classifying thousands of slides of his travels and expeditions, or occasionally resting on a small bed set in a corner. Covering the walls were large color photographs he had taken of the jungles he had explored and the tribes he had met. There were close-ups of Amazon Indians, colored faces of smiling Papuans, wild rivers, and his favorite campsites. Examining nostalgically the many gifts brought back from his explorations—masks, arrows, bows, spears, multicolored feather headdresses—displayed on tables and stored in boxes and cabinets, it was his turn to tell stories of expeditions.

He invited me for lunch the next day and we became simple friends, talking about normal subjects like movies, books, or music, but always we came back to recounting the thrills of exploration, the smells of jungles, and the smiles of natives. (Since then my expeditions have been undertaken under his patronage. And he became my godfather, introducing me to the Explorers Club of New York, which accepted me as a Fellow.)

I told him I was dreaming about an expedition to Borneo, where the headhunters have their largest kingdoms.

Leopold became almost as excited as if he himself were about to go off to Borneo, its wildness still in his memory from the time he went there many years ago. He opened a closet and took out a box that contained military maps of the island.

"Look at that, Douchan," he said. "These are the latest and most detailed maps of central Borneo. Look! This small spot . . . and this one . . . are still unexplored. And look at that. Nobody yet has crossed the central mountains between the Mahakan River on the south and the Kayan River on the north. Probably one hundred fifty to two hundred miles of wild and uncharted jungle, valleys, and mountains to cross!"

The map showed blank areas with these notes: "The elevation is believed not to exceed 7000 feet." The drawings of some rivers suddenly stopped with the notations: "Relief data incorrect" or "Unknown territory."

He explained that these areas, almost always hidden by dense, heavy clouds, weren't easily investigated by air. The mountains, valleys, and deep canyons make low-altitude surveys very difficult. Business interests always go first to the most accessible places. So the lack of knowledge about their features and the difficulties of transportation have completely protected these territories from oil, timber, and mineral exploitation. But when easily accessible areas run out, businesses begin to explore uncharted regions. And if that turns out to be a profitable operation, they spread through the jungle a string of supply and refueling bases, and conquer with bulldozers the last sanctuaries, chasing away the natives or using them as workers.

"This uncharted region of Borneo must be filled with headhunter tribes. Some are probably still unknown to us. I am sure you will discover at least one. What a dream!"

The king's blue eyes were dreaming. I am sure he was thinking, Ah, if only I were a little younger! (He was then about sixty.) His bright face was bent over the map, but he was not in the room any more. He was in Borneo. With his white hair glittering in the daylight, he was walking ahead of me into the unexplored jungle.

I put my hand on his shoulder as if he were a beloved father.

"Sire, I shall go there. I shall bring you the smells of the trees and the smile of Dayaks!"

He too smiled, not with envy but with love. More than once the memory of his look helped me while crossing through the green hell.

CHAPTER FIVE

Preparing for Uncharted Borneo

To love life much more than one fears the threats of death is
to deserve life.

ELIPHAS LEVI

The only one who did not share my happiness was
Daniele.

"You really want to risk your life in Borneo, don't you?" she
asked.

How could I convince her I was not going there to play with
death? How could I share with her the certainty that death only
happens to others, not to me? I was going to Borneo with love
and faith in myself. But she would not believe me because she
had seen how I behaved in the Sahara. Each time there had been
a choice between a safe straight passage and another route more
dangerous but perhaps filled with more excitement, I had opted
for excitement.

"Before the baby, it didn't matter if we died, because we
always were together. But now we have a baby! You don't have
the right to take risks any more! Besides, I don't think I will
be able to bear the long time you will be away, risking your
life."

Maybe I would be scared to lose my life sometime, but I knew
I wasn't going to meet death. Death scares me since the time I
saw my father dying, despite his strong will to live and his love
for life. When he died, he was still filled with dreams and yet he
lost his battle.

Thinking about death and fearing it, I came to a conclusion
that satisfies me. I believe at the very instant of our birth, the
day our life will end has already been determined. Therefore,
the day when I must die I shall die wherever I am and whatever

I am doing, whether walking down Sunset Boulevard to go to a movie or crossing a deadly swamp to reach an unknown village of cannibals. The day of my death, I shall not be a victim of adventure, or of nature, or of headhunters, but only the victim of my destiny.

In the in-between of this journey from birth to death, we are free to live as we want: nothing we do will put our life in jeopardy. According to our state of mind we can transform our lives into perpetual joy or never-ending misery. Of course we are even free to die if we wish, just by giving up our love for life.

However, the whims of fate often throw us into the middle of adversity, to test us, putting in our way great difficulties—misfortune, sickness, or other obstacles—that can endanger our minds or our lives. But if we handle these difficulties properly we will gain the necessary wisdom to move into a higher consciousness. All experience leads to some growing. Moreover, a powerful desire for being alive and staying alive, the thirst *to live,* can prevent us from being hurt by adversity. If my rage to live were not so strong, I wouldn't have survived wild rapids, dangerous jungles, volcanic accidents, ferocious pirates, distrustful headhunters and cannibals, tropical maladies and gangrene, deadly bites of scorpions and cobras, and auto crashes. On the other hand, constant struggle and disappointment may push us to give up the fight to stay alive. If we accept being defeated by life, we put ourselves into a state of accepting sickness, and perhaps death, for as the saying goes, "A man with no dreams is a dead man."

By living life fully, beautifully, deeply, and without self-imposed limitations, one is protected and fed by the powers of life. To live intensely is perhaps the best prayer and the purest act of love that a man can offer to the Creator. And if He exists as I would like Him to, I am certain that at our death His only question will be: "What have you done with your life?" And according to our answers, He will reward some by opening the doors of Eternity, while others will simply vanish. As Eliphas Levi wrote, "Inertia is the real evil without cure. God has often made saints from rascals, but nothing ever from the apathetic and cowardly."

Sometimes I wish for a God whom I could call on the telephone and say, "Give me all the lives of those who do nothing with life, for I have so many things yet to accomplish."

"What is it that pushes you to go toward danger? Why do you need to constantly risk your life? Do you have some sort of psychological problem?" asked a worried Daniele.

I was unable to answer her, because at that time I had no need to rationalize my attraction to danger. I was doing it and that was enough for me. I nevertheless became obsessed by her question and tried hard to understand myself. And by the process of elimination, in analyzing myself, I found some answers.

Aside from the misfortune of losing my father, my childhood was very happy. I love my family with the same passion that I love life. I have no problems accepting myself, I am not suicidal, and have nothing to prove to myself or to others. And like everybody, I am subjected to two opposite forces which by turns possess me: an extreme masculinity—perhaps man's old heritage from those times when nature had programmed him for hunting and fighting—matched by an extreme femininity.

Eliphas Levi wrote: "Human equilibrium is posed between two enticements, one toward death, the other toward life. Fatality: that is the vertigo that attracts us to the abyss; freedom: that is the mindful effort that raises us above the fatal attraction to death." I would add this: extreme masculinity is that vertigo that attracts me to the abyss, whereas femininity is what raises me above the fatal attraction to death; femininity being, in essence, the power of creativity. The struggle between these two opposite and extreme forces fuels the passion that makes me like a warrior as I fight my way through a jungle without breaking a single leaf.

Although I am certainly aware of the real dangers of exploration, I do not believe I am risking my life, because of the "magic of innocence" and the "alchemy of naïveté." The "magic of innocence" is my ability to believe that nothing bad can ever happen because of the purity of my intentions. The "alchemy of naïveté" is the faith I have in life and in myself. Both the "magic of innocence" and the "alchemy of naïveté" give me the ability to be passionate but prevent passion from blinding me. They transform my system of logic, my system of thought, my perception of "reality," giving it other values. The very same "reality" will "be," but according to other principles.

When I face wild nature or unknown people, strangely enough I get a different perception of the idea of *danger*. It's as if, in this other world made of primal and natural senses, feelings and emotions, the meaning of the word *danger* gets dimin-

ished to the meaning of the word *obstacle,* as if the danger were
now to my own scale of measurement. I think to myself, How
can I go through this without disturbing the harmony of which
this danger is a part? I believe that by respecting primitive
values I will be capable of going through the danger without
becoming its victim.

If I know others have been killed in a place where I am about
to go, I still think I will never get hurt. When you go to the
beach, do you think that you are risking your life by driving on
a freeway? Would you abandon your automobile if one of your
dearest friends died in a car crash caused by a drunk driver?
After all, where is the worst danger? In the jungles or in our
modern world? Out of balance and in complete disharmony, the
modern world is made of people whose warm hearts are frozen;
who have lost faith, dreams, hopes, and illusions; who hide their
faces with social masks, and end up walking behind themselves,
running after paradises where friendship is not a matter of
loving but of profit. Where is the real danger?

"Let me do Borneo. Please! I have just started my life as an
explorer. I must do Borneo. Now! Later, perhaps, I will need
nothing so dangerous. I promise. After Borneo I will change!"
And I believed what I said. I repeated my pleas to Daniele over
and over again but to no effect.

At that time, in 1973, I was lecturing in Belgium
with my film about the Tuareg. I received a letter from a fellow
named Max who said he had seen my film several times and
wanted to meet me. I agreed and met him in a restaurant in
Brussels.

I had first heard from Max a year and a half earlier, after the
publication of my book on the Sahara. A student in Economic
Sciences at the University of Brussels, Max expressed in his
letter an intense desire to join me on an expedition. I wrote back
offering him the same advice that my mother had once been
given: "Finish your studies first. Then if you still have dreams
of adventures, you will find ways to fully live them." He never
directly responded, but persisted in arranging a meeting.

Max had black hair and a triangular face that ended with a
slightly protruding chin. He was not very tall but his large
shoulders were well-developed from paratrooper-commando
training during his military service. Now he was working every

night in a restaurant so he could buy a Land Rover and cross the Sahara.

During our meal he proposed accompanying me on my expedition to Borneo. Though I knew I needed at least two companions to serve as assistants, I didn't feel ready to conclude a deal with him.

It is hard to choose the perfect companion for an expedition. In normal everyday life, roommates have a difficult time dealing with problems caused by lack of privacy and long, close cohabitation. On an expedition these problems are multiplied a thousandfold every day. Therefore, as in the adventure of marriage, the chemistry of companionship must involve a kind of love, which allows the entrusting of one's life to another. Each person must live in the full and deep conviction that he is willing to put his own life in jeopardy to save another's. Companions must, in personality and skills, complement each other and yet be of the same spiritual caliber and level. Moreover, male friendship must be based on a deep and full trust, confidence, and respect for the expertise of the head of the expedition. Sharing the leader's dreams, his companion is there to help him reach his goal.

Above all, I must feel that he has blind trust in me. Sometimes his life and mine can be saved by a command that I do not have time to explain and that may seem strange or ridiculous. And if he does not completely trust me, he will lose precious time before doing what I have asked him to.

Twice I have seen lives nearly lost because a companion took too much time to analyze my commands before obeying them. Once while taking a nap at the foot of a tree in the Amazon jungle where I was looking for the Jivaro headshrinkers, a companion and I were awakened by painful bites all over our bodies. We had gone to sleep in the path of a column of carnivorous ants whose vanguard was already sampling our flesh. Nobody is able to know in advance the path of the three-foot-wide and several-hundred-foot-long column of billions of ants during their massive migration. Urged by a mysterious instinct, they follow the vanguard blindly, going straight ahead silently and without rest, eating while they march.

By the time we managed to spring to our feet, our bodies were covered by these inch-long insects, whose giant heads are armed with powerful pincers so strong that, when you try to pull the ant off, the head separates from the body and stays hooked by the pincers driven into your skin. I started to run, and screamed at my companion to follow. I knew that if we attempted to tear individual ants away before escaping from their main column, we could be eaten alive. Stories about carnivorous ants leaving human and animal skeletons behind are not mere legends. Before moving away with its mouthful of flesh, each insect secretes a drop of formic acid into the wound. As large quantities of this acid penetrate your flesh you get increasingly dizzy, and with enough you can be rendered unconscious and fall amidst the column of ants which, tiny bite by tiny bite, will clean your bones. So you must ignore the excruciating pain and the disgust of having your body covered by hundreds of tiny carnivores, and you must run as fast and as far as you can before you fall to the ground, safely away from the deadly colony. Only then can you safely take time to remove them.

When I had reached a safe place, I became aware of my companion's absence and called to him . . . but no answer. Knowing he was in danger, I ran back to where I could see him still standing in the midst of the column and ordered him to run to me. But he would not heed my words. He was so crazed with pain that all he could do was tear helplessly at the increasing mass of insects who attempted to devour him. I had to go through the advancing column of ants and grab him. Finally a few blows from my fists were able to rouse him from his stupor and make him run to safety.

On another occasion, a companion and I were crossing a dark river covered with an almost impenetrable canopy of trees. I saw something move in the water and had a sudden premonition. Yelling out "Crocodiles!" I screamed at my companion to slap the water with his hands. Instead of obeying my command, he tried to make for the shore. When you are too far from the bank, you never try to run from a crocodile. It only incites him to attack. My companion was lucky he wasn't killed; but in escaping as he did he put my life in danger, for I remained alone in the water, slapping like a wild man. That technique, learned from my Philippine friend Amok, is the best way to scare off the crocs, unless they are used to hearing slaps resounding under the water. In that case one's best chance is a giant leap or an emergency call to heaven.

I told Max that there is a world of difference between the dream of becoming an explorer and the reality.

"Make your Saharan trip first. Prove to me that you're ready for the worst; then we'll see."

A few months after Max and I first met, I was scheduled to lecture throughout the French-speaking African countries with my movie about the Tuareg. I planned to stay about three months, combining lectures and photography. Daniele was going to join me for December and January.

Max's face was completely transformed when Daniele and I met him in Lomé, Togo. He was shining with happiness, and he wore a moustache and a small goatee, which was all the hair that would grow on his baby skin.

When we met up again in Douala, Cameroon, I became impressed by his perseverance and the depth of his desire to prove he was ready to become my assistant. Although he was nervous and easily angered, I had the feeling he would be a perfect companion. He had the trust in me that I required, and thanks to his military training in an elite fighting unit he was experienced in matters of survival, rescue, and mountaineering.

"But you must realize that the expedition involves some risks. So think about that. After all, you are only twenty-five. Too young to maybe die."

"Danger is everywhere, and I'll die only when I'm ready to," he answered, smiling.

I shook his hand. "Then let's go to Borneo and meet headhunters together."

Because of our baby, Maroussia, it took some time before Daniele alone could join me in Africa, and after only two weeks she was in a hurry to return to Brussels. During our time together I knew something was going deeply wrong between us. What was it really that changed our relationship? She asked me a few times to change my life-style, to become a sedentary, responsible person who could take care of his family. Perhaps by living so closely for four years we had used up one hundred years of a normal life together. Or was it my determination to explore Borneo? Maybe a little bit of everything, including the fact that I wasn't always acting as a good husband should.

Coming back from Africa in March 1974, I landed in Brussels at 6:00 A.M. She was there with the baby.

"So what are your plans?" she asked.

"Well, you know them already! I must head to the north of France right away. Tonight I am starting a one-month lecture tour."

"Are you still going to Borneo?"

I nodded.

"Listen, darling, if you don't care about us, I want a divorce. It's not worth living together. I'll give you the month to think about it."

I tried to change her mind by coming home almost every night, even when I had to drive a couple of hundred miles. After a week, physically exhausted, I had an attack of malaria at the end of a lecture. The lecture had been organized by a doctor whose son, Jean-François, was studying to become a doctor. He agreed to serve as my assistant and driver until I recovered my health.

Jean-François and I traveled together for about ten days and came back to his home every night whenever we were not too far away.

One night, in a small hotel room with Jean-François, I couldn't stop talking about Borneo, which was obsessing me. He expressed his desire to have at least one great adventure before taking over his father's practice. Although he had traveled with his family in East Africa a few times, he now claimed that only Borneo could fulfill his dream. Jean-François was perfect. A medical student. Totally trusting. Young and strong. I couldn't refuse him.

"Okay, my friend, you'll be my doctor in that expedition . . . if I do it."

"If? What do you mean by 'if'?"

"Oh, just nothing. Nothing," I said, remembering the smile of my wife and the face of my baby. "By the way, J.F., what will your family's reaction be?"

"I am coming regardless!" he replied.

Tall and thin with blond hair and a small beard, Jean-François was twenty years old. Besides skiing a lot, he already had climbed Mont Blanc, and was to do it again just to prepare for Borneo. One thing bothered me: J.F. still had his appendix. That may be of little consequence when living within reach of a hospital, but in the middle of nowhere it may kill you if it becomes infected. Since a radical change of food can affect the appendix, I insisted that he have it removed before our journey. That would be one less problem to confront.

His father absolutely refused.

"I can understand," I said. "But then, I want you to sign a paper allowing me to operate on your son if he has an appendix attack in the jungle."

"You are crazy! You are not a surgeon!" he yelled.

"With a sharp knife, my sewing kit, and my medical survival manual, I should have a good chance of success. Trying to save Jean-François's life will be better than seeing him dying from appendicitis."

Although I would attempt surgery to save the life of a man in an emergency, I was only hoping my words would change his father's mind. And they did. Jean-François had surgery a few days later. The surgeon notified him that his appendix had already grown too large and he would have needed an appendectomy in less than six months.

I began again to hesitate about Borneo when I saw my not yet six-month-old Maroussia looking at her mother with her toothless smile, trying awkwardly to grab her hair.

My God, what to do when one has to make a choice that risks turning three lives upside down and drastically changing their destiny? I thought to myself, How can I choose between changing my way of life now or remaining an explorer. Go to Borneo, explore a region still unmapped at the end of the twentieth century, meet headhunters and live with them, share their customs . . . all that would fulfill a dream. I would be happy for the rest of my life. But would I be happy if I were divorced and my family broken in two?

Maroussia smiled at me. She stretched out her two small, plump arms. My misted eyes couldn't see her deep blue ones any more. If I change my life I will witness her growing, step by step, word by word. I will be there whenever she needs me. I will save my marriage and have more babies like her. No more Borneo! That's it, I have made my choice! I whispered in Maroussia's small ear, "I'll stay with you."

But at night when you hear all around you the slow breathing of those with whom you share your life, who are dreaming their own dreams far from yours, their motionless figures point out your ultimate solitude. You are born alone and you die alone. You are alone in joy and alone in sorrow. As you die by yourself, so must you finally live.

"It's my life after all!" I whispered to my pillow. "My life! Sure, I may save my marriage and keep my family intact, and witness the growth of Maroussia. But then what? I am only twenty-seven years old and already forced to give up my dreams. How long will I be able to carry my regrets, deception, and bitterness without poisoning the lives of those for whom I give up my dreams? I will only be able to bring them happiness and joy if I don't carry these feelings inside my heart. It's my life! My first duty is to make myself happy. Otherwise I will not be able to keep those I love happy. I must create harmony in myself if I am to keep harmony with those I love. Regardless of the consequences, I shall go to Borneo. They will hate me today, but tomorrow I will light them up with my inner peace. Love is not changing another but accepting him. I must go to Borneo. Otherwise I'll die with my dream and the gangrene of my bitterness will poison their existence. I'm going to Borneo!"

That decision brought me before a lawyer. Daniele wanted an immediate divorce. In the midst of preparing for my expedition, I had no time to ponder how much suffering and remorse I was condemning myself to, especially by the separation from Maroussia.

For two days I searched the U.S. military supply stores to find the insulated metal containers used to carry food during the Vietnam war. These I transformed into water/heat/humidity-proof containers to carry and protect my film stock. I tried to promote free movie and photo equipment. No luck. I tried to promote free airline tickets and succeeded. By the time I had my gear plus a portable generating set and the radio-transmitters piled in the middle of a friend's garage, I realized that I had no more money left for the expenses I would have in Borneo: paying porters, renting canoes, and so forth. But I got that money too after one week of negotiation with my banker and after friends signed papers which put their cars, houses, and necks on the line.

I still needed permission from the Indonesian government to explore central Borneo. For military reasons, this region was forbidden territory. Because of the existence of uncontrolled headhunting tribes and the presence of Communist rebels, permits were given only by the Department of Defense. But first I needed permits from the Department of the Interior, which needed an okay from the Ministry of Information, which wanted the "go" from the Foreign Affairs Office, which wanted an agreement from the Tourist Bureau! And that was taking a lot of time, even though my expedition was under the moral patronage of King Leopold III. I say "moral" because it involved not financial aid but priceless help, such as the king's personal recommendation to the Indonesian government and various services of the Belgian Ministry of Foreign Affairs. In exchange for this, I had to bring the Museum of Natural History some samples of water from jungle rivers and as many as I could of insects and flora.

While waiting for my permits, I filled up a large box in the middle of my living room with whatever small items came to mind, things one can buy in any corner drugstore but, if missing in the middle of a jungle, may jeopardize an expedition. Most of the items were necessary to repair lenses, cameras, tape recorders, and other equipment. They ranged from a pair of scissors to glue, adhesive plaster, screws, small nails, nail varnish, and rubber bands. And I came to use all of these afterthought purchases.

There was just a large blank spot on the map to indicate our objective, the unexplored area of central Borneo, so I didn't spend time studying the detailed map that the king gave me. I hoped that as the Indonesian government was giving me permits, it would likewise provide me with some useful information about that region. I read many books given to me by King Leopold about headhunters and Borneo.

Seven or eight weeks passed after I started preparing for my expedition, and I was still waiting for the Indonesian government's permission to enter Borneo. Finally King Leopold himself told me, "Tourist Bureau and Foreign Affairs said yes. As for getting the permits from the other departments, you will be in a better position to speed them up when you are in Jakarta. Our embassy there will help you. Good luck!" People are always wishing me good luck. They must think I need it.

"When are you coming back?" asked Maman, speaking Slovak to me.

"I really don't know," I answered. "Perhaps in six or seven months . . . maybe sooner . . . maybe later. Don't forget that I love you!"

My loved ones and friends accompanied me to the airport.

"So, Max and Jean-François, stand by and come as soon as I get the permits," I said, hugging them.

"Don't forget, Douchan, if something happens to my Maxie, I shall kill you," said Max's mother with her Austrian accent. "Wherever you are, I shall find you and kill you. I really will."

She had told me that many times since the day we met. I felt more and more certain that she wasn't joking.

CHAPTER SIX

Crocodiles, Monkeys, and Flying Snakes

True strength, real courage, the only genius in our immense
jostling, is to go wherever we want, whenever we want, at the
speed we want.

G. DUHAMEL

Through the airplane window, I looked out on a
most amazing and beautiful gallery where the gods display their
billowy art. Powerful statues made of clouds with white, gray,
and blue shadings. The airplane would emerge from mist revealing cloud mountains, their steep slopes covered with virgin
snow. It is not astonishing that man has always dreamed of
flying, for the gods' perspective demands to be seen.

Then came Jakarta, capital of Indonesia, a country of so many
islands of beauty and adventure: Sumatra, Java, Bali, Komodo—
the home of twelve-foot lizards—the Celebes, and the Moluccas
islands, the half of New Guinea called *Irian Jaya*, and the largest
section of Borneo called *Kalimantan*. (The third largest island in
the world, Borneo is politically divided into four parts: the
sultanate of Brunei, autonomous but under British protection;
Sarawak and Sabah, ex-kingdoms that now belong to the confederation of Malaysia; and Kalimantan.)

Jakarta the fantastic—sensual, multicolored, noisy, smoky,
smelly, hot, humid. Jakarta, whose taxis' meters seem linked not
to the odometer but to the speed of the motor, which my taxi
driver wildly accelerates after each stop.

Like any city that has grown too fast, Jakarta is a mixture of
comfortable, modern, air-conditioned buildings; small colonial-
style wooden houses with colonnades, balconies, verandas, and,
suspended from the high ceilings, fans that slowly stir the thick,
humid air; slums with children playing in dirty pools left by the

frequent rains; unfinished building sites; never-ending road-work; abandoned and dirty buildings where transvestites hide; bordellos that look like healthy, innocent massage salons. Jakarta is a city of misery and wealth struggling against each other.

I prefer Jakarta at night. When sunset covers the city with a dark veil, even misery takes on exotic colors. Small nomadic restaurants set up their well-worn tables, half on the sidewalk and half in the street. You eat by the light of candles or oil lamps, bathed in delightful smells. In the poorest district, my tea was made with water left in large holes in the streets after the daily rainstorm.

For almost three weeks I ran crazily from one government building to another—they were always miles apart—battling the warriors of the bureaucratic jungle. Third floor, second door on the right, after the long corridor. Fourth floor, right at the top of the stairs: "Sorry, closed, come back tomorrow!"

"What time do you close?"

"Four o'clock. Come back tomorrow, I have said."

"But it's only three!"

I didn't have time to complain, as the clerk had already closed the window. The administrative maze was staggeringly intricate, and, as in Europe or anywhere else, each functionary had the objective of doing a minimum of tasks in the maximum time.

In spite of the heroic efforts of the Belgian embassy, another obstacle to obtaining my permits to explore central Borneo was that no official wanted to commit himself by stamping and signing a paper without "full authority" from some other official. When I finally faced the official who had that "full authority," he wouldn't sign without still more information about my itinerary and all that I intended to do in every area. When I gave him my story, I felt the suspicious eyes of someone who really couldn't understand what was pushing me to spend months in the dangerous jungle. Therefore, I decided to change my tactics. When I reached the highest authority, which was the Department of Defense, I told the man, "I just want to go and visit the west coast of Borneo."

"But it's written here that you want to cross central Kalimantan."

"I've changed my mind."

"That's much better, and you lose nothing. That area of Kalimantan is still uncharted. Nothing there. Just jungles, snakes, and primitive people. This will make it easier to approve. In two days you'll have your permits. With these, however, you can't go inland without authorization from the military governor of each district. Understood?"

"Thanks!" I said, thinking, Sure I understand. But at least we shall be in Borneo, and then we'll see! And I sent for my companions who were back in Belgium.

The evening before we left Jakarta, Max, J.F., and I reviewed our plans. Our first stop in Borneo was to be Balikpapan on the west coast. It is one of the main oil cities, where we were to be the guests of the Shell Oil Company. I got that invitation when, hoping to get more information about the territory we wanted to explore, I went to Shell's Jakarta headquarters. Unlike the other oil, timber, and mineral companies that have research or exploitation bases in Borneo, Shell gave me a good reception. I even met with the president, who said that in Balikpapan, their headquarters in Borneo, I would have a better chance of getting the information I was looking for by meeting their geologists and prospectors.

The uncharted territory we aimed for was wedged between the Kayan River (which had been explored in the sixties by Pierre Pfeffer and his crew) and the Mahakan River (the one explored in the mid-fifties by Pierre Ivanoff). From Balikpapan we would find a way to reach Samarinda, the first town on the Mahakan, rent a boat, and journey upstream to a small river leading to Tabang, the last outpost of civilization, where we would hire porters. Tabang was south of the region to be explored. From there we would walk straight north until we reached the Kayan River, on the other side of the unknown. And by going down the Kayan, we would reach civilization again.

"That's all we have to guide us," said J.F., pointing to our map unfolded on the table. "Just a blank spot with a few unfinished lines of rivers and some indications of mountains, but no specifications as to their number or height. Hmm!"

"We'll have to create our own map," said Max. "But what if the porters don't want to cross that region?"

"In that case we'll ask them to lead us to the first Dayak village, where we will hire new porters, and so forth up to the Kayan," I answered. "Anyhow, I hope we'll find Dayaks on our way, stay with them, study and film them. That's one of my goals, after all."

We became silent, dreaming about our expedition.

"Oh, by the way," I said, interrupting my two friends' reveries. "I almost forgot to tell you that we can't take our radio-transmitters along." I explained all the bits and pieces I had learned about Borneo while visiting the different government offices. Rumors were that its jungles, especially those of central Borneo, hid Communist guerrilla bands traveling through the island to join other guerrilla bands in Java in their revolt against the Indonesian government. Consequently, if we were found with radio-transmitters, we could be regarded as enemies both by government forces and by guerrillas. They would treat us the same as if we were carrying guns.

"In that case I suppose you don't intend to buy guns for the expedition, as we planned," concluded Max.

"Not for this trip. Sorry."

Hunting for fresh meat is the only reason I bring rifles and revolvers on most of my expeditions. However, it is very important not to carry guns where there are natives, for without guns you are less likely to be considered an enemy. Therefore, when I am about to enter tribal territory, I bury my weapons at the foot of a marked tree, so that I can find them on my return. Unfortunately, since it usually turns out that I can't find my hiding places again or that I am forced to come back by a different route, I own quite a nice collection of guns buried and lost in many different jungles.

On the plane carrying us and our expedition gear to Balikpapan, I started the first of a series of letters I had decided to write to my daughter during my expedition, without any intention of sending them. A kind of last will and testament of a man who has nothing to leave but himself. In case something should go wrong in Borneo, I wanted her to know who her father really was.

74/ In the airplane, somewhere
between Java and Borneo . . .

Maroussia, my beloved daughter,

How much time seems to have disappeared since I last kissed you under the sun of St. Tropez! How many thousands of miles traveled in only a few hours! I am the bird I have dreamed of being ever since I was your age.

Jakarta would have been a pleasant city to stay in if my obsession to live in Borneo had not been stronger than the temptation just to enjoy my sinfulness. I was exhausted by the waiting, and very impatient to descend at last into these jungles that raise the fevers of my imagination.

If Borneo must become the exit from my life on earth, I shall not be able to return to explain to you who I am. So, let me impress on you now that for me each exploration is the expression of my need to go beyond love and passion, to go beyond custom and normality and to follow the call of my heart, which will not be refused!

I am not trying to escape from duties or from anything or anybody. I am not driven by hate or frustration. I am called by love. I am going to make love to the forest and to the people who live in it.

> I love you,
> Dad

Balikpapan's airport was crowded with the oil companies' helicopters and aircraft. Oil rigs were scattered everywhere. Incessant flares blazed along the coast and offshore where by night they obliterated the stars and the emerald glow of the waves. No tropical sunsets through coconut trees here, only the silhouettes of giant tankers gliding slowly by, agitating the thick humid heat with their loud sirens. The too-quickly-grown-up town, with new offices and dormitories, was surrounded by the tumbledown shacks of natives lured by the black-gold rush.

A car was waiting for us at the airport, and we drove straight to the Shell Oil administrative headquarters where we met its manager, a busy man who quickly explained that he had no time to spend with journalists.

"I have instructions to help you as much as I can if it doesn't interfere with our activities. I have two rooms available for you. Be my guest."

Perched at the top of a hill, Shell's air-conditioned guest house was truly a warrior's resting place, with a classy bar, a luxurious club room, and comfortable quarters for bachelors and for married men whose families had stayed behind in Singapore or somewhere else while the men stood a four-week stint in the jungle. Other men, who had brought their families with them, lived in a colony of pretty bungalows with gardens, built on the other side of a wide green lawn across from the guest house.

That night we spoke to an American helicopter pilot who

maintained a weekly liaison with a refueling station about two hundred miles north of Balikpapan. Since it was still most profitable for the company to confine its onshore activities to within one hundred miles of the coast, he had never been in central Borneo. We asked about wildlife for filming, and he replied that while traveling in the jungle he had been surprised not to encounter many animals, aside from giant pythons and cobras. He said that if we wanted to film the jungle fauna (the main reason for this part of our trip), we should go into an area that was about one hundred miles west of his refueling station. Although almost the whole east coast was covered by oil derricks, that large wild area stretching east to the sea, with marshes, jungles, rivers, and mangroves, was still unviolated by industry. The lights of the flares had not yet dazzled the eyes of the fauna. The sounds of bulldozers and falling trees had not yet disturbed the wild game.

"A kind of giant Noah's ark, is it?" I remarked.

"That's exactly it! There's even an abandoned hut that was built some years ago by some scientists who went there to study orangutans. You could sleep in it."

"How can we reach it?"

"A river goes straight there from our station. We have a few speedboats. One could be available right away if you're lucky. Otherwise you'll just wait a day or two."

"When is your next flight?"

"Tomorrow morning. And I've got free seats in my Puma."

We joined him the next morning after buying some rice, noodles, and canned goods in a local market.

We were lucky. As we arrived at the refueling station, the mechanic had just finished repairing the motor of a speedboat, which the local manager then made available to us. I asked the manager to pick us up again in three weeks. Five or six hours later the boat dropped us into the wild area.

While the sound of the retreating speedboat grew softer, my companions and I looked at one another and smiled, relieved to find ourselves at last in a jungle that smelled and sounded like a real jungle, away from those we had flown over that were lifeless, murdered by oil exploitation. Before the sound had entirely died we became aware of a strange buzzing, something like an airplane approaching from far away. Then a fast-moving, large black cloud, humming louder and louder, came zigzagging toward us. A million bloodthirsty, malaria-carrying mosquitoes within moments covered our skin, stinging ferociously wherever they could. Abandoning our gear on the riverbank, we ran like madmen and took refuge inside the scientists' abandoned hut in a small clearing a hundred feet from the river.

No natives live in these unhealthy coastal jungles filled with large expanses of marsh and many dead rivers, the home of tens of millions of mosquitoes carrying malaria and other fevers such as *falciparum*, which in most cases is fatal to humans. It was against this threat that three weeks before heading for Borneo, we had started taking quinine in quite high doses. Not that it protects one from getting malaria or falciparum, but it does get one used to the medicine, so that in a crisis the body will be able to take the massive quantities necessary to fight malarial fevers.

There I experienced the worst mosquito attacks of my whole life. When they do not travel in massive packs of millions, they fly solo and never miss their target. Often, especially while we were motionlessly watching the fauna, we had to keep our hands in our pockets and wait until the insects were tired of us. Our faces were hidden behind a protective mask-helmet, its circular frame of thin bamboo plates covered with a mosquito net. These were U.S. Army supplies for the Vietnam war.

The first night, we tried to sleep with a small buzzer next to us that imitates the sound of the female mosquito. The sound is supposed to attract all the male mosquitoes in the neighborhood, and the females, the only mosquitoes that bite, stay away. Although this gadget seemed effective, we soon stopped using it because the mosquito bites were more bearable than the buzzer's irritating sound.

The hut was in fair condition and bigger than we expected, more like a cabin with two rooms. One had beds, the other a table, chairs, and a bookshelf with a dozen books—American novels and a well-thumbed volume about jungle survival.

This was to be our base camp. During our exploratory trips into the surrounding jungle, we slept in hammocks, with a stretched, tent-shaped mosquito net covered by a large sheet of plastic above each of us as protection from the squadrons of mosquitoes and the almost nightly rain.

We spent the first day getting used to the heat and the heavy humidity of the jungle, and checking our gear. My companions,

new to their jobs, had to be familiarized with their new func-
tions. J.F., who had studied tropical diseases especially for this
expedition, was to carry the movie camera's heavy tripod and
the stereo tape recorder. In addition, he would keep a diary and
act as my technical assistant, loading film and operating the tape
recorder. Max chose to be the cook, but he would also be my
second still photographer and second cameraman. Since neither
of them had ever operated this kind of equipment, they would
have to learn quickly.

The second day we started into the jungle, which is made up
of a mass of small areas, each defined by the trees and vegetation
immediately surrounding it. Whenever we spotted signs of the
regular presence of some animals or birds, we built blinds in
which I would hide, my body rubbed with aromatic leaves, and
wait with the camera and sound recorder while my companions,
acting as beaters, drove the local fauna in my direction. These
blinds were constructed on a circle-shaped stick frame. We
drove a series of thin branches into the ground, tied their ends
together, and then covered this frame with large leaves: a kind
of jungle igloo.

When in areas covered with swamps and water, we used one
of our two inflated canoes for beating, the other as a blind,
building a wigwam-shaped stick frame over it and covering this
with a green mosquito net.

Amazing in its variety, power, and rhythm, the symphony of
a pulsating jungle is made of the melancholy hootings of gibbons, the croaks of *calaos,* the screechings of multicolored parrots, the songs and calls of unseen birds or animals, the
background bustle of insects, and sudden, inexplicable silences,
sporadically rent by the sound of wild boars engaging in deadly
duels. Sometimes, when the wind blows and the leaves caress
one another, you can hear the jungle whispering. Sometimes it
cries desperately when a hundred-foot-tall tree, hollowed out by
age, humidity, and insects, finally loses its balance and crashes
to the ground, pulling dozens of surrounding interwoven trees
down with it. The crash reverberates from the green peaks to
the valleys, and the echo of its fall is followed by the sounds of
birds and animals awakened from their watchful repose. The
jungle symphonies, never the same from one hour to the next,
become familiar as the days pass.

After a few days of waiting in our cabin for a tropical rainstorm to pass, we were finally ready to film. I lay on my belly

in the bottom of my inflated canoe under a green mosquito net, covering everything but my lens. My companions had moored my floating hiding place in such a way that I could observe both the river and the bank. But the funny thing was that now I floated over what had been the beach when we debarked from the Shell Oil Company's speedboat. Two days of heavy rain had caused the river to rise almost fifteen feet.

These fast-rising floods are a common phenomenon, especially when a river is supplied by many other rivers farther upstream. When the torrential rains stop, the river falls to its normal level very quickly.

The sight of the surging river was apocalyptic. Everything was flooded. The tops of the small trees on yesterday's riverbank now fought against the current. In the middle of the muddy, tormented river there were countless whirlpools and floating islands made of whole trees.

Instead of being pulled along by the current, my boat bobbed silently in the same place. This happens sometimes in swiftly moving rivers and rapids when the speed and power of the water at bank level create whirlpools that go back upstream and stabilize floating objects.

Violently, a blue bird with a berry-red crest plunged into the water and came out with a small fish flapping in its yellow beak. A crocodile, using the side whirlpools to move upstream, slowly passed and glided to the river's new bank. Only his eyes and nostrils were visible, the rest undulated under the water, moving just enough to keep his head from going beneath the water. After a moment of complete immobility, he slowly raised his head and let his lower jaw drop open. This is the only way a crocodile can open his powerful mouth, for though he possesses tremendous muscles to close his mouth, he only has weak ones with which to open it.

This crocodile's jaws were now wide open. I could see his sharp teeth, and through the telephoto lens could even make out small leeches glued to the top of his mouth. Looking at his fascinating green eyes with their cleft and hypnotizing pupils, I understood why crocodiles are sacred in so many different religions. The Egyptians mummified them. In Pakistani monasteries crocodiles are worshipped. In some areas of Africa they are divinities and are offered sacrificial victims.

A crocodile's open jaws don't always represent a defensive or hunting position. Just as those of a dog, its open jaws serve as a thermal regulating mechanism that allows it to lower its body temperature by venting humidity through the mucous membranes of its mouth.

Usually crocs start hunting before sunset and continue until sunup. They use their powerful jaws to break apart small victims and make them easier to swallow. Larger prey are taken underwater and held there until they drown and are then stored in aquatic hiding places until the meat becomes rotten enough for the croc to eat.

One of the problems civilized humans have is the ease with which they can acclimatize to danger. All too quickly the senses become lazy and quiescent. Even in the jungle where danger is imminent, apprehensions soon disappear. The intimate cohabitation with what can suddenly become a killer seems to put the alarm systems of the body and spirit to sleep. And that is the real danger: that you no longer remain aware of your peril.

On my first night in the jungle, I will usually pee from my hammock, not wanting to put my feet down in the dark. After a few nights I become less wary and walk some distance away with my flashlight. A few nights more and I am walking without a light, carrying my tape recorder, absorbed in recording whatever sounds I can find.

At first, the sight of the crocodile made my stomach shrivel. A cold wind passed through my body and out through my mouth. For a few seconds it was hard even to breathe. I was appropriately afraid and totally in awe. Then slowly, incredibly, I found myself getting bored. I forgot the danger. I only wanted the croc to move, to do something interesting that I could capture on film. My camera had begun to function as that protective screen between myself and my subject.

Now, as I surveyed this crocodile, I wondered what would happen if I made strange noises. Would he swim away or, pushed by curiosity, come closer? I imitated the sound of a bird, and at first there was no observable reaction. But then I saw the rhythm of his breathing alter slightly. The nasal valves at the extremities of his mouth, which close when he goes under water, began to move. Suddenly, with amazing speed and force, the monster raised his body and throwing himself backward plunged his head into the water, which exploded with the impact. His tail erupted out of the frothy surface, beating the air, and then it disappeared in a flurry of violent whirlpools. Through the telephoto lens I could follow the eddies created by the propulsion of his tail as he moved upstream. For a while I lost sight of him. Too many floating branches and foliage, too many treetops agitated by the current. But then I noticed him heading toward the boat of my two companions about one hundred fifty feet away among other floating trees. Max had his feet dangling out of the boat trying to clear a path through the vegetation. I had endangered them with my own recklessness.

I shouted as loudly as I could. "Max! Crocodile!"

He couldn't hear me because of the noise of the river.

"Max! J.F.! Careful! Crocodile! Crocodile!!"

I jumped to my feet, breaking my blind apart. My heart raced in terror. Instead of getting into the canoe, I could see Max, his still camera flopping around his neck, plunge into the muddy water. Then I couldn't see him any longer. J.F. had jumped into the center of the boat and I imagined the worst. But in a moment, I saw Max safe on the shore. The croc had passed him by.

Five minutes later, standing on the bank, I asked Max, "What happened? Didn't you hear me?"

"Just once. Between the water, the birds, and the branches, as I was trying to break my fall. I just slipped. The worst was when I realized that I wouldn't be able to get back into the boat and that I would have to make for shore. I felt so many things rustling against my legs as I swam. God, I was scared!"

Slowly the color came back into Max's face but almost instantly a cloud of black mosquitoes covered our skin. In little bits or large gulps, the jungle is ever ready to eat intruders.

Our canoes seemed especially heavy when we carried them out of the water. Our near miss with death had sapped all our energy. The mud was too slippery. The heat and the humidity were oppressive. Sweat burned our eyes. Then we stripped to inspect for leeches. Counting those we found dead in our socks crushed by our feet, those that were still living and gorged with our blood, and those that were just about to dig in for their meals, we found more than forty apiece.

In a few days we had already had enough of this torrid hell . . . enough of being in this stinking steam bath . . . enough danger. I knew that my companions were sharing my thought: What the hell are we doing here? Although we still had two hours before sunset we didn't feel like filming any more and returned to our cabin to play cards. That's it, we are in Vegas, with matches for imaginary money, each representing a one-hundred-dollar bill. The naked female mosquitoes entertained us.

The next morning, with the level of the river considerably lower and the current not so strong, we decided to explore the mangroves where the backwaters of the jungle mingled with the waters of the sea. We spotted groups of big beige monkeys that are unique to the mangroves of Borneo. As skillful in water (for he loves to swim) as he is jumping from tree to tree, he is named *proboscis* for his long pink nose that reaches down to his chin when he grows older. The natives call him *Dutchman*. His nose is used as a trumpet when he is angry; when he wants to mate, he flares it out to declare his amorous intentions.

Because they subsist on the leaves of a specific tree that grows nowhere else, these monkeys can survive only in the Borneo jungles of this particular coast. These trees are being eliminated by timber and oil exploration; except for zoos, the proboscis monkey will soon disappear from the face of the earth.

The giant sea crocodile, which I was lucky to film from our canoe, is also confined to the mangrove swamp because of the brackish water, but it exists in other countries with this particular type of coastal jungle. Considered to be the longest crocodile, with a length of twenty-three feet or more, this beast is able to do battle with sharks when they both search the coral reef for giant sea turtles.

We also observed many *Varanus Salvadors,* a species of lizard that can swim, walk, and even climb trees. Usually seven or eight feet long, they live mostly near the water, eating fish and small animals. You can spot them lying on the limbs of trees along the river banks with their four-clawed feet hanging down, a funny but dangerous sight. Generally they avoid humans, but they will attack if they feel endangered. At first they give warning by inflating their necks and hissing. If they still sense danger, they bite, claw, and try to knock their prey down, lashing out with their long tails that are strong enough to break a human leg.

After a few days of filming the mangrove rivers, we went back to the jungle. Using a blind we built on the edge of a clearing where we had found the remains of fruits, I was able to film orangutans. We spotted a few very venomous species of snakes, such as the thirteen-foot-long royal cobra, several water snakes that we didn't recognize, and the amazingly beautiful *bugare*. The latter belongs to the cobra family and has a long body decorated with multicolored circles; while hunting, the bugare hides its head under its body, then raises the end of its tail and moves it to attract its prey.

With its high, dense jungle where some trees reach up to two hundred feet, Borneo is the right place to find several species of animals that have adapted themselves for gliding through the air. Although we always tried to be ready to film them, we were never able to catch them in flight, because they appear too suddenly and then quickly disappear, merging into the darkness of the jungles. One day, for instance, while we were walking beneath a series of lianas hanging down from large branches, several spearlike objects fell from the trees above and, flying obliquely, touched the ground somewhere about thirty feet from us and slithered off. These happily nonvenomous flying snakes are called *paradise snakes*. They can swim as well as climb trees from which they drop and glide, curving their abdomens, their long and mobile ribs spread out. Not the kind of snake that was in my paradise.

Another time we saw a monkey that glided more than a hundred and fifty feet, thanks to a membrane joining arms and legs on each side of his body. And we watched a small red frog that uses its wide palm and webbed fingers to glide from tree to tree; with leaves and resin it builds small aquariumlike nests for its tadpoles on the tops of trees.

One morning, I caught sight of a small flying lizard that landed on a tree bole just in front of me. Through my telephoto lens I was able to observe all its details. When this lizard, called a *flying dragon*, gets ready to fly, it unfolds small membranes on both sides of its neck, which act as rudders, and two larger ones on the sides of its body between its front and back legs, which serve as wings. These enable it to glide for distances up to one hundred feet.

It is said that only about ten percent of the amazing fauna and flora sheltered by the jungle of Borneo is known to science. Professor Capart, the head of the Belgian Museum of Natural History, told me the day I departed for Borneo, "If you tell me that you have seen a dinosaur, I will believe you!"

Just as we were about to leave the area, we found in a twenty-by-twenty-foot marsh the tracks left by a huge snake, probably one of the giant pythons. Nearby were tracks made by wild boars. Since boars are the favorite food of pythons, we decided to attempt to film one of their momentous encounters.

I placed Max, with one camera, in a tree overhanging the marsh. From there he would be able to cover whatever happened. With a camera, I lay at the other end of the marsh with mud and foliage to camouflage my body, my head protected by the helmetlike mosquito net. J.F., whose odor was also hidden by fragrant leaves, stood machete in hand some distance away in the bushes, but close enough to hear me call for help. The python has sharp teeth but is not venomous. Like other snakes belonging to the species that includes boas and anacondas, the python is deadly because of its powerful constricting ability, which it uses to crush its prey before swallowing it. It has several ways to hunt. Sometimes it will let its body fall from a tree on top of its intended victim. At other times it will lie in wait and then suddenly lunge at its victim and crush him to death. Its human prey can usually be saved by a companion, since it takes some time for a python to crush him.

We waited for the python to come, also hoping for some wild boars that could become the snake's prey. Because all three of us were excited, already imagining the scenes to come, the first hour or two of waiting went by fast. I wasn't even bothered by the mosquitoes that tried to bite my hands where the skin wasn't covered by enough mud, or by the swarm of insects that came with the mud. With boredom, however, I began to suffer from the disgusting movements of mosquitoes, insects, and worms all over my skin. At first my limbs, and soon my whole body, began to hurt from my cramped position. It was hard to keep my head up as my elbows sank into the mud. We waited for six hours, until 4:00 P.M., but then gave up. The python had not come. The next day we started again, keeping the same positions, but still in vain.

"Let's try for one more day," I said.

"For the last time?" asked Max.

"Yes," I answered.

"It's a promise?" called J.F.

"Sure."

The next day, after one hour, a python appeared and passed next to me, moving his enormous body in slow motion into a spot of sunlight at the foot of a tree. Then, slowly, this thirty-foot-long snake rolled himself around his head in coil after coil and settled down to wait. He was about twenty-five feet away from my head. I was overwhelmingly excited, but if I had known then what the Dayaks told me later about the python's technique for hunting, I would never have stayed there, lying defenseless elbows down in the mud. When something the python wants to eat passes close by and the distance that separates him from his prey is shorter than his whole length, the python suddenly stretches his body and with enormous force smashes into the prey's head with his muzzle, before recoiling back to his original position. He strikes again and again until his victim is knocked unconscious. Then he grasps the prey with his teeth, and uses it as a fulcrum to bring his whole body over to it. He coils himself around it, breaking all its bones, shrinking its size until he can swallow the victim whole. This technique explains how wild boars, panthers, bears, and even men have been found inside their stomachs. Two whole human bodies were once found together inside the stomach of a forty-five-foot python killed by a bulldozer in the Caltex oil company's exploitation territory in Sumatra. Fortunately the python I was filming remained unaware of me. After a while, possibly disappointed at not meeting his lunch, he slithered back into the jungle and we slithered back to our cabin.

When the time had come to leave, I had a bunch of film cans filled with images of orangutans, a thirteen-foot-long Royal cobra, several water snakes, and various birds and insects. However, our memories only will remember all the other wonders of the fauna that we saw without being able to record on film. Equal parts of elation and disappointment are the salary of a documentary filmmaker.

When we came back to Balikpapan, Shell's guest house was crowded. The manager of the base, with whom we had dinner, said that no helicopters were available to drop us on the Mahakam River. However, he said we could use their speedboat, which was leaving the next morning for Samarinda, the only large town situated on that river, a few miles inland from its mouth. There we could easily rent a small boat for our journey to Tabang. We accepted his proposition. Then he introduced us to the company's geologist, who had worked at one time for a mineral company and had attempted to explore central Borneo in search of uranium and other precious minerals. We spent the evening getting his encouraging advice.

"You are crazy to go there. The Punan don't even have villages. They are dirty, bloodthirsty nomads. Nothing else. Primitive bastards. And not only the Punan but the Dayak tribes who live there are also devils. When we tried to enter the region, they sprayed us with showers of poisonous darts."

He called over a group of prospector enthusiasts who had tried to enter the territory and also had been driven off by warning signals: poisonous darts stuck in circles on the ground and spears driven into trees.

"Did you notice any animals or birds?" I asked, hoping to change the subject before Max and J.F. changed their minds.

"No. Nothing but leeches. Fucking leeches everywhere. Why the hell don't you go up there by helicopter? It would save you days of shit going up there by boat."

"It's out of range for our helicopter," another man answered.

"Anyhow, I would lose more time waiting here than going to Tabang by boat," I said. It was also out of range for my wallet. Even if I could afford such an expense, I wouldn't do it. A gradual approach is important. It allows you to prepare yourself for other people's customs, life-styles, and languages. By meeting other tribes living along the route, you enter a world of differences incrementally instead of being a victim of culture shock.

"You must be very well paid for risking your life like this," said an oil prospector.

"Not really," was all I answered. Had I told him the truth, they might have sent us back to Jakarta in a strait jacket.

The truth is that I am at war with these oil men. Without qualm or remorse they travel from one virgin land to another, ravaging it and inflicting indescribable misery on its animal and human populations. It is a war of the heart and the spirit, an invisible war between predators and lovers. A strange war because the two sides nourish each other in so many ways. We depend on their planes and helicopters to move us closer to our destinations. We use their artifacts and machines to bring word of the jungle people to the world. They rely on us, in turn, for a kind of infusion of the spirit. It becomes clear when talking to them that they support us in our adventure. They want to believe in us and our values and the purity of our motives. And yet, as much as they want us to succeed, they also want us to fail because our failure would prove to them the folly of hoping for a different world. Even so, I know they would mourn us in their own way if we didn't return.

I understand those oil men who work in the jungles. They are inside me. All their cruel lusts, the barbarous force of their will to dominate. I sense all that inside me and I say, No! Never! I will leave everything as I found it. The only trace of ourselves we will leave behind with the Dayak will be their memory of our love and respect.

In my room, my two companions joined me over a bottle of Scotch. The room was like any luxurious hotel room, with a large and comfortable flowered sofa and armchairs. Flowered everything. Even the bathroom's wallpaper was flowered. But not the pictures hanging on the flowered wall, pictures of tankers, pipelines, flares burning in the jungle.

That night, in the face of the unknown, we felt a desire to talk and share episodes of our childhood and adolescence and intimate memories, as if revealing ourselves would better help us to confront tomorrow. Released by the alcohol, we imagined the adventure waiting for us. The sound of our own voices, the assurance of our past as guarantee of our future, was what we heard.

What a wonderful feeling it is to be able to decide your own life and destiny, obeying without limitations your own mysterious calls, and dreams, and passions. What a wonderful sensation to feel the fires of happiness burning inside the body. We were not happy as a sleeping or eating dog is happy. But happy as a dog is when greeting its master, jumping everywhere like a maniac, yelping and barking. We were wild with joy because tomorrow we would leave the known world behind. Our bodies felt too small for such an overflowing of love, joy, and friendship.

"I am so happy to go with you, my friends," I said. "Yes! Yes! Yes! I don't care about anything else. I would gladly die simply to be able to feel the way I do this very moment."

CHAPTER SEVEN

"Long Ears" Land

There are so many things between the sky and the earth that poets are the only ones to have dreamed of.

FREDRICH NIETZSCHE

In Samarinda, because of the presence of the oil, timber, and mineral exploitation companies, it wasn't easy to find a good boat that I could afford. And since I didn't have the megabucks of a National Geographic or Cousteau, I finally had to settle on a forty-foot "yacht," which soon revealed itself to be a leaky old bucket. The deck was covered with a rotting, low wooden roof. At the stern the kitchen and next to it the poop deck consisted simply of upended crates that hung precariously above the water. To steer, two rusty wires joined the front steering wheel to the back rudder, each running along one side of the boat. To control the motor speed, neutral, forward, and reverse, an old clothesline was strung from the front berth to a small bell hung above the motor, which was located near the end of the boat and protruded above the deck. Each different way of ringing the bell was a message for the cabin boy who then manually controlled our speed and direction.

A great deal of space on the deck was taken up by the top of the noisy diesel motor (a relic from pre–World War II days that coughed and sweated grease through the deck) and four sixty-gallon fuel tanks. Giant bunches of bananas, hanging from the roof next to stinking dried fish, and our expedition gear completed our cargo. The deck was so crowded that there was just enough space to stretch one hammock between two of the poles supporting the roof.

Our crew was composed of three Malayans who didn't speak a word of English. Kim, the thirty-year-old captain, confined his desultory piloting to the early morning and late afternoon. The rest of the time he spent rubbing his hair with half a fresh pineapple, plucking hairs from his chin and admiring himself in a mirror. His assistant used much of his day washing and re-washing a pair of white gloves that he wore at all times except when eating. All the real work was done by the fifteen-year-old cabin boy who labored from dawn until late at night.

Our crew was so intensely curious about us that we could never make a move without causing all eyes to turn in our direction. Time and time again, because of their fascination, we came perilously close to colliding with other boats, the banks of the river, the wharves, and the big timber rafts floating toward us.

Each morning around eleven, they would lower the boat's speed to a crawl. To save fuel, they said. They knew we were renting the boat on a daily basis, so they were trying to prolong the voyage. We would then order them to go faster. Impercep-tively they would lower the speed again and we'd raise it again. No words were spoken. None of us lost his temper. It became a daily routine, a game without arguments. We simply accepted that we had different points of view.

According to Kim it would take ten days to reach Tabang. Ten days to rest. Ten days to keep busy. Ten days to watch others doing what they do.

J.F. was often silent. His attitude hinted at inner problems, but in spite of trying many times, I never succeeded in reaching his soul deep enough to understand or help. He spent most of the time writing to his family, especially his girlfriend. Later, I finally understood that, when facing something that for Max and me was a source of joy and emotional excitement, J.F.'s sudden and long silences were because he was no longer with us. He was with Nana, revealing with tender words the sights he was admiring. He was her eyes. And when he lapsed into long silences, closing his eyes, perhaps was it to whisper under his breath, "Nana, I love you. France is not so far away. I can hear your heart." It was hard for him to accept that true explor-ing means putting out of your mind everything behind that is a reminder of one's past.

Max was a tougher character. He lived only for our discover-ies. He had left behind family, girlfriends, even his civilized persona. Impressed by the harmonious and natural behavior of the natives we met, in each village he spotted his "perfect woman" to take back to Europe with him. Unfortunately, he regarded anything that came between him and our goal—mosquitoes, mud, heat—as personal enemies. Sometimes I found myself wondering how he would survive in the jungle where the very air, laden with heat, humidity, and bugs, might become the object of his wrath. His teeth ached. His jaw was swollen. To buoy him up, J.F. and I constantly praised his cooking saying, "We loooove your food," but often that failed to impress him.

On the voyage upriver we made a startling discovery. Here we were, in fresh water, one hundred miles from the sea, and we saw a porpoise on the riverbank dying from wounds made by boat propellers. The natives explained that porpoises were a common sight and that before oil and timber exploitation on the banks of the Mahakan, they were seen as far as two hundred miles upstream.

To pass the time I started to read J.F.'s book on tropical medicine. It described so many unusual ways for us to die that death seemed long overdue. Beginning with the first chapter, I learned that to survive birth itself is just luck, to be born in good health is a miracle, and staying alive is almost impossible. Before I finished even a quarter of the work, I started to feel the symptoms of so many obscure diseases that I began to despair of reaching Tabang.

After the first day going upstream, the Mahakan was still crowded with taxi-boats, jet-boats, and other river cargo carriers used in timber exploitation. Long rafts made of logs from massive jungle trees passed by slowly like funeral processions. Sometimes we met canoes, pulling behind them large quantities of fresh, white floating rubber. All along the banks of the river, the jungle bore ugly scars of exploitation. The native villages were covered with rusted, corrugated iron roofs.

Fortunately, the fog, which lasted from dawn to the middle of the day, concealed much of this twentieth-century apocalypse. Sometimes, we would close our eyes and dream of the healthy, primal jungles that awaited us.

For an hour just before nightfall, the wide opening of the river allowed us the daily feast of the sky, which exploded in color. The heavy tropical clouds catch fire in massive conflagrations of red and orange. Colors flash back and forth like the bodies of lovers in amorous embrace. The sky becomes the theater for a love ritual between the spaces of light and those of darkness.

We spent our first night on the boat moored along the riverbank. J.F. had chosen the only hammock; Max and I lay on the deck. But the first stars were not the prelude of a new poem but the beginning of a nightmare that would be ours every night until we reached Tabang, for the still, humid, heavy air carried armies of unavoidable mosquitoes.

On our second night on the Mahakan, instead of stopping as he did the day before, the captain attached an oil lantern to the small mast and another just above the motor and, despite a heavy fog around us, continued to cruise upstream to Tengarong.

"Kim!" Mixing my English with the Indonesian words I had already learned, I asked the captain, "Don't we stop for the night?"

"No," he answered. "We must reach Tengarong tonight."

"I think it's very dangerous to navigate without visibility," said Max in his own gibberish.

"Tuan, we must reach Tengarong tonight," Kim repeated. "The authorities' offices are closed after one o'clock. And we still have about five hours to cover. Unless you don't care about waiting in Tengarong."

"What authorities?"

"Military control post. We must report to them. All boats must report, and you too," he answered.

"OK. But go carefully."

I didn't understand this reversal of Kim's desire to go slowly until the next day when the cabin boy, pointing at Kim, formed with his fingers the signs universally known to express lovemaking. Kim had had a girlfriend waiting for him in Tengarong.

The fog rising from the large river and condensing in layers hung on anything floating, giving the trees along the bank heads of white hair. In spite of the full moon appearing between dark clouds, the fog was so heavy that standing in the front I often couldn't see the back of our boat. But each hazy glow of light, each noise across the water, each darker shadow was a landmark used by Kim to avoid obstacles and determine his exact position. Sometimes, just at the right moment, he switched on the battery searchlight hanging next to his hand and swept it over the water's surface. The beam created new forms, unexpected silhouettes. Here was a pirogue he barely avoided. There was a raft carrying a whole family. Sometimes our boat was shaken by a submerged tree trunk. At last the lights of Tengarong appeared through the halo of mist.

Creaking, our boat rubbed its hull against giant algae-covered poles that supported the dock. It seemed to be too high in relation to the water level. With difficulty, Kim's assistant climbed the six feet that separated us from the dock and attached the boat's ropes to it.

"Hey, Kim," I asked. "Why don't you attach the ropes directly to the poles? The boat would be much more secure for the night!"

"Tuan," he explained, "whenever it's raining here in Kalimantan, the water can rise very high in a short amount of time. Then the ropes will break or the boat will sink."

Very early the following morning, we were awakened by a strange and heavy din mixed with screams and laughter. The boat was shaking as if we were in an earthquake. I opened my eyes and saw Kim smiling in front of me through the mosquito net.

"*Salamat Paqui, tuan! Apa Kabar?*" ("Good morning, sir. How are you?")

"*Baik sekali, terimakasih!*" ("Very good, thank you!") I replied apprehensively, seeing all around me people running in both directions across the boat's deck, zigzagging between our gear. "But what's going on?"

"No problems, tuan! No problems. Me look!" he answered in English, pointing with his finger to his eye.

A large taxi-boat had parked alongside our boat. Our deck and roof had become the gangplank for exiting passengers to reach the pontoon dock and for passengers-to-be to board the taxi-boat.

"You see, tuan?" said Kim, showing me that this morning our boat was at the same level as the dock. Without a single drop of rain in Tengarong, the water level had risen six feet in one night.

Since we couldn't tell the local authorities our real destination, I decided to tell them that we only wanted to visit some lakes along the Mahakan, located a few miles beyond the mouth of the Belayan River which leads to Tabang. I asked Max and J.F. to pretend not to understand English in case they were questioned.

We met with the district commander when his office opened at 8:00 A.M. Since he turned out to be a scholar interested in the Dayaks, I said we wanted to visit some of their villages farther up the Mahakan River.

"No Dayak villages before the lakes. Beyond that point starts the restricted area. You can't go there unless you are accompanied by an armed escort. We don't want anything bad happening to foreigners."

An explorer must be able to lie convincingly, so I laughed and promised him that after visiting the lakes we would come back and obtain an escort. Of course I had no intention of visiting Dayaks with an armed escort. Natives equate uniforms with the conqueror, and soldiers scare them.

Nine-thirty A.M. Visit to the police officer. Lots of smiles from me. "Yes, we'll certainly come back after filming the birds and lakes." The processing of documents took only forty-five minutes.

Eleven-fifteen A.M. To the army commander. "No, we wouldn't dare go into the restricted area." I told a dirty joke. In my experience, to avoid the severity of controls, one must be able to talk about tits and ass, have a great sense of humor, and carry plenty of official papers with many stamps on them. The more official papers you give them, the kinder they become. Too late I understood that I should have given them fewer official papers, for a stiff-fingered orderly began to copy them.

Happily, everyone got hungry at one P.M. and closed the office, allowing us to leave.

"So, we are going to see the lakes?" Kim said, smiling. He was already aware of the authorities' restrictions. I nodded my head, wondering how I could persuade him to go all the way to Tabang.

One hour later, although I had not yet decided what to tell him, Kim said, "Here's the Belayan River. We go?"

I hesitated to answer, not knowing if this were a trap or a friendly invitation.

"No problems to go to Tabang," he said, interested only in getting his salary. "I'll say nothing. And anyway you don't come back by here any more. So, we go?" I nodded yes.

As we left the Mahakan and went north on the Balayan, the river scene changed dramatically. The river narrowed so that we could almost reach out and touch the banks, whose vegetation rose in walls two hundred feet above the water. Sometimes the trees' disheveled heads joined above the river, blocking the sun. We entered a realm of eternal greenness. We traveled in a series of dark, zigzagging tunnels as the river curled back and forth in a seemingly endless labyrinth. Here and there a jagged chaos of stones jutted out from the riverbank waiting to assault the boats of unwary travelers. Dead trees floated on the water and others lay decomposing on the banks, nourishing and replenishing the land with the substance of their bodies—part of the endless cycle of birth and renewal. We heard the whispers of the jungle, its slow breathing rising up into swollen clouds, distended by the weight of vapors rising from the jungle floor. Snakes swam around our boat. Hundreds of monkeys cavorted in the trees. Multicolored birds screamed incessantly. Giant lianas hung from the branches overhead like a vast net. It was as if we were entering the realm of an enormous spider.

Little girl,

My joy would be greater if only you were with me to share the peacefulness of this tropical river voyage . . . if you were here to share the heartbeat of the jungle which is our escort . . . to share the breeze that carries the smell of the water, the scents of the dead leaves, and the perfumes of mists and hazes . . . to share the odors of a soil beaten by the brief but violent tropical storm, the fury of the thunder, the brutality of the lightning, the sad deaths of butterflies lying in the mud.

Each morning the panorama is hidden in a heavy fog, which recalls to me the atmosphere of my childhood. I am becoming intoxicated by my memories.

Love,
Dad

No more villages ahead. The last was barely visible behind the trees. Tabang was only one day away! But would we make it? After the rain stopped a few days earlier, the level of the river had dropped dangerously low. Everywhere on its surface we saw whirlpools forming around submerged rocks.

The captain's assistant stood at the front of our boat driving a long bamboo stick into the water to test its depth. "Five! Four feet! Three!" he yelled out his reports to the captain. The bell rang, signaling to change the engine's speed.

Suddenly the heavy boat jumped on some invisible rocks. The bell rang again. The captain shouted. The bottom of the boat shrieked as it was scraped by sharp rocks and beaten by the current. The waters suffered visibly, battling rocks. The bell rang and rang. . . . Panic on board, for the boy had too rapidly reduced the speed of the motor, which coughed and then stopped. The current mastered the boat, taking it against more rocks and throwing it askew. The motor coughed but died again, and the current began to turn the boat on its side.

We were going to sink. The motor awakened again, suffered, made the boat tremble. The propeller tore at the riverbed and was damaged by stones. The waters boiled around it. The boat jumped again and again. Our equipment slid across the deck, the tape recorder banging into the motor. The boat seemed ready to turn on its side, a prisoner of stones and a captive of the whirlpools. The bell shouted . . . the captain rang. The boat was trembling . . . crying . . . suffering. It didn't want to die here but was too tired to fight. The motor tried to help. The propeller begged . . . whined . . . fought. The boat jumped again with a sudden screech. The bell fell down. The captain was sweating and talking to his boat, which was all but ready to give up the battle against stone and current. The motor shut off. But the gods were with us—the boat ended its frenzy against the bank, captured by a net of dead limbs. We were saved.

"So what happens now?"

"The motor is powerful enough," said Kim, "but it's water that is lacking."

The captain sat down and smoked one of my cigarettes while the crewmen attempted to restore order.

"So now what?" I asked again, sweating under the heavy heat of the burning noon sun.

"Must wait, tuan."

"Wait for what?"

"Rain, tuan. If it rains we'll have more water to pass the barrier of stones."

Desperate, I called to the young boy, "Do you know a prayer to make rain?"

His laughter was my answer.

An hour later a thirty-foot canoe with less draft—powered by a forty-horsepower engine—came alongside. The Chinese owner was wearing a dirty hat with a *Playboy* insignia. He did not have to smile. All of his upper front teeth, capped with gold, leapt brilliantly in his mouth, smiling for him. He spoke only Chinese and Malaysian, but in a few minutes we learned that he lived in Tabang, where he had a shop.

"How much to get us to Tabang?"

"Twenty thousand rupees."

"What? How far is Tabang?"

"Three hours." The man with the gold teeth spoke calmly without moving his facial mask.

"Twenty thousand for three hours? You're crazy!" I said the words with a smile so as not to put him in a bad mood. "You know how much I paid for this fucking big boat? Seven thousand a day! Be serious, man! I don't want to be screwed just to cover your other teeth with gold."

To show him that we didn't need his boat, I asked J.F. to bring the cards, and with Max we started to play poker, trying to laugh as much as possible to hide our nervousness and anger.

One hour later, while mosquitoes attacked, I made a counter-proposal. He refused. For the next hour, I counterproposed, he refused, I countercounterproposed again, and again he didn't accept. I returned to playing cards. He countercounter-proposed, I ignored him and went on playing cards, he counter-countercounterproposed, and so on. Finally we agreed on ten thousand rupees.

But my worries were not over. While Max and J.F. shifted our gear to the other boat, I paid our rent to the captain. Seeing how nicely the Chinese gentleman had done with me, the captain asked me for triple what we had agreed on.

"You must understand, tuan. The boat has suffered. We used more fuel. You need to pay for our wait here until it rains and we can make our way back . . . and pay for our way back."

All this was said with smiles and firm resolution. Suddenly I noticed his assistant was standing with my tape recorder in his hands at the front deck. He was smiling also. Psychological warfare had begun. How could I win, here in the middle of nowhere?

In my childhood I learned from the African *palavers,* or never-ending discussions, that keeping one's position is a question of honor, because by accepting the other's argument, one admits defeat. But, at the same time, by remaining prisoners of their positions, two adversaries can reach resolution only by a fight. "Like two stupid roosters!" they used to say in Africa.

In order to avoid a situation where the adversaries keep re-peating their "no's" to each other, a palaver allows an evolution of the situation by creating an intellectual space in which each adversary is able to demonstrate to his opponent the benefits that will come from the opponent's accepting the other's per-spective.

A palaver must move to the point where one adversary can

win the case without forcing the other to admit defeat. This is only possible if the other feels that by giving up his argument, he reaches a different point of satisfaction. Thus palavers, which can take hours, are peaceful, almost chivalrous tournaments where the adversaries' humor is all important. Their humor will be valued and often acclaimed by the listeners, who always assist the palavers and testify to the great quality of the intellectual exchanges.

I put my hand on the captain's shoulder and with a wink I asked, "Listen, Kim, we are friends, right?" He confirmed with a nod, so I continued. "Between friends we don't lie, right? So if I don't pay, you keep my machine?" I pointed at my tape recorder still in the hands of the cabin boy.

He said yes. I shook his hand and said with a bigger smile, "Okay. You win. I'll pay you." I went toward the motor. With a wrench I had picked up on my way, I started to remove a piece of the fuel system. "Yeah, I'll pay you. But at that price I become co-owner of the boat, so I am taking some parts with me."

I knew I was playing with fire. It could be a bloody battle, or they might appreciate my ploy. I heard loud laughter of the captain, followed by the laughter of the ship's boy and the assistant, who approached me and presented my machine. I had won.

In this part of the world, as everywhere else, foreigners are fair game. They had tried to exploit me because the only strangers the people of Borneo are accustomed to seeing are those who work for rich and powerful companies. Getting as much of their money as possible, in almost any way, is basic to the culture and the economy.

Tabang, the last outpost of our civilization, was not three hours away, as the Chinese man had said. We were there in thirty-five minutes. One soldier, one policeman, one "mayor," one mosque, and one *mullah*. A small hut where the Catholic priest, who came once a month or so, performed mass. One shop owned by the man with the golden teeth. Another trading shop. A school. The inhabitants belonged to a Malayan ethnic group, but were not Dayaks. The Dayaks lived a few miles away from Tabang in their own village.

According to Indonesian law, each time we entered or left a district our first obligation was to show our papers to the army, the police representatives, and the *bupati* (chief of region or district commander). We were concerned because we had not returned to the Tengarong bupati and wondered if he would send a command to all inland official posts to arrest us. In Indonesian, a language I had started to master thanks to our boat's crew, I asked a boy who came to watch us disembarking from the Chinese's boat, "Who's the highest authority here in Tabang?"

"The kepala compound," he answered. The *kepala* is the head of the village, a kind of mayor.

"Good. Lead me to his house."

Leaving Max and J.F. behind to watch our six hundred pounds of precious materials, I went to the kepala's large house in the modern part of town, next to the school and the military and police offices, which were linked to a telecommunication antenna.

Still wet from taking a shower, the mayor greeted me with elaborate courtesy. Ten minutes later, our belongings filled up a corner of his large living room and my two companions and I were drinking tea brought by a female servant.

Soon the stuffy room was crowded with people who came to see the white foreigners. The previous visitors, who had come a year earlier, were two geologists from an oil company. They had stayed only a few hours; we were clearly going to offer considerably more entertainment. All the village notables were present, along with the policeman and the army officer. The onlookers included almost all the children of Tabang. Since there were not enough chairs, the important personages sat on the floor all around us. The others stood wherever they could squeeze themselves in, filling up doorways and windows. With a long stick, the mayor's male servant tried vainly to clear the windows and the entrance, chasing out the screaming children, but they returned as quickly as they were chased away.

In a loud voice the mayor read everyone my recommendation letters, including those from King Leopold, the Belgian government, museums, and so on, which were translated into Indonesian. The reading gave rise to nods and verbal reactions. Men, women, and children—now more than thirty in all—stared at us, sharing impressions, laughing, talking, smoking, chewing betel, burping, and farting. This is common behavior among people of tradition whenever they gather together and for whatever reason—political, religious, or purely social.

When there were no more letters to read, formality gave way

to warmth with the mayor insisting we stay in his guest room. While the whole population of Tabang passed through to look hard at us or stayed to stare, we ate rice and fresh grilled fish and joked about our boat ride.

When night began to fall, the mayor turned on the town's only electric generator, which lighted his house's three electric light bulbs. The generator supplied electricity not only to the mayor's house but also to the administrative buildings, which were really just two wooden cabins sheltering the police and military police offices.

The rest of Tabang was lit by oil lamps and flashlights, which moved about in the darkness like will-o-the-wisps.

After our dinner the visitors continued to come and go and the notables now sat on chairs they had brought with them from their houses.

"Does anyone play chess?" the mayor asked, looking at the three of us.

Max and I shook our heads. Surprisingly, J.F., who was a good player, shook his head too. So we started to chat. My knowledge of the Indonesian language didn't allow me to have any deep conversations, and after an hour of having repeated everything at least twice, we ran out of things to say. The long silences started to distress our host. He seemed to feel that these pauses might be interpreted by the villagers as proof of his inability to be an honorable host.

Once more at his request I explained our intention to cross the uncharted mountain region.

"Something occurs to me," he said. "Why did Tengarong's authorities, whom I know very well, not tell me of your coming?"

I began to get nervous.

The military man responded, "Maybe they tried but our transmitter is broken. The spare parts will be here soon. Perhaps tomorrow. *Inch Allah!*" ("God willing!")

I was relieved. Nevertheless, the way the situation was developing made me decide to betray J.F. "Kepala," I said, smiling, as I put my hand on J.F.'s arm. "My friend is a chess player. His shyness prevents him from admitting it. But I know he is dying to play with you."

In French, I added, "J.F., old friend, you must play for the mayor, who is so nice to us."

Noisy shouts greeted the news. When the pieces were set on

the table, the clamor increased, and the number of assistants too. I knew that my friends were as tired as I was, but we had to entertain our host before he asked too many embarrassing questions.

"We are staying with you, J.F., to cheer you on."

"Bastard!" he replied. "I am so tired, I don't feel like playing chess."

The assistants commented on each move. I was ready to bet my grandmother's trousers that as many verbal chess games were played that evening as there were people in the room.

In any case, it was a long game, J.F. battling for the honor of Europe but all the while thinking it might be a good idea to lose. The children and half of the assistants who commented at length about each move eventually went to sleep on the floor. Max and I fought to keep our eyes open. Finally it was over.

"Thank you for having lost, J.F.," I said with warmth.

"I didn't intend to. He's very good."

From then on, every evening for the whole week we spent in Tabang, J.F. was condemned to play chess with the mayor. During the day Max's duty was to play ping-pong with our host, except when we were too busy visiting a neighboring Dayak tribe in a vain search for porters.

The name *Dayak* designates a mass of various ethnic groups estimated to contain more than three hundred different tribes. While some have very distinctive language, cultures, and lifestyles, others are closely related. Some groups are peaceful, others are fierce warriors. Some are cultivators, some hunters, and some nomads. Of all the Dayak tribes that once were headhunters, only a few practice this ritual today.

Many of these tribes live in villages made up of only one long rectangular house built on a platform raised high on pilework. They are made completely of wood. The roofs consist of small tiles of ironwood that Dayaks cut and shape patiently with their *mandau,* a kind of saber. The ironwood tiles have amazing resistance to humidity, insects, and time.

The long house contains several two-room apartments side by side. One room is the bedroom, the other a living room, part of which is also used as the kitchen. At the back of the long house, each apartment ends in a bathroom, just a hole cut in the floor; at the front, each apartment opens onto a veranda, which runs the length of the long house. The platform—including the veranda and the house—is about thirty feet wide.

Some tribes have large square areas of hard-packed surface in front of and below the veranda. Others, especially warrior tribes, have an uncovered porch just in front of and on the same level as the veranda. In this case the width of house, veranda, and extension can be as wide as one hundred feet or more. The length of a long house is generally one to two hundred feet and varies according to the number of its inhabitants. (During my third expedition in Borneo, I lived in one that sheltered two hundred people and extended over eight hundred feet.)

Generally, the height of the pilings is at least six feet. But a warrior's long house may be raised as much as sixteen feet off the ground. For security, there is only one access to the platform by stairs carved into a tree trunk.

I always have a hard time walking on floors made of bamboo sliced lengthwise. Because of my size, the floor bends inward at each step, and I have the uneasy feeling that I will fall through—it had already happened to me once in another village.

Allowing for variation, all Dayak tribesmen are about five foot three and have Asiatic features with slit eyes, long black hair, and skin almost devoid of body hair. The men wear only a long, narrow piece of cloth which passes between the legs and is attached around the hips. For women, the customary dress varies from being barebreasted with a small skirt, to wearing also a kind of blouse, sometimes covered with glass pearls or silver coins. All fabrics are multicolored and made of cotton that they weave themselves.

In many respects, the Dayaks resemble the mountain tribes of the northern Philippines. They all have the same kind of houses built on pilework. Their tattoos, especially the spirals which symbolize the beginning of the voyage beyond death; their clothing; the way those who have taken human heads distinguish themselves by wearing wild boar tusks in their ears; and their necklaces attached to small hats made of willow—all are the same. Later I found similar customs among the Toradjas in the Celebes and Burma.

Of course, one might wonder why so many similarities exist between peoples living for the most part deep inland and in countries that are often separated by large seas. I believe the existence of houses built on high pileworks is a clue. Inland there isn't sufficient reason to build houses on pileworks, but this kind of building is necessary when living in coastal swamps or near the sea. This suggests that Dayaks and similar mountain tribes once lived on the coasts. Perhaps their villages were only bases from which these sea people traveled from island to island. One could speculate that they were chased into the inland jungles by more numerous and powerful enemies coming from the sea. They simply retained their way of building houses, even though there was no longer any reason to do so. This maritime origin could also explain why so many tribal houses have the shape of an upside-down canoe or boat.

The only long house near Tabang was inhabited by members of one of the main Dayak tribes, called *Kenyah*. They were once ferocious warriors and headhunters, but nowadays only a few, lost in the deep jungles, continue the practice. These people are noted for their amazingly beautiful works of art: wooden sculptures; motifs of their tapestries and cloths woven on archaic weaving looms; and beautiful designs of the exceptional paintings which adorn their walls, embellish some of their sculptures, and decorate the coffins of their dead. The various colors are made from different vegetable dyes.

Besides wearing tattoos as men do, the Kenyah women elongate their ear lobes—as do many other Dayak tribes. When very young, girls have their ears pierced by a hot knife or red-hot iron, which prevents infection. As the years go on, heavier and heavier rings are hung from the ear lobes, stretching them to remarkable lengths. I saw women with ear lobes long enough to touch their breasts. As the hole in the lobe is excessively stretched by the weight of the jewels, the skin around the pierced hole becomes very thin. If it breaks under the weight of the rings, a woman may reconnect the two ends with a string of pearls. Even as adults, the Kenyah women continue to hang numerous heavy, wide rings, often made of shiny copper or more rarely of gold, from their ears. In some tribes, instead of hanging heavy rings the women elongate their ear lobes by inserting larger and larger disks.

Men also elongate their ear lobes, but only about two inches. Some men also have small holes in the tops of their ear lobes, into which they put the tooth of a panther or bear, or the tusk of a wild boar. In more remote villages, the old men confirmed that this mark indicates that its bearer has had the courage to cut off at least one human head.

It is said among Dayaks that ear mutilation is only intended for beauty, but I am convinced it has another significance. Everything that people of tradition do to and with their bodies has a deep meaning, because for them there is no distinction between the sacred and the profane. Although all the people I questioned say they have forgotten its original significance, based on the similarity of meanings that often exists between different tribes and sometimes different ethnic groups living far apart, ear mutilation can be seen as a way to prevent malicious and sly spirits from penetrating the human body through the natural openings of the ears. Attracted by something shiny, evil spirits prefer entering the rings' holes than the ears. Perhaps by widening the ear lobes, people create more chances for these bad spirits to get lost. This probably holds true for nose rings as well.

The long house of the Kenyah was almost empty when I arrived after an hour of walking from Tabang, led by the mayor's servant. The men, women, and adolescents were working in the rice fields belonging to the whole community, leaving only the very old and the very young.

This group of Kenyah, like all Dayaks converted to "modern civilization," were much influenced by the code of Islam, which forbids many of the practices that were basic to their culture, drinking and sexual freedom among them.

Once they practiced headhunting, but now they must hide their last skulls, turned yellow by passing time, and just dream of them. They have been forced to abandon their old traditions that led their souls and provided reason for being since the dawn of their tribe. Only the old people have stretched their ear lobes. The young people don't even tattoo their bodies. But what about tribal celebrations? What about traditions?

"All of these are remembrances of the pagan gods and of an impious life," say men of the new religion. "Get repentance! Get repentance by hard work and prayer!"

Some of the Dayaks, to protect their inner balance, live a double life. Outwardly civilized, they continue the old ways in secret.

Before civilization they were hunters and warriors, but now they cultivate rice fields. No one here has had the genius or the will to sculpt the mountains the way they do in the northern Philippines, so each year these people attack a new part of the jungle covering the mountainsides, cutting and burning the trees. In that soil they plant the rice, sometimes using secret rituals. Then they harvest their efforts with furtive celebrations. Within a year the waters of the monsoon will take away the fertile topsoil. The next year they will need to go farther away, to attack new jungle, kill new trees, burn new soil. Today, their rice fields are three miles of hard walking from the village. In another year they will be four or more miles away.

I saw them, under the strong sun, working hard for no other reward than a few rupees. They had been civilized. Their last consolation was to chew the betel nut. Soon it might be to drink Coca-Cola.

It is hard for people to maintain their traditional ways of living in the face of foreign religious and modern civilization. The new society tells man that what was once for him the wisdom of loving life and living it fully, while watching the growth of his children, is now just a lazy kind of behavior that society severely condemns. The new society forces him to be an element that must be profitable, and nothing else, without taking full care of him as his tribal society did. And the foreign religions, which he did not choose but which have imposed themselves upon him, deeply disturb his state of mind, logical processes, faith and beliefs, by decreeing that now is bad what for him and his fathers and his fathers' fathers was always good, now is paganism what for him was always truth, now is evil what for him was only a search for connecting himself with nature, universe, cosmos.

When I asked these Kenyah if some among them would be willing to be hired as my porters for the few months of my expedition, they smiled, shook their heads, and left me alone without an explanation. They had had enough of serving civilization.

Two or three evenings after we arrived in Tabang, I saw a group of five half-naked Punan enter the shop of the man with the gold teeth. The Punan are the nomads of the jungle, and very little is known about their culture. Morphologically they are very different from the other Dayak ethnic groups. Their skin is lighter, probably due to the fact that they live deep in dark jungles. Smaller and squatter—about five feet tall—the Punan are known as the fastest walkers of all Dayaks. They are said to "walk as fast as the wild boars" and, like the wild boars, they walk straight ahead without becoming anxious to skirt around mountains. Their powerfully developed thigh and calf muscles attest to the truth of the saying. Equally remarkable are their feet, which are almost as wide as they are long.

The Punan collect from a specific tree a resin called *damar*, which is something that all Dayak tribes use. It is their oil lamps' fuel and the dye used in tattooing. It is a part of offerings to divinities, and an important ingredient in their native remedies. It is also their currency of exchange. From village to village, from mountain to valley, this resin brings them everything they can't produce themselves. Through this trading, even the remotest tribes can come to have the products of modern civilization. Damar has so much value that some Chinese traders in the last outposts of civilization will travel upstream on the rapids in order to obtain it in Dayak villages that have never been contacted by the modern world. The resin sells for a fortune in China, Taiwan, and Hong Kong, where it is used to make the lacquer for Chinese traditional furniture and various art objects.

The Punan are everybody's black sheep. Everybody humiliates them. The traders take advantage of their disinterestedness in money. I had already been surprised by how badly the inhabitants of Tabang treated the Dayak, but I was astonished to see how much scorn the people of Tabang had for the five Punan. I was told that they usually appear every month or so carrying damar and nuggets of gold, which they trade for T-shirts, plastic ropes, plastic gadgets . . . plastic everything. Then they leave as quickly as they come, disappearing back into the jungle.

I stretched out my hand to salute the Punan. Surprised, they just looked at it. Through an interpreter, I asked them if they would be willing to be my porters. These simple people of whom everybody took advantage asked for ten times the price I expected to pay. I offered them the usual price. They rejected my offer and started to leave, without looking at me. Disappointed by the abrupt end of what could have been a great first contact with the Punan, I rushed after them to accept their first offer. They didn't even answer and, walking faster, were out of sight in a minute.

Now I had no other choice but to recruit porters from among the inhabitants of Tabang. However, as I was about to start, the mayor called me for a small conversation.

"I want to help you in regard to your search for porters."

"Oh, thank you. Thank you very much," I said, smiling.

He lit a cigarette. "So, you really came here officially, did you?"

"Jakarta said yes . . . and . . ." I cleared my throat, which had suddenly dried, "and in Borneo, nobody said no."

Governmental caution can be justified as a protection for Dayaks from unscrupulous armed adventurers in search of gold or native artifacts; or as protection of foreigners from being lost or even attacked by a warrior tribe. This would oblige the government to send out a search party or take reprisals. But whatever the administrative reasons of the Indonesian government to forbid entry into this "restricted area," I didn't feel guilty at all about lying to the mayor. We were not entering that region for political reasons, we were no danger to the Dayaks, and, moreover, we were not asking for vengeance in case we had an "accident," or for special search efforts if we became lost. Thus, I didn't think it right that anyone should stop us from taking our own risks.

Choosing porters is a matter of instinct. Many explorers who have disappeared were not killed by natives or wild natural elements; they were murdered by their bearers for guns and money. The porters are, of course, aware that an explorer carries all his money with him in cash and the temptation could be very great.

A porter usually carries between seventy and eighty pounds. With the weight of our technical material and the food and gifts we were taking with us, we needed ten or eleven of them.

Twelve strong, young men were gathered in front of the mayor's house. These were the only ones that I had succeeded in recruiting in two days of long palavers. After I explained our goal, three of them left, claiming that the Dayaks were headhunters and much too dangerous. None of the remaining porters had ever entered the unknown territory before, but one of them, Roustan, whom I appointed head porter, knew the location of an important Dayak village. His information was from one of his friends who knew someone who had a relative who knew one of its inhabitants very well.

With only nine porters, my two companions and I would be carrying heavy burdens. But I was still not at the end of my troubles. The nine guys wanted what I had offered the Punan. When I refused, they too all went away.

I had the feeling that we had ended up with desperados. After two days of hard negotiations I reached the point of paying the nine porters a little bit less than they wanted, but more than I wanted to pay. On top of the salary—half to be paid immediately, the other half on arrival at our destination—I had to provide their food: five ounces of sugar and one-and-a-half pounds of rice per porter per day; six pounds of dried fish per porter per week; one pound of salt for all of them per week; and pounds and pounds of tea and noodles. They would take care of providing all of us with fresh meat by hunting.

While J.F. and Max went to buy all our food in the shop, I began creating a map with the help of the mayor and Roustan.

The itinerary looked simple. We had to cross about thirty rapids obstructing the Belayan River upstream to reach a spot called *Djelini*, an unpopulated rock promontory at the foot of a huge mountain, where the river became impassable because of a waterfall. From there, our plan was to walk into the jungle and proceed north, trying to locate and follow the paths left by Dayaks. Then, according to Roustan, we would reach a river and go downstream, on bamboo rafts that we could build, to the Dayak village he had heard about. The most precise map given to me by King Leopold showed only a blank spot for the area we intended to enter, with notations indicating several mountains whose elevations were "believed not to exceed 7400 feet." I assumed that there would also be valleys, swamps, and marshes to cross.

My idea was to use the Dayaks living in the village known by Roustan to guide us to the next village, and then leapfrog from village to village until we reached the Kayan River on the other side of the uncharted region. We should then be near the border between Kalimantan, Indonesian Borneo, where we were, and Sarawak, which belonged to the confederation of Malaysia. Once at the Kayan River, we would build another large bamboo raft on which we would go downstream to the first main city, where I could rent a boat to carry us to the east coast of Kalimantan. We would leave our porters there with enough money to take them back to Tabang.

We decided to depart at seven the next morning. Fortunately, the mayor allowed us to go to bed early. "You are aware that you're entering that area at your own risk," said the mayor. "We will not be responsible for whatever happens to you. Since I have received no instructions about you, I cannot give you an official escort or promise any help in case something should happen to you. Ah, if only the transmitter worked, I would feel better!"

I was unable to sleep that last night in Tabang. Instead of excitement, I had the blues. As I watched the river waters sparkling under the moon, I was depressed. I had an overpowering need to talk to someone. Far away from anyone who really cared for me, I needed love. I wanted to scream at the stars to calm the loneliness I was experiencing. Now I was feeling the high price I was paying to be eternally the lover of new lands. I cried for my daughter. I needed the smile of my child right now! Yet I was filled with so much joy that I was about to realize my dreams. My breath was short with the possibilities. So many contradictory emotions.

Suddenly, as when someone is about to die, I saw my whole life passing through my mind, and my images were not only of joy but of the suffering I had given to others. I hoped that Leila, the princess of Sulu, would not send me a bad curse because I left her island. . . .

Why did I make Daniele suffer so many times? Did I have the right to choose adventure over marriage?

And what of Maroussia? Will this adventure damage her fragile growth?

Forgive me Maroussia, but . . .

I jumped. Roustan had touched my shoulder.

"What are you doing, tuan?" he asked in Indonesian.

"Oh, nothing," I answered in a mixture of English and Indonesian. "Nothing . . . just thinking."

"You never with girls? You make love with your friends?" he asked very seriously.

"No, not with my friends," I said.

"You want a girl for tonight? I know a beautiful girl for you."

I looked at him. "Yes. I want love tonight. Bring her!"

I had seen her face many times behind windows, but I had never done more than smile. And now here she was, smiling and willing. As soon as Roustan disappeared, I took her to the edge of the forest.

When I left, I told her she was sweet and lovely. I could not tell her the truth, that I had been making love not to her but to myself, that I was emptying myself of all my shameful violence. When I screamed, it was not for her. I screamed to persuade myself that I was not alone in that tropical night. And because the power of sexuality had not yet fully healed the sufferings of my soul, I made love to her again, and this time my sorrow was gone.

How beautiful the stars were behind the clouds. The fish seemed to rise to the water's surface blowing bubbles of ecstasy. The frogs, crickets, and insects of the jungle joined in this symphony of relief. Perhaps it was when he felt so good for the first time that man invented prayer.

Entering the Forbidden

It is not that a man should fear, but he should fear never beginning to live.

MARCUS AURELIUS

In Tabang there was only one motorized canoe powerful enough to carry us with our gear and crew beyond the rapids up to Djelini, and that craft belonged to Mr. Golden Teeth. At the last moment he refused to rent it to me. Given the waters between Tabang and Djelini, he didn't think he would ever see it again, so he sold it to me for a fortune.

When I raised my head to look for the last time at the small cliff that overhung the river, I was surprised to see that half the village was there.

"I never would have thought we managed to make such a powerful impression!" said J.F.

"Perhaps they are there to be sure we are finally going away," Max said, laughing.

We had caused much trouble in that small town in our search for porters, but still about fifty people were there to say fare-wells to their fathers, sons, and husbands who were going with us. I searched among the faces to see if my night girl was there. My male pride was wounded when I couldn't find her. Before we shoved off, an old lady called J.F. out of the canoe. Singing a short but monotonous chant, she put a little necklace around his neck and then she showered all of us with rice. The safety of our journey was entranced, if not assured. Slowly, the people, the cliff, and the river disappeared behind the dark blue breath of the motor. As we pulled into the river, I finally saw my girl running toward the bank and felt better. The mayor yelled, "Hope you'll come back one day soon. Inch Allah! [If God wills it]," and we were off.

The thirty-foot-long canoe overflowed with our gear, nine porters, one boatman, my two companions, and myself. Our

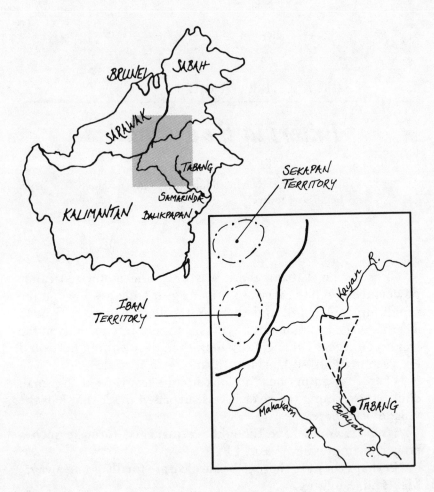

Map of Borneo. Dash line indicates the trail of the expedition.

first stop was in Ma Atan—a small Dayak town located one hour upstream from Tabang—to take on an extra boatman, supposedly the only one in the town who had the expertise to lead us safely through the rapids to Djelini. I was told that he could tell exactly where the reefs, rocks, and stones were just by the color, opacity, and motion of the water.

Going to Djelini was like going upstream on that part of the Colorado River where everyone else goes downstream. Invisible rocks created deadly slipstreams. It was difficult to zigzag between rocks and tree trunks and giant branches while fighting the current at the same time. Often the current was so strong that the canoe was held motionless while the pilot maintained the canoe perfectly head-on against the current before making a decision about how best to proceed. A small mistake and we would have been taken by the powerful current and thrown sideways against the rocks, where the canoe would have disintegrated. In order to advance in spite of the current, the pilot had to slide the canoe very carefully toward the dangerous rocks and, just grazing them, use the slipstream to propel the canoe forward. At best he would gain a few feet before the next slipstream and another dangerous rock.

Sometimes the rapids were simply impassable. We had to carry the canoe along a steep bank, bypassing the barricade of rocks on foot. At other times the water was eerily calm. Above us, the lianas hanging from trees were like giant cobwebs that darkened the whole river, and we had to lie down in the canoe to avoid being hit by the branches. At one point, a six-foot lizard plunged from a bank into the river and let itself be carried alongside the canoe by the current for a few minutes before disappearing.

Finally, at the end of the day, we arrived safely in front of a high waterfall careening down a narrow canyon. It was the end of the possible. It was the beginning of the unknown. The place: Djelini.

Although I had had a few flashing thoughts that the expedition would be broken by rocks and sunk in the furious water, we had made it. Perhaps we made it because none of us was ready to accept failure. Perhaps the will to reach the jungle and start the exploration was so strong that it allowed for no other possibilities than to win against manmade obstacles and the elements. Victory always starts in the head. It's a state of mind. It then spreads with such radiance and such affirmation that destiny can do nothing but obey.

I was overpowered by new confidence in myself. I loved this feeling: to win not by vanquishing but by becoming an ally of the forces of nature. We hadn't vanquished the magic power of the rapids but instead had combined our strength with its dangerous force, and so we had triumphed. It was in this state of mind that I was about to enter the forbidden jungle.

Rain started as we climbed the small rocky promontory of Djelini, twelve feet above the liquid chaos of the torrent. All our boxes, containing about six hundred pounds of material, were spread out on the ground: our small electric generator wrapped in a plastic sheet; a plastic jerrican filled with thirty liters of fuel; oil in a small container; three giant water-proof thermos containers with our stock of films and magnetic tapes; three well-padded aluminum suitcases, each protecting a 16-mm camera; a case with a tape recorder; two cases with still cameras; a heavy camera tripod; a bag filled with ropes and other climbing gear, and another containing an inflatable boat, des-tined for J.F.'s back; a heavy trunk of food, rice, sugar, tea, dried soups, and various cans; another trunk with the second inflata-ble boat; various smaller boxes with tubes of concentrated milk, tubes of highly concentrated meat (one pound of this paste has the nutritional value of twenty pounds of fresh meat), and a bunch of army survival kits; a heavy portable battery and all accessories needed for filming at night; a small solar battery recharger, an extra tape recorder, many sets of lenses; various gifts—namely tobacco, betel, cigarettes, and pearls—to smooth our way with the jungle tribes; a small bag with an old-fashioned wind-up movie camera and a modern still camera. Besides all of this, Max, J.F., and I each had a rucksack containing our per-sonal belongings, clothes, a hammock, a mosquito net, a sleeping bag to keep us warm in the cold jungle nights, a plastic cover, and a few extra survival kits.

After a quick meal of cold rice mixed with a can of tomato sauce and tuna, the porters unpacked their own rattan baskets, which they carried on their backs, and tried the weight of each box, each suitcase, each pack. After having made their choices, they attached their new burdens to their baskets.

While the porters were still completing their preparations, I started to write in the plastic pages of my personal notebook. From my journal:

> The stream is strewn with tree trunks like cadavers thrown there by the hazard of a storm. What a strange feeling. As if one were following barbarian conquerors who left the bloody marks of their victories behind them.

J.F. called out, interrupting my reveries. "Hey, Douch!"
"What is it?"
"You better come, the porters are already moving on!"
In Indian file, the porters were disappearing through a dark hole in the vegetal wall while the crew of "my" canoe were heading downstream back to Tabang.

I brought up the rear. When it was my turn to penetrate into the living challenge, I closed my eyes for a second to make a wish. I love you, jungle, I love you and I fear you. But I am determined to make love to you. To creep into your sex which smells of the dampness of caves. I came to tell you that I exist and that I want to know the pulsations of your ageless heart. I came to discover your own treasures and the men and animals you are hiding. But spare me the evils that you have brought forth to protect them, for I am not coming as a warrior but as a lover.

"Douch!" J.F. yelled again, becoming quite nervous.

"Yeah! Coming!"

"You'll get lost and we have just started!" he yelled again.

"Don't worry, I'm following."

J.F. walked in front of me carrying the long, heavy camera tripod attached to his rucksack. From the first step J.F. was suffering because the tripod was always catching in the lianas and pulling him off balance.

That first walk was a tough one. We climbed the steep slope of the first mountain, walking through giant ferns linked by lianas covered with thorns of all dimensions, born to tear at our hair, claw our flesh, and break our flight to pieces.

The soil slid under our feet. To avoid falls, we clung to tree trunks but found them covered with slippery green foam or glutinous moss. Sometimes we grabbed onto vines that left a nettle rash on our skin. Other lianas caused even more painful rashes, sometimes almost instantly bringing forth drops of blood.

At one point, through a small hole in the vegetation thirty feet below, we could see the wild white river zigzagging in its fury: an impassable whirlpool of foam. But I couldn't even hear its thunder because of my heart deafening my ears. Still I was happy, like a child at Christmas waiting for his wonderful gifts. The jungle of Borneo was the gift I had given myself.

That first impression of a deep joy boiling inside my body soon disappeared with the terrible effort required to climb the soft, muddy terrain. It was still raining, the cold shower freezing my overheated body. I was bathed in sweat, already exhausted, and we had only walked for one hour.

"Shit! Fucking tripod!" This time J.F. didn't have the time to finish his poetic sentiment. In forcing a passage through some vine tentacles and fighting simultaneously to free the tripod from a tangle of lianas, he reached out to a thin tree trunk that turned out to be rotten. It broke, and preceded J.F. in his fall six feet down. He came to rest hanging upside down against a muddy slope with nothing between him and a mass of rocks a few dozen feet below. Max came at J.F.'s scream, and we were able to haul him up before he plunged to his death.

As easy as it is to walk through primary forest, it is hell to try to go through secondary forest. There the daylight enters and fertilizes any seeds, and the space between trees is packed with dense vegetation. Though Borneo jungle is a primary forest, and the trees stop the daylight from transforming this vegetal cathedral into a dark sauna, we still could not proceed without the help of sharp machetes. Because it rains here more than three hundred days a year, Borneo is a primary forest inside of which a secondary forest is interwoven.

Each time a giant tree is felled by rot or wild elements, it creates a small entry point for fugitive daylight, which gives birth to new forest. From the stinking darkness, a new secondary-type of vegetation starts to develop, weaving its webs with poisonous lianas and thorns as sharp as razor blades. Then, slowly, the newborn trees find enough energy to survive the vegetal drowning. Slowly they grow up through the fifty or sixty thousand species of known and unknown plants, carnivorous vines, and lianas, their heads trying to reach the light. If they succeed, they will embrace the sky, creating new shadows beneath them.

When we didn't have to wade through mud that tried to suck the boots off our feet; when we didn't slip on the wet and rotten soil, always in danger of breaking bones and equipment; when the ground didn't give way beneath each step; when we didn't have to climb a vertical muddy cliff, helped and hindered by lianas and errant roots; when our machetes didn't have to sculpt a narrow passage inside the thorn cathedrals; when we didn't have to cross dead waters in which we sank up to the waist and sometimes deeper; when we didn't have to pass over wide, deep crevasses, inching slowly along narrow tree trunks that became natural bridges covered by a gelatinous mass of slippery moss and fungus: then the jungle became a paradise.

Noticing that we were constantly about to slip and fall because the soles of our shoes were hopeless on that kind of terrain, the porters suggested we march barefoot. Their toes seemed to hang on to any kind of slippery surface. The soles of their feet had become a hard bark, so they could survive the sharp-edged, pointed stones and the thorns and splinters of wood that hooked in the skin and made it split. The immune system of their bodies, not weakened by chemical medications, could quickly eliminate any possible infection. If we had used their barefoot technique, after just one day our feet would have been bloody wounds. But it would not have been long before we got septicemia. In that climate infections grow as fast as the vegetation.

Exhausted, I walked far behind my friends and the porters. As I wondered when at last we would have our first pause, the porters' laughter and the sound of their conversation seemed to get closer.

Here I am almost in tears, I thought, suffering from exhaustion, listening to the laughter of porters who are having fun and getting paid, when I could have been in Bali for much less money.

The porters were waiting for us in a small clearing, behind a tree so large that just one of its visible roots was big enough to hide me even when I was standing up.

They had laid all our boxes on the muddy soil's carpet of leaves. Each leaf was a different size and color: green, gold, copper, red, brown. The rotten ones were black. Max sat on a box, his face glossy with sweat and rain. J.F. was still standing, but his eyes were hazy and his face was distorted by his body's efforts to overcome the ordeal of the last hours.

"How do you feel, J.F.?" I asked.

"Up my ass!" he answered.

"I never thought it would be so difficult to climb these damn mountains," I said.

"The porters are crazy. Have you seen how high we are now? We have climbed the way the Punan do!" said Max, smiling in spite of exhaustion.

"They want to kill us," added J.F.

"Happily, it's four o'clock. End of the first hell," I said, putting my camera back in its case that hung from my shoulder.

"Did you film anything?" asked Max.

"A lot in the beginning. Vegetation, thorns, a little bit of everything in the jungle. But as we climbed, my camera was getting too heavy. And you?"

"I made a few shots of you and J.F. walking."

As I placed the camera box on the ground, I saw the porters' bloody feet and knew that, notwithstanding the fact that they were used to walking barefoot, they too had suffered from sharp stones, splinters of wood, and leeches.

While most of the porters were working with their machetes to widen the clearing, two of them lit a campfire so that Roustan, their chief, could cook the meal of rice and a big lizard they had caught during our jungle walk. Depending on what had been caught each day, our menu was composed of rice and monkeys, rice and big snakes, and rice and lizard. It was all surprisingly delicious.

"And now my revenge on the leeches," said J.F., whose canvas shoes looked as if they were bleeding. He took off everything but his underpants. Just from between his toes on one foot, J.F.'s harvest was amazing: ten leeches, or to be more accurate, the remains of ten leeches. Max and I also took advantage of the daylight for our mutual leech inspection, which would become one of our main evening occupations. Each day we killed an average of thirty leeches. It was never enough to satisfy our need for vengeance.

The intermittent rain started again while the porters were building their dormitory, a wooden floor raised about eight inches above the ground, on which they would all sleep side by side. The height off the ground was meant less as protection from insects or snakes than against being awakened by a sudden flood. The roof was made from plastic sheets interwoven with branches.

Max, J.F., and I stretched out our hammocks between some trees. About twenty inches above each hammock we strung a rope to hold a mosquito net and a large plastic sheet that was our umbrella.

"Shit!" said J.F., coming to me. "Douch, I've lost my plastic cover."

"How?"

"I don't know! All I know is now I don't have anything to protect me against the rain."

"Have you looked everywhere?" Max asked him.

"Did you look among the porters?" I added.

"Everywhere! Maybe I lost it when I fell . . . or maybe the boatmen stole it."

"That's possible, too," said Max.

"You can hang your hammock beneath Max's or mine," I told

him. "That way, you too will be protected from the rain. Let me see . . . yeah, I think you should attach your hammock beneath mine. My trees seem stronger than Max's."

Between the two trees, the ground was cluttered with bushes and branches. Since the hammock bends, I had to attach mine about six feet or so from the ground. Above that point I fixed the rope to hold my mosquito net and the plastic cover that would also shelter J.F. I accomplished this while standing on an unstable scaffolding of various tree trunks with J.F. holding my buttocks. Then, J.F.'s mosquito net was attached beneath my hammock.

Just before dinner we washed ourselves in one of the many small streams that ran through the jungle. This was the same water we used all day long to quench our thirst, without purifying or boiling it or adding any chemicals to it. If it were too muddy and rotten, we used a small portable filter to clean it. Although very reluctant at first, Max and J.F. accepted the idea after I had explained the reasons.

After our bath, while J.F. was taking care of two porters whose feet were badly wounded by sharp stone fragments and wood splinters, I noticed that the trunk containing our survival food was not closed. I opened it all the way just out of curiosity and checked its contents. Two big tubes of concentrated milk had disappeared. We had been robbed.

The porters swore that they had never seen them, but we searched and J.F. found them under the wooden floor of their dormitory.

Apart from use in emergencies, the concentrated milk tubes had no intrinsic value. But it was stealing. And where is the difference between stealing two tubes of milk and something else? Would our lives be forfeited just to get hold of the money I carried in a small leather bag hanging around my neck?

The porters had seen me paying for the food in Tabang and giving some money to the boatmen of Ma Atan. They knew where I hid my money, which for me was just enough to finance the rest of the trek but to them was a real treasure. All of them together, including their whole families, could live on it for at least two years. So it was important to deal with it immediately in order to avoid problems in the future that could put our lives in jeopardy. We were in the middle of nowhere without weapons, facing nine armed men who could be sweet and obliging guys or could suddenly become fearless desperadoes.

Therefore I convened a meeting of the entire party to play a "game," one I had often played during previous expeditions and to which I probably still owe my life. The game is based on the fact that among the societies of tradition the power of "respecting others" is tremendous. It can protect a man from theft and even death. It concerns everyone who is linked to another by cultural identity or tied to another by family, clan, or tribe. Everyone is involved because it had been installed by authority—whether it is the myth represented by an authority or the authority itself—as a code of life, or a rule to follow on pain of severe punishment. (In our society, "respecting others" finds fewer and fewer adherents, except for believers who belong to religions in which "respect" is a basic commandment.)

So, my "game" consisted of defining the limited society that the nine porters and ourselves composed. I dictated rules and codes of life—no lies, no robbery, no disobedience to the authority—to be followed by everyone without question. Being the guarantor of these rules, I automatically became the authority. To help make authority unquestionable, I needed my two companions. We agreed that from then on I would talk with the porters as little as possible, except to congratulate them or scold them if someone were to commit a fault. Max and J.F. would act as intermediaries. They would tell the porters stories to confirm my power and severity. They would spread the news that I was carrying a mysterious gun, so powerful that we could not even use it to hunt animals. That mysterious weapon hanging on my belt was, in fact, my light meter, which had the shape of a strange revolver.

Also, to show the porters that we were constantly keeping an eye on them, I established a night watch on the camp with each of us taking a turn for three hours or so.

The rain stopped just as I was the first one to start.

My first night in the unchartered territory.

My daughter,

The pulsations of the jungle sometimes scare me. Perhaps because I still cannot understand "her" language. As soon as possible, I will identify myself to her, the better to feel her and touch her, the better to hear her vegetal whisperings and slow breathing. Soon I will discover her shudders of dread, her warnings of possible danger. I will cross her without disturbing the order of her thick hair. I will break her resistance to be better caressed by her shadow.

Your Dad

Nightfall is announced by a strange sound like the whine of an electric saw or the kind of piercing siren that increases its volume by pulsations. When it reaches its maximum amplitude, it repeats the last notes a few more times and then suddenly dies. The sound spreads farther and farther. Made by an insect three times as large as our giant cicada, this sound—which lasts for only a few minutes—starts around 6:00 P.M. and then again around 6:00 A.M., marking the transitions between day and night.

With these calls, certain other sounds would die and others arise. The music of the light is different from that of the darkness, for Borneo's opera is made of an inimitable chorus whose rhythms mark the different states of the night and of the day.

Engendered by the strident cry of the cicada, the jungle's nocturnal symphony resounds in the cathedral of trees with an astonishing diversity of sounds, tones, and volumes. Each sound is distinct but somehow perfectly integrated into a chorus. Some sounds are dreadful solos when heard in isolation but perfectly adapted to the whole. Others are like a never-ending, melancholy moan, a symphonic base line composed of the unending chatter of crickets and frogs.

In the morning, we were awakened (even Max who slept through his guard duty) by the porters relighting the campfire that had been drowned by the never-ending night rain. As they worked they talked and laughed, recounting our falls and mishaps of the previous day, punctuating their remarks by loud explosive farts and never-ending belches.

Our canvas shoes were sopping. Our clothes had started to mold. (Always wearing humid or wet clothes is one of the toughest prices to pay.) In a desperate attempt to wear a dry, warm polo shirt, I got too close to the flames and burned it. I was left with a still damp but now charred polo shirt.

After a copious six o'clock breakfast made of rice and the remains of our dinner (it had to be copious, since we did not really stop for lunch), we broke camp.

And each day it was the same. Although we were using up

supplies, each day our burdens got heavier. Usually for the first
hour or two we had to walk through a mist, sometimes lighter,
sometimes denser, but always wet. The slow white smoke would
rise from the cold soil and from all the organic beings expiring
with the first heat of the sun. Breathing like locomotives, we
would renew our duel against exhaustion, our hand-to-hand
combat to keep our balance and prevent falls into the rotten soil.
Our faces burned under the bite of sweat and rain and the heat
of the vegetal sauna.

Often the steep slopes were slashed by large, deep fissures,
whose bottoms were filled with small streams or stagnant water.
Sometimes, instead of passing through all these barriers, we
could cross above them by walking very carefully on tree trunks
covered with moss and fungus. Other times, thanks to networks
of fallen trees, we could walk faster over flat swamps. Some of
these trees had fallen by chance, but others had been put there
deliberately by Dayaks or nomad Punans to ease their own
passages. Thanks to these signs, we knew we were on the right
track even when there was no track at all.

The poisonous vines called for our blood; the smells were
lost in our mud-clogged noses. With the mud, the slippery
dead leaves, and the leeches, it all seemed endless, each hour an
eternity.

The walk was more brutal. The straps of our rucksacks burnt
our wet skin and seemed about to tear away our shoulders. We
searched through our rucksacks for something we could throw
away. We even discarded our toothpaste and brushes and
cleaned our teeth as our porters did, by using a special small
root. We left a trail of debris that would almost have allowed us
to find our way back to Djelini.

O̲ur first days of jungle had been bathed by the
excitement of confronting a new element. I was filming everything that caught my eye. And everything did. Everything had
to be filmed because it carried such exotic beauty. The lianas
hanging with backlighting. Thorns seen in close-up. Colorful
flowers. Various insects, birds, butterflies. A snake frozen motionless on the trail by our noise. Big ten-foot lizards sleeping
on branches overhanging streams. Because of the lack of light
inside the jungle, filming was difficult; but we succeeded thanks
to the high-sensitivity film we were using. Even for close-ups I

shot as much as I could without using the tripod, because the mud, the steep terrain, and the lianas, vines, and other vegetation and bushes provided poor footing in the jungle. After a while exhaustion took over, driving out not my wonder but my will to film.

Soon I didn't even want to shoot pictures of a python that moved slowly on a branch above us, or the crocodile, who, perhaps was hoping that one of us would fall from our thin bridge made of a dead tree lying high above his stream. The screams of monkeys and the calls of birds were lost in the strenuous efforts of my heart. Its beats resounded under my skin and behind my eyes and drove all thoughts from my brain. We had only one obsession, the next halt, when we could lie down under the rain of sweat and water. But after a few minutes, we would be called by porters, and we would have to lift our heavy bodies once more to follow them. Even if one of us had just drunk so much water that he was about to vomit, he was already looking forward to the next stream where he could drink again.

The mountain slopes became so abrupt that we were obliged to move almost perpendicularly on the sides of deep canyons. J.F. fell again and again. I moved ahead of him, trying to show him exactly where to put his feet. Still he fell. Through a hole in the forest, I saw the porters cutting their way with machetes on the far slope of a narrow canyon. I stopped, took my camera out of its case, and, needing the tele lens, called to J.F. to bring the lens box quickly. I waited patiently. Then, realizing that shortly the porters would be out of my sight, I screamed out to him. No answer. Furious to have missed a great shot and suddenly worried, I stumbled back the way I had come. Five minutes later I found him sitting on the ground, leaning on his rucksack, and sucking a giant tube of concentrated milk, his face gaunt with exhaustion.

"What are you doing here?" I yelled, possessed by a sudden anger.

"I can't take it any more . . . sorry!" he answered, ready to break into tears.

"Max and I are making efforts to keep the milk for emergencies, and here you are, sucking it as if it was a feeding bottle."

"Sorry, I couldn't resist."

"Then don't carry them. Come on and follow me with the tripod. You're here for that."

I raved on, provoked by my own exhaustion, until we reached a stream where Max was waiting. Without a word I drank and then went on, leaving my two friends behind.

(Extracts from J.F.'s journal) . . . I take a small ten-minute rest with Max next to the river. More patient than Douch, he helps me and gives me advice. The porters are already far away! Many times we must stop, unload, and search for the way. I stagger, fall, my feet are so heavy. I have only one obsession, to reach the next stream, drink and rest. Sometimes my tongue sticks to my palate, the saliva, what little there is of it, is rare and thick. I can't stand that tripod, which is the source of a great number of falls. I get Max to exchange with me and then realize that his case is filled with still cameras and is heavier than the tripod, and I ask Max to return it to me.

After a half-hour walk from the stream where I left Max and J.F., I suddenly couldn't find a single mark left by the porters. I called to Roustan. Then I called to J.F. and Max. Nobody answered. After first being amplified by the jungle, my voice disappeared into the vegetation. It was as if human voices had no right to exist in that vegetal world. I waited motionless, sitting on a dead trunk. Suddenly a liana started to move like a snake. It took me a while to realize that it *was* a snake. Often called "liana snake" or "minute snake," it is supposed to kill quickly according to the natives. Whenever it falls on a man from a branch, its small mouth bites on the face or the neck, and there is no way to make a tourniquet to slow the progression of the venom. I was ready for its bite now.

During our progression through the dark jungle, the porters would scream often. It was a way to warn snakes, bears, panthers, and other deadly animals of our passage. At their screams, the jungle became silent; the fauna had time to devise the best camouflage and reach the most protected place from which to watch. They froze, literally stopping their breath, and waited for the danger to go away before coming back to life and moving again.

In the Sahara Desert, even at ten feet a viper can still be dangerous, because it doesn't feel protected by the small stones. Its insecurity can push it to deadly attack. Here in the jungle, we could stop two feet away from a cobra and the snake would not even think of biting because it feels secure, hidden in the vegetation.

I have experienced this amazing slow awakening of the jungle's fauna many times. Sitting on the ground to relax, deafened by the screams of my heartbeats, I would lie in perfect stillness, not even chasing the hordes of mosquitoes which darkened my hands. In the silence, I would witness the coming back to life of the frightened fauna. What was just a branch would start to breathe. A long forked tongue would come out of a mouth to "feel" if the danger had gone. An invisible python would reappear by moving its head. In a small stream, a piece of vegetation would slowly come to the surface to take a breath.

Max and J.F. finally appeared. My anger returned when J.F. proposed that he carry my camera instead of the tripod.

"You're crazy!" I yelled at him. "I need to carry the camera myself so I can grab it whenever needed! Listen, guy, you're here to carry my tripod today, tomorrow and forever!"

"I don't give a shit about your tripod!" he yelled, throwing it in front of me.

"Listen, Douch," said Max, "this tripod is not—"

Without leaving him the chance to end his sentence, I jumped to my feet, grabbed the tripod, and moved on. "Next time, I will take real men with me!" My anger helped me find the porters' tracks.

To move fast with the tripod on my shoulders was impossible, but I wanted to give J.F. a lesson. After several more falls and a long struggle to free the tripod from ferns, vines, and lianas, I abandoned the cause of my trouble.

In spite of our daily arguments and disputes, each time we pitched camp, anger and irritation gave way to peace and friendship.

Each time we approached a mountaintop, the weather became colder and the forest afforded more space between the trees. The parasitic vines, instead of strangling the trees, decorated them from head to foot with long, dark-green tufted ornaments, as if for a tropical Christmas. The clouds hung on the treetops like spun glass.

The walk became easier. But not for long. As if the vegetal rear guard were assigned the duty of stopping any human parasites, the clawed vines continued to bite our hands, our arms, our shoulders, before lodging themselves deep in our flesh. The thorns drew bloody furrows through our perspiration-soaked shirts. We were not the only victims of this organic savagery. The trees themselves had to fight against the lianas, which strangled and then sucked out their vital substance. We crossed many corpses that had lost the battle.

The porters finally understood that we were not in this jungle for a marathon, but to make a movie. Many times each day we found them sitting on top of the mountain or in a clearing complaining about our frequent halts. For them, the stops were more tiring than the walking. Bent over by the heavy loads, their bodies would reach a cruising speed we never obtained. Then, at my order, they would have to break their forward motion, stop, unload the boxes, wait, load their weights, regain their feet, and regain their momentum . . . to stop again . . . and again.

So we found a compromise. Each morning we all left camp at the same time but the porters kept going, clearly marking the trees with machetes so we could follow. At two in the afternoon, they would stop and set up camp. If by four we hadn't joined them, one of them would come back to find us. In that manner, at last we could appreciate the forest and rediscover the sounds of the wildlife that had been silenced since the beginning of our trip by the porters' loud voices.

Often exhaustion threw us down to rest on the rotten soil. It rained sweat and heat. When would it end? At each small stream, clean or dirty, we plunged our heads into the water and drank . . . drank up new energy . . . new consolation.

And the daily leech inspection. And the porters' feet carrying bloody wounds. And guard duty under the nightly rain. And the cold awakening. And the wearing of damp clothes in the foggy morning. However, I could find the strength to film and collect plants, insects, butterflies, samples of water, at the request of the Belgian Museum of Natural History. I also found the peace to dream.

We almost lost J.F. again but soon found him hanging by the tripod to two old trees that had saved him from rocks one hundred feet below. A porter also lost his balance and fell. He slowed his fall and finally stopped it only by driving his fingers into crevices in the rock. In the abyss below him, his load exploded. No more electric generator now, so I got rid of the gas to operate it. Two days later it was the turn of another porter, who in similar circumstances lost his basket containing the powerful batteries and lights for night shooting and also one of our inflatable boats.

Almost every day had a special danger. One afternoon we found the fresh marks of a panther, which hunts only in the dark. We hurried on, eager to find our camp and rest. That night, I was awakened by a soft growl. I felt my hammock trembling! Something big was in the tree to which our hammocks were attached. Lying on my back in total terror, I squeezed my large dagger in my hand, pointing it above me. Soft growls approached my head just on the other side of the thin plastic sheet. The hammock trembled again. The thing *jumped* on me! I screamed. In the hammock beneath me J.F. screamed. With my two hands I drove the dagger through the mosquito net, through the plastic cover, and into . . . the *panther!*

Everyone awakened! And a few seconds later, everyone laughed!

The rope on which both hammocks were stretched had started to slip down the trunk. The move made the hammock tremble, resulting in a noise that in my head became the growl of a panther. With the shaking, an old branch from the tree had fallen on top of me.

J.F. imagined another scenario. Lower down, his hammock had come into contact with the bushes beneath it. He imagined that he was being bitten on his bottom. Both of us were victims of imagination in the wild black night.

O ver the next few days we slowly trained our bodies to endure the ordeals. We climbed higher, with much more ease. Since the last valley, we had been able to find more markings of Dayak trails. Here we would find cuts in tree trunks. There we would find three thin trunks linked together in a long footbridge over crevasses or deep swamps. Farther on we would discover traces of passage along dead trees that served as natural footbridges. By following their zigzagging maze from one tree to another, we moved more quickly than by trying to walk straight north.

I hoped that these Dayak trails would lead us to one of their villages, but none did. I knew it was a hopeless dream—Dayaks never leave clear trails because that would show their enemies the locations of their villages.

During our climb J.F. almost collapsed, his eyes full of bright stars. Our heartbeats galloped, our temples buzzed, there was pain behind our eyes. Were we victims of excessive doses of quinine? Possibly.

Once again, the secondary forest gave way to more open spaces and fantastic displays of flora and fauna. We saw deer, wild boar, and a Borneo bear which, although belonging to the smallest species, can weigh as much as two hundred pounds. These bears, which the Dayaks call "sun bears" because of the yellow spots on their chests, are—to our misfortune—good tree climbers. (Later I was to discover this exceptional talent of the bears under most unhappy circumstances.)

We photographed the *nepenthes,* a huge carnivorous plant formed by a tube six or seven inches long and two inches wide. Its inner surface is smooth and filled with liquid enzymes that digest the insects attracted by its perfume. While we watched, it captured an unlucky worm.

We observed gibbons, orangutans, and other monkeys. And inch-and-a-half-long carnivorous ants, in never-ending columns two-feet-wide. Multicolored, noisy parrots were everywhere. We saw the flight of the *calao,* a big bird whose screams haunt the jungle. Its strange large beak is prized by the Dayaks for ornaments and by the Chinese who believe it to be an aphrodisiac. The most amazing species of calao is the *rhinoceros calao,* a three-foot-long bird that has a red or orange horn covering its beak. When the female is laying eggs, the male confines her inside the nest with a covering of his excrement and leaves only a small opening for the food he brings to this future mother.

On my camera box one morning there was a deadly black *death's head spider,* about six inches in diameter including its legs and wearing on its back a white skull. The porters wanted to kill it.

"Very dangerous!" said Roustan.

I stopped them at the last moment, explaining that I wanted to film it first. I discussed with Max and J.F. how we could immobilize it so that I could shoot some close-ups without risking that it would jump on my face and bite me.

"The best way would be to put it asleep," said J.F. "I have some ether in my medical supplies."

"Good idea," I said. "Max, find a small saucepan to cover the spider, so J.F. can slide a cotton ball soaked with ether underneath it."

Max came back with a pan. With a stick, I pushed the spider away from my camera box. But the spider moved with such speed that Max kept missing it with the upside-down saucepan. Finally, after many attempts, he succeeded. While I changed the lens on one of the movie cameras, J.F. carefully slid the ether-soaked cotton under the pan. The spider escaped, and the chase began. Finally, it was trapped and the ether ball placed underneath the pan.

"Are you sure she is asleep?" I asked after a while, quite nervous.

"She should be!" said Max, slowly taking away the saucepan. And she was indeed. After I took a few shots of her whole body, I worked up enough courage to approach within a few inches of her head for some additional close-ups.

"What bothers me is that she doesn't move . . . she looks dead," I said. "J.F., bring some sewing thread, we will tie her down."

We tied a thread—attached to small sticks driven into the ground—to the end of each of her legs. Then we waited for her to wake up. This way I was able to make, safely, some extreme close-ups of the spider moving.

On another day when I was alone, I stopped to pee, making a game of it. My boyish game was to try to drown the ants walking on the roots of a bush, similar to a fern, whose one-inch-long leaves were separately attached all along the central stem. Suddenly, touched by the drops of urine, the small leaves along the central stem started to close, squeezing themselves against the stem. Then the foot-long stem itself bent down as if the whole bush were dying. In a short time the bush was lower by about one foot. Marking the spot, I went looking for my companions and found Max.

"Max! Follow me, quickly!"

"What for?"

"It's astonishing, or maybe I'm becoming insane!"

"What happened?"

Leading the way to the spot, I explained. "While I was peeing on some ants, a bush moved as if it were dying!"

When we returned to the marked spot the bush had resumed its former position.

"Max, I promise, it moved as if it were dying. Pee! You will see! Pee!"

"Easy, Douch. Come with me, you need a rest."

"How much do you want to bet?"

Finally, Max urinated and the bush died again. This plant belongs to the family of the *mimosa pudica*, generally called *the sensitive*. In Borneo, it can grow to giant proportions.

Remembering an interesting article by an American researcher about the odd behaviors of plants, I squatted next to the leaves and brought the flame from my lighter close enough to burn some of them. Immediately, the whole bush bent over. Then, with my lighter not burning, I approached close to the leaves of a similar plant a little farther away. No reaction. I came back to the plant whose leaves I had touched with flame, and before I had even touched the lighter the bush bent down. As a last experiment, still without a flame and without touching the leaves, I approached from another side of the plant that I had already burned. The leaves, which were about eight feet away from those I had burned, also started to bend—slowly at first, and then faster, until the whole plant had completely bowed. Somehow the plant had recognized the danger.

Moving toward a high mountaintop, we entered a new kind of jungle, this one a strange, dead forest. No noise. Just silent tree trunks with almost leafless branches covered by a luxuriant moss as thick as a coating of wild lichens. Tentacles of moss fell from branch to branch, giving again the impression that the trees were decorated for Christmas.

The trees were prisoners of the exuberant moss that linked them together with its gigantic webs. In some places the brown-green vegetal cobwebs actually seemed to hold a dead tree erect. These giant wooden candlesticks stretched into a sky of mist, sending wordless prayers to the divinities. Such sights of nature reaching toward the gods must have inspired men to build pyramids and stone cathedrals.

Farther on and higher up, a chaos of gigantic stones separated sky and mountain. I could no longer measure how high we were for we had lost our precision altimeter with the last box that had fallen, but the air told us we were climbing higher.

From this stony mountain peak, rising from the middle of the dead forest and bathed by shreds of cool, sticky mist and fog, we finally saw the blue sky and what was still to be crossed: more mountains, more deep valleys covered by unbroken vegetation. The puffy treetops spread out like a soft carpet rolling to an infinitely distant horizon. Somewhere beyond that carpet was the Kayan River. Looking at this endless virgin space yet to be crossed, we wondered if we had the strength and will to reach the other side.

At the beginning of our trek, I was too excited to think about the far future. Then, while trying to adapt my body and mind to the ordeal of our journey, my thoughts became muffled by exhaustion. Now acclimated to our daily efforts, my mind started to function again.

I began to have another, deeper appreciation of life. Living in the jungle seemed to scrape away the old, heavy bark that long had wrapped my thoughts, feelings, and reactions. I had lost my "civilized" coating. Life here seemed easier to handle, less complicated to understand. I felt ready to utilize nature's secret teachings, to restore the most primal parts of myself.

I started to become aware of the smells that indicated the proximity of a swamp, the differences in heat that announced a portion of jungle cloaked by thorny bushes; the size of leaves gave me a sense of our altitude, the thin breath of freshness that signaled the presence of a nearby stream. Without even seeing the sky, I felt myself moving throughout the entire cosmos. It was like walking inside the book of the universe.

Even though Max and J.F. were also experiencing new awareness, being changed in subtle ways, we didn't talk very much with one another about this. Perhaps we were too tired to do so. Perhaps one can only talk about a new birth when it is over.

Going down the mountain, at 4:00 P.M., we made camp on the sandy shore of an ocher stream, probably colored by an underground deposit of rusted iron. We swiftly entered our evening routine. The porters built their dormitory, washed themselves, prepared the fresh monkey meat, and cooked the food. We stretched our hammocks. J.F. wrapped the films I had shot and put them in the container. Max made notations about the pictures he had made. I took note of what I had filmed. And already it was dinner time. Then the sun disappeared as we moved to sleep, except for whoever had the first guard duty.

CHAPTER NINE

Abandoned by Our Porters in the Middle of Nowhere

What is freedom? Freedom is the right to choose: The right to create for yourself the alternatives of choice. Without the possibility of choice and exercise of choice a man is not a man but a member, an instrument, a thing.

ARCHIBALD MacLEISH

With the passing weeks, the joy of our discoveries started to diminish. Although our now well-trained bodies allowed us to fight the rough terrain with more ease, we started to be weakened by dysentery and by bouts of despair. J.F. was the most frequent victim. Fortunately, discouragement didn't touch all three of us at the same time or we would have had to abandon ourselves to the jungle. On the contrary, when one of us was despondent, the other two reacted with a boost of optimism and courage to fight their own despair.

I was becoming paranoid about my filmmaking, wondering if the films would be able to endure the high humidity of constant rain. In spite of all precautions, there was so much moisture in the lens that as soon as the heat started, the inner surfaces were covered with condensation. I spent hours heating them with the flames of our campfire to clear them. Three of my best lenses were already unusable. The inner surfaces of two were covered with fungus and a small ant had penetrated, grown, and died in the third lens.

In the silence of one march I became an accountant. With much less money than the cost of this expedition, I calculated I could be bathing in Bali or lying in the shadows of coconut trees on some lost Brazilian beach, my body sensually caressed by feminine fingers. I pictured exotic women of the Tropics created by Aphrodite, the goddess of love, and formed by Eros, the divinity of holy sexuality. I became a sex fantasist. I could be loved by three women. No, by ten! Ten women to make me forget the hell I was enduring. And fifteen more to make me forget that I must walk barefoot to diminish the pain from the deep crevices that a fungus had cut between my toes. And twenty more women to make me forget that I must walk bare-chested because my sweat-impregnated polo shirt burned my skin, also torn by fungus.

Perhaps the porters, also weakened by exhaustion, had similar thoughts while walking through the bottom of a valley in intense humidity. Fantasy and paranoia grew in my mind like jungle vegetation. I was worried by J.F.'s condition, and yet I didn't want to admit it in front of him and perhaps push him over the thin borderline between success and failure, sanity and loss of control. It was sufficiently difficult for me to admit that, after all, we were totally at the porters' mercy.

Just as we thought we were about to leave the inhospitable valley, the worst came: a large marsh-covered area. Before crossing it, the porters coated their anuses and buttocks with tobacco juice to fight the vicious leeches. Having no more soap to coat ourselves and knowing that tobacco juice would burn our sensitive parts, we made plugs from gauze and adhesive plaster.

The crossing of these swamps was a horror. Although increasingly nervous and depressed, J.F. was still able to drag himself about. But often Max and I had to help our porters, who were bent under their loads. Trembling under the effort, their feet would disappear into the thick, sticky, stinky earth. At each step we had to help one another pull our feet from the mud.

Our faces—bent at more than a right angle by the weight of the material pressing on our shoulders, the backs of the neck and our heads—were pushed toward the mud. On all fours, we moved forward like the beasts of burden we had become. Fully as dirty as our feet, our hands would touch our faces, depositing a layer of mud that made us look as if we were at a health spa trying to get rid of wrinkles. The dirt drying inside of our noses and ears made a buzzing sound as if an animal had introduced itself into our bodies.

On the other side of the valley, we reached a new forest and slowly began climbing its slopes. One day around three P.M., we arrived in a small clearing in which there was a wooden structure similar to the dormitory built daily by our porters. Next to the shelter were the remains of a campfire with still unburned wood and dry ashes. The last rain had stopped only around four or five in the morning.

"Roustan," I called, "*apa?*" ("What's that?")

"Punan, tuan! It's a camp of Punans!"

"How do you know it's a Punan camp?"

"Because nobody else would live in this area. Look, tuan!" he said, showing me a big terra-cotta jar sealed with bark and wrapped in leaves. Inside there was cooked rice and a piece of smoked meat. "You see, tuan?" he continued. "It's their food. This is a Punan passage camp!"

"What do you mean by a 'passage camp'?" asked Max.

"This food left here means this camp is on their route. Whenever traveling, they stop here!" answered Roustan, suddenly very excited.

"Douch, come over here!" yelled J.F. Bent over the campfire, he seemed to have made a discovery.

"What is it?"

"Touch that! The stones and the wood are still warm."

I called Roustan and asked, "Roustan, if Punans camped here last night, would they come back soon?"

"Yes, if they are on a hunt. Punans are hunters! With blowguns! So, never know!"

I could see in his eyes that he was becoming more and more uncomfortable.

"What's going on, Roustan?"

"Ah, tuan, Punans are wild. Savages! *Orang bodo!* [Insane men!] They're ferocious in their own territory."

"We have not come to hurt them."

"You must understand, tuan, if they don't catch anything while hunting, they think we have chased away their game, and they will kill us."

I had never seen Roustan behaving like this before. He rarely showed his emotions and now he was clearly disturbed and, I feared, even on the edge of losing control.

I came back to my two companions. "Well, my friends, I hope Roustan is exaggerating. If not, I hope the Punans kill enough wild game."

Max pointed out that the porters had gathered together for a meeting in a way that they had never done. To break the tension of the moment, I yelled to them, "Okay! Let's go!" But the porters stood motionless while Roustan stepped up to approach me as a spokesman on their behalf.

Looking aft in our boat on the Mahakan on the way to Tabang.

Max asleep in his hammock on the way to Tabang.

J.F.

A porter, cigarette in mouth, carrying a sixty-pound case across the swamps in the uncharted region.

Small author in large jungle.

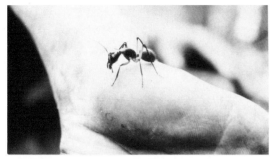

Giant ant on the side of my hand. They are almost big enough for dessert.

Flying lizards climb trees and then glide to their next destination sometimes over 100 feet away.

Roustan carrying our fresh caught dinner—a giant water lizard.

A Sekapan in ceremonial dress.

A shoulder carrier for Punan babies, with panther and bear teeth.

An old Punan woman
with elongated earlobes
and flower.

A Dayak woman with elongated earlobes.

Dayak ancestor pole protecting the village from evil spirits.

On the day of my initiation, the Iban women put on ceremonial dress.

An Iban warrior with blowgun. I borrowed his poisonous dart before taking this picture.

A garland of human heads hanging from the veranda in the Iban village.

The pilework underneath
the Iban long house.

The chief, holding his most recent trophy; Tawa, with his mandau;
and the author looking concerned.

The tattoo indicates that this man has cut more than 200 heads. He is sharpening a mandau.

The neck tattoo that will free the wearer's spirit if he is beheaded.

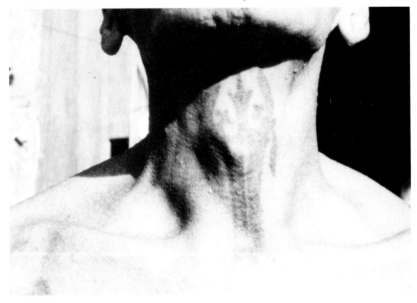

"*Tidak,* tuan [No, sir], we better camp here!"

"But we still have time before halting."

He looked at his companions and said: "Tidak, tuan, we're tired."

Rather than fight with the porters and possibly lose my command of the party, I accepted their proposal and offered each of them a pack of cigarettes as a way to calm them.

My insecurity made me edgy. I started an argument with Max because he had left behind the rope and the snap hook used to attach his hammock to the trees. J.F. said that I was acting like a stupid child. That increased my anger. I argued even more fiercely.

Finally, realizing that my two companions were getting as crazy as I was, I decided to walk around the camp and hang on the trees some of the gifts that I had carried since Tabang—tobacco leaves, betel nuts, pepper leaves, and lime—so that Punans, if they came, couldn't miss these marks of our good intentions toward them. If we were to meet the Punan I would have preferred to be in front of their village, because then it's easy to learn where one stands. Here things were less formalized, and they might feel more threatened and become more dangerous.

We could divide the people of tradition into three different groups. To the first group belong the tribes who have never heard of or had any contact with a white man. To the second group belong the tribes who have never had any contact with a white man but who have heard about him in positive or negative ways. To the last group belong the tribes who have had contact good and bad.

My past experiences had shown me that the first group will not kill the white man when they meet him. Having white skin he resembles an albino and amongst traditional people albinos usually enjoy great respect, because their skin is the color of the day, the sun, and the stars. Also, physical difference is often a divine mark. Instead of being rejected, the "different" is considered an asset to the tribe. Some tribes even believe that the different one has magical power, even though he will not or cannot display it. In the Bolivian and Peruvian Andes, as in many places around the world, the shaman often has a physical handicap.

At his first contact, the white explorer does not have his life threatened by the second or third groups either, if they have heard something positive. However, it can happen that a tribe doesn't want the explorer's presence. In this case, instead of killing him, they will threaten him or indicate that they want him to go away by some symbolic actions—for instance, not accepting the gifts he has put around the camp.

Of course, approaching a tribe that has had a negative experience with a white man is risky and one never knows to which group an unknown tribe might belong.

Upon first contact with an explorer, a tribe will often simulate an attack. It is a sign both of respect and fear, for they too have no way of measuring the invader's power. And the basic hope-infusing threat is: if the foreigner came with bad intentions, he will not be afraid of the simulated threat, while the bad spirits that may have accompanied him will be frightened and leave.

After all my gifts were hung around the campsite, I started to walk back to the camp. On my way, I encountered a narrow track so well drawn that I didn't know if it had been made by Punans or by wild boars. I followed the path in the opposite direction of the camp and, after a short walk, reached a small stream whose banks were crowded with animal footprints, mainly of wild boars.

Both relieved and disappointed that the track was made by animals, I followed it back to the camp. Just as I started to hear the porters' voices, my eyes were attracted by something strange in front of me. An eight-inch-long poisonous dart was driven into the center of a small circle drawn on the middle of the track.

I touched the dart's flight-stabilizer "feathers." They were made of a soft, light wood and they were dry. That meant the dart had been put there some time since morning. It was a message for me, a warning, a prohibition not to go farther. Seized by a sudden anxiety, I looked around for signs of an ambush. My legs became like rubber and I sank to the ground, staring at the dart, afraid to move and afraid to stay.

The only sure think was that if Punans wanted to kill us, they could already have shot us with their poisoned darts. Were they trying to give us a chance to fly away before they killed us? We had two courses of action. We could run and show them how scared we were. Or we could ignore their warning, continue our walk through their territory, and somehow try to show our desire for friendship. Then they would have to guess how scared we were. If they had seen me on my knees, they would not have had to guess.

There was no doubt about what I wanted to do; however, I decided to take only my two companions into my confidence. If I told the porters, who were already very scared of the Punans, they would certainly fly away. Hoping that neither porters nor Punans could see me, I buried the poisoned dart and erased the circle drawn on the track.

"Douch," said Max, upon hearing my report, "I think you're wrong."

"What do you mean?"

"I really think Punans placed their warning sign after we arrived in their camp. If they really wanted to scare us away, they would have put the dart in the middle of the camp so we couldn't miss it. But they put it where we would see it on our way out tomorrow."

"Well," I said, quite relieved, "if that's true, our lives are not in danger, at least not tonight."

As we were ready to eat the evening meal, I asked the chief of the porters, "Tell me, Roustan, how far is it still to the first Dayak village?"

"Very soon, tuan! Maybe one day, maybe three!"

Hoping to keep their spirits up for the days ahead, I said, "I have a proposition for you and your friends. If we find enough Dayaks at that village to carry our stuff farther, all of you who want to go back to Tabang are free to do so, okay? I'll pay all of you what I promised. As for those of you who want to go on with us, I'll discuss a new salary with you. Go now, tell that to your friends."

In spite of this good news, our porters didn't laugh or tell jokes during dinner as they usually did. They were as quiet as if it were their last meal. One of them told stories about his father-in-law who had been killed by Dayaks a few years before. And Roustan remarked again that the Punans are vicious, ferocious, and savage.

As soon as I awoke, I went to check the gifts I had hung, hoping that some had been taken. According to what some missionaries had told me, if they were gone it would signify that Punans had accepted the gifts and, consequently, a possible contact with us. If this were the case, they would replace our gifts with theirs.

Nothing was missing. However, I found evidence that Punans had come during the night and walked around the hanging gifts. I knew that they were Punans by the huge, wide size of the footprints left on the muddy soil. The mayor in Tabang had told me how to recognize Punans' footprints, which are shorter but wider than those of other Dayak ethnic groups.

After a large breakfast, the porters, as usual, loaded their baskets and attached them to their backs. Since I didn't want to carry anything that could make the Punans believe I was armed, I attached the box containing the movie camera to one of the porter's baskets.

Roustan came to me and said that, in spite of my offer, we must all return to Tabang. Besides, he added, the porters had too little left to eat.

"What? How come you don't have any more rice?" I asked. "I gave you 10,000 rupees to buy rice."

"We didn't spend all that money to buy food."

"Why not?"

"We wanted to leave more money for our families."

"Well, that's your problem. We are going on."

"Give us more rice, tuan, and we'll stay with you," added Roustan.

In other circumstances, I would not have given in so easily, but this was a crucial moment. I had no other help and had yet to contact the Dayaks or even the Punan so I asked J.F. to bring out our reserve of rice.

"Shit, Douch," he said, looking in our reserves box, "there's almost no rice!"

"What?" I yelled.

"It's a fact, man, all the reserves are empty, even those we kept as gifts."

In a fury, I called all the porters to gather around me. "Someone has stolen rice! I want to know who!"

No answers.

"Did you take it or not?"

They remained mute, staring almost challengingly at me.

"Well, in that case, I will take 1000 rupees out of each of your salaries."

The porters' response was to untie their baskets and drop them to the ground. The box containing my movie camera came loose and almost fell into the remains of the campfire. Now seething with rage, I went to the porter who had dropped it and stopped in front of him, my six-foot-three towering over his five-foot-five frame. With a threatening gesture, I stared at him and slowly said, "Take your load back!"

Without a word, he bent down, took the movie camera box, attached it to his basket, and once again positioned it on his back.

Then, casting an angry look at each porter in turn, I said, "Now we are going on! Understand?" They exchanged a few words among themselves and asked that I pay them right away. I refused.

"In that case, we're going away back to Tabang!" they said, abandoning their loads and moving away.

I was seized with a sudden fit of anxiety. I thought it unlikely that they would go back to Tabang without the balance of their pay, which, according to our deal, was to be paid only at the end of the crossing of the uncharted territory. I believed they were thinking that I was going to give in out of fear of being abandoned in the middle of the jungle and accept all of their conditions. But that was their mistake. I was not at all ready to give in to their blackmail. Besides, by doing that I would show them our inferiority, thus our vulnerability. I told Max and J.F. to sit on the boxes, light a cigarette, and act as if they didn't care, as if we were on a picnic in a park in Brussels. We must have given a great performance because after a while, the porters, who had hidden in the jungle to see what we would do, returned to the camp.

"Roustan," I called. "Ask your friends what they intend to do. As far as I'm concerned, I want to go in ten minutes. Understand?"

"They . . . hmm . . . they want a double salary," said Roustan, visibly embarrassed.

I slowly rose to my feet. "For what?"

"To carry your stuff as far as the first Dayak village. Otherwise . . ."

"Otherwise what?" I asked, moving closer to Roustan, almost touching his chest with mine and looking at him from my whole height.

"Otherwise . . . they said they will leave right now for Tabang."

I yelled at them that I didn't want to see them any more and that they were free to go back.

"Are you paying our salary then?" asked one of them.

"You have not respected your contract, you shall not be paid! Now get out of here!"

Convinced that I would give in, the porters sniggered and slowly started to move away again, stopping behind bushes where they roared with laughter. Angered by my apparent helplessness and their mockery, I ran after them and grabbed one. Holding him firmly by his shirt, I lifted him off the ground and yelled: "Roustan, tell them that if I see one of them in front of me today, I will smash his face in!" Frightened by my size, my strength, and my anger, the porters immediately disappeared.

Still shaking with rage, I joined my companions.

"Well done, Douch," said J.F., "well done. Just what will we do with six hundred pounds of stuff in the middle of nowhere? I think you should pay them."

"Pay them?" I yelled. "I refuse to give in to their blackmail. Besides, if I do pay them, what will stop them from starting the same game again tomorrow?"

A few seconds later, starting to calm down, I looked at my friends and saw their eyes gleaming with anxiety.

"Max, J.F., listen," I said. "If you want to, you are free to follow the porters. Take all the survival food you need. I'll give you enough money to reach Balikpapan and your tickets back to Brussels. I understand."

"What about you?" asked J.F.

"I don't fucking give up now, my friends. I am too close to my goal, close to Punans, and nobody will stop me from joining them. Even if I have to abandon all our boxes. I don't give a shit about my cameras and the rest of my stuff! It's too late. I can't go back. I'll cross this damn jungle alone!"

"Cool down, Douch!" said Max. "Nobody is going to leave you. We came together, we'll stick together. But do you realize that we're alone in the jungle, in the middle of nowhere?"

"Listen to me. Perhaps we are alone in the jungle, but we're not *lost!* I listened to the porters talking yesterday. I know where to go." I suddenly became excited. "Are you aware of the luck we have? What we have done is easy to do with porters and guides. Any tourist can follow a guide. But now we can live a real adventure and do it on our own."

"Even Livingstone followed a guide!" J.F. said.

"My friends," I said, feeling a sudden strong love for my companions, "I promise we will make it! It will be the greatest adventure, the most smashing feat ever dreamed. Be happy we have no porters. But we must organize ourselves."

While I was still talking in this crazy way, a move in the bushes gave us a start. It was Roustan.

"Tuan!" he said, approaching me.

"Roustan? What the hell are you doing here?" I was suddenly afraid that we might be in store for an unpleasant surprise from the porters and put my hand on the large hunting knife hanging at my side.

"Chut! Tuan, the others don't know I'm here. They are not my friends. I don't agree with them. They were not right to break the contract. They want money, they are only interested in money."

"Was I right, then?"

"Yes, tuan. Tomorrow they would have started bargaining again because they are scared of Dayaks. But you are my friends, you always were nice to me and I don't want you to have problems."

"Good. Are you staying with us?"

"No, tuan, no! They will beat me, perhaps to death, if they learn that I don't like them. But I want to help you." Bending over the ground, he started to draw lines. "You must take this direction. You will find a river."

I looked at the compass hanging around my neck. Roustan's direction was north.

"How long to that river?"

"One day. Then you go down the river, half a day, and you will find the Dayak village."

"Are you telling the truth, Roustan? Swear it on your ancestors."

"Yes, tuan!" he said, pointing his fingers toward the sky.

"How do you know this information? Have you been there before?"

"No, tuan, none of us has been here before. But I know because Punans coming to Tabang have told me."

"So it means that until now you have only followed the Dayaks' tracks of passage?"

"Yes, tuan!"

Looking at my friends, I saw that they too didn't know what to think about Roustan.

"Listen, Roustan," I said, fixing him with a penetrating stare, "to reward you, I will give you your money and much more."

"Really?" he asked, smiling for the first time.

"But not here, not now. In Samarinda I know a Catholic priest who often comes to Tabang. When I get there I will give him the money for you. All the money and a nice bonus. You trust me?"

"Yes, tuan, you say the truth. I trust you. But what if you don't get to Samarinda?"

"You will get your money only if we can reach Samarinda with the help of your information."

"I am telling you the truth. I am not like the others. The others are bad. Cowards!"

Putting my hand on Roustan's shoulder, I asked Max to give him two packs of cigarettes. Then we shook his hand.

"Tuan, be careful. Punans don't want you here."

His remark worried me. "What makes you think that Punans don't want me?"

"Signs, tuan, many signs everywhere."

"Where?"

"Everywhere, tuan. I must go!"

As he turned to leave us, I called out: "Oh, Roustan! Before you go, look at this." I took the revolver-shaped light meter out of its case, which was shaped like a holster. "You remember what I said about this weapon?"

"Yes, tuan! Very dangerous!"

"Indeed, it's so powerful that with one single shot I could kill thirty wild boars. They would be completely torn to pieces. That's why I never used it for our hunts."

"Hoo!" he said, his eyes expressing admiration and fear.

"Before you go, I want to tell you a secret. If your friends come back here with bad intentions, this is what I shall use to greet them."

"Yes. . . . Yes, tuan. You're right!"

"Goodbye now, and don't forget you're my friend."

"We need to solve a few problems," I said to my friends as Roustan disappeared into the underbrush. "The first one concerns all our equipment. There is no way to take it with us, even carrying it piece by piece up to the river. We have only one small canoe for three men and gear. On the other hand, if it stays here without a close watch, there are great chances that if the porters are waiting nearby they will steal it. After all, who knows if they are spying on us."

"I'm sure they are," said J.F., ominously.

"That's why one of us should stay here. Since he will be armed with the dreadful weapon, none of them would dare to come near," added Max.

"Thanks, Max. I'm not ready to sacrifice the equipment since the Dayak village is so near. Okay, now that everybody agrees that at least one of us must stay here, we have two possibilities. I can go alone in search of the Dayak village and, once there, I will get porters to come back and collect our stuff, or I can go with one of you. That would be much safer. No one knows what kind of difficulties I'll encounter. No need for two of us to stay here and wait."

"Yes," said Max. "It would be safer."

"J.F., what do you think?"

"Looks okay to me," replied J.F. with a shrug. "No objection."

"In that case, J.F., I think you should stay here."

"What?" J.F. looked startled. "Why me?"

"Because you are exhausted." I didn't want to tell him that he would never make it. "You can rest here. To reach the village, I need a strong guy with me who has survival skills, like Max. Since it is my intention to stay there and make friends, Max will be the one to bring the Dayaks back. Okay?"

"Okay, okay . . . easy to say okay," mumbled J.F., not happy at all with the idea of staying alone in the camp. Uneasily, he asked, "How long will I be alone here in the middle of nowhere? When will Max be back?"

"I don't know. Let's see, tonight at the river, tomorrow night at the latest at the village. That means two days to reach the village, but three days to come back here because they will be going upstream."

"If Roustan hasn't lied about the distances! You know very well that two of his days have often meant four or five."

"That's a possibility," I said.

"And what if the Dayaks don't want to accept you?"

"Then we'll just come back alone. Anyhow, there is a difference between accepting us and being ready to serve us as porters. Perhaps they'll move fast if we can explain to them that it's a matter of life and death for the person who has stayed in the camp."

"Yes, but what if they are having a hunt, or whatever, and there are no men available to serve as porters?" J.F. asked.

"J.F. is right," added Max.

"Okay, I buy that. In that case, J.F., count on five to eight days before Max comes back with Dayaks. But I beg you, don't move away from here. In fact, that's not a request, it's an order. You understand?"

"Yeah, but what if you get lost? I won't wait here an eternity. Maybe this isn't such a good idea. I can't wait forever."

"Of course, if something happens to us, you must not go moldy here. But listen to me carefully: You must stay here at least two weeks. You have enough survival food for that. That will just allow for . . . for. . ."

"For mistakes perhaps?" J.F. started to shake with anxiety. "Four days just became two weeks. What am I gonna do after two weeks? Have you thought about that, Mr. Gersi?"

"Calm down, J.F. We have absolutely no intention of dying or of abandoning you. We'll be back." I put my hand on his shoulder, wanting to tell him even less of what could go wrong. "However if . . . I mean *in case* we're not back in two weeks, then of course, just get out of here. And then you have to make it to civilization to get help for us."

"Yeah . . . and could you tell me how?"

I didn't have an answer but we really didn't have an alternative, so I said without too much conviction, "The porters' tracks will still be fresh. You just follow them."

"But what about the Punans or whoever? Am I in danger of being attacked by them?" J.F. asked, making a last attempt to change our mind about his duty.

"Listen, my friend, besides the dart left by them yesterday, and in spite of what Roustan has said, I have seen no more of their marks. Besides, if they want to attack someone, it is Max and I who are in jeopardy, certainly not you," I reassured him, "because you are not disobeying their no-trespassing sign. We are."

"Well, if I have to stay . . ." Realizing that he had no choice, J.F. reluctantly asked for Max's mosquito net and all our torn clothes so he could spend his time repairing them. "At least I will be useful to you," he said, smiling. Then, while J.R. was setting up to make himself comfortable, Max and I filled our rucksacks with what was needed for our trip. We took our inflatable boat, the manual air pump, a stock of film for movie and still photography, sleeping bags, mosquito nets, hammocks, one plastic sheet against the rain, all our ropes, including two that were thirty feet long, snap hooks, and our only small water filter. We had one sweater and one bathing suit a piece in addition to the shirts and jeans we were wearing. We filled another bag with two tubes of concentrated milk, tea, sugar, three kits of army rations; and tobacco, pepper leaves, limes, and betel nuts as peace offerings for the Dayaks. We also packed one movie camera, one Nikon, and the lenses for both.

Max and I had our machetes hanging at our sides. I also carried a large hunting knife attached to my leg and a compass around my neck.

After we tidied up the rest of the boxes and trunks, Max helped J.F. stretch out his hammock and attach the rope to support the mosquito net and the plastic sheet. Moving some distance away, I placed the movie camera on the tripod, set it on automatic, and filmed a message to my family. It was a kind of living testimony in which I tried to explain all that had happened to us, including the departure of our porters. I gave the reasons we had to leave J.F. alone in the camp and explained that Max and I were about to go in search of the Dayak village, seeking help. I wanted my family to know about the circumstances in which we made such decisions and about my reasons for not wanting to abandon my expedition.

"I'm sure I can make friends with the headhunters. If they wanted to kill us, they could have done that already. My daughter, if people tell you that your father was crazy, you tell them I am not, I am simply a man who makes his dreams his reality. I must finish this exploration. Remember that I love you very much." I finished the message, unloaded the camera, and put the film and the tape in a plastic bag, which I handed to J.F.

"J.F., whatever happens, *please* take all the exposed films with you. Find a way to sell those of the expedition and keep the money for my baby. Also, don't forget to bring my mother this plastic bag and the box filled with my letters to my daughter."

"That's encouraging," said J.F., laconically. My funeral must have sounded to him like his own.

"By the way, J.F., always keep the fire alive. It will stop animals from entering the camp. The smoke will keep them away from you. Understand? Don't ever let the fire die!"

We kissed good-bye and left.

CHAPTER TEN

The Separation

Hope is the pillar that holds up the world. Hope is the dream
of a waking man.

PLINY THE ELDER

After no more than half an hour, the small track
leading north that was to lead us to the Dayak village simply
disappeared. Staying within shouting distance of each other,
Max and I searched for clues or marks that would show us the
right direction. There was nothing but dozens of confusing
tracks made by the passage of wild boars and deer that disappeared beneath bushes.

"Douch, we should move back to the camp and start again."

I refused Max's proposal. If J.F. realized that we had lost our
way so quickly, he would never again agree to stay in camp
alone.

"Let's walk north, since that's what Roustan said. We should
find the river."

Taking no chance that in the future we would lose sight of
our present location, Max used his machete to cut notches along
our path so he could find his way back to J.F. As I filmed that
walk toward the enigmatic river which did not appear on any
map, I reflected on what had taken place during the last few
hours. Soon a jungle of unanswerable questions grew in my
imagination.

Although it had happened to a few of my explorer friends,
this was the first time I had ever been abandoned by porters.
Had the porters noticed some of the mysterious warning signs
Roustan had talked about, but which we had missed? Had they
seen me burying the poisonous dart? Had they found another
dart somewhere in the camp or near it? And if so, then why
would they hide it from us? Suddenly, everything became clear
to me. The porters had thought that if they shared their discovery with me, I would have gone back with them. Therefore, they

would have lost the opportunity to blackmail me for more money.

I began to worry that they might return and kill J.F. No. They knew I was carrying the money and that's what they would be interested in. If they were ready to fight for it, they would have done so before fleeing. After all, it was nine against three. Also they were frightened by my mysterious "gun." However, if they knew that I had left it with J.F., then my life was in danger. Indeed, they could be following me, waiting for the best occasion to attack and kill me.

I hope they are so scared of the Dayaks that by now, they are far away, I thought, searching desperately for relief from my racing mind.

Then I started to wonder if it had been such a good idea to ignore the warning of the Punans. Their message had been put there for the porters, but going ahead could still be deadly for us. Even though Max and I were still alive after having penetrated the forbidden territory for about a half-day's walking, perhaps death was just on the other side of the next clearing.

Following Max who, with a sixty-pound pack on his back, was fighting through a thick barrier made of one-inch-long thorns, I started to envy J.F. I imagined he was quietly resting. He was not in danger as long as we could come back to him within the time limit of two weeks. And if things went as I hoped, Max would be back to him much sooner. Then I thought how great my two companions were. Although free to go back to civilization, they chose to stay with me.

"What the hell are you mumbling?" asked Max when he saw me. Thorns had drawn two bloody lines across his face.

"Oh, nothing special. I was just saying we deserve to make it."

"You bet," Max said, mopping his bloody face.

Around four-thirty, a cleanly slashed trunk at the bottom of a narrow canyon revealed that other human beings were using the area for their passage. Ten minutes later, we arrived in a large clearing surrounded by bamboo trees. At the center were the stick frames of two abandoned Dayak houses. Three hundred feet away was the peaceful river that Roustan had predicted. Max and I congratulated each other. We didn't need guides after all.

Since it was already late, we decided to camp and agreed to do so on the riverbank, so that if Dayaks decided to use their camp they wouldn't be angry to find us sleeping in it.

Joyfully we put down our rucksacks on the wide pebbled

bank, which sloped gently down to the water. As we collected dead wood for the campfire, we conducted a quick tour to make sure the terrain was not already chosen by crocodiles.

The sun's heat, amplified by the reflection from the pebbles near the water, was tremendous. We put on our bathing suits and stretched our clothes out on the warm bank to dry. Just as Max was about to light the fire and I was getting out the mosquito nets and sleeping bags, a swarm of giant wasps, attracted by the salt in our perspiration, swooped down on our clothes and also covered our bathing suits, with us in them. While I was carefully peeling off my suit, some of the wasps ventured onto my skin and one, without provocation, stung my stomach. Controlling our rising panic, Max and I slowly moved into the river, keeping only our heads out of the water. We stood there, petrified, for over a half hour until darkness fell and the wasps left as suddenly as they had arrived. For that whole time our conversation was limited to exchanges of glances, for we were scared that our voices would excite the ferocious wasps.

That night for the first time, we opened the army survival kits I had purchased in Belgium. Food from halfway around the world. There was a piece of chocolate, cigarette and matches inside a small glass container, and two paper packets. One contained powdered soup, a gray powder with small pieces of something hard, about one-eighth of an inch square. Some were green, some red, others black. We poured everything into hot water and sat back to watch. The tiny green things became green peas, the reds became carrots, and the blacks were transformed into tiny pieces of meat. But it was much more fun to watch than to eat, and our monkey dinners now seemed like a feast. Still, we were at the river and surely within only hours of fulfilling my Dayak dream.

At five o'clock the next morning, Max inflated the canoe, made of many separate sections, or rolls, which had to be filled individually. In this way, if one roll was punctured by a sharp rock or stick, the other rolls would keep the canoe floating. I cut two long bamboo poles to use as paddles and poles. Then I wrapped the cameras, lenses, and film in plastic bags especially designed for diving. We roped it all together in the middle of the canoe with the bag of food and the camera cases between our rucksacks.

Wearing only our bathing suits and our walking boots, we carried the loaded canoe to the river. Our hopes were high. In order to keep visual memories of this part of the trip, I set the automatic camera in position to record that fragment of our journey. We were tourists enjoying what promised to be a great adventure.

Since our gear almost completely filled the small canoe, which was about three feet by seven, we sat with our backs to each other, dangling our feet over the sides in the water. The wide river slowly moved east. The banks quickly gave way to curtains of high trees and we floated in and out of narrow canyons of vegetation. The morning sun was so hot we had to splash ourselves with water to prevent our skin from burning. Then the river would disappear beneath a dark canopy that brought a sudden coolness. Above our heads giant branches, linked with entangled lianas and vines in hanging loops, supported a paradise of birds, mostly an amazing variety of noisy calaos with strange and varied beaks. Although I wanted to doze we had to be careful, for it was difficult to distinguish a root or a liana from a giant python sleeping above the water.

The river was as slow as the heat, as slow as the sweat that dripped from our noses onto our chests. Two dragonflies landed on one of my feet, mated for a long time, and flew away. The hours passed in the timelessness of the river and the jungle.

Max and I didn't question what Roustan had said to us. Everything was meant to be easy. Even without the aid of landmarks we had found the river. There was no reason to miss the Dayak village, yet by 3:00 P.M., we started to worry.

"Shit!" said Max. "Roustan said that we would find the village after a half day of going downstream. We are already a half day late."

Half an hour later the river suddenly increased its speed and we hit a stretch of rapids, rough whirlpools, just enough to satisfy our need for excitement. At each ragged passage we screamed as if we were riding big dippers in an amusement park.

"Max, real rapids ahead," I called out, "and the river is splitting!" We jumped into chest-high water to slow the canoe and pushed it toward another pebbled bank. While Max hoisted the canoe onto the bank, I went ahead to investigate. I walked in the river, which rapidly doubled its width and at that point was only one foot deep.

I returned to report that there was another river, coming from the north, which joined ours. Farther on they separated again. Our river seemed to go south with a strong current, the other one headed gently east. The problem was that both seemed to be of the same size, and we had no way of knowing on which one the Dayak village lay.

"Hell! Roustan never talked about this. And we could not possibly have missed the village. What do we do, Douch?"

"I don't know. Let me see the map."

I took out the small map which I had been filling in since the beginning of the exploration. "The only sure thing is that we are still on the high plateau. The conifers around us prove it."

"I wonder," said Max, "if the river going south would not be a tributary of the Balayan or the Balayan itself. In that case, since we could be at the end of the high plateau, we should not even consider following it. Besides, Dayaks would not build a village along rapids, would they?"

Max was right. Everything pointed to the fact that the river going south had something to do with an impassable torrent that began above Djelini, where we had started to walk through the jungle. So we chose the river going east.

We pushed the canoe until we reached chest-deep water and the river's current carried us. After a large loop, the river entered a narrow pass with high granite walls. One hour later the current increased at the exit of the gorge. The whole of the river, about forty-five feet across, became flecked with frills of white water. Because of the difference in river levels, we couldn't see how bad the rapids ahead were. We didn't want to take too great a risk so we stopped the canoe on the bank and attached the two long ropes at each end. While I kept the canoe back with one rope, Max held the other rope and moved ahead, walking on the bank until both ropes were stretched out. Max was then about 60 feet ahead of me, halfway down the rapids.

"Okay! Let the rope go!" he yelled. I did, and the canoe, carried by the strong current, passed in front of Max, jumped over rapids and then stopped, restrained by the rope he was holding. I ran down to the other end of rope, which was floating in the rippling waters. Then Max let go of his rope and it was my turn to hold it until the canoe again stopped farther on.

"It's stupid. We have lost valuable time. The rapids are not so bad. The waves were three feet at the most. We could have passed on the boat."

"Yes, Douch, but we couldn't have known that."

We stayed in the canoe to cross the next rapids. Our screams of joy disturbed a group of wild boars and two deer that were peacefully drinking on the bank.

Since the sun was disappearing rapidly, we decided to bivouac on the next large bank. We held a long conversation to prove to ourselves that we had done the right thing. Then, more exhausted than convinced, we climbed under our mosquito net and went to sleep.

When we awoke the next morning, we found ourselves at the water's edge. The river level had risen almost five feet in one night. Half the canoe was already floating, our shoes were in the water, and Max had just time enough to rescue his socks.

"One hour more and bye-bye canoe!" said Max.

Max sat silently during breakfast, his face a mask of anxiety.

"I guess the village is not far now," I said. "We should find it today."

"I hope so. But Roustan said only half a day downstream."

"Don't worry, Max. With these guys, time and distance are always relative."

"Yes, of course, he was wrong many times before. We'll be in the village soon. Right, Douch?"

"Right, Max."

This time the rapids were rough. Often we had to use our feet to push the canoe away from the big and sometimes sharp stones crowding the middle of the river. Enjoying ourselves, we secretly hoped the rapids would not end before they deposited us on a beach in front of the village.

"Max! A house! We made it!" I screamed. Indeed, on top of a cliff at the other end of a beach appeared the silhouette of a small Dayak long house built on pilework, surrounded by trees.

After having firmly attached the heavy canoe to a large stone on the beach, I took out of my rucksack some of the peace offerings for the Dayaks. No one came to greet us. Bringing the gifts, we crossed the beach, climbed the muddy cliff, stopped and called a few times. As there was no answer, we moved toward the house. The path was covered with lemons: small green ones and others the size of a grapefruit hung on trees.

Seen closer, the Dayak house looked dilapidated from storms

and winds. It had been abandoned for some time. Next to the entrance, a large turtle shell was lying on the rotten floor.

"A souvenir for my little darling!" said Max, grabbing it. Farther on there were two wonderfully sculpted pestles about three feet long, which I took with me.

Max looked at the deserted house and suddenly seemed possessed by a deep discouragement. We scouted around, found nothing, and returned to the canoe. On the way back Max filled up his turtle shell with the green and yellow lemons.

Back on the river we went over the rough rapids with an excitement that burst like the waters against the rocks. We couldn't stop screaming. Still sitting on the sides of the canoe, opposite each other, we used our feet and the bamboo poles to steer clear of rocks obstructing the rapids. The canoe spun in the swirling waters. Once past the rapids at high speed, the river spread and slowed somewhat, but when we were too close to the bank, an opposite force stopped the canoe and pushed it upstream. Gradually our strength was failing to get us out of the large, powerful whirlpools and back into the current.

Three P.M. The banks covered with dense jungle were growing higher and steeper. More and more big rocks held floating dead trees obstructing the river which by now seemed to be plunging toward an invisible chasm. The rapids were becoming a succession of five- to ten-foot swells, more dangerous with every foot we traveled.

We felt the same excitement, the same anxiety, the same breathlessness as one feels on a rollercoaster, but without the security of knowing that the ride will end safely. The canoe glided over stones polished by the savage waters; then it plunged into swirls as violent as those that battered and moved the rocks and the banks. The waves were more than five feet high.

Suddenly, as I was filming, the current picked up speed, causing the canoe to go out of control and strike against the sharp rocks. We used our feet and Max his bamboo pole to repel the danger; but in a move to avoid crashing into a sharp rock, Max broke his pole and was thrown into the raging waters. The collisions were so brutal that the canoe disappeared for a second under a big wave. Everything was soaked except my camera, which I was still holding high. By a miracle, Max was able to grab the small rope around the outside of the canoe. I quickly put the camera back into its case and then jumped into the river to help Max pull the canoe to the bank.

We unloaded the boat to empty the water from it and counted our losses: the turtle shell, the lemons, the bag of survival food, the two Dayak pestles, and our machetes.

We sat down next to our drenched sleeping bags stretched on a giant uprooted tree, and started to argue.

"We must stop and go back, Douch. Otherwise we'll kill ourselves. Do you see this river is going south?"

"Then what about the village?"

"Roustan must have lied. Be reasonable, man. This river is as deadly as the one above Djelini. The one our porters called *the rapids of death* or something like that. I bet it's the same river. Listen to the sound of the rapids down in the valley. We're at the end of the high plateau. Let's go back to J.F. on foot."

"Think how many miles we've already covered. It will take us forever, and there's no food."

"It's better than drowning."

In fact, Max was probably right. There was no way to go on. "Okay, Maxi. If you say so."

We deflated and folded the canoe. Then, since it was impossible to walk along the rapids because the narrow bank was crowded with obstructing trees and rocks, we started to climb diagonally up the steep, muddy cliff. I was following Max, who is a well-trained mountain climber. When we reached a gentler slope, we moved along parallel to the river. The rucksacks cut against our skin, burned by two days of sun. The soil and stones constantly disappeared beneath our feet as we pulled ourselves up an arm-length at a time, gaining support from rocks, lianas, or tree trunks.

After two hours of struggle, of uncontrolled skidding and painful slips, as the sun was disappearing behind the mountain, we started our descent toward a small sandy beach that Max spotted through a break in the trees. Once there, we realized that we had gone little more than a half-mile from the point where we had decided to make our move back to J.F. The place of our canoe accident was still visible just before a large bend in the river.

"No way, Douch, we'll never make it. What will we do?"

"We'll see tomorrow, brother. Let's camp here and get some sleep."

While I set the mosquito net on the white, soft sand, just at the edge of the jungle, Max gathered some dead branches scattered on the small beach, which was covered with hundreds of animal footprints. We could recognize those left by deer and wild boars, and the undulating track of a very large snake.

As calmly as we could, we discussed the river and the Dayak village we were trying to find. Where the hell had we made a mistake? Roustan had said to move downstream. We had done it without seeing anything more than the one abandoned long house. Now what? Was the village on the other river?

"Douch, remember we have nothing to eat. What will we do tomorrow?"

"Walking as we did today, we'll never get back to J.F. Do you realize how much effort it will take, being so loaded down? We can't even go along the river. It's impossible. Too much effort. We have no food. Max, I think we have to go downstream. We should arrive soon where there are people."

"Douch, where the hell are we?"

"I don't know. The only sure thing is that we're going south. Maybe this is the Belayan or a parallel river. I don't know. It will certainly be less exhausting to go downstream, even if we have to walk on the banks and hold the canoe back with ropes, like we did in the beginning."

We talked until we were afraid to say another word. The truth was as frightening as our worst fantasy.

A gentle noise from the jungle awakened me. Still lying on my belly, stretching both hands up to my hunting knife, I slowly lifted my head. Something moved, next to a tree trunk ten feet away. While I was trying to see through the mosquito net what made the noise, the moon pierced the torn clouds and suddenly a ray of its light was reflected by two eyes shining with a greenish gleam. Two wide-open eyes.

"Max," I said in a hushed voice. "A black panther!"

"Tell me rather that there's a pussy."

"I swear," I said, laughing nervously.

"Where?" said Max, as he straightened up with a jolt. "Where?" But the eyes had disappeared.

"Right ahead in front of us. Don't move."

"I don't see anything."

"Wait."

Suddenly I saw a dark shadow climbing the tree whose branches were stretching up above us. "Did you see . . . ?"

"Yes, yes."

"She may be above us."

"Shit! We . . . we should do something. We can't stay like this beneath her."

"Listen, Max, we should get the fire going again."

"Yeah, you're right!"

But no one moved. We had a deep-seated fear of moving out from under the mosquito net. The net by itself could hardly have protected us, but it was enough to offer psychological security.

"Get out, Max. I'll cover you with the knife."

"How do I get out?"

"The same way we came in."

"Then you get out."

"Me? Well, if you insist." Scared to move backward without seeing behind me, I made a quick U-turn under the tent-shaped mosquito net and ended up kicking Max in the head. Still holding the knife pointed toward the invisible panther, I stood up but not completely so as to be ready to lie down on my back and impale the beast with the knife if it came at me.

"Follow me. I'll go get some wood," said Max, out of the fragile shelter.

The fire illuminated the beach, projecting mysterious and scary shadows all around us. I raised my knife to every noise. We moved the mosquito net so close to the water that a five-inch rise in the river level would have flooded us.

We had an awful night. Max woke up several times to stoke the fire. In the morning, I emptied a can of film and used it as a pot to heat some water. That was breakfast.

"So, what's your final decision? Do we move back or do we move on?"

"We move on, Max."

"Ok, since you want to. But I'm telling you it's damned stupid."

"What else do you want to do? You have a suggestion? You have to admit it's better to go downstream, even though it may mean walking along the rapids, than it is to walk for days, loaded like donkeys. If only we had our machetes, we'd be able to cut some bamboo poles and build a raft . . . instead of carrying that heavy canoe."

"I knew it. It's always like that with you. Improvising lousy things. My mother told me your expedition would be botched up."

"What is botched up?" I screamed. "Come on, say it! You can do whatever you want, but I'm going down the rapids!"

The dispute was only the residue of a night of anguish. It ended quickly, and we inflated the canoe. Using snap hooks and ropes, Max firmly tied the camera cases and the two rucksacks all together to the boat.

"Ready?"

"Let's go!"

With the new morning strength, we charged the first rapids. The canoe plunged into the noisy explosions of furious water. Once again we were at the mercy of whirlpools trying to break us into pieces. Again we used our feet and Max his bamboo pole, as we tried to master the boat and avoid collisions. Holding the movie camera in my right hand to record the water furies, I lay on the equipment trying not to be thrown from the canoe.

At a break in the liquid chaos, we took a rest. I emptied the movie camera and wrapped the finished roll of film in a water-proof plastic bag that already contained the other exposed film.

"You better help me steer the canoe instead of that damn filming."

"Okay, okay! I have enough pictures anyway," I answered, wrapping the movie camera in another waterproof bag and put-ting it back into its case.

Taking turns, we left the canoe and climbed the chaotic rocks that crowded the bank to examine how the next tormented passage would be. Twice we both had to leave the canoe, letting it slide alone through the rapids while we moved up and down the bank holding it with ropes.

Then it was my turn to leave the boat and investigate the difficulties of the next passage. "We should be able to pass all right. Waves seem to be the same as the last rapids: four or five feet high. Just hang on."

The bumps became more violent. Spinning out of control, the canoe drove into a wave and then, with a sucking noise, slid over some rocks and plunged into more swirls. I lost my balance and, losing my grip on our only bamboo pole, fell onto the equip-ment and lay clinging to it. Meanwhile, Max used his feet to try to protect the canoe from the sharp-edged rocks. The exploding, roaring waters spun us faster.

Far ahead, the right side of the river seemed to be violently tortured with high waves, while the left side was almost as calm as a lake.

"On the left side!" screamed Max, trying in vain to move the canoe toward that quiet pool of water. I heard myself calling my father and begging for his help. Slowly we moved toward and arrived on the peaceful waters.

"Max," I yelled, "we are not going to crash, we are the best, we are the . . . Max, *Max, we must stop the boat . . . Max! Careful!*"

At the last moment, directly in front of me I saw the peaceful-looking waters disappearing over the edge of a ten-foot waterfall that crashed into shining whirlpools below.

Leaning backward and holding onto the side of the canoe, I saw Max, barefoot, pass over my head, flying as if shot from a gun, into the falls below. Riding the canoe all the way down, I fell into the luminous liquid, which exploded against rocks sharp as razors. My heavy walking shoes dragged me to the bottom of a hell of liquid fire. Sucked down by whirlpools, I struggled for my life. Suddenly I found myself on the surface, at the foot of the waterfall. I couldn't see Max, only the canoe, spinning in the deafening tumult. I grabbed the thin rope along the side of the canoe and tried to pull myself up, but my feet were too heavy. Then, as if pushed away by a new force, the canoe strained to escape without me. It pulled, it struggled. The thin rope tore my fingers, burning and cutting the flesh. I had the feeling that my fingers were stretching, that my hand was being torn from my wrist. Not able to take the pain any longer, I let the canoe go and saw it moving away, riding on high waves. Then a new force sucked me down into the waters, which pounded me so brutally that my body doubled up as if I were being pummeled by giant fists. I saw the white surface of water disappearing far above me. My knee smashed against my jaw. Badly in need of air, I tried swimming upward toward the white shining surface that taunted me by moving away. I needed air, I was being torn apart. Something had caught my foot, something was holding me to the bottom . . . *a rope* . . . a rope was binding my foot. A rope, perhaps attached to the heavy camera box, was caught between rocks, and my foot was snagged in a loop. I needed air. The light all around me was becoming brighter, the luminosity so brutal that I wanted to clench my eyes to lessen the pain inside my skull. The water pressure was too strong. I will die, I thought, attached to that hidden under-water gallows, rolled around like the hair of a mermaid, I am dead forever.

That image gave me a new strength for the supreme effort to reach my thigh, my knee, my foot. . . . I felt the rope and finally got my foot loose. Although I was swimming like a madman, I still couldn't reach the surface. It was as if a strong hand were holding me under. Then, still as if in slow motion, I smashed into a big rock. A few seconds later, a force pushed me up along another giant rock and I came at last to the shining surface. I had just enough time to breathe in a little air mixed with water when a new violence sucked me again into the bottom of a whirlpool. Death was coming after me, but I didn't want death! I begged my body to give me the strength to get me out of there. I beseeched my father's help. Rocks bumped into me, rolled all over me—as if they were seeking revenge. I wanted to scream, but I kept my mouth shut tight.

When my head once again reached the surface of the river, the water was quiet with a gentle current that carried me toward the right bank. As I relaxed I heard the horrible noise of a powerful suction and realized too late that the current was forcefully pushing me toward a high rock ahead that blocked part of the river. I tried with all my strength to swim away, but it was as if I were swimming backward, sucked by the force of the whirlpool. My feet were already inside the siphon. I stretched my arms wide, my fingernails clawing a rock for safety. The waters passed over my head, pushing me inside the deadly inlet. I knew that if my fingers lost their grip, I would be drawn in, stuck to the bottom of the hole. "Papa, help me . . . I don't want to die . . . *please, not to die!*"

"Douch!" Max's loud call pierced the noisy fury of the siphon.

My last strength went into my lungs as I screamed: *"Max! Help!"*

Somehow Max caught hold of my shoulder and pulled me from the river. When I opened my eyes I looked up and saw Max's smiling face covered with sweat and tears.

"Douch, you're alive! It's wonderful! I . . . I really thought you were dead. I called you and looked for you everywhere. . . . But thank God, you're alive!" Max was holding my head between his hands. The light hurt so much that I had to close my eyes. "Are you all right?" he asked, suddenly worried by my silence.

"I don't know. . . . Let's see!" I answered, as I tried to stand up, helped by him. A deep pain in my back distorted my face, but I hugged Max, squeezing him against me for a long time.

"Max, my brother, we are alive! Thank you, God. Thank you, Dad!" Then, looking at the deadly surging river, I said, "It's a miracle we survived that!"

"You're right, we should have drowned! . . . How do you feel?"

"Pain in my back and neck."

"Shit, I hope nothing is broken."

"I don't think so, but it hurts."

"Do you know we've lost everything? I don't even have my shoes. Just my bathing suit. That's all. You're lucky, at least you have something to protect your feet."

I looked at my shoes, still laced up, and at my bathing suit hanging in miserable tatters on my buttocks.

"Sorry about that," he said, glancing at it, "but there was no other hold to get you out of the water!"

We sat on the bank and looked silently at the murderous water. "You know, Douch, the more I think about it, the more I'm sure this river is the one to Tabang."

"What about the other one? It was going south, too."

"Yesterday, going through some rapids, I saw a tributary coming from the right side, from the west. It could be it; I forgot to tell you about it. Now let's go, it's time to swim."

"Swim? What are you talking about?"

"Well, look around you!" said Max. He was right: there was no other way to move downstream than to swim. We were inside a hundred-foot-deep canyon, and on our bank, huge rocks obstructed the whole space between the river and the unclimbably steep cliff.

Without waiting for me, he entered the river. I tried but couldn't follow him, so terrified was I by the water and its noise. In water up to his neck, Max used one hand to swim downstream along the huge rocks and the other hand to hold onto them.

"Wait! Max, wait for me! Please!"

"Follow me!" he yelled. "We have to get out of here!"

"I can't! I'm scared!" I started to cry like a child, asking my father why he had allowed such an accident to happen to me.

Suddenly I was in panic, for Max had disappeared from sight.

Frightened by my solitude, I screamed: "Max, *wait!*" When he didn't answer, I slowly slid into the cold water. Terrified, I did not dare swim. I moved downstream holding onto crevices in the rocks. Rapidly regaining my confidence and courage, I started to swim calmly and even dared to cross a whirlpool so as to join Max sooner.

I found him on a rocky overhang. Once next to him, I heard him whispering: "Mama, Mama, I want to get out of here!" I hugged him, my brother in fear.

This time it was my turn. "Max, don't cry, please! Come on, swim!"

"Leave me alone!" he answered.

From where we were, we could hear the wild screams of rapids. I climbed the bank's rocks and discovered that about three hundred feet below us, the river was once again blocked by an impassable and furious chaos; in addition, our side became large rocks with abrupt drops, whereas the opposite bank, crowded with only small rocks, was more passable.

I came down and told Max what I had seen. "There is a strong current in the middle, but there's a place where we can cross before the rapids. Come on, Max!"

The speed of the current carried me toward the rapids faster than I had expected. But the fear of experiencing a new accident gave me the strength to double my efforts, and I was able to reach the other bank just in time. Having seen my maneuver and how close I had come to the rapids, Max went back upstream about one hundred feet in order to increase his distance from the rapids. Then he plunged into the torrent and swam across faster.

While he was taking a short rest, I climbed the small rocks of the bank and moved ahead. As I passed the rapids, I saw a red rucksack slowly spinning in a whirlpool farther downstream. I called Max and while running to the boat began to realize how many important things I had lost in addition to it: the case containing two still cameras, a set of lenses, the movie camera, three thousand feet of unexposed film, my rucksack containing the five hundred feet of film shot since we left J.F., the quinine and all my money in the small leather bag that usually hung around my neck. How great to have found it.

"It's mine!" yelled Max, joining me.

"Are you sure?" I asked, deeply disappointed. "With the waterproof bags I have in it, it's mine that should be floating."

"Positive!" And indeed it was Max's bag, containing his pull-over, the two sleeping bags, one mosquito net, one hammock, the small water filter, and a tube of aspirin. Damn!

As the sun passed to the other side of the mountains, the canyon started to darken. While Max was spreading our soaked belongings on some rocks, I went back, running on slippery rocks, as far as I could toward the waterfall where we had had our accident, searching every nook and cranny in the hope of finding my rucksack. If we had found Max's rucksack, why not mine as well?

Empty-handed, I came back to Max and began to search downstream. Six hundred feet farther down in an infernal din, the torrent hurled itself into a terrifying waterfall. Terrifying because the water fell twelve feet down against rocks that held many dead trees, whose sharp branches stretched toward the sky like hundreds of lethal spears. Our accident had been lucky. Here, we could never have survived.

While mentally congratulating God and my father for having permitted our accident, I noticed something moving in the water a few feet away from the waterfall's foot, next to the opposite bank. Because the river was sixty to seventy feet wide there and was growing dark, it took me a while to identify the strange thing as a still-inflated piece of our canoe, which floated and struggled against the current. By the way it was moving, the remains of the canoe appeared to be attached to something that was holding it back.

Max joined me. I said: "One of us should cross the river and see what is holding back that roll. Try to remember how you attached our stuff to the canoe."

But my request made him bloody mad. "You're crazy! Do you realize that, since we crossed it, the river has become a string of rapids? Listen, Douch, if being alive is not enough and doesn't mean very much to you, that's your problem! But *I am alive,* and I don't fucking care about what could be attached to the fucking roll because I am not crossing that river! We are half-naked, without food, in the middle of nowhere, on an unknown river, with nobody searching for us, with nobody even knowing where we are, and you are asking me to find out how I attached your rucksack? To hell with your crummy expedition. I don't give a damn about your film! I'm going down this river until I reach civilization, and I don't care how long it takes! I want to live, you hear me?"

Disappointed and desperate, I retreated into my silence. It was 5:00 P.M. My watch was still working, another miraculous survival.

Night had fallen, and Max was still sitting silently by the river. I slid under the mosquito net that he had set on the only sandy spot, just the size we needed. Suddenly, a giant wasp appeared inside the tulle cage. As it hung on one side of the net, I screamed: "Max, help! A wasp, kill it!" He came over and, from the outside, smashed it between two stones. Less than a minute later, the wasp was there again. "Hell, Max, you didn't kill it!" He came again and smashed it so brutally that its body stayed stuck to the net. "Thanks buddy!" Hardly had I ended my sentence than, coming out of a small hole in the sand, I saw three wasps following one another—then four, then five, and . . . I rushed outside the mosquito net.

It was too dark to search for another place to pitch the mosquito net, so we stretched the still-soaked sleeping bags on a long flat rock at the foot of the steep jungle-covered slope, lay down on them, and wrapped ourselves in the mosquito net. We were stuck together, shivering from the cold.

"Max, please try to remember how you attached our stuff."

"Your rucksack was tied with a short nylon rope and a large snap hook to the front handle of the canoe. My rucksack was hooked to yours with a small snap hook. That's all I remember. The still camera case was under everything. I had to put the extra Nikon in your rucksack. Okay?"

"In that case, there is a good chance that my rucksack is what is holding back the inflated roll. If it's my rucksack, it also means my money, the exposed film, the Nikon, the . . ."

"I said it's not my problem any more. Tomorrow, I am going to go back to Brussels, get married, and keep my nose clean for the rest of my life. Perhaps I'll talk to you again in five years—or twenty."

A thunderstorm burst with a sudden peal of thunder, bringing a cold rain that pelted our bodies. We pressed close to each other. Somewhere above us, we heard the fall of a tree, killed by the explosion of the sky's anger. Then small rocks came rolling down the cliff. For safety we left our rock and sat under a giant tree whose wide trunk was large enough to protect us from other falling stones. Each time sleep seized me, it was to throw

me again into the raging waters . . . I dreamed a thousand deaths
. . . I slept a thousand drownings. . . .

The thunderstorm stopped around 5:00 A.M. We
awoke again at 8:30 A.M., exhausted. In spite of all my attempts
to talk to him, Max was still sulking and wouldn't say a word;
so, whistling, I went to quench my thirst at a small spring
nearby, whose limpid water tumbled down onto green moss. All
around the spring high grass grew. I took a bunch of stems and
started to chew them on my way back to Max. They were soft
and a little bit sweet.

"What the hell are you eating?"

"Me? Oh, just some grass. My breakfast. You want some?"

"No, I want to go before the sun heats up. So what are your
genius plans?"

"We'll follow the river downstream. Judging by the position
of the sun, the river is still going south, therefore, to Tabang
. . . well, I hope. In Tabang, we'll organize a rescue expedition
to search for J.F. But before we leave here, we'll cross the rapids
and get my rucksack!"

"No way!" Max started to scream again, "I am alive. You are
alive. Consider yourself fortunate! Don't mess around. Let's just
get to Tabang, rescue J.F., and then back to Brussels."

"Max, listen to me carefully. When I was about to drown, my
only problem was to stay alive, and I did everything for that. I'm
sorry, but now that I'm alive, my main problems are to join J.F.
and finish my expedition and my movie. It won't take so much
time to cross the river and regain the film and the money before
we head for Tabang. And if you decide to abandon me there,
you're free to do so."

"If you want to kill yourself, you're welcome. Therefore,
adios, asshole!" With that, Max took his rucksack and hurriedly
filled it with everything it had contained when we found it.
Then he stood up, put the rucksack on his back, and said, "By
the way, I have taken your sleeping bag, so you'll have to follow!"

It was funny, in the middle of nowhere, to see Max, barefoot,
wearing just a swimsuit, disappearing along a riverbank, with
a rucksack on his back. However, my first reaction was to insult
him. I hoped that he would react by coming back and insulting
me. That at least would open a discussion, but he didn't. He

disappeared behind a mass of huge rocks, without even looking back.

Furious, I ran upstream along the beach until the bank became impassable. Max was right: the river consisted of a succession of small rapids, which nevertheless looked passable. Feeling that my distance upstream from the waterfall was not enough to allow me a safe crossing, I started to climb, obliquely, the muddy slope. I fell down many times, for the rage I felt at being abandoned was shaking my whole body so much that my movements had become clumsy. When my passage was cut off by a deep gap in the slope, I moved down to the river and found myself standing on top of a huge, twenty-foot-high wall of rock. To jump from there would have been suicide, but there was no easy way to move down from where I stood atop the rock wall. So I had to climb the steep slope again, moving back toward the deadly waterfall. Finally, after all these efforts, I was almost back to the spot where I had begun my climb.

Not at all sure that I would be able to cross the river, I began to talk with my father. Since his death, when facing an insoluble problem or in need of help I have surprised myself by having conversations with him, as if he were always accompanying me. And I often hear his answers—or believe I do.

"Papa, I am scared to death! What would you do if you were me? Advise me, please! I am your son. And I know that you see everything. You know what I am risking! Do you hear me?"

"Everything depends on you," came his response. "Would you give up now and later have to remember, each time you face yourself in the twilight hour, that you could have done it but didn't?"

"But, Papa, tell me what you would do!"

"Like you, my son, I would go on."

Cutting off our conversation abruptly, I said, "Papa, help me!" And then jumped into the torrent and swam like the devil.

Reaching the opposite bank, about thirty feet from the waterfall, I screamed, almost in tears, "Thanks, Papa! . . . I love you!" Blood was flowing from my shins, for the skin had been deeply cut by sharp stones while making my way over the small rapids.

I looked up. Water dripped and trickled down a cliff of rotten sandstone that overhung my landing spot and rose one hundred feet above me. All along the cliff, a mass of rocks formed the riverbank. It was too dangerous to swim along the bank because the waterfall was located nearby, so I had to climb the rocks. As I was about to start up, I heard somebody whistling on the opposite side of the river. It was Max. Having seen that I had crossed the stream, he had come back to direct my climbing. It made me happy to know that he remembered I was clumsy at this. He was of great help, for sticking close against the rocks, I could not easily evaluate which ones would get me to the waterfall.

I yelled to him: "Do you hear me?" He said yes, but his answer was quite inaudible, perhaps because, unlike me, he had no cliff behind him to magnify his voice. I screamed: "Guide me with gestures!"

I took about one hour, following Max's instructions, to reach the closest place to the floating inflated roll. Unfortunately, it still was about six feet from the bank. I slowly entered the cold water, but it was too deep, with a strong current, and I had nothing to hold onto. I picked up a branch, which I wedged into a small crack in the rocks. Once into the water, holding onto the branch, I was able to stretch one leg and search with my foot for the rope beneath the inflated roll. Having hooked it with my foot, it took me a few attempts before I was able to grip the roll with one hand. And there was the rucksack!

Holding it up, I screamed to Max: "I have it!" In answer, he joined his hands above his head.

All the waterproof bags were torn up, perhaps because of violent shocks, and everything in the rucksack was completely soaked. The water hadn't had time to get into two of the lenses, but the Nikon and the other lenses were broken. Because the water had penetrated all their cans, the unexposed film—3000 feet of it—had to be discarded, but I kept the exposed film in case the lab could do something to save it. Once more, I hung around my neck the small leather bag containing my money. My waterproof notebook—containing pencils and the map I had drawn as we traveled through the uncharted area—was also there, but I couldn't find the compass.

Max whistled and signaled me to come back to him. Now I was facing a dilemma. I had to choose between two possibilities. First, to struggle with the torrent, rejoin him, and together move on to Tabang where we would find people to help us get back to J.F. But this didn't require both of us. Second, I could try to find J.F. on my own. Who knew how long it would take Max to reach civilization and then come back? With the porters we were always heading north; then following the river, we had gone east, and then south. With the map I calculated that by going west, with luck I would cross the tracks left by our expedition when we were going north. Following those tracks I couldn't miss J.F.'s position or I would meet him on his way south, back to Djelini and Tabang.

"Papa, what shall I do?" I asked loudly. Any voice, any clues would have been welcome advice, so I sat by the river—next to the boxes that each contained a hundred feet of unexposed film—and hoped and waited for an answer. I opened each box one at a time, and unrolled the film into the water, tying one to another end-to-end. "If this river leads to Tabang, Max is saved, unless he gives up from lack of strength, and I am sure to meet our track leading to J.F., unless I miss it. If this river doesn't lead to Tabang, how long will it take Max to reach the town, gather enough people, and come to save J.F.? In fact, if this isn't the river to Tabang, how can I find my way to J.F.? Staying with Max would be safer for me, in spite of his temperament. Because negativism gives him the courage and strength to go on, he needs to repeat to himself that he's finished and will never make it. I need to repeat to myself that what I am in search of is just around the next corner! Whatever the case, together we will be able to find help and search for J.F. On the other hand, J.F. has been alone four days already! Will he have the courage and patience to wait ten more days? If he won't wait and starts out alone, will he be able to make it to Tabang by himself? Small chance! And will I, without a knife, matches, or clothes, be able to make it back to him? If not, at least I have tried!"

Holding the end of the last roll of film, I said to myself: Amazing to think that the other end is already 3000 feet farther down the river. That is one kilometer! Then I let the film go, and since I had made my choice, I stood up and yelled: "*Max!* Do you hear me?"

Although I could hardly hear it, his answer was positive: "Whenever you don't hear me, just stretch up both your hands! Okay?"

Then, yelling as loud as I could, I told him my intentions.

This time, I was able to hear: "You're crazy! You'll never make it! Come back!"

"In ten days J.F. will be leaving the camp," I yelled, "and he'll need help. I must go! I would rather die trying to find him than come back without him!" Seeing his gestures, I guessed he was not happy with my decision. "Max, I love you! God bless you!"

I couldn't hear what he said, but he stayed there, as if waiting for something. Perhaps waiting for me to give up.

CHAPTER ELEVEN

In Search of the Garden of Eden

Hope is independent of the apparatus of logic.

NORMAN COUSINS

I felt good about my decision. After all, Max and I had survived this river because we had had the accident before reaching the waterfall that fell onto the tree spears. Moreover, I had found my rucksack; these were omens of good luck.

I tried to find an easier slope to climb but there was only the hundred-foot-high vertical cliff that slightly overhung the bank. I remembered having seen along the shore a small mound of earth with a few wild banana trees on top and decided to head for it.

Climbing the rocks with difficulty because of my wet shoes, I realized how much Max's instructions had helped me before. Now all I had were my blind, torn fingers. After going back and forth a number of times searching for the easiest passage, I finally found the clump of banana trees, the object of my quest.

When I reached the top of the small mound, I could see Max on the other side of the river. The fact that Max was about to witness my climb encouraged me. Suffering from vertigo, and terrified of climbing, I considered my attempt to make the top of the hundred-foot cliff a test of strength. As I climbed I began an incessant inner monologue.

About one hundred feet of climbing with soaked shoes. Too bad, but I must go. . . . Damn, it's not easy to climb with my fingers so sore. Blood is flowing again from the places where my nails are torn away. . . . Don't give way, root, don't give! I still have not found a grip for my foot. Shit, it's slippery! My dearest Papa, be there for me. It's not time to drop me off. . . . Holy ghost, Douche, you have reached halfway! Now it will be easier.

During the whole climb I was pestered by hundreds of minus-cule flies and enormous mosquitoes that noisily swarmed around my face and body, which streamed with sweat, dirt, and mud. After biting me, many of these creatures remained stuck to my skin.

Uh-oh, a slight overhang. The wall is curving. Let's go . . . not the right time to give up. Damn, the stone is coming loose!

The stone loosened and in falling carried a few cubic feet of earth with it, landing on the banana trees and rolling into the river.

Damn, better get down a little bit and find another way to pass over that overhanging, otherwise I'll fall off, too! Hey! My holds have fallen off! The wall is streaming with water. It's too smooth . . . I'll never make it! . . . God, Papa, help me!

Searching for a way down so that I could find another way up, I suddenly realized that the weight of my body had loosened all the holds I had used for my way up. I was stuck there, spread-eagled, both hands grabbing a root, my body stuck against the cold stones, humid soil, and soaked moss. Panic struck.

Do not panic! No point! Smell the cliff, Douchan, that humid rotten coldness is so good. It excites me a lot. Come on, Douchan, climb! Okay, okay, guys, don't push me. I am climbing . . . I made it! Bravo! Thanks Papa, thanks Lord! I would be ready to pray, but don't have the time. I must hurry!

My idea was to walk along the cliff to the dark ocher river, which would bring me up to the small beach where we had pitched camp. According to the map I had drawn, we only met one river of that kind, and it was going east, toward the torrent. Just before the small beach I should find the trail that would lead me back to J.F.

I saw Max waving his hand to me, before heading south along the stream. Poor Max, he has a long way to go, I said to myself in a kind of curious intoxication and angelic compassion. It was not clear that I was heading anywhere at all, but it was absurdly delightful just to be alive. While I walked I looked at my watch often.

I am lucky that my watch is still working. I hope the batteries will last forever. It's a companion. I don't feel lonely with it on my wrist. Although I am hungry, I feel great today. What incredible vitality I have. I am now walking with much more balance than in the beginning. Could suffering give me new strength? Could it be that fear of dying is giving me new strength? But who will die? Certainly not me.

A deep and extensive fissure interrupted my progress. Scared of getting lost, I made a wide detour around it. After a while I was stopped again by another impassable gorge.

Impossible, really impossible to go along the cliff. Max is walking somewhere along the river. Where is he? Can I see him? The jungle goes up to the edge of the cliff hiding the river. I am scared to fall off. Okay, I'll walk west. Then I will find the track we followed one or two weeks ago. Or whatever. . . . Shit. This time it's not a fissure blocking my way but a high wall. Never mind, I will go around it. The most important thing is to keep heading west. North is always indicated by the larger amount of moss on the tree trunks. Yes, ladies and gentlemen, the side of the tree where the moss is the most abundant always establishes a north/south axis. To move west, one walks at a right angle to the left of that axis. The left, of course, always goes west. . . . My legs are covered with these leeches. Without a knife, a cigarette, or salt, I must tear them away without having the satisfaction of cutting them to pieces.

Blood was still flowing from the deep cuts on my shins from the rocks in the rapids. This part of the jungle was filled with long, sharp thorns. More and more of them. I could not go through any more. I had to break the thorns in my path before moving; otherwise I would lose the skin off my shoulders.

Aiee! Not easy to break thorns with bleeding fingers. In fact, I should suck them later to stop infection. Hell, my shoulders are bleeding. . . . Ah, nice clean water to quench my thirst and wash my wounds. It's so good to fill up my stomach. It kills the hunger. However, I should eat something. But which grass? The porters had told me that some are poisonous. What's that? Hey, a group of gibbons! They are lucky. Wonder what kind of leaves they eat? I should try the same. What they can eat, human beings should be able to eat as well. Little bit sour. If only I could have a small piece of steak I would feel much better. . . . No more hunger. I feel good! . . . It's already 5:00 P.M. I must quickly find a place to sleep where animals will not hurt me. Perfect! This half-fallen tree will be perfect. I'll sleep on it so that animals will not attack me. I'll be safe with my feet off the ground. . . . Waiting for darkness to come, I write, write everything that has happened today. . . . Ho-ho! Time to go to sleep. Like a chicken. No, like a baby.

I took from around my waist the short nylon rope and snap hook with which my rucksack had been attached to the floating roll, and which I was now using as a belt to hold up my bathing suit, and put them into the rucksack. But I kept my rucksack on my back, as a cover against the nocturnal cold. I lay face down on the bent trunk that rose about six feet above the ground, my hands and legs hanging down like a giant lizard, hoping no such creatures were down there.

It's cold and dark. What time? 7:00 P.M. I have slept only one hour. I must sleep more to gain strength for tomorrow. My hands and legs are stiff. I should walk a little. . . . No, too scared. What if an animal hears me and comes over? No, I must stay like this and sleep more. . . . Shit, too cold. And nothing with which to cover myself. Even the rucksack I had kept on doesn't heat my back. I am shivering. What time is it? 8:00 P.M. I'll never make it, never. If I get a cold I will die of illness. I must find a way to sleep through the night. . . . I should have stayed with Max. At least he can sleep stretched on a flat rock. And what about J.F., who has the best situation? . . . What time? What, only 8:45 P.M.? I have only slept twenty-four minutes? No, twenty-six! I can't spend the night like this. Okay, I know what I will do. I will get down from my tree and I'll scoop out a hollow in the loose soil, then I will lie down and cover myself with soil and dead leaves. At least that will keep my body warm. But what about animals? What if there are animals sleeping just beneath my tree? Okay, don't worry, I will clap my hands. Not loud enough to alert other animals, just enough to frighten away those who may be sleeping beneath me.

Wet leaves and mud. No! No! No! I am not digging my tomb. It is just a bed. Damn, I have forgotten the leeches and other insects. I must find a way to stop them from penetrating my body. But how? Ah, I know what I will do about them. Here's a large leaf. I can clean it by putting it in my mouth, then I will roll it to block my anus. . . . Aiee! Not agreeable at all. Painful, I should say. Okay, now let's cover my whole body with the muddy soil and dead leaves. Cold. Now, two leaves, clean, to obstruct my ears. And two others to block my nostrils. Perfect. Now I must learn to breathe through my mouth, but without opening my lips too wide, and keeping my teeth squeezed together. . . . Okay, guys, have a good night. So good to stretch the body. Alea Jacta est. Good night, Julius Caesar. It's Douchan Gersi talking.

I was freezing in the beginning but after an hour or so my body started to warm up. I slept until morning. I was fortunate it didn't rain that night.

I see light through my closed eyelids. Perhaps it's morning. I am scared to open my eyes because I feel so good and so warm that I am certainly dead. And if I am, I don't want to know it. What's that strange noise in my ears? Screeching. Throbbing. Buzzing. Do dead people have buzzing ears? This is ridiculous, I must open my eyes but

I don't dare. What if an animal is staring at me? I know what I will do: I will open my eyes just a slit. I see nothing. Open more. Yes, like that. I see monkeys. Monkeys all over the trees and all around me. Monkeys everywhere. I bet they will be surprised to see a dead man waken.

After a breakfast of leaves, I started walking again toward the west. Later, I filled my stomach with water from a small stream. Making my way slowly through a jungle of thorns that led toward a valley, I began to question whether the river I had left behind me was really the Belayan.

If it isn't, then I will meet it somewhere ahead and have to cross it. It would mean that I am lost. I shall meet nobody. Help! . . . Max! . . . J.F. . . . Answer me! . . . Punans, help!

I screamed like that until my voice was gone and my throat hurt. Then, realizing that I should calm myself, I decided to think about my life, starting with my parents in Czechoslovakia. Then our wild exile to Africa. Then memories of my childhood.

"After all, if I had to die, it would have happened at age seventeen when I got meningitis," I said aloud in the loneliness.

Or I might have died later in a volcanic accident or with gangrene that infected my leg. The bites of scorpions and snakes. I could have died of thirst in the Sahara or in car crashes. Or just a few days ago in the rapids. . . . Great, that means I will make it.

A light rain started to fall in the late afternoon. I went to sleep buried under more soil, mud, and dead leaves. Now I knew how to make my bed. This time I covered my head with my rucksack. My natural cover kept me quite warm in spite of a cold rain, which lasted almost the whole night.

When I awoke I was not really hungry. But since I scheduled my three daily meals by my watch, I ate. For breakfast, lunch, and dinner, I ate just good simple food: water, fresh leaves, and grass. Although there were many kinds of fruits all around me, I was scared to eat them because so many varieties were supposed to be poisonous and I had no idea how to tell them apart.

My stomach was still doing a good job, but to fool my appetite I ate grass and leaves and chewed some tender roots, pretending it was a feast. I fantasized about gourmet menus. I remembered all the times when I hadn't finished the food on my plate. I was determined that would never happen again, even if I had to force-feed myself.

I am starting at 6:00 A.M. my third day alone, with amazing strength and morale. For the first time I don't feel brutalized by the jungle's aggressiveness. On the contrary, I perceive deep in myself something like a need to communicate with the jungle.

If I were to personify the jungle, I would call it *she*, femininity—the feminine element. I wanted to talk with her, to befriend her, because that would help me survive. But perhaps talking with her would not be quite intimate enough. Sometimes we can understand each other by glances, gestures, or caresses. My situation called for a total merging. Since awakening, I had had an erection. But instead of masturbating as I sometimes did before, I decided to maintain my erection as long as possible. For the inner awakening of senses that possessed me seemed intended not merely for personal satisfaction but for an exchange. I had an infinite tenderness to give and receive. It was like being next to the very beautiful body of a woman and feeling an invisible connection growing between you and her, pushing you to a more precise contact with her. First with the eyes, then with the light touch of fingers, then with lips that tremble before they touch the petals of sweet female skin. I no longer saw trees, branches, and vines around me, but the hands of women, the bodies of women. I felt that burning yet tender glance that suddenly creates shivering in the deepest part of my being, shivering that slides, explodes, and is then consumed in the bursting of sex.

Strangely attracted by the freshness of its sweat, I stuck my naked body against a tree. The tree became the body of a woman. I slowly sucked her humid moss and drank a few drops of its bitter liquid. I rubbed my body against hers, searching for caresses. I did it until I could master my sexual desire no longer. Then I drove the messenger of my soul into a soft mossy cavity . . . and started to mix my dreams of survival with the act of love. Slowly at first, then faster, harder, until I felt on my body the rain of her cold sweat mixing with mine. And as I gave the jungle a part of myself, my inner dream melted into the dew still clinging to ripples of the bark since the cold dawn.

Transformed by the act of love, I felt happy, happy to be living, happy to be alive. I lay down on the ground for a short rest. Then I moved toward the west.

Later, my efforts and exhaustion broke my confidence apart.

I started to think about my dearest friends who might have to be told that I was dead. I saw them in mourning. I saw them watering my empty coffin with tears of friendship and love. Suddenly I yelled, "No! No, I want to live!" The morbid pictures went on, and I felt good seeing my friends crying, while obviously I was still alive. "Hey," I said. "They are not crying now. They will cry only when they learn of my death. No! I don't want to die!" To chase these nightmarish images from my mind, I started running. Running through the thorny vegetation. And I felt good when the thorns tore my skin before driving deep into my flesh. I felt good because the pain testified that I was still alive.

I want to be stupefied with pain . . . stupefied by pain, which chases morbid thoughts away. I want to stop the clock of distress . . . break the order of things . . . I want life!

I ran like that until lunchtime. But I didn't want to stop because the pain was not yet enough to kill my despair.

Not even the thorns tearing fiercely and unrelentingly at my hair, my shoulders, and my legs could stop me from thinking that I would die. Lost in the jungle, drowned in waves of lianas, trees, bushes, deep crevices and fissures, with wild screams and silence all around me, I hallucinated. My flesh was ripped by thorns and tears. Blood and sweat mixed together. Each trunk, each liana, all vegetation was covered with moss, and twenty or thirty times I stopped and tried to discover if a leech had penetrated my anus. The place where they liked to gather most was behind my knees. I was scared by everything. By my own moves and noises. I was paranoid. I felt like vomiting and crying. I felt like staying at the same place and giving up the fight against myself. But a great force still pushed me to walk. I stumbled. I fell. I extricated myself from bushes and thorns in order to climb a steep slope or to turn around and go back in order to move on. I tried to bathe as much as possible in the momentary flashes of the sun's rays, but most of the time it was dark in the sea of foliage. First silence, then the scream of birds and the drone of insects. Then silence again. Then screaming. How could I stop the process of my death? How could I get out of my never-ending dying?

Okay! I get it! I know how!

I remembered something very strange and mysterious that I had seen one night in a small village in the southern part of France. A dead cat, probably killed by a car, lay in the middle of a deserted street. It was surrounded by eight live cats who sat silently regarding the dead body. I don't know how long they had been in that position, but suddenly one cat stood up. It came over to the dead body and began a symbolic copulation. When the cat was finished another took its place, and so on, until they had all completed their mass ritual of love. Then, although the rain was falling, they began all over again. They conducted their ceremony in complete and solemn silence. It was as if they expected the magic of procreation to bring the cadaver back to life. They went on until the light of dawn started to appear. Then, all the cats departed, leaving behind them the dead cat to whom each of them had made love six times.

Holding my head between my hands, I tried to concentrate my mind on erotic images. I wanted to have a hard-on! For I thought that as long as I was able to have an erection, I would be more alive, because I had the potential to create life. By keeping and protecting that potential, I would be able to stay alive. Having an erection became my way to exorcise my own death. Lovemaking with the tree was a celebration of life.

I regained confidence in myself. I was feeling wonderful until my body froze at the sound of a monstrous scream. It was the same scream that Max and I had heard one night coming from the other bank of the river. The scream of a bear. The scream sounded closer, but I didn't know from which direction it was coming. I tried to guess which way to flee. Desperately I looked all around me but could not find any natural spear. There were only roots or thorny bushes. A new scream. A new shot of fear. From the bushes, a black bear appeared, with its mouth wide open.

In a panic I threw myself through the foliage and thorny bushes. I fell. I stood up. I ran. I fell and stood and ran again. The bear's scream changed to ferocious growling. It was closing in on me. I jumped on a narrow tree, trying to reach its top. My rubber soles couldn't grip the slippery, moss-covered trunk. I squeezed my thighs harder. I don't know how I got the strength, but I was able to reach the first branch about six feet from the ground. The bear ran around and around the foot of the tree. Fear squeezed my throat. I was a living dead man. I was already feeling the pain of my leg being torn off. I said prayers to God, to my Papa, and everyone I could think of.

The bear stood up, roaring. It had a white "V" on its black chest. I could see that it was about three feet tall. Visibly furious, it went back on its four feet. Growling, it continued to circle the tree. Then it stopped and went away, came back, and started to climb the trunk. Each time it roared I could see its teeth coming closer. A nightmare! Trembling with fear and screaming, I battled with my shaking hands to open the snap hook and the rope that served me as a belt. Holding the rope with the heavy snap hook at the end, I waited until the bear came closer. Then I beat its mouth as hard as I could. Our roarings mixed together. I sweated. I spit on it. Losing my grip I started to slide down. I grabbed and climbed again, higher. Beat. Scream. Pray. With blood flowing from its nose, the bear calmed down. Me too. A respite, a hesitation. The bear circled, wondering how he could get me.

He continued to besiege me for three hours. Three hours during which I wondered why the bear was attacking me. Three hours to understand that perhaps, being a male, he had decided not to allow my presence in his territory. Three hours to dream of killing him. Three hours to fear his devouring me as revenge. Three hours during which all the prayers of my childhood welled up in me. Three hours to become a Christian again.

And then death simply walked away. And I began to cry. I was a child in need of tender love, clinging to the sweetness of a mother. I swore that I would never leave home again. No more expeditions. No more nothing. Just stay quietly at home, wrapped in love.

For a few minutes I remained paralyzed. Then moved by an incredible strength—and running as fast as the mud, the thorny bushes, the hanging lianas, and the dead trunks allowed me—I hurtled straight ahead, remembering to notice the direction the moss grew.

I spent the night vomiting bile and suffering from a burning diarrhea. Without a doubt I was suffering a liver crisis provoked by terror. Waiting for my strength to return, I went back to my journal and tried to write in the dark.

The morning of the fourth day I found new energy in digesting my grass breakfast. I hung the rucksack on my back and moved on again toward the west. Each steep slope was painful to climb. The wounds all over my body, the large cuts on my shinbones, and the deep scratches made by thorns had all become infected.

The thorny bushes have torn my right shoulder again. I must walk carefully on this long trunk covered with a slippery moss. I must be careful not to fall down into this deep crevice. I must be careful. Careful. I wonder what time it is. Without looking at my watch I would say 11:46 A.M. Hey! Almost right, Douch! It's 12:03 P.M. Okay, time for lunch. "What about starting with a tomato soup, then lobster, then a thick, juicy steak, with crispy french fries and a lot of mayonnaise? And a magnum of Beaujolais Village, please!" I ask the maître d'.

"Sorry, sir," he says, smiling stupidly, "we only have grass."

I stand up, yelling. "What? Don't tell me that you are only serving grass!"

"Sorry, sir. But all over this town you'll find only the same thing: restaurants for vegetarians."

"What about wine?" I ask, shaking.

"Just water, sir."

I sit back and say, "In that case, give me a glass of water 1947, and a thick grass steak . . . with a salad."

A new sound reached my ears. It seemed to be coming from inside the ground like the noise of rapids. A doubt suddenly crossed my mind. Did I walk back toward the rapids that almost took Max's life and mine? Was I back to my starting point? *No!* That couldn't be! While searching for an explanation I moved on, like a sleepwalker, through the vegetation, which seemed to clear a little. Then I saw a small red river. A red river, the same color we once encountered when we were with the porters and where we had bivouacked. The river, ten feet wide and three feet deep, led southwest. I walked downstream into its sludge, moving faster than I would through thick jungle. Now the sounds of waterfalls became clear. The current grew faster. Another small river joined mine, and together, a hundred feet farther down, they fell thirty feet in extraordinary jumps and then broke into pieces in a deep fissure where they surged and blew into a torrent in a gigantic splash—like an immense vomiting.

Back at the fork of the two rivers I decided to go upstream on the new river. This too was an ocher color. The waters became deeper and deeper. Too deep for me. I climbed the bank and continued walking, even though it was covered with plants with long leaves whose thorny edges lacerated my legs. The river flowed between two rock walls whose summits were covered with a very thick vegetation. Back into the river. Thanks to the water, my wounds didn't hurt any more. I moved on, disappearing up to my chest, carrying my rucksack on my head.

Suddenly a splash. Then a second one. I just had time to see a crocodile's tail disappearing into the dark waters. With a superhuman jump I left the muddy deep and found myself hanging on the rock wall. Images came to my mind. I saw my legs devoured by the saurians. Without taking time to find out if they were deadly crocs or merely harmless *gavials*, I climbed the slippery wall. Then with tears in my eyes I walked on the cliff, cutting a passage with my hands through the dense, thorny vegetation.

It's 4:00 P.M. I must stop, I am dead exhausted. What about having an early supper?

I am naked. I am freezing. I am about to vomit again.

Each noise gave me a start. Since my encounter with the bear, I feared the night. I remembered the black panther Max and I had seen. It's strange how good I felt about J.F. He had everything needed for camping: food, campfire, hammock, sleeping bag, warm clothes. I wondered, What is Max doing right now? We split up four mornings ago. Is he worrying about me?

I wanted so much to be joined by him. And yet, I knew it was impossible for him to follow my track that was no track at all but only a drifting wherever my falls pushed me, wherever my fear or madness led me. It was not the jungle that scared me. I feared being lost. I feared my weakness.

I was overcome by the impossibility of surviving without weapons in a jungle filled with animals. Where will I sleep this night? Sudden and ferocious screams gave me a start. I froze. The screams seemed to come from the right, from the river. I prayed. That stimulated me. The solitude was the worst thing. One is not scared when there is someone else. Happily I still can think aloud.

No panic, Douch! Please! Okay.

My heartbeats banged in my head. I moved on, slowly, toward the river. By the water, two powerful wild boars were fighting a duel. They smashed against each other, heavily, their tusks as long as daggers. One had a deep slash in its side. Suddenly they stopped the fight and looked in my direction with their small, villainous eyes. After a last roar they dashed away, one following the other. Their company and then the solitude further intensified the feeling of being lost.

Am I really lost? No! I start to whistle. Then I scream: Help! Help! . . . J.F.! Max! Help! I scream again and again until my throat is sore. Now, because of my screaming, the jungle is silent. But not for long. What's that sound? Gibbons! All the trees around me are filled with gibbons. About thirty of them. It's great to watch their agile jumps from tree to tree.

I realized that night was about to fall. It was too late for my dinner, I had to dig my bed. Especially at night, I was scared to death. It was horrible to feel thousands of insects crawling all over my body. I couldn't scratch myself without breaking my cover of wet soil and rotten leaves. Mosquitoes used my face as their landing field, worms used my nose as a ski slope, ants used my forehead as a dance hall.

Exhausted, I fell asleep with moral tortures crawling through my mind, my life's worst parts projected on the screen of my memory. Waking during the night, my heart beat in quiet panic as I tried to identify the noises around me or explain the too deep silence. I imagined a thousand deaths. Diarrhea kept me awake part of the night. Unable (and too scared) to move, I simply defecated in my "bed."

The dawn came slowly, announced by an extraordinary concert of animals, birds, and insects not heard later in the day. At dawn and at dusk, the jungle assaults the ears. Screams answer one another, echo from tree to star, from cloud to leaf, from moss to drops of dew. I started the morning of that fifth day by bathing in the river and then searching for my breakfast.

Strange. I don't feel like making love to the jungle today. What's going on? Did I become impotent? Or have I just grown a little bit weaker? That's it. I must eat protein this morning. Anyway, if I want to be able to make it, I must eat something more nourishing than grass. . . . Courage, Douch!

I forced myself to eat two long worms I found by the water (it's just spaghetti, Douch, just spaghetti, I said to myself), a bunch of huge ants, and a few leeches. I drank water and burped loudly in rhythm with the melancholy hootings of the gibbons. I started my walk along the river, but the rain came, pouring down so heavily that it would have been dangerous to move on. I took refuge inside a cavity in the small cliff and went back to my internal monologue.

. . . And if it isn't the right river, never mind. I shall return and follow the other one. But today I want to believe in miracles!

I felt great, filled with confidence in myself, in God, in my father, and, most of all, in the jungle, which appeared to me as a friend and not as an enemy. I was ready to combine with its energy.

Impatient to go on, in spite of the pouring rain, I moved out of my shelter and started to follow the muddy bank of the red river. I had hardly covered one hundred feet when the sky was suddenly torn apart by a series of lightning bolts followed by a deafening explosion of thunder. I moved back into my shelter.

Oh, woman-jungle, you caress my hair in thorny confusion. Your eyes reflect a deep sadness that bruises the heart. I have forgotten if you have a body. My hands are too weary to caress you, too heavy to embrace you. How long will I last in this sinister sleepiness? Perhaps until your face evaporates in the boiling soil. My dreams are becoming crazed. They carry me to the gate of delirium. I am afraid of falling into the dwelling place of madness. Yet I would like to become mad.

I walked in the river as long as I could, sometimes disappearing up to my chest in the swirling water. Its depth and sticky sludge forced me to move back to the jungle, along the almost impassable bank. As if I were not already suffering enough from other wounds that covered my body from my face to my swollen ankles, the claws of the vegetation stuck deep into my already torn flesh. Sleeping in the mud and walking in the dirty waters, I had become a mass of pustulant infections. Yet strangely enough I was possessed by amazing physical energy.

The jungle was covered with heavy clouds that day. It was so dark that I was literally overjoyed to meet a single sharp ray of light. That narrow beam crossed the fog and slid beneath the tops of trees, like the holy beam in religious paintings that lights the praying forms of saints. The strange beam fell exactly on a small hillock covered with light green moss. The whole of my surroundings, filled with a smooth silence, created an atmosphere of miracles about to happen.

Perhaps the Virgin Mary will carry me with her to the sky. A helicopter of angels will save me from the rot in which I am lost. I want to be ready for her. I'll try to neaten my hair. Tangled by sweat and rain and heavy with dirt, it doesn't want to come unstuck. Never mind. I put down my rucksack and kneel on the moss lit by the divine beam. The scabs covering the wounds on my legs break open, releasing pus. But so what? The Virgin won't care. I pray, kneeling on this holy pillow, enlightened by the bright countenance of the God of Gods, Lord of divinities. I pray to my heart's content, I cry out my most secret convictions. I pray as I have never prayed before.

After a while, I realized that I was stupid to wait in that

position for the Virgin Mary. By kneeling on the moss, I had taken the place of the Holy Virgin. That's why she hadn't come. Making fun of myself and my arrogance, I moved into the darkness of the forest, knelt again, and continued to pray.

I waited.

The beam of light moved and grew weaker.

"Shit!" I said loudly. "How stupid I am, waiting here like an imbecile. I have just lost an hour being off my rocker. Eh, Douch, shake yourself up. Move on. Walk."

The experience of coming close to the limits of sanity frightened yet impressed me. Going on along the red river, I couldn't stop thinking about madness.

Perhaps insane people are not sick. They are just people made fragile by a lack of love, or whatever, and weakened; people whose protective envelope of will or personality or position has given way under the pressure of forces they can't handle, endure, or accept. Their only way to survive is by taking refuge in stories they invent to combat these enemy forces. Madness is becoming someone else, experiencing another kind of reasoning, reasoning that protects and gives back one's self-confidence. Madness is entering a new world, a land of dreams, souls, or nightmares.

My thoughts were disturbed by the loud noise of branches cracking. I froze, thinking the noise could only have been produced by the fall of a tree or a large branch. As I started to move on, the noise resumed with even more volume. It sounded like a bulldozer coming after me through the jungle. I started to run in the opposite direction. Falls and thorns soon covered my body with more mud and bloody scratches. I knew that if I didn't stop my wild flight, I would either kill myself or break part of my body. Again I took refuge in a story of my own creation.

What if the noise is a helicopter, a very special helicopter, landing to rescue me? No, impossible. The most special helicopter couldn't do that. Well, why not, after all? A helicopter with parachutists has come to save me. But then why didn't they call me? I know why. Before saving me, they are filming how I am coping with the jungle. Yeah, people are observing while filming me. I must show them that I don't feel miserable at all. [I laugh loudly.] No, no, I am not miserable. Besides, I should do some fitness exercises to show them that I was just running for the pleasure. [I stick out my chest and yell like Tarzan.] But where are they, so I can show them my best profile? I will turn when I reach that tree,

*so they will certainly catch my best profile. I will act as if I were
examining the moss on the tree trunk. That's it. Now I look like a real
explorer searching for his way, without panic. Now I will move on with
style, showing my muscles. It's a pity these scabs covering my body look
so dirty.*

I went on imagining in that manner for a couple of hours,
until I forgot the story I built to protect myself from fear.
Happily, my watch was still working. I, who had always hated
watches, hung onto the time now. I kept checking it as if I were
late for an appointment. It was great to have a watch that
worked so precisely after five days. Five days? Shit, it felt like
five months.

I thought of J.F.'s cushy life. So much food. Concentrated
milk. I was not worried for him but for Max. Max is not sensitive enough to become occasionally insane in order to release
tensions. He could die from being too realistic, too rational, a
too-serious pessimist. Dreams give a new strength to the batteries. It was strange to notice every morning how much I enjoyed
life. I loved the trees and smells of the jungle. The sounds and
colors. I loved it all.

"Forest, I love you!" I said loudly.

And what if the forest were a praying mantis?

I realized that I was not going west any more. Yet
I felt I should follow that river. I had the vague impression that
this river, now a lighter red, was the ocher one with the small
sandy shore, which I call a beach, where we had camped once.
A few hours later I stumbled on a small sandbank.

*What's this? Hey, it's the beach! It's my beach! I am sure of it. But
if it is, I should find proof of it. . . . Nothing. Yes! Something! A small
piece of the pink toilet paper I had used! And there, the stick frames of
the shelter built by the porters. Yes, it's my beach.*

Like a child, I threw myself on the sand and rolled all over
the small beach. Then I knelt and, in tears, said, "Thank you,
Papa, thank you! I love you!" It was not my time to die. It's lucky
the beach was there, for I had crossed our trail without noticing
it. Without that beach, I would have walked in the jungle till
death caught up with me. The water was more red than ocher
now. But so what? Perhaps the color changed depending on the
kind of earth the rain brought into the river. No time to lose.
I tried to think about my situation.

To the north is J.F. with the food. He is one or ten days from here. No. I'm stupid, he's farther than just ten days. Let's see my map. He's about one month from here. But that was one month with porters and many long stops to take rest or take pictures. Alone, walking nonstop, J.F. is ten days from here, maybe less. Walking north I will meet him. It will put his mind at ease to know that Max and I are alive.

But maybe Max is in danger. If Max needs me, going to find J.F. will make me lose several days, which will add to Max's agony. What if he has broken a leg? What if he has abandoned the rapids, climbed the cliff and walked through the jungle, following my suggestion? My God, what to do? Papa, help me make a decision. So what if J.F. is worrying, he has everything he needs to wait comfortably. His life is not in danger, but Max's may be. Therefore, I must go to Tabang and get a rescue team to Max.

I was so worried about Max's life that I ran toward Djelini from where I could easily reach Tabang. About two hours later, I found the cave where we had slept the evening before stopping at the beach. That meant that in only two hours I had covered what had taken a whole day to cover with the porters. The desire to save Max gave me wings. I was ready to move on in spite of the approaching night, but a thunderstorm forced me to bivouac there. Later, as the night fell, it became so cold inside the cave that I brought in handfuls of dead leaves to cover my body.

Before this experience I would never have believed in the power of the will to survive. The will is so much stronger than muscle or bone. I am feeling much better and stronger than when I first arrived in Borneo. In addition, I have an amazing sense of balance that allows me to move over obstacles which, two weeks ago, I would have stumbled over.

I am freezing, but God how wonderful that thunderstorm is. Extraordinary. I am happy to be living and shall live more intensively from now on. I shall make the most of my family, of their presence, of my daughter Maroussia. I will also make the most of all the affection offered to me.

In order to travel lighter, I kept only the notebook and pencils, my money, and two yellow plastic bags—in case I needed to leave a visible message somewhere. I left the rest of my gear and film wrapped in a broken plastic bag, in the deep end of the cave.

I am starting my sixth day walking like crazy. I mean running. This is terrific. I have the kind of energy that leads people to victory and life;

toward the secret sap that prevents death. What does that mean? Yes, I am filled with confidence. I would be feeling totally great if only this fire were not devouring my guts.

I found the small trail overlooking the river. I was high above it and thought perhaps that by another miracle I would see Max. But the river wound too much. By sliding down the steep muddy slope, I reached the edge of the rapids.

My exhilaration grew as I imagined seeing Max, my friend Max, walking on the bright stones. I called, I yelled, I screamed. I wanted to make him appear in front of my eyes, through the limitless power of love. Death did not exist that day. It existed only for the weak and the unlucky. Death was for others.

"Max!... Max!..." Nothing. Nothing but the echo of stones turned upside down by the tumult of the water flying away from the falls. "Max!... Maaaaaax!..." Still nothing. Nothing but the water roaring like a mad dog that should be killed. A rumbling of foam that troubles my nerves. "Maaaaaax!..." Could he be dead? No, that's impossible. He's stronger than me. A paratrooper-commando. Unless he has smashed his face on these slippery stones or been eaten by one of the crocs that sleep in the dead water or hunt in the rotten mountain crevices.

I left him a message on one of the broken yellow plastic bags: "Max, I've found the small trail, we're saved. Just climb the slope and you'll meet it. Taking it to the right leads to J.F., to the left is Djelini. Wait for me at Djelini. I am going to find help. Douch."

I put the yellow plastic bag, with the message written on it, on top of a huge rock, in such a way that he couldn't miss it even if he walked by on the opposite bank. Then, with an easiness that surprised me, I climbed the steep muddy slope to pick up the small trail again.

Damn these wild boar trails, they always end in impassable thorny bushes or in deep crevices. Okay, now. U-turn. Now where is that trail? That's it, I will invent a new direction through dense vegetation. Invent the road of life. I am running as fast as I can. Great, Douch, since morning you have already covered the distance between three of our previous stopping places. Now you've got it made.

Trying to hold on to a rotten branch, I fell ten feet, landing hard on my back. When I hit the ground, something like a brutal electrical shock crossed the nape of my neck, immobilizing me with my hands and legs wide apart, in the ridiculous posture of a man killed by a deadly fall.

I lay a long time without being able to move my fingers or my hands, which were ravaged by inner pins and needles. I was on my back, my arms stretched out to my sides, attracting a thick cloud of mosquitoes that I couldn't even chase away. When I awoke an hour later I was able to move again. I started running toward Djelini, which I knew was closer.

At 2:00 P.M., exhausted, I arrived at the rocky overhang—Djelini. All my wounds were painfully and deeply infected. I intended to lie down in the sun for just a few minutes but instead I slept for two hours. I was awakened by hunger burning my stomach and the need to vomit bile again.

Before leaving Djelini, I abandoned my rucksack in a conspicuous place on the top of a rock to encourage Max if he found it and to give him what I didn't get: the friendship of hope. In a plastic bag that I was able to inflate a little bit, I kept only my money, my notebook, and one pencil.

The riverbanks seemed impassable. The only way to move on and reach Tabang was to swim downstream, but I was still afraid of rapids.

Not knowing how I got such an idea, I tore out a pubic hair and threw it into the river, as a substitute for my life. Then I inflated the plastic bag containing my treasures and hung it on the snap hook of an improvised belt so I would have my hands free for swimming.

Half an hour later, I saw the silhouette of a Dayak long house on the top of a huge hill—a long house that we had seen on our way to Djelini without paying attention to it, because we had been in such a hurry to start the expedition. "That's it!" I yelled. "Here is my garden of Eden. I am saved. It's the end of my sufferings." Climbing the hill, I called, "Eh! Dayaks! *Eeeh!*" But in vain. The long house was deserted. I found eleven nuts on the broken floor. They were my dinner. I chose the veranda as my bedroom. The bamboo floor was like a soft mattress after what I had slept on over the last days.

On the seventh day I slept until 10:00 A.M. But instead of having renewed my strength, I awoke from that long sleep in a kind of deep numbness. I was weak, and my whole body hurt deeply. The pain was especially intense in my groin, where I found several very swollen and painful sores the size of pigeon eggs, four on the left side, five on the right. These "alarm signals" indicated the gravity of the infection I had in my legs. But I had to move on.

Several bamboo poles and pieces of cord made of flexible bark scattered around the house gave me the idea of building a raft to reach Tabang. So I picked up all the material I needed and moved down to the river while eating some roots gathered on my way. By noon I finished my three-by-three-foot raft. I lay on it chest down, able to paddle with feet and legs.

I had hardly started when I noticed a small cascade on my right side whose clear water slid over green moss before falling and mixing with the torrent. Compared to the muddy river, that water was what I wanted to quench my thirst. But since the bank was made of huge rocks, I had to stay on the raft, holding on to the rocks to stop myself from being carried away by the current at the same time as I drank.

With my stomach filled at last, I stayed close to the bank and let myself be carried toward a line of foam that crossed the whole width of the river. Suddenly, I saw that my partially inflated yellow plastic bag with my money and notebook had fallen off the raft and was whirling and jumping in the water ahead of me. Then it disappeared into the waves and whirlpools before reappearing, floating on quieter water.

"Hey!" I screamed loudly. "My balloon! It is going to the other side of the river. *My balloon, my money, my notebook!*"

Blinded by tears of anger and frustration, I paddled like crazy with my hands while being carried faster and faster by the current toward the middle of the river, which was about sixty feet wide. Waves smashed my face, stones hit my knees. The poor raft was being torn apart by violent whirlpools, waves, and the shocks of rocks that obstructed the rapids. I was about to drown again, but, enraged by my misfortune, I paddled desperately toward my goal yelling, *"My balloon! It's my balloon!"*

Only my wild madness gave me the strength to move over the barricades of stones, raging waters, liquid storms, and bright and luminous whirlpools. My frenzy removed all sensation of pain from my battered body.

And then, close to the opposite bank, it appeared, slowly spinning on a series of small whirlpools, held almost stationary by the countercurrent along the crowded sides of the river. I succeeded in catching the balloon, but holding onto it, I was unable to stop my raft from being carried away by the current into new rapids.

The foamy water smelled like the blood flowing out of my nose, coloring the water, as if the stones had their throats cut. One eye seemed to be removed from its socket and was hanging on my chin, which had lost all feeling. I was inside an elevator crashing down into a cellar flooded with water. Its sides were exploding in slow motion; then, in a crackling of a thousand cannons, the elevator tore down a ravine of giant cliffs. Each tumble—a spurt of fire, blood and rocks, water and vomit—entered my nose, my mouth, and even my lungs. A hand was strangling me. My hands gripping the balloon were dead. I was dead.

When I awoke, I was lying on the bank, legs still in the river, hand still gripping the precious yellow plastic bag, my body covered with leeches. I had slept all night. It was 7:30 A.M. of the eighth day.

As soon as I stood up, my legs started to tremble. I vomited. Frightened even to look at the rapids, I entered the thick jungle and started walking parallel to the river, my heavy legs stumbling at every step. After a while, I encountered a small trail that disappeared into the bushes. Hoping that it would be the way to reach human beings, I followed it without caring about its direction.

An hour later, I caught a whiff of smoke mixed with burning hair. Overjoyed, I left the small trail and searched frantically in various directions to find where the smell was coming from. Finally, the precise, cracking sounds of burning wood confirmed that I had found the right track.

Moving with care through the bushes, I spied a group of five long-haired Dayak warriors, wearing only dark red loincloths, the rest of their bodies covered with tattoos. One of them was tending a wild boar cooking over a campfire. The others were sitting around the fire laughing, spitting reddened saliva, and obviously enjoying their successful hunt. Each had a long, sharp machete. Their deadly blowguns were leaning within reach against a nearby tree.

I hesitated before signaling my presence. I was inside their territory without having been invited. My appearance alone could frighten them so much that they would kill me. So I decided to remain hidden in the thick vegetation, so that I could think about my next move.

I didn't have that time. To my horror, a warrior suddenly jumped for his blowgun, brandished it like a spear, and began moving toward my hiding place. In less than a few seconds, he was joined by three others, holding machetes or blowguns into which they had inserted poisoned darts. The fifth one disappeared into the forest, no doubt to find out if I were accompanied or alone.

Their smiling faces had become motionless masks. Nobody was chewing betel any more. I stayed motionless, too exhausted even to complain had they decided to end my heroic adventure by taking my life.

They looked at me and then at one another. Then one of them said a few words that I couldn't understand.

I knew that my life as a life per se had no value for them, and that killing me was not in itself an immoral or forbidden act but only a matter of what bad consequences might befall them and their clan. Whether I lived or died was now a matter of what their imaginations told them. I had to appeal to them as a human being, for I was not in a position to intimidate them. I slowly moved out of my hiding place, lifting my hands, palms wide open to show that I was unarmed, and fell on my knees, bursting into tears. I whispered weakly, *"Makan . . . makan . . ."* ("Food . . . food . . ." in Indonesian language) without knowing if they could understand. They remained motionless, holding their breath, ready to kill me either by driving the blowgun's long iron blade through my chest or by sending a poisoned dart into my flesh. I looked into their eyes and detected a sort of apprehension. In spite of their position, these men were also scared, and it was their fear more than anything that could unleash their spears and darts.

"Makan . . . makan . . . ," I repeated in the gentlest tones, slowly using my left hand to show what I meant. The warriors exchanged a few words without looking at one another but continuing to watch me like a wild animal. Then one of them screamed something. A faraway answer disrupted the silence of the jungle, coming from the one who had gone off to scout around.

"Makan . . . ," I repeated, pointing to my stomach and my mouth. Other words were yelled again by the scout, still searching the jungle. This time, all of them together answered him. By hearing the calmer sound of their voices and also by seeing them start to spit their red saliva again, I had the feeling that they were becoming reassured that I was alone.

I have no idea how long I waited for their judgment, but when the Dayak scout returned, the atmosphere became markedly more relaxed. Putting down their weapons while talking all at the same time and smiling at me, they gestured with their hands that I was to follow them to their campfire. Once there, they motioned me to sit down and then sat down all around me.

Immediately, one Dayak cut off a piece of the wild boar meat and put it on a large leaf, next to a portion of rice removed from an iron pot. In the meantime, my answers to their many questions were bringing smiles. I ate everything gluttonously and that made them roar with laughter. They served me a second and much larger portion of rice and meat. By the time the second helping had disappeared, they were guffawing so much that they could hardly eat their own meals.

My stomach filled, I took a break during which I tried to tell them my whole story, using gestures and drawings on the ground. But suddenly, feeling sick from having eaten too much too fast, I stood up and ran to vomit behind a tree. That, judging by the ringing level of their joy, was my biggest hit.

They told me they were Punans and I learned each of their names. They were able to memorize and perfectly pronounce my name and those of my two lost friends. Then, after they finished off the rest of the meal, they invited me to follow them.

A half hour later, called to us by the shouts that my escort yelled all along our way, five other Punans came and greeted us as we entered a wide natural clearing. In its middle was a large Dayak shelter of stick frames covered with leaves, used by hunting parties or groups to gather the damar resin. Leaning along the interior wall were five or six huge baskets filled with small blocks of damar, the harvest of several weeks of work. In one corner was a small basket of gold nuggets, probably gathered from the middle of rapids.

Noticing my infected wounds, one of the Punans immediately covered them with a native medication, a strange dark paste he had mixed with dirt. I felt total trust that he knew what he was doing; normal concerns about getting dirt into a wound didn't apply in the jungle.

Meanwhile, each of us, including myself, had to report my misadventure several more times for those who had missed hearing it. Thanks to these repetitions, I ended by learning so many Punan words that we were able to understand one another quite well.

I learned that same day that they were about to carry a load of their harvest up to Djelini, where they had a meeting with a Chinese trader from Tabang. Once the first exchanges had been concluded, they were to bring him a second load the next day. And so forth until, having nothing more to exchange, they would go back to their faraway village. By now we were the best of friends, and they invited me, Max, and J.F. to go and live with them.

As soon as I understood their invitation, I dared to ask them to aid me in finding my two friends, hoping deep in my heart that they would accept. And so they did. We decided on the following plan. With orders to call Max's name as loudly and as often as possible, one group with food and a written message from me was to run back along the river, find him, and then bring him back to Djelini. Another group would do the same thing for J.F., except that they were to follow another path. They would also carry my material along to Djelini.

The most difficult task was to make them understand that in case one of my companions was found dead, they had to bring his body back; for when a Dayak dies, it is not usually with his body that these people deal, but with his soul.

After having made them repeat my instructions to be sure they understood everything, the search parties set out, and the rest of us went with the first load up to Djelini. There we met the Chinese trader whom I had seen a few times in Tabang. I recognized his motorized canoe as mine and told him so.

"No, it's mine," he said.

"Hey, I bought it from Mr. Golden Teeth. You can ask him in Tabang."

"He sold me his whole business and this boat and moved out of Tabang a month ago. This boat is mine."

I stopped arguing. After all, I could do nothing except act friendly if I wanted him to bring me back to Tabang. In taking me aboard, he was losing the place of my weight in precious damar. Since he probably believed my story, he accepted without complaining too much.

It was the best season to move downstream over the rapids. The river was high, and the Chinese trader knew the locations of all the dangerous passages so well that, moving almost at full speed, we reached Tabang very late that night. My friend the mayor was away on vacation, but I was greeted by Ahmed, a damar and gold trader and the merchant from whom we bought the food provisions when we left Tabang. He offered me warm hospitality for the few days I had to spend in Tabang while waiting for my companions to be rescued.

I spent a very bad night. In spite of the accumulated exhaustion, in spite of having taken some antibiotics from Ahmed's stock, I found my sleep a torment of feverish jumps and frightening nightmares. I drowned many times that night. Again and again I was sucked into a raging whirlpool. I also dreamed of Max's various deaths: devoured by a panther, torn into pieces by a bear, killed by exhaustion and hunger. Then I dreamed I was in court, first condemned for having continued my expedition in spite of Max's death, then accused of his death. I awoke terror-stricken.

Max had been alone for eleven-and-a-half days, J.F. for eight.

M y first morning in Tabang, I made a reluctant visit to the police officer, to whom I had to make a report. He said he couldn't do anything more to help me than to let me send whoever I wanted to find my friends. He also said that our misfortune was our own fault, since Roustan had told us to go *mudik* (upstream), but we had mistakenly gone *muller* (downstream). There was no point in arguing. The police are always right.

I recruited new porters. Except for Roustan, those who had previously accompanied us had become invisible. We searched for a motorboat to rent.

Finally the Chinese owner of "my" motorized canoe agreed, for a high price, to carry the group of rescuers up to Djelini. However, he would not agree to wait there for them. I had no choice but to accept all his conditions. When I started to argue, he said, "Then swim upstream."

At last, eleven newly recruited porters with a large provision of food were put aboard. I repeated the orders I had given to the Punans, and the overloaded motorboat disappeared upstream.

In spite of my intense desire to accompany them, I didn't. Weakened by infection and still shivering with fever, I wouldn't have been much help in that search. The canoe was already heavily overloaded without me, and I was convinced that my friends were already found by the Punans and would be waiting at Djelini when the boat arrived.

I decided to take a nap, but I couldn't find sleep because of my inner nervousness. I lay on my bed and, half-awake, half-asleep, daydreamed about what we would do as soon as my friends and I were together again.

My Punan saviors will lead us into their village. There, we will take the time to recuperate, all of us, quietly. Meanwhile, I shall create strong contacts with them and film their daily life. After that, we will finish our crossing of the uncharted region. It will be the triumph of which I have dreamed.

But what if Max is really dead? No, that can't be! If I was able to survive all my shit, then he's still alive! . . . Sure! . . .

Tomorrow, the canoe will bring Max and J.F. back to me.

That evening I heard the motorboat's roar as it returned. I ran out to see my friends, but the Chinese trader was alone except for his crew and a load of damar.

Tonight, in my dreams, instead of drowning in bright and savage whirlpools, I am murdered by Max's mother. She follows me everywhere to avenge her son's death, screaming: "I told you I would kill you if . . ." Without giving me time to explain, she drives a knife into my abdomen.

Pouring rain slowed the Chinese trader's second trip to Djelini and his return. At last, on the morning of the fourth day after the rescue team left Tabang, he returned with his motorboat.

"Tuan," he said, handing me a folded piece of paper. "Here, a message for you."

"What?" I said, my whole body suddenly trembling with a deep emotion. Using Ahmed's flashlight, I unfolded the piece of paper and discovered that, in fact, there were two messages. The first one had been written by Max:

"Douch, the nasty Chinese didn't want to take us in his boat. We're waiting for you at Djelini. Everything is all right. Come quickly. Your pal, Max."

I was wild with joy. But not for long. The second message—written in English and signed by the teacher from Tabang, who was part of the rescue team—said that Max was feeling great but that J.F. was very sick.

"Can we go now to Djelini?" I questioned the owner of the boat.

"No, tomorrow."

"Why tomorrow?"

"Because it is night now."

"How come you're able to come back from Djelini at night but not to go there at night?"

"With the moon it's okay to go downstream, but not upstream."

"Tomorrow I am renting your boat. Be here at 6:00 A.M., okay?"

"Okay, okay. Same price. But for the return, I—"

"I know, I know. You still have your damned damar to carry. But don't worry, once I'm at Djelini I won't need your boat any more."

I couldn't wait to reach Djelini. Until I did, my life was to remain a torture, for I was mad with worry for J.F. and at the same time wild with joy at the idea of meeting up with my two friends again. The day upstream seemed endless.

In the late afternoon the Chinese trader said, "There's Djelini," as if my eyes hadn't seen the rocks from the moment we started out.

"I know, man, I know. You don't need to tell me that."

The sight of the Punans standing on the rock overhang with Max and the rescue team was exactly as I had imagined it, except that one detail was missing—J.F.

"Max! J.F.?"

"Douch!" Max was so wasted away that he seemed to have grown smaller. "Douch, you have lost so much weight!"

"You too, brother!" I answered, as we hugged each other tenderly with tears in our eyes. "Where is J.F.?" I asked.

"There, somewhere," he said, pointing at the jungle. "He's acting strangely."

"What do you mean by that?"

"Go see for yourself."

I spotted J.F. standing near the edge of the jungle, looking at the ground. I ran over and hugged him, but he didn't seem at all pleased to see me. "So, brother, are you all right?" I asked, kissing his cheeks.

"Yeah . . ." he answered, with a faraway look in his deep blue eyes.

There were no traces of emotion. When I stopped holding him, he looked at the ground and muttered to himself.

"What are you seeing?" I asked.

"Me? Um . . . I am careful not to swat the ants. Otherwise, they will suffer, and . . . and then complain . . . complain to the jungle." He looked at me from far away. "Do you understand?"

"Yes, J.F. Sure, I understand."

I was disturbed by his attitude but convinced that he was just suffering from a momentary psychological shock and, with a little rest, would recover. "J.F., are you feeling good enough to come to the Punan village with me and rest there?"

Too passive to argue, he replied, "Sure. I am your assistant, aren't I?"

"Thanks, J.F."

I left him by himself and moved to my expedition gear, checking to see if everything were there. Then I went to thank each of the Tabang rescue team members and those of my Punan saviors who had remained in Djelini. They seemed really happy to meet me again.

"You're right," said Max, joining us. "It's time to say farewell to the Punans. Let's go. I never believed I would say it but I can't wait to get back to Tabang."

"No, Max. I have brought along large provisions of food and gifts for the Punans. We're going to be their guests."

"Where?" he asked, looking at me with deep suspicion.

"In their village. We're invited to stay in their very comfortable village."

"What for?"

"Well, I'll try to learn about their life and customs, and . . . and I shall film them. You and J.F. will rest as long as you need, as long as you wish."

"Don't bullshit me!" Max said, raising the tone of his voice. "If you intend to finish your fucking exploration, don't count on me."

"Max, my friend, my brother, calm down. You're free to do whatever you want. I am just asking you, would you be pleased to recover in the Punan village?"

Max said nothing. Anger was making him mute. I knew that I would do better by leaving him alone. As I was going toward the Punans, someone touched my shoulder. It was Max.

"You are really going on?"

I nodded *Yes.*

"Really?"

"Yes, really."

"It's crazy."

"I know."

"Insane."

"Of course."

"Okay, then as long as you admit it, let's go. Besides, I've had enough of this shitty place."

As soon as the roaring of the motorized canoe disappeared in the never-ending noise of rapids, about twenty other Punan men, women, and children timidly appeared from the jungle where they had been hiding. One of my rescuers explained that they were from his village, and their help was needed to carry all my stuff. Escorted by these people, we took an easy path to reach their village the evening of the following day. The night of camping and the day of walking were filled with hearing of Max's adventures.

Listening to his story, I realized how much he was a man without an open door to the land of dreams or folly. The military rigidity and discipline Max had learned during his training in the Belgian army as a paratrooper-commando had robotized him. However, that is probably what had saved his life. During the ten days in the jungle, he had thought only of survival—at any cost and no matter what. To walk, to walk, and to walk, and to survive.

Here is Max's story as he told it to me.

"I knew that energy was all I needed to make it. I had no idea how many days or weeks it would take me to reach Djelini, Tabang, or anywhere else. When I saw you crossing the torrent just in the hope of saving the films in your rucksack, I thought you were insane. Insane and damned stupid. You might kill yourself. I couldn't do anything about that, my goal was to stay alive. I understand that for you, once sure of 'being alive,' the next main concern was the success of our expedition. But it was not the same with me. I lived long enough in the army to understand the problems we were facing. When I saw you examining that high rock cliff blocking the jungle, I realized that our ways were about to part. Instead of trying to cross the jungle, I preferred to follow the security of the river, even if that increased the number of days or weeks it would take me to reach safety.

"Every day I started early in the morning, around six, and I continued until about eleven or noon. Along the river there is no protection from the sun. At noon it becomes so strong it knocks you down. I would take a nap for two or three hours and then start to walk again. My tube of aspirins was filled. At each of my breaks, my menu was one aspirin with as much water as I could drink to fill up my stomach. That's why I slept so well.

"On the third day the riverbank that I was following became impassable. I had to cross the torrent again. I don't know why, but I tied the mosquito net wrapped with my sweater and the portable water filter around my wrist. Then I started to swim, pushing the rucksack in front of me. Suddenly the whirlpools started to carry me toward the rapids. In order to swim faster and harder, I jettisoned the rucksack containing my hammock, your clothes, and our sleeping bags, but I made it across the river.

"The nights were cold. I slept on rocks, wrapped in my sweater and the mosquito net, both of which were soaking wet and cold. I broke into tears once or twice. I experienced two or three terrors. I encountered a ten-foot-long lizard who was more frightened than I. When he saw me, he made a powerful U-turn in the sand and disappeared into the water. My heart pumped for ten minutes. Another time I had to climb a slippery stone chimney, thirty feet high. Just as I was about to reach the summit, I met a snake. I almost fell and killed myself on the rocks. Let me tell you that I survived only because of my military training.

"I often thought about you. I was waiting to see you appear almost any time at the top of the cliff.

"On the eighth day I saw a yellow spot shining on a rock and knew it was a message. It took me about two hours to reach it, but how happy I was to learn that, indeed, I was on the Belayan, leading to Tabang. It was almost more than I could have hoped for at the moment. I climbed the cliff, just at the place indicated by your arrow. But I couldn't find either your landmarks or the small trail. So I continued my walk along the river. Besides, walking on slippery stones, even in darkness, was more attractive than walking in a jungle filled with thorns and snakes. I got used to walking barefoot on stones and sand or in water.

"On the tenth day I heard someone calling. I didn't react at once. Too many times I had imagined hearing you call my name. I was sure it was an auditory hallucination. Then I saw some people running along the top of the cliff. I hid myself behind a rock and waited. Who were they? What would they do if they found me? Ten minutes later, I distinctly heard my name, so I answered. Roustan ran from the jungle carrying a message. He was happy to find me again and he hugged me. Then his friends arrived with warm rice. I ate too much. When they told me that we had to walk farther to reach Djelini, I started to cry and then I vomited.

"During the walk I collapsed every five minutes. My heart beat so hard I thought it was going to fail me. Finally they had to carry me. Then we were joined by J.F. and the rest of the rescue group, followed by Dayaks.

"The worst was the three days of waiting at Djelini. The rain and my waiting for you never seemed to end. I thought a lot about everything. The jungle, my folks, our friendship, what I've done with my life. I spent the rest of the time sleeping, eating, and throwing up."

When we arrived at evening in the Punan village we were greeted by the wild barkings of their native dogs. Unlike other Dayak villages that consist of a long house, this village was composed of twelve houses on pilework about six feet above the ground. The houses were built side by side, their balconied entrances facing a central plaza not far from a river. Internal walls, of bamboo frames covered with palm leaves, divided each house into two, three, or four rooms.

My material was put inside one room of the house of one of my Punan rescuers. Then, sitting half in the house and half on the balcony and observed by all the villagers who awoke to see us, we shared a copious meal of rice and wild boar meat.

We went to bed on thin matting stretched on the bamboo floor, under two joined mosquito nets. Our room stretched the length of the house, squeezed between a small hall that gave onto the balcony, with a large kitchen on the other side. The entrance to the kitchen was through our room. It had a stone hearth set in one corner where two or three couples were sleeping. On the opposite side of our room, instead of a wall there were steps that led outside to the balcony. In the third room, which occupied the other end of the house, someone was playing the melancholy *sapeh*, a Dayak musical instrument with three strings, similar to a lute.

The melodious music, mixing with the nocturnal symphony of the jungle, was interrupted by the wild howling and barking of dogs fighting. The Dayaks do not teach their dogs Western manners. As J.F. and I were talking before sleep, a dog entered our room, urinated on the mosquito net, and wet my shoulder. We chased him away, but half an hour later he was back with three other dogs who came to fornicate at our feet, tearing away our mosquito net in their mating frenzy. Between the farts, sonorous burps, children's screams, brutal coughings, human and animal lovemakings, barking, howling, and other nocturnal noises, it was not particularly pleasant to share the hospitality of the Dayak village.

That night Max, J.F., and I didn't feel like sleeping. Max and I kept telling our stories, adding forgotten horrors with each retelling. We begged J.F. to share his tale with us, but he refused. Even during the three nights he had spent with Max at Djelini, J.F. had said almost nothing. By now Max seemed to have recovered psychologically from his ordeal, but J.F. hadn't. His thirteen days of solitude had marked him deeply. I tried to ask him questions, but he rarely answered. And when he did, his explanations were in vague snatches, with tears in his voice. He acted as if he hated me.

"You must understand," he said. "I thought you had forgotten me. I trusted you so much that I was sure nothing could ever happen to you. To Max, maybe, but not to you. I believed that you didn't want to lose the time to come and take me with you. Do you understand?" What could I tell him?

Most of the time J.F. was perfectly lucid. He was able to diagnose the sicknesses of the Punans and was a perfect technical assistant. But every now and then he would plunge back into a faraway universe of dreams and madness. More than once I noticed that he tried to avoid stepping on insects. His lips would move as if he were talking to them.

Psychologically speaking, his waiting was certainly more difficult than the physical struggle to survive. For Max and me, our survival, up to a certain point, belonged to us. We had our destiny in our control: to walk or to give up. J.F.'s survival was in our hands. His only recourse was to endure the terrors of waiting. Every single day, after we had left him, he had gone to the precise spot where we had disappeared into the jungle. He would wait there, repeating thousands of times the same sentence with which he intended to greet us: "Hey guys, it took you so long to come back that I was about to call you up on the phone!"

Months later, after our return to Europe, he let me read his jungle diary. Through the reading of some extracts from his journal, one may understand how he came to enter into another consciousness.

. . . But the real fear, the Fear with a capital F, the one which lowers, paralyzes, gnaws, and destroys the brain; the one which weakens, makes one fly away, abandons, crashes, kills, is the horrible feeling of seeing oneself becoming diminished, ridiculous. It is intolerable to one's self-esteem. I shall try to forget that fear, but I will never be able to forget it completely. I am scared of this fear, I am scared of the marks that it will inevitably leave.

I thought I would never know what fear was. I thought I was strong enough to fight it and win. My fear is caused by not knowing; I don't know where Douchan and Max are. I don't know what they are doing, I don't know when they will come back. I don't know if they will ever come back. I would be able to keep going for days and days, if only I knew exactly when they would be back.

I am responsible for the equipment. Therefore, I am responsible for the continuation of the expedition. But that is Douch's job and a great part of his future. Even if I knew where to go, I can't wander off. I am stuck here, in ignorance. At least they know where I am. They know that I have enough food. Although I don't eat. They know that nothing terrible can happen to me. I wish I could believe that.

The waiting pushed J.F. to take sleeping pills at night and other medications and stimulants every day to keep him going. These destroyed his appetite and he grew weaker and weaker. He forgot that the fire was necessary and let it die. That was his biggest mistake. Without the smoke to chase wild animals away, they became accustomed to J.F.'s silent presence. More and more birds and even small animals started to enter the clearing to visit him, without fear.

It's hot. I decide to open my watch to dry it out. Maybe it will start working again. It must be noon. The shadows are almost vertical. I shake my watch. It works! I jump with joy. I put it on the right time, 12:00. I hope it will keep running.

I am lying in my hammock, silently, looking at a big lizard climbing one of the tree trunks. I am listening to the songs of the birds. It is amazing how many different songs one can hear in the jungle.

I really don't understand what could have happened to them. If they hurry, Belinau, the Dayak village, is only one long day's walk. Roustan said so. Maybe they fell off a tree or something. Douch dead? Max dead? That's not possible! Okay, they are not dead, but in that case they have no more food. No more film. Then what the hell are they doing? They should have been back a long time ago.

I know what's going on. They are making a monkey out of me. I don't want to think about them any more. They are certainly dead. No, that's not possible. Shit! And shit again! What the hell do I do now?

I have decided to stop writing my journal. I have the impression of writing this journal for the time after my death and I don't give a damn about that. It's for me that I am writing it, not for others. I will start writing again when I shall be alive. I am scared to write. I don't want to see myself any more.

Each day, as if they were reconquering lost territory, more birds, snakes, deer, monkeys, and wild boars came to visit J.F.'s camp. Their incursions gradually plunged him into a deep terror. He had the feeling that everything, even the trees and lianas, were becoming aggressive. He began to imagine that everything was watching him intently.

In order to escape from these dangers that seemed to be getting closer and closer, he had only three possibilities: to fly away into the jungle; to fight back against plant and animal adversaries with his machete; or to enter the world of madness, dreams, and imagination. J.F. chose the latter, a refuge of hallucination.

I had also entered this domain of imaginings, dreams, and madness, but I had to leave this psychological "refuge" to face the reality of my own survival; whereas J.F. had no other reality than his never-ending waiting, surrounded by adversaries. His psychological survival was made possible only by remaining merged with an organic and animal world where there was no longer anything to frighten him.

Unconsciously, perhaps, he began to humanize and personalize his plant and animal adversaries. By assuming a nonaggressive position he created deep emotional contact with his aggressors and called for their understanding. To communicate with an adversary is already to be in less danger. One can see the foe and create limits to one's fear.

Perhaps this saved him from an irreversible madness. Had he refused this gift of imagination, it's possible that the external aggression would have broken through his protective envelope and sent him into a world with another level of logic.

No one will ever really know when J.F. passed from one logic to another, but I believe it was the day when a black panther entered his camp. J.F. was lying in his hammock when the panther began to sniff the air, then the boxes, coming closer and closer to him. According to his own memories, as J.F. talked to her, she came back again and again as if to protect him. One day she presented him with her cub. Here's the first passage that he wrote after having closed his journal for a few days.

For the thousandth time I hear them [Max and Douch] walking, talking. I lift my head, but see nobody. Again I have the feeling that I will die. I am crying. I have a headache. I am either boiling or freezing. I can't take it any more. I hear too many things. I am thinking about my mother and crying again. I am delirious, going out of my mind, experiencing absurdities. A helicopter is coming to save me.

I am chatting with a black panther. I have told her to watch out, for I have a fire stick [rifle] in my hand and if she makes one single move I will shoot. Slowly we are reaching the point where we understand each other. However, I still don't trust her completely. I squeeze my stick, always ready for a possible ruse from the beast. Finally we talk about men in relation to animals. Is she trying to deceive me? She tells me that she has a cub, and because she finds me likable, she is offering it to me as a gift. I am scared to vex her by refusing it.

. . . I am scared to continue this relationship. Yet I feel so good in these moments of madness. As soon as I come back to earth again, it's utter fear and depression and I become crazy!

Very soon there will be only two solutions for me. Either I will die here slowly, mad, or I will get out of here alive and end my days in an insane asylum. I must get out of here! It's my only chance. Feverishly I prepare all the stuff to bring along with me: vitamin C, peanuts, sugar, rations of U.S. army survival food, matches, cigarettes, sleeping bag, plastic cover, quinine, airline ticket, and passport, antivenom serum, syringe, alcohol, canteen, concentrated milk, bowl, spoon, rice. That's it. I think I have forgotten nothing. Now I shall put all of that inside my rucksack. I feel better. I shall go away tomorrow.

. . . Night is coming. The animals start to scream again. It hurts inside my head. I am scared. My ears can't take it any longer. I shake them but it gets worse. For sure I am leaving tomorrow. I am getting away from here. I don't give a shit about Douchan and Max any longer. I don't want to see them any more. It's their problem to get out of their own damned mess. I am going home.

. . . It's the tenth morning. How much longer should I wait? A whole day? Two? Three? Ten more? Just thinking about it makes me throw up the two small spoonfuls of rice I have eaten. I am ready to scream so loud that everything will stop. The joke should have stopped long ago. What have I done to this jungle to make her so nasty to me? The jungle is alive, watching me intently, and waiting to kill me. I have done nothing to her, apart from crushing a few ants. Only a few ants . . . and many, many mosquitoes. And now she is frightening me.

On the morning of the tenth day, J.F. wrote on one of the large film containers: "I am leaving!" Trying to reach Djelini, he got lost, but fortunately by a true miracle my Punan saviors found him three days later and brought him back, along with our equipment.

To this day, J.F. still affirms that he really had conversations with the black panther. I believe him.

CHAPTER TWELVE

Living with Punans, the Jungle Nomads

Treat the other man's faith gently; it is all he has to believe with.

HENRY S. HASKINS

I have always been fascinated by nomads. This attraction for people who travel endlessly, often for reasons that are unknown to them, has pushed me to share the lives of Gypsies and the Tuareg people. I don't really know what it is about these travelers that fascinates me, but I believe it is their faculty to move on and on, always farther and farther, without caring for ownership that keeps the rest of the world in place. They belong to the world and the world, they feel, belongs to them.

The Punans are nomads of the jungle, silently marking trees over hundreds of years—nobody really knows for how long—to record their passage throughout the deep jungle.

At last we were living with them. They protected us as if we were their own—giving us shelter, food, and freedom—for much longer than the period covered by the laws of hospitality.

Weakened by exhaustion, diarrhea, and the parasites that had begun to travel through our bodies, we didn't have the patience to study as we might have in a healthier condition, but we nevertheless learned a great deal.

This group of Punans had come from the north. Their long trip had lasted for almost two generations. With their women, children, and old people, they carve passages through the thick jungle. They carry their meager belongings, their culture, memories, and divinities over raging rapids, deep waters, and almost impassable mountains, stopping sometimes for months, to give birth or to bless a death. Some groups always camp in temporary shelters. Others build small villages in areas well-stocked with game and abundant fruit and stay for years before moving on.

Their nomadism drives them from these villages for days, weeks, or longer, in search not only of food but of resin and gold. They find gold grains or nuggets along rapids or behind small dams they build to filter the riverbeds.

Seemingly incapable of—or perhaps simply uninterested in—farming, the hunter Punans undertake long travels to reach other tribes to exchange meat for rice. In exchange for resin and gold, they get iron blades for their machetes, plastic shoes, T-shirts, and other goods from modern civilization. In this way, without ever having been visited by foreigners or ever having been in direct contact with the twentieth century, many Dayak tribes have had their beautiful clothes of beaten tree bark replaced by machine-made atrocities. Uncertain transistor radios that pick up more static than music interrupt the jungle quiet. Flashlights scar the blackness of tropical nights. Yet, in spite of these attractions, the majority of Punans and other Dayak tribes refuse to leave their traditional world.

During their travels for hunting and barter, they spend rainy nights under the small wooden structures we encountered throughout the jungle. The caravans of Punan travelers are preceded and followed by armed men whose duty is to protect them from enemy tribes.

The morning after our arrival, we toured "our" village in its jungle clearing. The first thing we noticed was the cleanliness of the village and throughout it the abundance of colorful flowers, mainly hibiscus. Nests of orchids decorated some verandas. The village sheltered about fifty people. Because sooner or later they will go back on the move, they don't have a village chief, but instead a type of organized anarchy where everyone does what he wants so long as it doesn't disturb the freedom of others. We made friends by offering tobacco, which the men liked to chew, distorting their cheeks with the tobacco squeezed between teeth and upper lip. The women preferred to smoke it rolled in leaves. From them we received large smiles that revealed the betel chewers' reddish lips and dark teeth.

Many of these Punans had never seen white men before and some women and children hid inside their houses. The men expressed neither aggressiveness nor apprehension, for we were their village's guests. They stared at us with intense curiosity, astonishment, and, in a few instances, suspicion. Many stayed cautiously on their verandas, both fearful and threatening. Only one man reacted with overt hostility, brandishing a long knife each time we approached. No words were needed to make his warning clear. With the exception of this one fellow, after a few days even the most suspicious Punans became friendly.

Blowguns are vital to Punan survival. Accurate up to one hundred feet, a dart can easily knock down a pigeon. The poison will paralyze a deer or a man almost instantly.

The Dayaks carve the blowgun from a single piece of wood and their technique is a marvel of traditional technology. An old man, one of the last in that area who knew how to make blowguns, allowed us to observe and film parts of the secret process. This brave man hadn't been aware of what would happen to his house when he accepted my filming his work. The huge frames used for making the Punan blowgun couldn't be moved outside because they were too high, but I couldn't film inside without additional lighting. "Well, take down some parts of my house's wall," he said. As more and more of the sun disappeared, we removed more and more parts of his house. By the time we had finished filming, two walls were stripped to the framework. We were about to rebuild them when he said, "We'll do it tomorrow." That night a violent thunderstorm not only soaked his furniture but blew out his other two walls and the whole roof!

The blowgun, which may be up to seven feet long, is carved from a perfectly straight branch of an iron tree, the strongest and hardest wood on earth. A branch is precisely carved until it is a perfect cylinder with a diameter of about two inches. This is tied vertically to a wooden frame that holds it firmly six or seven feet from the floor. The space between the floor and the lower end of the cylinder cannot be less than its length.

Sitting on a raised platform that positioned him at the base of the blowgun-to-be, the old man, using a double-edged chisel with a sharpened point, dug a quarter-inch-diameter barrel, starting at the lower end and going through its entire length. Carving that hollow tube is like drilling through steel.

One would think that the channel would be straight; but if it were, the blowgun would be unusable. In the shooting position, a blowgun sags under its own weight, resulting in a curve that would make it impossible to see through the barrel. To counteract this, the old man bored a hole that curved up, so that

Punan blow-gun maker.

in firing position, when the weight of the gun bends the wood, the hollow remains perfectly straight.

In order to determine the curvature of the channel, the old man must analyze the length, weight, and density of the iron-wood cylinder. However, since his empirical calculation allows for small errors, he attaches to one end of the blowgun a long iron blade whose weight corrects its inflection as well as indicates the firing position of the weapon. Besides firing poisonous darts, a blowgun can also be used as a spear.

The making of a blowgun can take months. It requires enormous patience, incredible skill, and almost infallible intuition, for a single crack in the wood can ruin months of diligent labor. Each blowgun is made according to secret traditions and standards handed down for countless generations.

Each hunter carves his own darts. Bamboo is carefully trimmed and whittled to a precise shape about eight inches long and one-seventh of an ounce in weight. For propulsion, a soft wood plug is attached to one end. This guides the dart like feathers guide an arrow. The tip, coated with a powerful poison, is designed to break off when it penetrates the flesh. Even if a dart is torn out of a wound, neither monkeys nor men have a chance to survive.

Punans are known to be great experts in the preparation of the poisons with which they coat the tips of their darts. They use a mild poison for killing birds, small animals, and monkeys, and a very powerful one for deer, orangutans, wild boars, and humans. Dayak poison, more potent than the curare used by Amazon Indians, is made of certain plant extracts mixed with the powdered pit of a fruit called *strychnos*, the favorite food of the calao birds. The fruit is edible, but the pit contains strychnine. The poison doesn't kill by itself, but penetrates the nervous system so that the victim dies slowly of asphyxiation. This allows the unpoisoned meat to be eaten. Long before the game would die, the hunter kills it with the blade of the blowgun or with his *mandau*, the traditional Dayak machete.

I tried to get the Punans to allow me to film a hunt, but they believed that it might disturb the spirits of the animals and that all the game would leave. However, I was allowed to join. For the hunter, the most amazing part of a hunt is not finding and chasing the game, but finally facing his victim. As a way of honoring his prey, the Punan will never shoot until he and his prey have made eye contact. Just before killing, he recites prayers asking forgiveness of the animal whose spirit is linked with his own system of divinities. Through his prayer this act of destruction does not disturb the harmony that reigns between men, nature, and the gods.

Filming wasn't too difficult, since we spent about a week behaving as the Punans did before taking out our cameras. Soon they were used to our "strange machines" and stopped looking at them whenever we were filming, although they never could understand what it meant to be filmed. I simply said that I wanted to show my people how Punans live in the jungle.

The daily life began early in the morning with the departure of three or four men going hunting together. All men take their turn at hunting for the village. Each family takes what they need of the meat. It's a perfected "community way of life," where a kind of well-ordered anarchy reigns.

Later in the morning, men, women, and adolescents go in small groups into the jungle to search for fruits and edible flowers and plants.

Larger groups of men search the jungle for damar and gold nuggets. These gatherers are often gone for many days. And if their harvest is important enough, other groups of ten or twelve men, each carrying baskets filled with as much as eighty pounds of damar, leave the village to exchange these goods with other tribes. Sometimes these traders are gone for weeks, always preceded and followed by an armed escort.

Those staying in the village spend their time preparing food, taking care of small children, making poison and darts for their next hunts, fishing in the nearby river, or just resting and chatting, like people do everywhere.

In late afternoon when the jungle starts to release its freshness, the hunters return, carrying enough to feed the village for another day. After each family has taken what it needs, fires are lit on the balconies and dinner is prepared with a variety of ingredients such as native flowers, fruits, and herbs. Before eating, the people go to bathe in the river, where the children play and scream in their own joyful prayer to life.

The ascent of the blue smoke, carrying the aromas of the cooking food toward the fawn-colored sky, is sometimes disturbed by the arrival of Punan traders bringing plastic reminders of the twentieth century to their otherwise almost stone-age existence. After the shadows have vanished with the setting of the sun, the darkness brings new symphonies to life in the jungle, and a large campfire is lit in the middle of the square, which calls out to the people who are still eating to assemble as they do every night for a musical gathering.

Finally, the whole village gathers around the fire to sing and dance, accompanied by the melodious music of the four-stringed *sapeh*. Covered with ornaments of feathers attached to their heads and wrists, the girls start to dance, their slow movements blending with the shadows of flames. For hours these girls continue to dance with the night, preparing with their sensual movements for the nocturnal intimacies to come. With music and dance, couples freely summon each other to enjoy the heartbeats of their sex. The following night each may taste other lips and other loves. This free mating will go on until a boy and girl decide to become a couple, with the hope of creating new life and sanctifying the joy of life together. Contraceptive methods are used to limit births.

Late at night, after the adolescents have gone into the darkness to exchange their embraces, the older men dance. Feathers cover their backs and are also tied to their heads and wrists so that they become "flying men." The story they tell with their dancing is always the same: the flight back to their original homeland, which they believe is another planet.

I found this same myth of flying men in Burma and on Easter Island, where a whole village is dedicated to remembering times when flying men came to visit the people of the earth. Even the Indians of North America and the Amazon have this myth, as well as the Incas and the Mayans. We, too, have these flying men, called *angels*, in our mythologies.

I gazed into the campfire and thought about these extraordinary similarities. Why have all cultures had such a myth? Why, so far from one another, have they all imagined their origin on another planet? Why do the Dayaks say they come from the Pleiades? The Dogons of Africa think they came from Sirius B. Two thousand years ago by unknown methods, they plotted its circuit around Sirius, the Dog Star. Indeed, according to their dated cave paintings, two thousand years before Jesus Christ, the Dogons had already greeted a man who came from the stars, who was symbolized by a fish, and who died on a cross.

So much dizziness in a Borneo jungle on a night of good-bye. Tomorrow we must go, but tonight we are joining our girls for the last time. How long will it take me to forget the freshness of their smoky skins?

A group of Punans agreed to help us cross the uncharted region. Following their trailmarks we were able to cross the high plateaus with ease. We were only two days' walk from our destination, the Kayaniot River, when for unknown reasons the Punans said they would escort us no farther. Since we were still under the emotional stress of our survival experience and didn't feel ready to take any more chances by going solo into the jungle with our heavy gear, we felt that we had accomplished our mission and headed back to Balikpapan.

We arrived in Balikpapan three uneventful weeks later. The Shell Company's people were surprised to see us alive.

"Some people of a timber company brought us a backbag and pieces of your inflatable canoe that they found floating along the Belayan's mouth. Since your name was written on the backbag, we sent it to your embassy in Jakarta. They have probably reported that you are dead."

Once in the Belgian embassy of the Indonesian capital, the first thing I did was send a telex to my family saying that I was alive. Indeed, at the embassy I found a month-old Belgian newspaper article headed: BELGIAN EXPLORER DOUCHAN GERSI REPORTED DEAD WITH HIS TWO COMPANIONS.

It took a few months for J.F. to return to the logic of our civilization, then he went back and finished his medical studies. Today he is a medical doctor in the north of France. Whenever we meet, he says to me, "Douch, I'll ask you very soon to take me to some wilderness where we can meet such warm-hearted people again."

Max had promised to accompany me again on another expedition, but he soon began to dream about making his own adventures. As I am writing this book, he's filming somewhere in China.

CHAPTER THIRTEEN

Third Expedition into Borneo

I am an idealist. I don't know where I'm going but I am on my way.

CARL SANDBURG

Man has always collected trophies of the hunt. Most lodges in America have a few of these on the wall. But in some areas of the world, the trophy is often the head of a man. To the headhunters, such a hunt is a religious ritual that can perpetuate life, but modern civilized men, mystified and shocked by this practice, have tried to stamp out what they consider barbaric savagery. They have almost succeeded. Therefore, headhunting still exists only in places isolated from the outside world. That's why I came into the interior of Borneo. I knew I would be risking my life to travel there, but I wanted to locate traditional natives and, by living with them, find out if the Dayaks of Borneo still hunt human heads. That was the question I asked these Punans. All affirmed that neighboring tribes, such as Ibans, Kenyas, and Kayans, were headhunters, but they remained silent about themselves. And, in spite of our meticulous searches throughout the village, we didn't find a single place, inside or outside of their houses, where they could have kept the skulls of their enemies.

However, thanks to pillow talks, I learned that Punans will behead their enemy headhunters when attacked—not for religious reasons, but to instill fear and respect in their enemies. Much later it was confirmed by a Punan friend that some of their groups need human heads for ritualistic purposes when someone dies. This was not enough for me to conclude that Punans were headhunters. The question was still to be resolved. Thus I knew I had to return one day soon to Borneo for my meet-up with headhunters.

It had taken me a year to rid my body of the unknown parasites that had chosen my skin as their new home and the unknown tropical amoebas which gnawed at my intestines.

The following year I was lecturing in Belgium with the movie of my first expedition in Borneo in search of headhunters. Prompted by my comment to the audience that I was ready to reenter Borneo since I had fully recovered physically from my jungle ordeals, a solid man in his forties approached me at the end of the lecture.

"My name is Bernard de Brouwer," he said. "I want to join you on your next expedition in Borneo."

He was president of a huge advertising company and father of a large and happy family, but dreamed of experiencing high adventures. In spite of his lack of physical training, he seemed mentally prepared to face almost any danger. So I agreed.

With two other companions we left two months later to explore the southern part of Indonesian Borneo. But still I failed to discover any active headhunters.

A year later, upon returning from a long trip in East Africa, I had learned that a region in the eastern part of Sarawak, the Malaysian part of Borneo, had been closed to travelers for security purposes. Rumors were circulating that although headhunting had been forbidden by the authorities, it was now permitted if the victims were communists. Had the government found a perfect way to stop the communist infiltration? Perhaps.

It was in exactly this region that the Iban people lived. They were considered fierce warriors and implacable headhunters. So I chose to return once more to Borneo.

Max had sworn he would never go back into a rain forest. J.F. was back at medical college. I decided I would return alone with my new girlfriend; her shining blonde hair would be a good passport, astonishing the tribesmen and stimulating their curiosity. I knew that traveling with my girlfriend would be safer than going alone or with other men, who could represent a potential danger. Entering warriors' territory with a woman would open all doors, I hoped, since we would represent a non-threatening traveling family. So we left together for Sarawak.

On our way to the Iban, who lived in the mountains straddling Sarawak and Kalimantan, we made a short detour along the boat route and stayed in the only remaining

village of the Sekapan tribe, of whom only four hundred in-
dividuals were still alive. Sekapan, who had been neither warriors nor headhunters, were disappearing, because their heads
were much sought after as easy trophies by the aggressive neighboring tribes. The village consisted of two long buildings facing
a river about two hundred feet away. Between the river and the
main long house, fresh eggs were left on a specially carved plank
every morning as an offering to their protecting divinities. Next
to the plank there was a pole fifteen feet high and fifteen inches
in diameter covered with carvings of grimacing figures with
large, mother-of-pearl–covered eyes. A wooden box at the top
contained the remains of the chief founder of the village who
had died three generations ago. The box was covered with masks
of grimacing figures similar to those I had found among the
Maoris in New Zealand and in the Marquisian islands.

Like those of the Punan, the ear lobes of the Sekapan women
were extremely elongated with the weight of heavy earrings.
The women wore even more tattoos than the men, and their
hands were so heavily marked that it looked as if they were
wearing lace mittens. Their feet were also covered with tattoos
to the ends of their toes.

Although they are also called *Dayaks,* the Sekapan do not have
the same cultural or ethnic origins as other Dayaks. Sekapan live
in the remains of a matriarchal system. Women lead all ceremonies and entertain at meetings. They speak among themselves a
different and secret language that is not understood by men.

The Sekapan use drugs all day long. Although cannabis smoking is part of most Dayaks' magico-religious ceremonies, it is
also used by the Sekapan for pleasure. Every day on awakening,
and sometimes even before the morning meal, we received a fat
strong joint. To refuse it would have been an insult to their
never-ending friendliness, so I got so stoned every morning that
I could not even consider lifting up my camera.

The most amazing thing about the Sekapan was their ability
to carry on their own customs and ways of life in spite of all
obstacles. (Although they are never visited by tourists, they
showed no real reaction or curiosity upon our arrival.) Years
before our arrival, the Sekapan had been in contact with missionaries but, unlike many other tribes, had resisted Christianity. The government had offered to help the tribe leave their old,
broken houses and move into brand new ones built near a modern city. When the tribe refused, the well-meaning government

built a school with houses for the teachers close to the Sekapan long house. But the Sekapan, like so many other tribes, were not willing to face the fact that one day their children or even their grandchildren might be forced to meet the modern world without adequate preparation. The teachers, who were not members of the tribe, had wanted to teach them the Malayan language. The tribesmen, however, refused the offer and finally scared off the teachers.

The will of the Sekapan to carry on their own culture is magnificent. But the question remains as to how to help people realize that they are condemned to disappear, that there is no way for them to retain their present way of life that is so in harmony with nature. The bulldozer of modern civilization driven by the profit motive is irresistible, and one day the Sekapan, like all tribes, will vanish. The surviving members will be merged into the proletariat of dispossessed people. They will have lost their name, their culture, their way of life, their identity, their dignity. We too will have lost all that as well as the knowledge they have carried since the dawn of their existence.

Living with these gentle people, I pondered their fate. The Sarawak government was, I feel, genuinely interested in helping them, but are good intentions enough? Do we have the right to separate these people from their culture? Do we have the right to impose new religions upon them? Do we have the right to take these people away from their own conception of the divine and sacred? Yet how else can they be protected and prepared for the inevitable?

After we had spent several weeks in their village, a Sekapan took us to their land of the dead. It was a forbidden place where every single plant, every single leaf, every single piece of soil was taboo. In the middle of this restricted area, hidden by high bamboo trees, stood an even larger and higher pole with another wooden box on top, which contained the remains of the village founder's son, who had been dead for two generations. The grotesque figures decorating this pole had their mouths wide open, showing four powerful teeth, very much like the grimacing gods of Tibet. Their duty was to chase away evil spirits.

This pole was surrounded by large trees in which the Sekapan buried their dead. After carefully cutting off the bark of the tree, they hollow out the tree trunk without killing the tree and place the dead body in the fetal position inside the hole. Then they replace the bark which, with the passing years, knits together with the rest of the tree. According to the anthropologists, this method of burying dead people might be linked to the belief that man is descended from trees.

Like the poles of the Ato in the Philippines, those of the Sekapan are symbolic of the tree of life and are also the link between the world of humans and the invisible world of divinities and ancestors.

After a few weeks of sharing the Sekapan's way of life, we decided to go on toward the territory of the Iban, entry to which was restricted by the government for reasons of security, for it was known that the dwellers were still ferocious headhunters and proud of it. It took us a day on a small launch to reach the last outpost of civilization. Then, after another day on a pirogue, we entered the deep jungle again at a point where I had been told I could perhaps find the Iban after a two- or three-day walk.

The captain of the pirogue clearly regarded our adventure as crazy. He wished us "Good luck." There was that phrase again.

After two days of weaving our way through hanging vines and thorny bushes, we came face-to-face with two calabashes hanging from a branch of a huge tropical tree. They were the first sign of man's hand we had seen. The gourds contained offerings left by the Ibans to the divinities for protection against evil spirits and were a signal to the evil spirits not to go farther toward the village somewhere nearby. Aware that people in this "restricted" region were well-known headhunters, I decided we should stop and wait, hoping for a meeting at this sacred and, I believed, safe place.

One calabash contained rice, the other old flowers, leaves, and chicken feathers in a mixture of oil made of damar resin. In gratitude for the magic of these offerings, the divinities had the duty to protect the village from evil spirits and worldly enemies.

I use the word "duty" because, in fact, the purpose of an offering is to put a person or a divinity in a state of debt and obligation toward whomever has made the offering. It is said that if you give to the gods, they will return what you give many times over, because they are more powerful.

This tree with offerings was more than a symbol. It was the invisible door, the invisible frontier of the village. The tree was like the gate that protects our houses. In our countries, we might add a sign with warnings such as PRIVATE PROPERTY or KEEP OUT, DANGEROUS DOG or ARMED RESPONSE. The headhunters' reputation made such a sign totally unnecessary.

If you see someone waiting in front of your gate, you may ask him what he is doing in front of your house. You may leave him there until he goes away, or call the police if you are worried. Perhaps you invite him in. It was the same here in the jungle of Borneo; but since there were no police, you had to be careful—the Ibans still cut off the heads of their enemies, real or imagined. There was not much choice: either we were friends or enemies! Thus, for our safety, we waited until the Ibans would come and invite us to enter their village. They could just as well have given us notice to go away. If they never showed themselves, that too would mean GO AWAY.

We pitched camp at about 5:00 P.M. The light was already disappearing behind the two-hundred-foot trees of this rain forest. It started to rain, as it does there three hundred days of every year.

This place, a short distance from the offerings, would be our "residence." If the headhunters didn't come after two weeks, we would go away to another village, if we could find one.

Everything was wet. Deeply wet. Even without active rain from the sky, you are wet by the trees which drip for three hours or more after it has ceased raining. I didn't even attempt to light a campfire. If it were still daytime, I would try my best to light one as a way to signal my presence, but I knew that at night the Ibans would never invite us to join them. Night is the empire of darkness, and darkness belongs to the evil spirits. Anyway, we had no need for fire. We were too tired to cook and just ate a bowl of cold rice and went to sleep.

As soon as I lit the campfire the next morning, it started to rain. We went back to the plastic-covered hammocks where at least we were a jungle version of dry. Sitting motionless, we could hear the gibbons playing in the tree above us. I played classical music and jazz on my tape recorder to help us make our presence known to the natives. The ways in which people of tradition react to jazz and classical music are surprising. Invariably, they love one and hate the other. I have yet to find a tribe that loves both.

Instead of lying on a warm, sunny Balinese beach next to my girlfriend, here I was again in a cold and rainy jungle, waiting for some headhunters to invite me into their village.

The rain stopped around noon and within minutes, as if they had been waiting for us to get out of our hammocks, two half-naked warriors approached us with sharp machetes hanging at their sides and spear blowguns in their hands. A head shorter than me, they were both well-built, with long black hair. They wore long, narrow pieces of cotton cloth, which passed between their legs and fastened around their waists. From their necks to their feet, they were completely covered with tattoos. I knew by the marks tattooed on their fingers and the upper side of their hands that these two warriors were headhunters, for that is the way Ibans indicate the number of their beheaded victims. Each small line represents a human head. One can learn the history and the warlike values of their wearer by the number of tattooed lines and extent of the tattoos on one or both hands. One man had both hands covered with pretty designs made of dozens of small lines. Whole fingers of the other man were darkened by his accounts. They were professionals.

"Don't be scared, and smile," I said gently to my girlfriend as I smiled at them with my whole body and slowly stretched out my hands, holding tobacco leaves and a pack of betel nuts. They took my presents and smiled. But the two Iban warriors were more interested in my girlfriend's long, blonde hair than in my presents.

"Don't move, baby, everything will be all right," I whispered to her as I saw her lips trembling with anxiety. They approached her, staring at her hair, which they touched with their fingertips and burst into laughter. Then they looked at me and said a few words to which I responded with only a smile and nods of my head, indicating that I did not speak their language. Putting a small ball of tobacco between their lips and teeth, they offered us the lime and pepper leaves that accompany the chewing of betel nuts. Then, as if we were old friends, they invited us to follow them. We packed our belongings and left, preceded by one warrior who led the way as the other followed closely behind.

There was no real path on the muddy soil, and we zigzagged through the jungle to avoid dangerous or difficult places. After an hour or so, we passed through the last natural barrier of thorny and dense vegetation and came upon a calm river where naked children were bathing. On the banks, a few women were washing clothes. Having only a few tattoos on their fingers, they were bare breasted and wore a kind of sarong wrapped around the waist. On the other side, hanging on the top of a tall cliff that fell straight down to the river, an Iban long house was built on a fifteen-foot-high pilework. It was an impregnable wooden fortress, seven hundred feet long and one hundred feet wide, along a portion of the river that flowed quietly between two impassable rapids.

Set between the river and the long house's foot, a path made of tree trunks carved into stairs climbed the cliff. A last tree trunk served as the only access to the long house's supporting platform, built on top of the foundation of pilework.

As we crossed the river on a small flat canoe, all the naked children bathing in the water scampered away, climbing the tree-trunk stairs to the long house. When we got to the other side, the guides indicated that we, too, should ascend. Hesitating on each slippery, narrow step, we made our way up. Above us, bending over the edge of the platform, a group of kids greeted us with laughter and screams.

As we were about to climb the last stair, the women we had seen washing clothes rushed toward us, and, taking my girlfriend along with them, they climbed the final tree trunk and disappeared on the platform, which the children suddenly deserted. I heard women's screams of joy and laughter. When I reached the supporting platform, I couldn't see where my girl had been taken.

This Iban long house had a sixty-foot-wide terrace. The floor was made of bamboo poles lashed one next to the other, stretching up to the veranda and along the length of the entire building. Half of the large terrace, used mostly for children's games, was covered in rectangular trays holding pepper grains for sun drying. In some places, the grains were still very green; in others, they were already completely dried and black. Walking on the pepper grains, a tattooed old man with long gray hair turned them with his feet. On another part of the terrace, cotton threads, each dyed a different color, were stretched for drying.

A few men sat on the floor and carved wood while others repaired baskets or fishing nets. One was sharpening his decorated machete. Only the oldest people and the children were there when I arrived. The rest were hunting, fishing, and taking care of the fields, as they always do as part of their daily tasks.

Although my appearance on the terrace obviously interrupted their daily activities, only the children took refuge under

View of Iban long house.

the veranda. A few men approached me with curiosity, still chewing their tobacco and spitting their betel-red saliva. At their invitation I followed them onto the veranda. Along its entire length, garlands of small rattan cages hung from the roof. Each cage contained a bunch of dusty human skulls, sinister reminders of Iban ferocity. Under each garland was a small basket that each morning was filled with rice, fruits, and flowers as offerings to the spirits of the heads.

As I started to worry for my girlfriend, I saw her exiting, completely disheveled, from one of the long-house apartments.

"They touched me all over and even wanted to see if my pubic hair was the same color as my head hair!" she said, pointing to the women who followed her, laughing. "I couldn't believe it," she added, her cheeks still red from nervousness.

"Were you scared?"

"Panicked at the beginning . . . but I calmed down."

"At least thanks to you they have opened their doors wide for us," I said, squeezing her tenderly in my arms to console her. "I'm proud of you."

The men and women indicated we were to sit on a small bench. We started to chat as naturally as at a Sunday picnic, using hand language and smiles. The children still kept their distance.

According to people of tradition, our protected status was to become effective only with the first meal. I later learned that we were already protected by this village's laws of hospitality, which covered a period of fifteen days. Not knowing this, we kept hoping they would serve dinner before they changed their minds.

As the late afternoon approached, more and more people, wet from their daily river bath, started to arrive. Only a few came near to observe us and smile. Some showed little emotion on their faces. Others ignored us, because they didn't want to offend us. Though I was used to this kind of behavior on the part of the traditional people, it still made me nervous.

By the way our hosts presented us to Aku, we knew he was the chief. But I would have known it anyway because of his charisma and his magisterial way of regarding his people. He smiled and invited us to enter his apartment.

Each of the forty doors on the veranda opened onto a separate two-room apartment called a *bilek.* Each apartment sheltered one family, which contained an average of seven members including parents, children, and other relatives.

The roof covering the entire length of the long house was supported only by the interior walls that separated each apartment from the next. Since the exterior walls didn't touch the roof, both air and light could enter each apartment. The roof overhung the veranda, protecting this area from rain and sun.

The ceilings were about fifteen feet high. Each of the rooms was the same size, about fifteen feet by twelve feet. The first room was the bedroom; the second served as the living room, dining room, and kitchen. There was no door between them. In the left rear corner of this second room was a stone hearth. Above it a human skull yellowed by smoke hung from the ceiling. The burning hearths were supposed to keep the spirits of the human heads warm.

Behind the second room, and separated from it by a panel of woven palm leaves, was a small porch where a system of bamboo pipes coming down from the roof collected the daily rain, used as drinking water, in large terra-cotta pots. One side of the porch opened onto the bathroom, where a hole through the floor

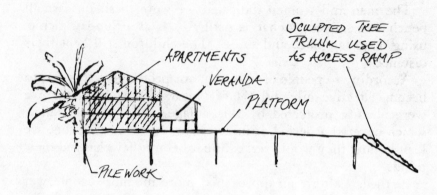

SCULPTED TREE
TRUNK USED
AS ACCESS RAMP

APARTMENTS

VERANDA

PLATFORM

PILE WORK

SERIES OF TWO-ROOM APARTMENTS
(AS MANY AS THERE ARE FAMILIES LIVING IN HOUSE)

KITCHEN WITH
HEARTH

SMALL COVERED PORCH WHERE RAINWATER IS GATHERED

TOILETS (JUST A HOLE IN THE FLOOR)

BEDROOM/
LIVING ROOM

COVERED VERANDA

PLATFORM

SCULPTED TREE TRUNK
USED AS ACCESS RAMP

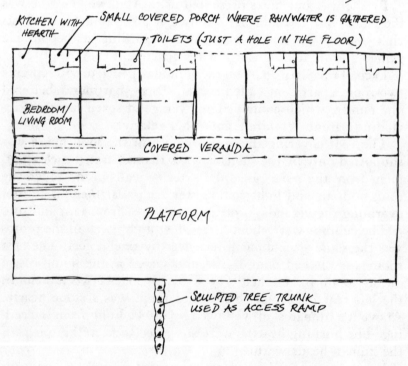

Typical Iban long house. Top, a profile; bottom, the long house seen from above.

served as a toilet. In that way, the fecal material dropped to the ground beneath the long house and was washed into the river by the daily rain.

The furniture was limited to straw matting used as beds. Frying pans and other utensils as well as their hunting and fishing instruments hung on the walls. Against the porch and kitchen walls was an impressive number of giant jars used as storage for water, rice, and pepper grains. As with those of the Kalingas in the Philippines, these beautifully decorated enamel jars were from the Chinese Ming dynasty.

Except when they slept or ate and on special celebration days, the villagers spent most of their days under the long, covered veranda where they met to talk, smoke, drink alcohol, and do their work.

In his apartment, which was the same size as the others, the chief introduced us to the more important men of the village: the shaman and four older people who were obviously members of the council of wise men. One of these was Tawa, the man whose family shared their apartment with us. This meeting was made according to their custom. While the women disappeared, taking my girlfriend along to the kitchen, the men sat around a large Chinese jar filled with *borak*, a highly intoxicating beer made of rice or a mixture of rice and sugar cane. A long straw, with small horizontal lines all the way up to its top, floated vertically in the bowl.

Using an empty straw as a tube, each of us had to suck up as much alcohol as possible. As we drank and the level of the bowl fell, the quantity each of us drank was measured automatically by the markings on the vertical floating straw. From the men's approving glances, I quickly understood that the more I could drink, the higher I would rise in their esteem. I did my best, as I was determined not to be just a guest but a great guest.

While we were getting drunk, female servants who were slaves captured from enemy villages prepared the meals with help from the chief's wife, two of his daughters, a few older relatives, and my girlfriend. Then our official acceptance dinner was served: tasty boiled wild boar's meat and a soup made of flowers and rice, washed down by more borak.

During our long stay among these warriors, we were amazed by the variety of meals they prepared: at each meal a different

Inside an Iban kitchen.

soup with different flowers or leaves. There was a variety of meat—turtle, python, bird, pig, deer, and big fat tree worms— always prepared with spicy sauces and served with rice.

The Iban eat twice a day, in the morning and at night. The morning meal, as copious as the evening one, is washed down with water, while dinner is always accompanied by borak. They also have a very strong rice alcohol, which is drunk only for some special events and ceremonies.

After dinner the chief offered us the alcohol. My girlfriend was permitted to refuse as women usually do, but I couldn't. I don't remember how I got to our apartment. I do have a vague memory of finding my girlfriend already asleep on one of the two mats of straw that Tawa's family had set on the floor of the first room. I also have a vague memory of the face of the girl who silently came to visit my bed, hoping to share it as part of her people's sexual hospitality.

When we awakened late the next day, the village was almost empty. We rolled up our two mats of straw and put them along the wall as the Ibans do. The owners of the apartment had left us some food in the kitchen, covered with a straw basket as protection from flies.

We spent the day quietly with the elders, taking advantage of the chance to learn new Iban words. The people had so much fun teaching us that we knew they would enjoy being our instructors for the rest of our stay. When Aku returned in the late afternoon, he took me to an apartment where there was a sick old man and made me understand that the villagers expected me to save his life. Almost invariably when I enter a village I am placed in such situations, and even though I am not a medicine man, I always try to do something. First, everyone in the room took his turn mimicking the man's symptoms. He didn't eat. He had been vomiting blood for a few days. He hurt here and there. By the time they were finished with his symptoms, I thought he would be better off dead. I examined his whole body and found swollen lymph nodes around his neck and at his groin, and strange, hard, egg-sized balls in his stomach. In gesture language I indicated that he was very sick. His relatives smiled, believing I could save him.

I had already accomplished many medical miracles during my life as an explorer. Because these people are not accustomed to our medications, a single aspirin can have a surprising effect even on diseases that, in our countries, need much more powerful drugs to heal. But the major key to my success as an apprentice doctor is their faith. No matter what I give them, their belief in me and in my medicines is what really heals their bodies.

The man swallowed my antibiotics and an effervescent vitamin C, which seemed to them to be the real magic. He found the strength to move his trembling hands above the drinking bowl to feel the thousands of small bubbles that emerged as the tablet dissolved. When the treatment was finished, our roommate Tawa took me away to share dinner with his family and my girlfriend.

After our meal, Tawa and his family, in a special act of kindness to protect our privacy, took their mats to unroll them in the other room. I hadn't noticed the same kindness the night before, due to my drunkenness. This time we stretched our mosquito net above the matting. I saw that there was a lot of malaria in the village. Because I have had attacks of malaria many times, I recognize the symptoms.

The next morning we accompanied Tawa and his family to their personal pepper field and worked side by side harvesting.

Although the Iban are warriors and hunters, they cultivate pepper by techniques taught to them long ago by Chinese traders. Once or twice a year, they carry their stock of dried pepper down the roaring rivers to isolated trading posts still owned by Chinese. Pepper for Iban is what damar is for other tribes, such as the Punan.

After our return from the field, we bathed with the villagers. Tawa learned that the ill man was feeling much better and had been able to eat some food without vomiting. As a result, when we arrived back at the veranda, there were a great number of ill people waiting for me. They all wanted to come in with us at the same time.

While Tawa's family prepared dinner, I examined my patients, who openly expressed their dissatisfaction whenever I didn't give them an effervescent tablet. Meanwhile, my girlfriend was acting as a nurse, and brought me each time smaller and smaller portions of vitamin C, which I called by a different name so that the people would think that I was giving a separate medication for each sickness.

Apart from infected wounds, the most common ailments with which I had to deal most often involved children with scurvy or whose bodies were covered with fungus or eczema. I have noticed that these skin diseases occur more often when people normally accustomed to going naked start to wear modern clothing or when they replace their natural fabrics, which are more adapted to the humid climate, with clothing made of synthetics.

Each patient either brought me a gift of chicken, eggs, rice, alcohol, and meat or sent me one later. Among these Ibans, as among other Dayak and Papuan tribes, chickens are not meant to be eaten but to be sacrificed to feed the divinities.

The evenings were spent in drink and laughter, the language of peace and friendship. We listened to their music and watched their dances and asked questions and answered them. I particularly worked on developing my relationship with Tawa.

During the day, we accompanied him wherever he went. I

went with him on hunting and fishing parties, and we helped his family and the other villagers harvest the pepper grains. I cut trees for a new rice field and acted as much as possible like any other member of the tribe. We took complete advantage of this grace period covered by the laws of hospitality, when we would automatically be forgiven for mistakes, to learn the codes that govern their way of life. In every way we tried to blend into their culture and become one with the villagers. I never used cameras or recorders during this time.

After the two weeks was up, they could have asked us to leave. But they didn't! On the contrary, our relationship with Tawa and his family was such that they insisted we stay and continue to live in their apartment.

Only then did I take out my camera and sound recorder, while my girlfriend used the still camera to photograph animals and the scenery outside the village. Of course, our strange new behavior aroused their curiosity.

"We are," I explained, "attempting to show the people of our world how different your world is from theirs."

A few days later Tawa said, "You should take pictures in the village too and show your people how we live."

This was the response I had been hoping for. From that day on we were allowed to freely film and photograph without anyone objecting to or even looking at the camera.

One day a ten-year-old girl moved into the apartment. We thought she was the child of one of Tawa's relatives, until Tawa said, "She's my daughter."

"Your own or your wife's?"

"Same father, same mother."

"How come? When you presented your family to us, why did you tell us that you had only three kids of same father and same mother?"

"I had three kids then, now I have four."

"Do you have other children?"

"No."

A few days later two more "sons" moved in, making six children in all, but the next morning one of his daughters, who had been living there when we arrived, left.

"Tell me, Tawa, how many children do you really have?"

"Now I have five."

It took us a great deal of time observing the life of villagers before we understood that my friend the headhunter was right in his answers. What I should have asked him was: "How many children did you engender with your wife?" For according to the Dayak custom, a child became his when he, Tawa, assumed his function as a father.

Generally speaking, among the societies of tradition, a couple makes children for reasons that often are different from ours. Children will be the parents' old-age insurance, because their main duty as adults will be to take care of their old parents. By making children, the natives guarantee the cultural and physical survival of their family and, by extension, of the clan, village, and tribe, which means each child belongs to that extended family. And the tribe, clan, and family are all responsible for him.

By this system, apart from his biological parents, the child has more than one father and one mother. If, because of occupation, sickness, disposition, or other reasons, a child's real father or real mother cannot give him the attention and teaching he needs, the child has the opportunity of going in search of the "father" or "mother" who has the opportunity and the desire to give him these things. With this system, neither divorce nor the death of one or both of his biological parents will destroy the child's balance.

Less than a week later the Ibans' attitudes toward us changed sharply. We suddenly felt we more like strangers than on the day we arrived. First the chief and then Tawa asked me when we were intending to leave their village.

"Did we do something wrong? Are you preparing a ceremony at which we cannot be present?" I asked Tawa.

I had guessed the reason.

An apartment had become too small for a growing family, and the villagers had just finished building a new one at one end of the long houses. But to move into a new apartment, the Iban needed a human head,[2] and strangers weren't permitted to be part of the ceremony.

In order to witness what was about to be performed, I proposed to them that we become members of their community.

2. For more information about tattooing, please see note 2 at the back of this book.

"That will take too much time, for our ceremony will begin very soon." He said, "If you want to be initiated, you must come back again. However, you both will be allowed to stay if you accept a tattooing."

We did. My girlfriend got a black point on one of her finger joints, and I received a stylized scorpion tattoo on the side of my right calf.

All Dayak tribes use similar tattooing techniques. With a dark mixture whose main ingredient is damar oil, they first paint on the skin the design to be tattooed. Then, using a small stick as a hammer, the tattooer repeatedly hits another small stick on whose tip is tied a thorn or needle. He continues this until the drawing becomes a wound in which the dark mixture has deeply penetrated. Each tattoo design, its placement, and the part of the body which it covers has a precise significance. For men, the designs are tribal codes of life, messages sent to the inner world of the individual. Those on fingers and hands represent the number of their beheaded victims. Tattoos also provide magical protection and totemic affiliations. Each individual is magically connected to an animal spirit. In the Iban tattoos, one can recognize the stylized forms of dogs, scorpions, dragons, and other animals, both mythic and real. As men gain more knowledge, their bodies are covered with more and more tattoos, for Ibans have initiations of many degrees. Tattoos also protect men from losing their souls to headhunters. Thanks to the magical power of the neck tattoo and the ritual which is performed at the time of the tattooing, a man's soul, instead of being "captured" by the headhunter when he is beheaded, has the ability to escape. In Borneo, each man is a potential victim of headhunters, so the neck tattoo is a good investment.

Ibans sent a message to our inner world. They gave my girlfriend the markings of a married woman. My tattoo represented warrior values. Having become an integral part of the long house, we were allowed to participate in the home-moving ceremony that was about to start.

Two nights later, warriors returned carrying the head of a Dayak who was an enemy to the clan. This was the cause of a huge celebration with music and dance. The head was plunged into a nest of carnivorous ants and so the skull was made ready for the ceremony.

Whenever an apartment becomes too crowded, one part of the family stays and the other moves to a newly-made apartment. This moving is celebrated as a rite of passage. In accord-

ance with traditions and divinities, all the members of the divid-
ing family, even those living in faraway jungle villages or in the
larger towns, are required to be present at the ceremony. For
days, people arrived from everywhere, some wearing modern
clothing and carrying automatic rifles that contrasted weirdly
with tattooed nudity and blowguns.

Each time a Dayak meets someone from his clan or his tribe,
he tells him all that has happened and all that is about to be. In
such manner, from village to village, news spreads easily
throughout the jungle. In the same way, villagers know if all
their guests have arrived or not, for there is always someone
announcing that someone else is still coming, until the arrival
of the last guest who knows nobody else is on the way.

The guests came carrying offerings for the spirits of their
ancestors and also various gifts, both for those who were moving
and those who were staying. Some of the gifts from the modern
world didn't make sense to the men of the jungles. One man
wearing jeans carried a brand-new mattress, which probably
would stay rolled up in its plastic bag forever so as to remain
undamaged.

When all the guests were present, the moving ceremony was
allowed to start. Early on the morning of the celebration day,
some villagers created a second but temporary access to the new
apartment, which would be destroyed at the end of the celebration. Meanwhile, in front of the old apartment, all the villagers
and guests gathered around two young women who beat gongs
to frighten away evil spirits. The shaman, accompanied by the
gongs and carrying a deer's skull intended as the home for the
spirits of the ancestors, led the procession to the new apartment.
Instead of going directly, the procession left the long house
through its main entrance, went to the river, and rowed upstream in canoes to the temporary access of the new apartment.
In this way the evil spirits were confused and unable to follow.

At the new apartment, the shaman hung a deer's skull on the
outside wall under the veranda. Then, followed by two women
still beating the gongs (as they would continue to do throughout
the night) by the family which was moving, their guests, relatives, myself, and some of the villagers, the shaman entered the
new apartment where, suspended from the roof by palm leaves,
the newly-cut human skull held a fresh white flower in its jaws.

In the new apartment the shaman purified our presence by
slowly waving a chick above our heads. Before sacrificing it, the

shaman asked me to prepare the offerings to all the various divinities, including the spirit of the human head. The eggs, cakes, and rice that I offered to these invisibles were served in Ming bowls.

Leaving the apartment we returned to the veranda and the real feast started. Meals were cooked for everybody and distributed along with betel nuts, borak, and strong rice alcohol. Later, there was dancing, singing, chanting, smoking of hallucinogenic herbs, and eating of psychedelic mushrooms. And we all flew outside our bodies reaching for the divine.

A few days later when all the guests had returned to their homes, Tawa and the chief took us on a small trip to visit the other Iban clans, with whom our village had peace treaties. In each village we were welcomed by the chief, who presented us his most glorious trophy and told the story of the headhunt. Very often these heads belonged to Japanese who, during World War II and much later, remained in Borneo. The heads were considered particularly glorious because the victims had been very well-armed and elusive.

My girlfriend's holidays were coming to an end, and I promised to accompany her as far as Singapore. On a one-day trip down the rapids, Tawa carried us in his canoe to a town where we caught another boat that dropped us on the coast. After a five-hour airplane flight, we were in Kutching, Sarawak. Seven hours later we were in Singapore. My girlfriend went home alone, her eyes, ears, and heart filled with memories of another world.

Still unfulfilled in my relationship to the tribe, still longing for some unfelt element of the primal experience, still hoping for I knew not what, I went back to Tawa. But I wouldn't have had I known what I was to experience among his people.

CHAPTER FOURTEEN

Initiated into an Iban Tribe of Headhunters

The hopeful man sees success where others see shadows and storm.

O. S. MARDEN

Against Tawa's excellent advice I asked the chief if I could become a member of their clan. It took him a while before he could give me an answer, for he had to question the spirits of their ancestors and wait for their reply to appear through different omens: the flight of a blackbird, the auguries of a chick they sacrificed. A few days after the question, the answer came:

"Yes . . . but!"

The "but" was that I would have to undergo their initiation. Without knowing exactly what physical ordeal was in store, I accepted. I knew I had been through worse and survived. It was to begin in one week.

Late at night I was awakened by a girl slipping into my bed. She was sweet and already had a great knowledge of man's morphology. Like all the others who came and "visited" me this way every night, she was highly skilled in the arts of love. Among the Iban, only unmarried women offer sexual hospitality, and no one obliged these women to offer me their favors. Sexual freedom ends at marriage. Unfaithfulness—except during yearly fertility celebrations when everything, even incest at times, is permitted—is punished as an offense against their matrimonial laws.

As a sign of respect to family and the elders, sexual hospitality is not openly practiced. The girls always came when my roommates were asleep and left before they awoke. They were free to return or give their place to their girlfriends.

The contrast between the violence of some Iban rituals and

the beauty of their art, their sociability, their kindness, and their personal warmth has always fascinated me. I also witnessed that contrast among a tribe of Papuans (who, besides being head-hunters, practice cannibalism) and among some African tribes. In fact, tribes devoted to cannibalism and other human sacrifices are often among the most sociable of people, and their art, indus-try, and trading systems are more advanced than other tribes that don't have these practices.

For my initiation, they had me lie down naked in a four-foot-deep pit filled with giant carnivorous ants. Nothing held me there. At any point I could easily have escaped, but the meaning of this rite of passage was not to kill me. The ritual was intended to test my courage and my will, to symbolically kill me by the pain in order for me to be reborn as a man of courage. I am not sure what their reactions would have been if I had tried to get out of the pit before their signal, but it occurred to me that although the ants might eat a little of my flesh, the Iban offered more dramatic potentials.

Since I wore, as Iban do, a long piece of cloth around my waist and nothing more, I had the ants running all over my body. They were everywhere. The pain of the ants' bites was intense, so I tried to relax to decrease the speed of my circulation and therefore the effects of the poison. But I couldn't help trying to get them away from my face where they were exploring every inch of my skin. I kept my eyes closed, inhaling through my almost closed lips and exhaling through my nose to chase them away from there.

I don't know how long I stayed in the pit, waiting with anguish for the signal which would end my ordeal. As I tried to concentrate on my relaxing, the sound of the beaten gongs and murmurs of the assistants watching me from all around the pit started to disappear into a chaos of pain and loud heartbeat.

Then suddenly I heard Tawa and the chief calling my name. I removed once more the ants wandering on my eyelids before opening my eyes and seeing my friends smiling to indicate that it was over. I got out of the pit on my own, but I needed help to rid myself of the ants, which were determined to eat all my skin. After the men washed my body, the shaman applied an herbal mixture to ease the pain and reduce the swellings. I would have quit and left the village then had I known that the "pit" experience was just the hors d'oeuvre.

The second part of the physical test started early the next morning. The chief explained the "game" to me. It was Hide and Go Seek Iban-style. I had to run without any supplies, weapons, or food, and for three days and three nights escape a group of young warriors who would leave the village a few hours after my departure and try to find me. If I were caught, my head would be used in a ceremony. The Iban would have done so without hate. It was simply the rule of their life. Birth and death. A death that always engenders new life.

When I asked, "What would happen if someone refused this part of the initiation?" the chief replied that such an idea wasn't possible. Once one had begun, there was no turning back. I knew the rules governing initiations among the cultures of tradition but never thought they would be applied to me. Whether or not I survived the initiation, I would be symbolically killed in order to be reborn among them. I had to die from my present time and identity into another life. I was aware that, among some cultures, initiatory ordeals are so arduous that young initiates sometimes really die. These are the risks if one wishes to enter into another world.

I was given time to get ready and the game began. I run like hell without a plan or, it seemed to me, a prayer of surviving. Running along a path I had never taken, going I knew not where, I thought about every possible way I could escape from the young warriors. To hide somewhere. But where? Climb a tree and hide in it? Find a hole and squeeze in it? Bury myself under rocks and mud? But all of these seemed impossible. I had a presentiment they would find me anyway. So I ran straight ahead, my head going crazy by dint of searching for a way to safely survive the headhunters.

I would prefer staying longer with ants, I thought breathlessly. It was safer to stay among them for a whole day since they were just simple pain and fear compared to what I am about to undergo. I don't want to die.

For the first time I realized the real possibility of death—no longer in a romantic way, but rather at the hands of butchers.

Ten minutes after leaving the long house, I suddenly heard a call coming from somewhere around me. Still running, I looked all around trying to locate who was calling, and why. At the second call I stopped, cast my gaze about, and saw a woman's head peering out from the bushes. I recognized her as one of my pretty lovers. I hesitated, not knowing if she were part of the hunting party or a goddess come to save me. She called again. I thought, God, what to do? How will I escape from the warriors? As I stood there truly coming into contact with my impossible situation, I began to panic. She called again. With her fingers she showed me what the others would do if they caught me. Her forefinger traced an invisible line from one side of her throat to the other. If someone was going to kill me, why not her? I joined her and found out she was in a lair. I realized I had entered the place where the tribe's women go to hide during their menstruation. This area is taboo for men. Each woman has her own refuge. Some have shelters made of branches, others deep covered holes hidden behind bushes with enough space to eat and sleep and wait until their time is past.

She invited me to make myself comfortable. That was quite difficult since it was just large enough for one person. But I had no choice. And after all, it was a paradise compared to what I would have undergone had I not by luck crossed this special ground.

Nervously and physically exhausted by my run and fear and despair, I soon fell asleep. Around midnight I woke. She gave me rice and meat. We exchanged a few words. Then it was her turn to sleep.

The time I spent in the lair with my savior went fast. I tried to sleep all day long, an escape from the concerns of my having broken a taboo. And I wondered what would happen to me if the headhunters were to learn where I spent the time of my physical initiation.

Then, when it was safe, I snuck back to the village . . . in triumph. I arrived before the warriors, who congratulated and embraced me when they returned. I was a headhunter at last.

I spent the next two weeks quietly looking at the Iban through new eyes. But strangely enough, instead of the initiation putting me closer to them, it had the opposite effect. I watched them more and more from an anthropological distance: my Iban brothers became an interesting clan whose life I witnessed but did not really share. And then suddenly I was bored and yearned for my own tribe. When Tawa had to go to an outpost to exchange pepper grains for other goods, I took a place aboard his canoe. Two days later I was in a small taxi-boat heading toward Sibu, the first leg in civilization on my voyage home.

I think of them often. I wonder about the man I tried to cure. I think about Tawa and the girl who saved my life, and all the others sitting on the veranda. How long will my adopted village survive before being destroyed like all the others in the way of civilization? And what has become of those who marked my flesh with the joy of their lives and offered me the best of their souls? If they are slowly vanishing from my memories, I know that I am part of the stories they tell. I know that my life among them will be perpetuated until the farthest tomorrow. Now I am a story caught in a living legend of a timeless people.

Postscript

So much for the explorer. He adapts and moves
on. But what is in store for the people of tradition who remain
in these unexplored areas? And how should we, the people of
progress and technology, deal with our brothers of tradition?

In their attempts to classify human societies, anthropologists
have applied the word *primitive* to the people who have not yet
or have barely found access to the tools of modern technology.
I don't like the adjective *primitive*. When it precedes the word
man it has a bad connotation. We associate *primitive* with wild,
stupid, rough, without intelligence or knowledge, without true
religion or sophistication. Yet even the slightest contact with
"primitive" men has shown that they are not wild (they may act
wildly, but never more so than "civilized" people), stupid (their
logic simply differs from our logic), and they do not possess any
of the other negative attributes we often ascribe to them. Indeed,
their cultures are highly workable and their religions satisfy the
soul. For them, living as a human being is a religious act: eating,
making love, working—all have sacramental value.

Lately, anthropologists have begun to replace the word *primitive* with the word *archaic*. Etymologically, *archaic* is the perfect
term to designate these societies, but in our language the word
is often misused and confusing. This is why I call the tribal
people "the people of tradition," and I wish the whole world
would do so. To speak of them in this way and accord them their
full dignity may be their final tribute.

They are intelligent and sophisticated. They do not have our level of scientific knowledge, but what they do know works for them, and their social information sometimes brings them more happiness and peace than our information brings us. They may lack our tools, but by their own evaluation they are not the worse off for it.

Although we have history, the cultures of tradition don't. Instead, they have their mythology: an essentially unchanging body of stories that tell them who they are and where they come from. The cultures of tradition have had to undergo some adaptation but basically have not changed in relation to their myths, because traditional people's lives are based upon the daily systematic repetition of these primordial stories. To alter details would be to stray from their point of original reference; to repeat the myths is to remain an integral part of them and thus belong to their divine world. Traditional man's life is the human repetition of what the divinities did and are *still* doing in the myths. Therefore, his life is innately religious, and there is no separation between the sacred and the profane.

Instead of focusing on technological advancements, the people of tradition search for more elaborate ways to deal with the divinities and the forces of nature. They use their creativity to keep themselves in balance, away from the chaos, and in harmony within their village as well as within society, nature, and the cosmos.

For traditional man, nature attests that living a life of repetition is perfect. Nature in the midst of which he lives and from which he gains his survival does not experience evolution but rather cycles of repetition. If nature doesn't change, why should man? In his attempt to copy the divinities' behavior, he lives a repetition of his own cycles.

In relation to our cultures, the state of mind of a man of tradition could be compared in many ways to our childhood. Indeed, the child has his parents to take care of his tomorrow, and the man of tradition has his village chief and his sorcerer to look after his future. Children usually create gangs in which each member has duties toward others. The man of tradition lives in a similar system that includes his family, clan, community, village, and tribe.

The man of tradition has his myths to guide him; the child has his fairy tales. Without a developed consciousness of the time space, the man of tradition—like the child—lives in the present time, free for the most part from adult preoccupations, anxieties, and worries.

The cultures of tradition are in danger everywhere. Progress is beheading the Dayaks of Borneo, eating the peoples of the Amazon, and executing the children of the Sun. Their homelands—the last wild territories—are shrinking, torn away by bulldozers and the industrial needs of the twentieth century.

Throughout the world there is industrial exploitation for precious wood, gold, oil, and uranium, the varied earth riches that we so lavishly spend. Starting from the most easily accessible places, exploiters spread farther into the sanctuaries of the tribes. Unless industrial and governmental policies change worldwide, someday soon the jungles will no longer exist to support the dwindling number of tribes. These policies intend to bring all "primitive" tribes into the twentieth century—the better to maintain "order" and "unity" and, of course, to supply the cheap labor required by the exploitation of natural resources. If the tribes resist, they are slaughtered by soldiers of the central government who are the partners of industry and not the protectors of people.

In a last desperate assertion of his right to exist, the man of tradition sometimes fights back. But what can his arrows do against the fury of our weapons? If he survives the sorrow and dishonor of defeat, he is conscripted into tomorrow's subproletariat with little chance of smiling again for generations. No more will he be what he was. Touched by our "evolved" society, he is compelled to join our solitude. (In the high mountains of Borneo, I saw people using psychedelics in religious ceremonies as a way to reach the divine. In the villages tainted by modern civilization, I saw people taking drugs continuously, trying to forget that there was no longer any purpose to their lives.)

Natives are thrown unprepared into another way of life, another civilization, another set of values. Forced to abandon their cultural identity and the traditions that have sustained them for countless generations, they become socially maladjusted by the thousands. When a culture built on tradition collides with a culture built on "progress," tradition always loses, and the witnessing heart cries out. Condemned to adapt itself to our system of values, the world of the man of tradition is sentenced to disappear forever.

Because I have witnessed the dramatic struggle of so many of these people of tradition, I am creating a foundation called Tribal Life Protection. Like the industrial corporations, this foundation will buy large portions of jungle throughout the world and turn them into sanctuaries that are forbidden to twentieth-century exploiters. In these preserves, endangered tribes will be welcome to stay as long as they want, protected from the outside world. We will prepare them to move into the twentieth-century world only if they wish it.

The foundation will give tribal people a respite, a place to dream and to live as they always have. They will be free to maintain their social structure so that the children of their children will still be able to witness the philosophy, magic, beliefs, and traditions of their forefathers.

These so-called "primitive" tribes live every day for itself, in harmony with their gods and with nature. They are proud to be, not proud to have. I wish we could say the same.

Notes

1. Tattooing

Tribal man is aware that his skin expresses the emotions of his inner world (such as fear, embarrassment, anxiety, etc.). He sees it as the thin border between the inner and outer worlds. Thus, he believes that the skin can be used as the canvas on which he paints pictures that symbolically express who he really is and what he truly feels, or on which he can hide what he is by picturing what he isn't.

And as the skin is the messenger from the inner world to the outer world, it is also used to send messages in the other direction, from the outer world to the inner. By covering the skin with symbols, the tribal man tries to limit or increase the powers of his inner world.

Of course, body paintings do not last the life of the individual, so many tribes use permanent means of marking the skin—tattooings and scarifications. These techniques have many other advantages over body painting: the message is not only written on the skin but into it. The deeper the message is written into the skin, the more chances that message will have to reach the inside world. Skin mutilation also produces pain. Pain is unforgettable and becomes a memory that forever carries all of what was said and learned during the ritual of "sending a message into the inner world." Thus, the markings are visible mnemonics that remind the individual of his death and rebirth.

Tattooing is practiced around the world where people's skin is light—except in Timor, Indonesia, where the skin is branded with a piece of red-hot wood or iron. Since tattoos cannot be seen on black skin, the darker races use scarification.

Depending on the tribe, the scar can be flat, carved into the skin and depressed, or raised. While a flat or depressed scar is easily obtainable just by cutting the skin or by clawing it deeply, the emergent scars result from more complicated operations. Raised with a claw or a thorn, each small piece of skin must be incised in such a way that it is partially detached. An irritating substance is then poured into the incision below each of these small flaps. This substance eats away at the exposed flesh and causes it to seal into a visible scar.

In some tribes, the various markings of the skin are made only to stress the individual's entry into adulthood; in others, each social "passage" is also cut into the skin. For women, it might be a wedding or the birth of the first child; for men, headhunting or other social initiations and personal exploits will be registered. Marking the skin is also used for magical practices, to exorcise evil and sickness, to win the favor of the gods, to signify a relationship to a special tribe or family, and even to express one's attitude toward the society in which one lives.

2. Headhunting

Civilized societies have proven their unlimited capacity for repeated brutality; nevertheless, our feelings of repulsion about headhunting and cannibalism prevent us from approaching the phenomena with understanding. These practices, when seen from within the structure of civilizations that engage in them, are clothed in more than the garment of human savagery.

Throughout mankind's history, all cultures have performed human sacrifices in one form or another. An entire book would be needed to list all of the different ways that human sacrifices have been performed and to explain what philosophies prompted these actions. Here I will address only a few limited aspects of headhunting, which is still practiced in many regions of the world: Borneo, Sumatra, New Guinea, the Philippines, Burma, the Northeast of India, Southeast Asia's mountain regions, the Amazon basin, and in some countries of black Africa.

Whatever the apparent reasons for this behavior, such as rites of passage, revenge between clans, or the need to express warlike values, headhunting always has magical and religious components.

The most common primal value attached to headhunting, one that is relevant throughout the world, is that human sacrifice is part of a fertility rite, a call for favors from the gods or an effort to appease their anger. For Apayaos, Dayaks, and the majority of the Asian tribes still practicing these rituals, the kill is inevitably a reminder of their creation myths. In brief, the myths say that the universe began with the sexual union between two cosmic entities. The result of this act was two worlds—one above (the invisible one, represented by a god and his lieutenants) and one below (the visible one, also represented by a god and his followers). After this creation, there was a "holy war" between the gods. Although they were immortal, the lieutenants of the two divine groups killed each other. These dead divinities gave birth to Man and his universe, and through this new creation, the two gods found a unity and balance. The destruction of the lieutenants (the destruction of immortality) engendered mortality (mankind).

The basic teaching of this myth of the creation is that *something* cannot start from *nothing*. *Something* can begin only if it follows the ending of *nothing*.

The following myth, which I heard among the Iban, has a similar but more easily understandable message than the primordial myth of the creation. It says: "In the beginning of everything, only the gods were living in their immortality. There was no beginning (birth) and no end (death). In order to create life—specifically, to create something that had a beginning (birth) and an end (death)—one god killed another god. His death allowed a birth to occur." The end of immortality created mortality. Again, nothing can start without being preceded by a death.

Taken to the level of daily life, this myth tells its followers that to start something new, particularly something that does not belong to everyday life, a death is required. So, whenever a human being is about to create *something*, he must first perform an act of *destruction*, the killing of a man. By sacrificing a human being, one becomes a god who kills another god. One lives the myth!

(Even in Christianity, we have a symbolic resemblance: only the death of a divinity—Jesus, the son of God—could save Man and allow him to be reborn.)

Among tribes practicing headhunting, human sacrifice is often performed to mark important events in the life of an individual or of a whole village; such events might include deaths, weddings and other rites of passage, building a new house, even a canoe, creating a rice field, harvesting, or going on a big hunt.

For example, when the Iban build a long house, deep holes are dug in which they will place heavy tree trunks to support the building's structure. When raising the first pole, they used to put a living woman into the hole (generally a slave captured from an enemy village) and crush her with the heavy tree trunk. During my stay in Sarawak, I learned from a civil engineer that to this day, when building a bridge, the Iban workers often request a human sacrifice—and to avoid interrupting the construction, they sometimes make arrangements to obtain a prisoner who has been sentenced to death.

The subjugation of the spirit of the victim is another primal value that one can find in headhunting traditions. Except during tribal conflict, when the warriors have too much to do, the attempt to become allied with the victim's spirit may start ceremoniously before the beheading. When the Iban go in search of a head, they form a group of about ten warriors who will try to find a victim, usually during the night. When captured, the victim is thrown on the ground. While one man prevents him from yelling, another drives a bamboo stick into his naval, piercing his abdomen but not killing him. This has the following symbolic meaning: in the fetal state, it is through the naval that a human being receives physical life and, therefore, also the evil spirits responsible for sickness and weakness. By piercing the abdomen, the warrior creates a hole, allowing these evil spirits to escape from the suffering body.

Then the warrior will try to get his victim's name and talks to him. He starts by telling his victim the myth he is enacting—he is about to be the god who will kill another god. He begs for the victim's forgiveness: "If you were killed by an enemy who would not behead you, your soul would be lost, and, thus, you would never reach your ancestors in the world above, for no one would perform your funeral rituals. The same would happen to you if you were killed by an animal. Allow me to kill you in order to create a new beginning. Allow me to kill you so that you can have rebirth as a member of my family, a member of my clan. And as such, I will honor you. Be mine, O spirit, be mine and give me your strength and your energies. Protect me and all members of my family, and I will honor you. Fight for me in this world and in the world of above, and I will honor you. I promise to take care of you by practicing the rituals which will keep your soul alive."

Just before the victim dies, the warrior cuts off his head.

The spirit of the slain man becomes a member of the headhunter's tribe. It is subject to the will of the one who beheaded the victim on the condition that he retain the head. By keeping the head—the home of the soul and spirit—and living with it, the headhunter magically transfers all of the victim's values and energies to himself. He has power over the spirit, which protects him, his relatives, and his clan from evil—not only in the visible world but also in the invisible one.

Consequently, headhunting is also a way to increase the warrior capacities. The more heads the hunter takes, the more energies he gets. Aku, for instance, the chief of my Iban village, claimed to have beheaded 250 enemies. He told me how he and his tribe once attacked a village, beheaded the men, and took the women as slaves. It was all very matter of fact—not barbaric. It was just the way things are in that culture. The victims, too, may be said to have understood their roles in the drama.

Holding power over the victim's spirit by keeping his skull, a head-hunter will venerate and take care of the skull, dressing it with flowers and offering delicious meals to feed the spirit living in it. A few tribes will even decorate it. Some people remove the jaw so that the victim's spirit cannot "bite" them, whereas others use the head as their pillow, since by magical osmosis the spirit of the victim can communicate with the owner's spirit and give him advice.

The skulls used by Asmats (a Papuan tribe) in ceremonies, such as initiations, are the heads of enemies, but those used as personal protection are always the heads of their family members. Indeed, their custom requires that their dead parents return home in this form. To disrespect that tradition would call forth anger from the deceased and would deprive the living of an invaluable ally. On the other hand, the Asmat knows that a relative's skull shields him from evil, malevolent spirits and protects him from dangers in the visible world, particularly during sleep. Therefore, he guards the skull by using it as a pillow. Whenever he goes on a headhunt or on a dangerous trip, he carries the skull hanging around his neck.

It is difficult for a headhunter to carry his cumbersome trophy, especially when hunting or fighting. Therefore, some tribes wear something that symbolically represents, and is magically linked to, the cut heads hanging in their houses. For instance, some Dayak tribes wear wild boars' tusks in holes pierced in their ears. For other Dayaks, the tusks are part of their necklaces. Warthogs' tusks hang around the necks of Papuan Asmats and India's Nagas, who also wear them as bracelets. Elsewhere, in Africa, Asia, and the South American continent, cut heads are represented by sea shells or small red seeds, wild animal or cat skin, or gold plates or feathers in the hair. For some tribes (like the Iban, who wear small tattoos on their fingers and hands), body paintings or tattoos also mark the possession of human heads.

The Jivaros and Munduruku of the Amazon jungle have found an easier way to carry the spirits of their victims with them by shrinking their victims' heads.

Although some other tribes perhaps have different ways, the Jivaros, whom I have met, use the following techniques: After beheading his enemy, the warrior makes a long incision from the neck almost to the top of the head in such a way that he is able to peel off the skin with the hair. Then, he boils the skin in a mixture of different plants. This operation shrinks the skin by eliminating the water which composes ninety percent of it.

Next, the Jivaro sews the eyes, mouth, and incision shut. The nostrils and ears are filled with a mixture of resin and rubber. In that manner, the Jivaro obtains something like a small skin "bag" the size of a fist. By filling and refilling it many times with hot sand—which will harden the skin—the warrior is able to shape it into the face of his victim. As a result, the shrunken head looks like his enemy's face in miniature. This long operation is usually accompanied by chants, prayers, and invocations to the spirit of the head and to divinities.

Scalps are even lighter than miniaturized heads. For the Maoris of New Zealand and some native American Indians, these hanks of hair or hair and flesh were trophies symbolizing the whole head.

As a substitute for a cut head, tribes have also kept other parts of their victims—such as the jaw (to decorate warriors' drums), various bones, teeth, or hands. While some Papuans used to tear the ears off of their still-alive captives, some Africans remove the nose or lips, and Australian tribes choose the beard, feet, or hands.

Although some Ethiopian tribes still emasculate their enemies, carrying their dried testicles around their neck, nowadays there are no records of people practicing phallotomy, the removal of their victim's penis. That custom was formerly widespread among many cultures, including Egyptian, Assyrian, Hebrew, Spartan, Abyssinian, Persian, and a few African tribes. For most tribes, the sacrifice of an animal has become the substitute for a human kill.